PHOENIX IN SHADOW

D1433025

PHOENIX IN SHADOW

Ryk E. Spoor

PHOENIX IN SHADOW

This is a work of fiction. All the characters and events portrayed in this book are fictional, and any resemblance to real people or incidents is purely coincidental.

Copyright © 2015 by Ryk E. Spoor

All rights reserved, including the right to reproduce this book or portions thereof in any form.

A Baen Books Original

Baen Publishing Enterprises
P.O. Box 1403
Riverdale, NY 10471
www.baen.com

ISBN: 978-1-4767-8037-5

Cover art by Todd Lockwood
Maps by Randy Asplund

First Baen printing, May 2015

Distributed by Simon & Schuster
1230 Avenue of the Americas
New York, NY 10020

Library of Congress Cataloging-in-Publication Data

Spoor, Ryk E.
  Phoenix in shadow / Ryk E. Spoor.
    pages ; cm
  ISBN 978-1-4767-8037-5 (trade pb)
  I. Title.
  PS3619.P665P47 2015
  813'.6—dc23

                                                    2015005954

10   9   8   7   6   5   4   3   2   1

Pages by Joy Freeman (www.pagesbyjoy.com)
Printed in the United States of America

ACKNOWLEDGEMENTS & THANKS

As always to my wife Kathleen, for giving me the time

To Toni Weisskopf, for ensuring Kyri's story will be told

To Tony Daniel, for giving excellent editorial advice

And to my Beta-Readers, for giving me encouragement and feedback—especially my Loyal Lieutenant, Shana.

This novel is dedicated to my son Christopher, who helped make Kaizatenzei what it now is.

CONTENTS

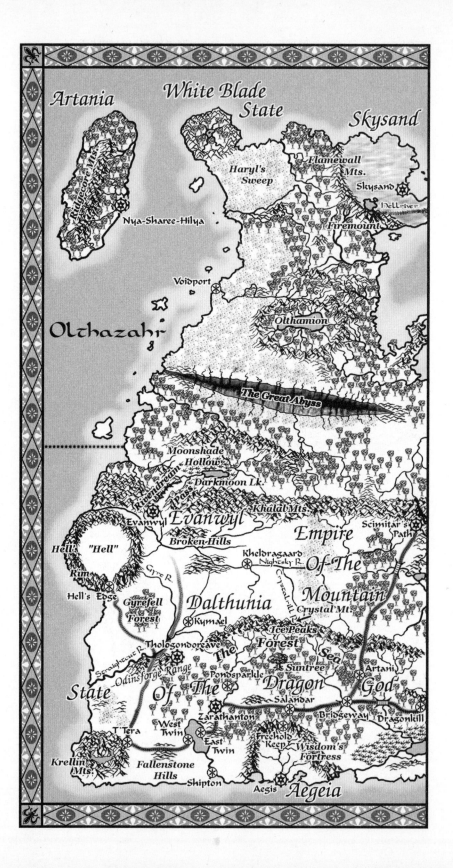

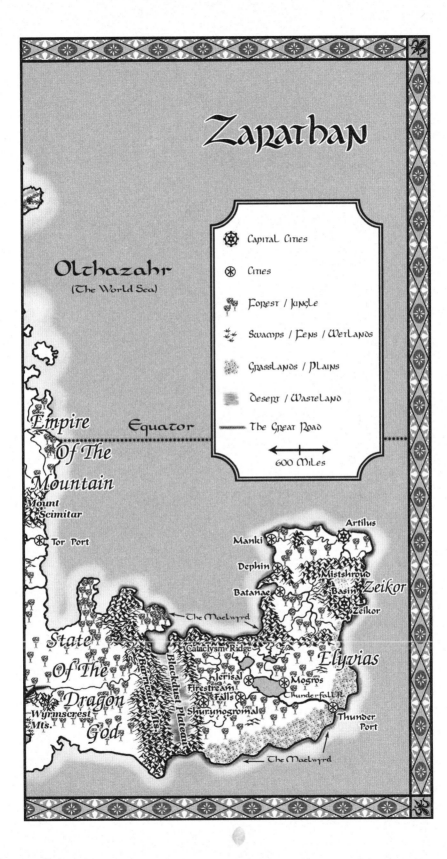

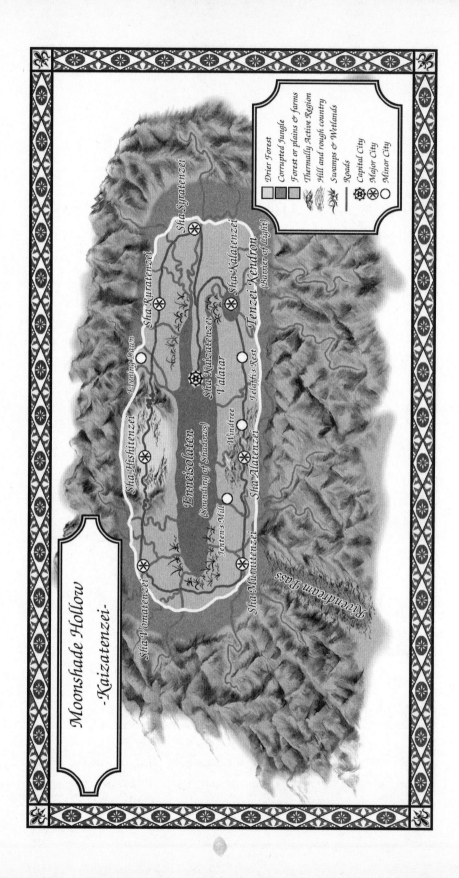

Moonshade Hollow
-Kaizatenzei-

Legend:
Drier Forest
Corrupted Jungle
Forest or plains & farms
Thermally Active Region
Hill and rough country
Swamps & Wetlands
Roads
Capital City
Major City
Minor City

Sha Syratenzei

Sha Ruratenzei

Sha Kalatenzei

Tenzei Kendron
(Burner of Light)

Evening Dawn

Sha Hishitenzei

Sha Kaizatenzei

Valatar

Telohi's Rest

Enneisolaten
(Sounding of Shadows)

Windtree

Sha Alatenzei

Jenten's Mill

Sha Mumutenzei

Sha Vomatenzei

Riverloam Pass

Previously in The Balanced Sword series

Kyri Victoria Vantage lost her parents to unknown attackers some years before; even the Justiciars of Myrionar, God of Justice and Vengeance, the patron deity of her country Evanwyl, were unable to discover the identity of the assailants. But she has moved on, and her brother Rion has become a Justiciar himself. But then tragedy strikes a second time, and during a sudden and monstrous attack on Evanwyl, something kills Rion, tearing his soul to shreds.

Shocked and now worried that her whole family is in peril, Kyri leaves Evanwyl with her aunt Victoria and younger sister Urelle, travelling to far-distant Zarathanton to begin a new life. But a chance discovery there reveals the hideous truth: that it was the Justiciars who were responsible, the supposed holy warriors somehow betraying everything they stand for. In rage and shock, Kyri demands Myrionar explain itself—and the god answers. Something far worse is happening; Myrionar is weakened, perhaps dying, but It promises Kyri that if she will be true to Myrionar—will become the one true Justiciar—then she will one day have the justice and vengeance she seeks.

Meanwhile, Tobimar Silverun, youngest prince of the country of Skysand, is forced to leave his country in search of the origins of his people—a quest that is thrust on his family once in a generation, and which amounts to exile for twenty-four years . . . unless he can discover their ancient homeland. The mysterious mage Khoros, once Tobimar's teacher, also warns Tobimar that the next Chaoswar is about to begin, and that this is connected to his quest.

Tobimar's search leads him to Zarathanton, greatest city of the world, and to a startling meeting with Poplock Duckweed, a diminuitive Toad adventurer who has already disrupted the plans of one of the Mazolishta demonlords, Voorith. The two seek an audience with the Sauran King, only to find that he has been assassinated moments before they enter the Throne Room!

Having accepted Myrionar's offer, Kyri realizes that if she is to be a Justiciar, she must obtain the magical and powerful Raiment—the armor of a Justiciar—that both symbolizes and protects a Justiciar, and sets out to find the half-legendary Spiritsmith who can forge the Raiment; after managing to discover him—and pass his lethal tests—she convinces him that she is indeed the first of the new Justiciars, and takes the name Phoenix as her new title (as all Justiciars have the names of birds).

As refugees from the Forest Sea begin to pour into Zarathanton in massive quantities, and word of revolutions or wars in distant lands begin to arrive, Tobimar and Poplock realize that they are seeing part of a massive, coordinated plan to destroy the State of the Dragon King and perhaps the peace of the world—certainly part of the Chaoswar that Khoros warned them of.

The small clues that Tobimar had for locating his country suddenly come into clear focus when he realizes that the god Myrionar's symbolism and location fit everything he has heard, pointing him and Poplock to Evanwyl. In the company of a new ally, Xavier Ross of Earth, they head for Evanwyl, confronting demonic pursuers along the way.

With her new Raiment and accompanying sword, Kyri begins her work of undermining the false Justiciars and preparing to confront them. She attempts to convince the first, Mist Owl, to change sides and help her, but he fears the force behind the false Justiciars too much to do this, and dies at her hand. A second Justiciar, Shrike, also fails to kill her, afraid that she will convince his adoptive son, the Justiciar Condor, to follow her, and this will lead to Condor's death. Realizing that her confrontational approach is making it almost certain that she must fight each one, she chooses to try another way: to approach them not as a Justiciar, but as their "little sister," Kyri Vantage. For this, she selects Thornfalcon, the least martial of the Justiciars.

At the same time, Tobimar and Poplock have arrived in Evanwyl, having parted ways temporarily with Xavier. They hear the rumor of a false Justiciar named "Phoenix" who has killed at least one of the real Justiciars, and, as this fits with the sort of thing they've already encountered more than once, offer their services to help hunt down this Phoenix. They come across Shrike's body and deduce where Phoenix is headed next—although they do not realize the truth yet.

Kyri makes contact with Thornfalcon, who seems open to her approach...until he reveals that he has set a trap for her. He was the one who killed her brother, and who has directed most of the operations of the false Justiciars (although there is someone or something above him).

Tobimar and Poplock arrive at Thornfalcon's just in time to prevent him from murdering Kyri, and instead find themselves in a fight to the death. But Kyri escapes her imprisonment and joins them; together the three kill Thornfalcon despite his nigh-demonic powers, but are then caught in a trap that is unleashing an apparently endless horde of monsters into the midst of Evanwyl. At the last minute, Xavier shows up, and together they locate the source of the monstrosities; Kyri calls upon the power of Myrionar and destroys the gateway through which they are coming.

Once all four have been introduced and understand each others' stories, Kyri, Poplock, Tobimar, and Xavier make their way to the Temple of the Balanced Sword where they confront two more false Justiciars, Bolthawk and Skyharrier, and reveal them for what they are.

The truth has been revealed, but they know that there are more mysteries—who was truly behind Thornfalcon, how a god's chosen emissaries can be corrupted, and how this all connects to the rise of war throughout the world. With Xavier now gone on his own quest, it falls to the three of them to find the answers...

PHOENIX IN SHADOW

PROLOGUE

This is . . . most interesting.

It surveyed the clearing, smoke still drifting from multiple scattered fires which had—mostly—died out by now, dozens of bodies of monstrous, twisted . . . *things* lying everywhere, and a huge scar of blackened earth that stretched from an underground opening to fan out all the way to the edge; ash, dust, and blood coated everything black, gray, and red-brown, shocking against the vibrant green of the jungle. *It appears I have arrived rather late for the party. What a shame.*

It . . . well, *sniffed* would have been an appropriate term, but while it did think of the perceptions it gained as scents, they were not; the senses it extended were far beyond those of ordinary creatures, born of its essence and power, and not limited to the physical. *A mighty battle indeed, and much more than I would have expected . . .*

In all honesty it *had* expected that—when the conflict came—one of two things would happen; either Thornfalcon would kill the Phoenix, or the new-minted Justiciar would somehow overcome Thornfalcon. If the latter, well, then his expectations would be fully met. But it had thought this confrontation still a bit in the future, and its arrival here was purely fortuitous—a morning conference with its most useful acolyte to make some further arrangements . . . which, it seemed, would no longer be necessary. *So let us see what really occurred.*

As the senses of magic and power, tracery of traces of past

1

conflict, began to impress themselves upon the being's conscious-
ness, it raised one eyebrow. *Oh, now, not nearly so simple as I
thought. No, not at all.*

There certainly *was* godscent here—it knew the particular
tang of Myrionar well. *Of necessity,* it thought with a smile, *for
it is rather hard to fool others with a counterfeit unless one truly
understands the original.* But there were a myriad of other scents.
Alchemical concoctions and materials had been used with abandon,
and it was impossible—with the god-fire's interference—to tell if
it had all been Thornfalcon's work, or someone else's. Other types
of magic...and was that another god-scent? It frowned. *No, it's
possibly* more *than one. Or a mixture, magic and god-power. Not
familiar directly...but there is a touch of the Mortal God about
it that I do not like at* all.

While it did not—precisely—fear any of the gods, there were
those it was very wise to take extremely seriously. The Greatest Dragons, certainly, Chromaias and the Four...but of them
all, perhaps the most to be feared by those—like itself—which
walked the darkest paths was Terian, the Nemesis of Evil, Light
in the Darkness, the Mortal God, the Infinite. *Yet it is not the
touch of a priest or a god-warrior. Something else, and that is
intriguing indeed.*

Finally it found one of the things it was looking for: Thornfalcon's body, headless and now burned almost beyond recogni-
tion. *Now, let us see...* It frowned. *Scarce anything remains. I
can barely sense his soul now. It desperately clings to the remains
still, which is why I sensed not his defeat before I came...but it
is nigh-obliterated.*

Reaching out, it drew in what remained, or tried to. But even
the effort of pulling in the traces caused them to fade, shatter, just
as touching the ashes caused them to collapse into shapelessness,
losing whatever they had kept of their shape in life.

It smiled with an edge of apology. *I had promised you power,
Thornfalcon, and of your people you had shown much promise...
and begun to learn true mastery. I am surprised your life has
truly ended. This should* not *have happened.*

One—*or more,* it corrected itself—of the weapons used upon
Thornfalcon must have been made in such a fashion as to break
even the most unique changes that the being had made to Thornfalcon's essence, to shatter that particular soul-hungry pattern and

make it impotent. *Were it otherwise, Thornfalcon would rise again, though it might have taken time. I would do well to remember this myself, for when the time comes.*

This did leave another problem, in that it could not simply ask Thornfalcon what had happened, what he had learned in that final and titanic conflict. *Must do this the harder way; depending on what the Phoenix learned, and how he, or she, chooses to act, I may be on a rather limited timetable now!*

It extended its senses further, to make sure there were no witnesses. *I do not want interruptions now; there are things that would need explanation.* Fortunately it had come here early in the morning and Thornfalcon's little estate was set at a distance from other residences, but there would be gawkers, or more purposeful visitors, soon enough.

Someone took Thornfalcon's head. Single cut, very clean, large blade. Definitely this "Phoenix" as described.

But were you fighting him alone, avenging Justiciar of Myrionar? True, you have killed two others, and it smiled to think of what would come of that second killing, one it had sensed only a short time before, *but Thornfalcon was undoubtedly much more challenging an opponent, and I did not read your prior battles as ones in which you had no difficulty. No, you had help, I think.*

It shifted form to one more comfortable for careful inspection of the perimeter. It was at the edge of the clearing that traces would remain of those who had come in . . . or left. It took some time, but finally it found what it sought: a faint set of marks and tracks leading away, into the jungle.

Two sets of feet . . . no, three . . . left here. And, it would appear, at very much the same time. Yes, my little Phoenix, you have acquired friends . . . and here, I have your scent.

It laughed aloud suddenly, a sound that was more tearing metal and shattering bone than human amusement. *Kyri Victoria Vantage! A perfect symmetry, and oh, it makes so very much sense of all things. Yes, an excellent choice, Myrionar, a well-played choice of your final piece in our game.*

The creature could now understand the exact way in which the prior Justiciars had died; they had been undone by their own sentiments, slowed or confused by the children they had known all their lives confronting them with their crimes. Mist Owl would have allowed his death as a sort of futile penance, while Shrike... It smiled. Shrike would have become emotional and desperate for another reason.

However, Thornfalcon... The figure shook its head. Thornfalcon would not have been so affected. He did have other interests which might have led him astray, but that of pure sentiment, no. She would have needed help, indeed.

It considered the scents of the companions. *Both young men, yes. Of a similar age, it would seem. The first... there is a general familiarity about it, but the individual is unknown. But it has been a long time since I scented this particular... could it be?*

It moved along the trail, finding that the three were traveling in a nearly straight line, and very purposefully... *Towards the capital, I think. Yes. Interesting. That may make things difficult... but I must learn more before I act.*

It retraced its steps, looking for additional clues that it might have missed. *Why is there a hint of the Mortal God on this one?* There was no immediate answer, though the faint scent taunted it maddeningly. *Never mind. Let us examine the third.*

The third young man... *Now that is most interesting. There is a scent with him of... plastics. Electronics. By my Power, this boy must be from the other world!*

Something about that bothered him. After a moment, he recalled what that was. Zarathanton... the five young people who had been, as they might have said, "framed" for the assassination of the Sauran King... his agent had been emphatic that they claimed to come from Earth. *It would be ludicrous to suppose that another such traveler could have come so soon, so this must be one of those five—one who has either escaped the inescapable, or been released.*

There was also some other energy, a sense, that sent a tingle of warning and anticipation throughout the creature. *Traces of something ancient, ancient indeed. Yet I cannot quite make it out.*

But that was not all. There was *another* trace of presence, another spirit-scent... *And this, too, something hinting of the familiar.* It allowed itself another good-natured internal complaint about the limitations it was currently saddled with. *Necessary for the way things must be done, yes, but there are times I am tempted...*

Too many feet—humanoid and otherwise—had trampled these grounds in that combat, especially in that endgame against a tide of unnatural monstrosities. *And that was* very *well-done, Thornfalcon. I have a suspicion as to the source of these things, but for you to have found it, been able to make the appropriate bargains... it truly* is *a shame you are dead.* It quickened its pace, criss-crossing the entire clearing, walking, sensing, sniffing...

A very faint scent caught at its senses now, and it glanced around and down, found itself looking at a tiny thing that glittered on the ground. Changing shape back to human, it reached down and gingerly picked up the little metal shaft. *Pointed. Notched at the other end.* It sniffed carefully. *Alchemical bolt. But how* tiny. *Now what could...*

For a moment it was no longer smiling. *Now* that *is too far for coincidence; first the child of Zaralandar finds his way here and is working with the last Justiciar, and now* this? *From the center of the Great Forest to here? With the Phoenix and whoever these others are? Voorith had no visible connections here, so what would have led this one hence?*

Its eyes narrowed and it looked around, suspicious. *And if that is the case, other aspects of the plan may be in more danger than it appears.* It sniffed again at the ground, and now, with its senses fully alerted, it caught the faintest hint, a chime and a flicker in the background.

That it recognized instantly, and it grinned savagely, realizing that all of their plans *were* in more jeopardy than it had imagined... and it was glad of it, in truth. *My oldest mortal enemy... is it truly you again, Khoros? Have you dared to try your hand once more? I must discover if it is so!*

It was even more glad, now, that its true goals were still buried layers deep, hidden behind the dozen other plots in which it was involved. *Kerlamion, o King, your plans proceed apace... yet they may be doomed to failure.*

As might be true of the other three branches of the conspiracy. It nodded. *I must find a way to have this possible connection discovered, brought to their attention. It would not do to make it easy on our adversaries, yet the King of Demons and our other... allies do not have any need to know how I have learned these things.*

It glanced up at the sky. *Time to leave; I have learned what I could here.*

More importantly, it guessed what the Phoenix was about to do, and if it was right, there was little to be done to stop her now.

However, if it moved very swiftly, it should be able to arrive at Justiciar's Retreat *just* ahead of someone else who must be even now approaching. *That should be very entertaining . . . and useful, if his performance is as expected.*

It strode into the jungle, chuckling, shape becoming something swift and terrible, arrowing towards the once-holy sanctum.

CHAPTER 1

Aran felt cold, cold inside, so cold that he was able to ignore his fear entirely. *There is nothing* to *fear here, not now. For what I want and what* It *wants, they must be the same now.*

Even so, he had to steel himself to knock at the great stone and metal portal which was the Hall of Balance, the innermost area of the Justiciar's Retreat...and the chosen quarters of their leader. He remembered the last time he had entered there, practically dragged by Shrike...

"Enter, Condor."

The voice sent a new bolt of fear through Condor's heart. *I'd expected* Thornfalcon. *Expected that I'd have to argue with him to reach...It.*

But in a way, this was better. He had no idea why Thornfalcon's patron would be here now, and even less as to why Thornfalcon would not be present, but at least now there would be no impediments to his purpose. He shoved the fear away, replaced it with the cold-burning rage, and entered.

The room was dimly lit, as it nearly always was. Part of him wanted to believe it was because the creature feared light, but he'd watched It in the sunlight too many times. "You must know by now."

It raised an entirely human-looking eyebrow over a pure-blue eye. "How bold a beginning; not even a hint of the courtesies. But yes, I know, Condor; Shrike has fallen. A terrible loss for you." The last words carried an *almost* sincere note of sympathy, that nearness to human feeling making it even more jarring.

He gritted his teeth. *I cannot get into a duel of words with It. It will enrage me if It so pleases, and then humiliate me, and I will still need to ask this of It.* "I apologize for my failure in diplomacy; I am empty of thanks or courtesy this day, for he was my father in all but blood."

"Of course." There was little irony in the voice now. "And I will tolerate...for the moment...a certain amount of personal clumsiness, Condor. But you did not come here to speak of the dead, I think, but of the living."

He knows, or guesses. Of course. Aran, the Condor, laughed suddenly. "Yes. Of those living who must soon die. This...this *Phoenix,*" he spat the name out as though it burned his tongue, "killed Shrike, left his body lying in the woods, didn't even *burn* it or bury it, like you'd leave some animal in the woods, no ceremony, nothing." Even as he said it, he heard his voice rising, and suddenly felt no inclination to restrain himself. "Well, I'll do the same to him!"

"Or her," the other responded with maddening equanimity. "And really, why the rage? You know perfectly well that in all likelihood this is the *true* Justiciar of Myrionar. You're the traitors and monsters. Didn't you say something like that...perhaps even here in this room?"

"Do not *patronize* me, monster! I'm beyond fear of anyone, even you!"

Its eyes narrowed, and the blue was like frozen sea. "Have a care, Condor."

"I have no care *at all*, for all that I had left to care *for*—once you and Shrike had done with me—is gone. I will at the least follow, for once, the true path of my name, for I want *vengeance.*"

It raised an eyebrow. "As do we all, in our own way. I have hardly barred you—any of you—from hunting down this Phoenix. Indeed, I urge you all to the hunt frequently, and have begun... my own little investigations as well."

"*NO!*"

Actual surprise showed in the falsely-human eyes when it found Skyvault at its throat, and Condor continued. "I don't want you involved at all! Phoenix is *mine!*"

It stood still, studying him.

"But I'm not stupid. This Phoenix killed Mist Owl, killed... killed my *sirza.*"

"And Thornfalcon, but hours agone," the creature said, its voice unaffected by the threat of the blade.

Aran paused in his rage, momentary shock forcing him to re-evaluate the situation. He knew—none better—just what a monster Thornfalcon had been.

But this only reinforced his current point. "So, he killed your favorite, too. Phoenix *broke* Shrike's axe, carved up one...no, *two* other Raiments now. I'm good, but I'm not that good."

It reached up and gently pushed the blade down with irresistible force. "Interesting. If I choose not to take your soul for daring to draw sword on me, what then is it you want?"

"You know perfectly well. I want power to match Phoenix's, to *out*match anything that Myrionar can give its last servant. I want to face Phoenix down, myself, and kill him or her and spit on their grave. I want to rip out their guts and let them die slowly and rot on some forgotten hillside the way Phoenix would have let my father rot." He had to force the words out through tears and a snarl of gritted teeth.

Their leader suddenly burst out in laughter, a sound so warm and human that Aran shuddered despite his rage and determination. *No wonder that no one suspects a thing.*

"And you think I can give you *that* power, Condor? Do you realize what Thornfalcon was? That I had already *given* him much power the rest of you lacked, and still he was finished—and rather handily too, or so it would seem—by this Phoenix?" It was smiling in a way that sent shivers down his spine, and a distant part of him was screaming that he should back down, change his mind, run. But in the front of his mind he saw a beloved face in a death grimace, black-caked blood around a shattered piece of metal, and flies hovering for the feast.

"If you can't, then *you* are finished too, because the Phoenix will find this place—and you—eventually, even if they don't catch you outside when you're fooling the rest of the world! You've openly mocked the Balanced Sword enough—are you going to back down? Tell me that Myrionar is, after all, more powerful than us, and we're all doomed?"

For a moment It regarded him, still with that gentle smile that seemed to imply terror beyond imagining. "No...no, I would not say that. Myrionar's power is vastly diminished, for in these centuries at my work it has been eroded, slowly, surely, but nigh-completely. This is a final desperation move, the only one left to a deity in Myrionar's position. But just as a cornered animal, even wounded, can be surprisingly dangerous, so it is with a near-ended god. All they have left will be devoted to this final Champion. I have many things to devote my own attention to, for—as you learned some time ago—this is but one small part of the grand design. I have such power, perhaps, but I cannot give it to you—especially since, alas, I have seen you are less than dedicated to our ideals, unlike Thornfalcon."

Condor wanted to lash out again at the urbanely-smiling mask in front of him, but he knew that would end any hope of revenge by ending his life. "So you're saying there's nothing you can do?"

"I am afraid..." It stopped, tilted its head, and the smile suddenly widened. "Perhaps. Perhaps there is. Not something that *I* can do, no, but..."

"What...what do you mean?"

The figure turned slowly and considered the polished mirror-scroll set on the desk at the center of the room, and Condor felt as though his guts were going to freeze. It looked back at him with that same smile. "Normally I would not call...but it is true that this Phoenix could be a significant hindrance to our cause, given time. *He* has the power you seek, do not doubt it."

"But..." He shuddered, but shook his head. "He has the power, but how could he give it to *me?*"

"We can but ask." Before Aran could object, the human-seeming figure passed a hand over the mirror. "Great Kerlamion, your servant begs your attention."

The shining surface blackened, became a room of darkness with something darker than any darkness seated upon a throne, the only light from eyes of screaming blue-white. "Viedraverion." The eyes shifted. "Why is this one before us again?"

"A...small problem has emerged in Evanwyl, oh Blackstar."

The eyes narrowed. "You begin with circumlocutions we expect from others such as Balgoltha. Do not follow that path, for we have no patience for it, even for one with such a record as your own."

Viedraverion—*if that is its real name*—shrugged and smiled. "You are of course right, King of Demons. As I had expected, the Balanced Sword is forced to make its final move, and has produced a true Champion. Now, while I believe I can maintain all as we desire it, this is certainly a crisis of minor but perhaps significant import."

The barely-visible head of blackness nodded. "Go on."

"I have many other duties you wish me to attend to, of course. There are so many... details involved across the world." He gestured to Condor, who flinched as the alien, deadly gaze turned back to him. "The champion, called Phoenix, has slain three of my false Justiciars. One of them was, in essence, the father of Condor." It smiled more broadly. "We can, of course, appreciate the strong bond between father and son."

The laugh from Kerlamion Blackstar was the sound of the very rending of air, and the smile a blue-white void of pain, and Condor very nearly did run then. "In our own way, yes, we can." It leaned forward, and though the mirror-scroll did not change at all, Condor felt as though something immense was looming over him. "And so from us you seek the power to avenge yourself, to counter the final throes of a failing god? Answer us!"

Condor swallowed. "Y-yes, mighty Kerlamion." *I am already damned, my soul must already be his as a false Justiciar.* "Something that will give me the strength to face the Phoenix, to shatter his or her power, their new-forged Raiment, break their sword and ... and tear their soul apart." *If my sirza will find no rest in the afterlife, no more will Phoenix—no salvation by Myrionar or by its allies in death.*

"And this is the one who thought to abandon us, that was drawn by the Light?" Kerlamion spoke to its servant.

"Even so. By a noble and courageous girl, even." It smiled.

Kerlamion chuckled again. "Then we are pleased, and we see that, though you tremble, Condor, you stand firm. Veidraverion sees that the time is nigh, and he is right. Come, then, to us, and we shall give to you the power you desire." The mirror went blank.

Elation warred with terror and confusion. "I ... thank you, mighty King ..." *But there is no way to Kerlamion's Throne that the living and human can travel!*

"Fear not, Aran," their leader said, with a smile even more chilling, and answered the unspoken words with a darker mystery. "You shall walk there on your own living feet, and stand alive before the Throne of All Hells itself."

CHAPTER 2

"Down!" Kyri shouted.

Tobimar reacted just in time; the huge serpent's venom sprayed above his head, striking the grass and bushes behind them, almost instantly turning them gray and brittle. "Terian and Chromaias!"

If that struck him, he could be killed! Not that getting hit by the thing's immense teeth or caught by coils the thickness of a strong man's thigh would be any better, but the virulence of the poison stunned her.

Also somewhat stunning was the pain in her heart at the thought of Tobimar dying. She was aware that this was something she should think about, should understand—but this was not the time.

The green-black monster's head swayed back uncannily fast, evading Flamewing's strike, then lunged forward; its teeth, in turn, rebounded from the Raiment of the Phoenix, and drops of venom dribbled harmlessly down and away. Still, the impact sent her tumbling away, a shock of pain echoing through her frame. *It's even stronger than I thought. And I thought a fifty-foot snake would be awfully strong.*

Tobimar took a twin cut at the creature, distracting it from Kyri momentarily, but the monster's scales rippled and deflected most of the force of the blow; what should have been crippling wounds became mere scratches. It slewed around and sprayed more venom at him, but the Skysand Prince anticipated the move and leapt *over* the downward-slanting spray.

Then the gray, dead bush reached out and grasped Tobimar.

Kyri charged forward, even as part of her stared in disbelief. *The bush became its* servant *upon death? What monstrous thing* is *this?*

The monster was forced to turn away from Tobimar at the last moment or have Flamewing's blazing blade take its head, but now Tobimar was struggling in earnest. *The hideous corruption in Rivendream Pass is worse than I imagined. I never thought of anything such as this. Poplock, where* are *you?*

"Come forth, Son of Fire, and consume our enemies!" shouted a voice from somewhere in the greenery.

A glittering little red crystal flew out and shattered, expanding into a low, squat, four-legged sinuous form that was formed of pure white flame. "*Ssssooo it sssshall be,*" it hissed, a voice of water striking white-hot steel, and lunged at the huge serpent.

Astonishingly, the monster's scales were at least partially proof against fire as well, for though it let loose a steamkettle whistle of pain and rage at the salamander's attack, it did not appear terribly burned.

But it had reflexively turned towards the source of pain, and *that* gave Kyri the opening she had sought. Flamewing streaked out and around, a meteor and lightning bolt in one, and with a terrific impact the titanic greatsword sheared clean through the serpent. She leapt back to clear the thing's death throes, and the salamander scrambled up and down the twisting coils, directing its flames and reducing the corpse to ash. It then bobbed in her direction and in the direction of the voice from the bushes, and vanished in a puff of smoke.

"Well, *drought,* Kyri!" the little toad said plaintively as he emerged from the bushes. "If I'd known you were going to kill it *that* fast I might have saved *him* for another time."

She shook her head with a grin. "It was that *distraction* that permitted the blow, o most cautious of Toads." She looked to Tobimar, who was now standing; the gray bush had fallen apart once its master was slain. "Are you all right, Tobimar?"

"Not...entirely."

She saw grayish trails across his cheeks and hands; fortunately the thing's tendrils had not reached the eyes. "Hold still."

She called upon Myrionar's power as she touched her friend. The power came, golden light that erased gray, eased pain, restored strength and health.

But she felt *resistance* this time—both from the dead grayness, a pushing and denial that tried to shunt the power of the God of Justice and Vengeance away, prevent it from touching the parts of Tobimar it had claimed, and from outside, as though Myrionar were more distant. She set her jaw and drove her will against the grayness, and it shattered, passing into darkness like that which she sensed all around, and then dispersing.

The strain on her face did not escape Tobimar's observation; one of his greatest talents was to see that which others hid, she'd noticed. "That was harder than usual, I see."

She straightened and nodded, looking around warily. "Yes. We were warned it would be."

She remembered how they'd finally decided it was time...a bright day, a good day, a day when things seemed right...

CHAPTER 3

The twin swords flickered at her like darting reflections from a pool of water, and Kyri realized just how very, very good Tobimar Silverun was with those weapons. In moments she deflected two strikes with her own sword, and still felt three, no, four impacts of those blades on her Raiment. *And I've already increased my speed some.*

His raven-black hair was pulled back in a long ponytail that swirled behind Tobimar as he pirouetted away from her retaliatory attack; his brilliant blue eyes measured her, calm yet with a hint of the laughing joy she knew he felt, that she echoed, at this chance to push each other to their limits against a foe worthy of their skill yet not an enemy to be destroyed.

"Heads up!" called another voice.

Oh, no!

The third combatant was so small that even with the hint of his voice she didn't see him; the sphere of swirling vapor hurtling at them, however, was all too obvious. She called the flame of the Phoenix and carved downward, slashing a safe haven through the spell; at her side, Tobimar did the same somehow, weaving a defense from willpower and the unique discipline of the art which the mage Khoros had taught him.

"Attacking us *both*?" Tobimar shook his head. "In that case, my lady, shall we?"

"Oh, yes, let's."

Now she and Tobimar ran stride-for-stride towards the source of that mystical assault, and a part of her remembered how—even when they had first met, before they had even been formally introduced—somehow they had *known* how to work together.

A tiny brown streak burst from a clump of grass on that side of the training field, and suddenly the mists erupted low and thick, covering the ground to a depth of two feet. *That's not good; we can't see him coming—*

She closed her eyes, letting the Truth of Myrionar guide her, even as she knew Tobimar would be extending his own senses...

There!

From the ground *behind* them Poplock Duckweed sprang, and he gave a flip in midair that, astonishingly, caused Tobimar Silverun's sword to pass *just* under him. Kyri's sword blocked the little Toad's path to her, but he wasn't aiming for the young Justiciar, but at her partner, Tobimar. Now he was *on* the Prince of Skysand, scuttling with startling surety *under* the arm, even as it swung, then around to the back—

And Tobimar flipped and came down *on* his back. Poplock *barely* got out from underneath in time, but he had Steelthorn out, the slender blade glittering deadly silver—

—and freezing, as he realized that the immense gold-red sheened sword Flamewing was an inch from his brown, warty hide. "Whoops."

"Do you *both* yield?" she asked with a grin, and she could see that Tobimar realized the way she was standing, she could simply run them *both* through.

"Yield," said the Toad, sheathing Steelthorn.

"Yield," agreed Tobimar. Once she lifted her blade, he rose. "Shall we try another?"

"Best four out of seven?" she asked with a grin. "No, I think this is more than enough for today. I'm quite winded."

"I think we all are." Tobimar nodded to Poplock, who then bounced to each of them, removing the safecharm from their weapons. "That vortex ball—I didn't expect that one. Where'd you learn *that?*"

"Sasha Rithair, of course," the little Toad answered, bouncing to his accustomed location on Tobimar's shoulder, as they walked back into the Vantage mansion. "She may specialize in summonings—and believe me, I've been learning those, too—but she's got all the magic basics down, and after what *we've* been through, I figured I couldn't just sit there and dabble in magic. Time to get serious about it." He gave an exaggerated sigh. "Not that it *does* much when you guys can just *cut the spell apart.*"

Kyri laughed, and let the Raiment flow off her and onto a nearby rack. "You *did* warn us in advance. I don't think you'll do that with our enemies. Besides, that doesn't always work."

She noticed that Tobimar was sheathing and unsheathing his swords; the motion seemed slightly uneven. "What is it?"

He held up the slightly curved, tri-hilted swords with a rueful grin. She saw that the shining perfection of the metal was marred with dings and one was slightly bent. "I am afraid that even the finest swords in the Skysand armory weren't really meant for contesting with Justiciars—real or false."

"Why didn't you *tell* me?" She was, truthfully, somewhat annoyed. Tobimar and she were allies against forces that even she barely understood, and the *last* thing they needed was one of them working at less than their top form.

"Oh, I kept meaning to get them repaired, but we've been doing so much putting Evanwyl back together it just never quite got done. You're entirely right, though, I should have told you and made sure it was done. My apologies."

His expression was so solemn that she couldn't keep the serious look on her own face. "Oh, fine, fine, you're forgiven. But aren't your weapons magical? I can't believe that Skysand has no mages."

"Oh, we have some magicians, of various types, certainly. But... Kyri, you *have* to understand that fighting things that play on *your* level just isn't the same as most battles. I've fought quite a few things—*mazakh*, graverisen, a few demons, once one of the least Wormspawn, a few other things—especially when we were traveling with Xavier—but you and Thornfalcon?" He shook his head ruefully. "My Lady, that is a *whole* different kind of thing. There were points in that battle where I knew if I had been too close, at the wrong angle, the power that you were both *deflecting* would be enough to kill me. Training with you... I think both Poplock and I have been learning just how very far we have to go."

Startled, she looked at the two Adventurers. Tobimar was completely serious, and the Toad bobbed an assenting nod.

"Well," she began, not quite knowing what to say. "Well... all right, I suppose there must be truth in that. If there wasn't something special about a Justiciar, we wouldn't need them. But really, training with the two of *you* makes *me* feel the same way. And sometimes I think that Xavier would have been worse."

"Oh, no doubt," said Poplock with a chuckle. His tongue snapped out to grab a flying insect before he continued. "He had some very nasty tricks."

He glanced at the two of them as they hesitated at the base of the stairwell. "Oh, that's right. Clean up or go to eat? Here, I'll help with that."

Kyri saw the Toad make a few gestures and a sparkling, cool mist enveloped her and Tobimar, evaporating to leave her feeling as though she'd just had a nice long shower. "Now *that* is impressive, Poplock."

"Sure more useful in most situations than calling the thunder down," Poplock agreed with a bounce, and held on as she and Tobimar headed for the dining hall. "So like I said, Xavier had some real nasty tricks. But *power*-wise? We were *totally* in the mud compared to you two, Kyri. You and Thornfalcon were way, *way* out of our normal playing level. Look at what you did at the end there, calling on Myrionar and wiping out . . . well, I don't know how many, but it was a *lot* of monsters in one big flare. I'd bet Thornfalcon could do stuff like that too, if he had prepped."

Kyri couldn't argue; whatever power had been backing Thornfalcon—whatever it was that lay behind the false Justiciars—had been able to fake the Justiciars well enough that no one could tell. She had to assume anything *she* could do, they could equal. She seated herself at the table and nodded to Vanstell to have the food brought out. "You're right. But I'd have been dead, dead, dead if you hadn't come along. I really can't see you as being *that* far below me."

The exiled Prince of Skysand grinned, and snagged a crispwing as the platter was set down. "I didn't say we didn't have some kind of edge. But my poor swords, *they* didn't have the edge."

"Or rather, they don't have much of an edge *now*," Poplock corrected, earning a poke from his friend.

"I really think you need to get them fixed soon, Tobimar," she said slowly, as she served herself from the other platters. "Evanwyl's pretty stable now, and I know time's slipping away."

Tobimar paused in eating, and nodded seriously. "I know. I wasn't going to push you—this is your country—"

"But maybe you should have. It doesn't do any good to help Evanwyl if the threat that's going to destroy it is still out there."

"No one's seen the other Justiciars, have they?"

She shook her head. "Not since they fled from the Temple before Arbiter Kelsley's wrath, no. But that just means they've been taking this time to figure out their next step, while we've been clearing up everything...without ruining everything." The two didn't ask what she meant; they *knew*, and she was incredibly lucky the two had been able to stay and help her.

The problem of course was that the Justiciars being utterly corrupt—and in the case of Thornfalcon, vastly worse than merely corrupt—was a *shattering* blow to the faith that held up Evanwyl. The faith of Myrionar, the Balanced Sword, god of Justice and Vengeance, was represented most clearly by two groups: the priests—Arbiters and Seekers and such—and by the Justiciars, the living symbols of the faith. The fact that the entire order had become corrupt, had committed murders for *years* and never been caught, had even been able to mislead and trick Arbiter Kelsley, undermined all the faith Evanwyl had relied on since before the last Chaoswar, at least.

So Kyri had had no *choice* but to stay, to shore up the damaged faith. It wasn't just a matter of keeping Evanwyl together and strong, though that would have been more than enough for her, but it was also a matter of the mission Myrionar had laid upon her. She had to be, as the god had said, the living representative of the Balanced Sword, and surely that included keeping the few remaining worshipers—the people of Evanwyl—strong in their faith.

"You still can't find the Justiciar's Retreat?"

She shook her head and sighed. "I'd *hoped* that I could find it now, because I'm a real Justiciar. But whatever corrupted the Justiciars obviously dealt with that; I get no sense of location even when I head to the West, which I *know* is the right general direction. Rion told me that all he had to do was *think* about going to the Retreat and he suddenly knew exactly where he was going. Only one of the other false Justiciars can find their way to the Retreat now."

"There has *got* to be some other way," Poplock said emphatically, voice slightly muffled as he snagged a large green darter out of the air and stuffed it into his mouth. "There's other gods, and magicians, and so on."

Kyri nodded. "Oh, I have no doubt there *is* some other way. I just don't know what it is. Neither does Arbiter Kelsley, or your new teacher Sasha."

Tobimar reached for another crispwing, to find that they were all gone. His expression as he looked down and realized he *had* eaten them all caused her to grin; she gestured to Sanhon, one of the three servers this evening, who whisked the old plate away and replaced it with another. "There you go, Master Tobimar."

He had tried to convince them not to call him "Master," but that had failed miserably, as she could have told him if he'd asked. So there was only a slight twitch before he replied, "Thank you, Sanhon. I don't suppose..."

"You want *more* crispwings? Don't you have them—"

"In Skysand? Almost never. They had to be imported from the Empire of the Mountain, at best, and maybe from somewhere in the State of the Dragon King. I think I got them three times before in my life, and these are just wonderful."

The older woman—*well, older than* me, *but not anything like* old—smiled. "In that case I'm sure I can get Dankhron to fry up some more, if you can wait."

"Thank you so much; I'd be glad to wait. I can always eat something else." She watched as he surveyed the generous assortment of fruits, vegetables, and cheeses in the center of the table. Grabbing a handful of *arlavas*—greenish berries with a frosty sheen—he sat back and looked over to Kyri. "Well, all right, let's leave that problem aside for now," he said with a quick smile that emphasized the clean symmetry of his face. "Do you think you could leave Evanwyl now? Are things all right?"

Kyri considered. The Temple of the Balance was fully repaired, and—more importantly—people were attending regularly again, and she *felt* their faith, especially when she was there, part of the ceremony with Arbiter Kelsley. Their doubts had slowly faded over the last month or so; she knew this was because pretty much everyone in Evanwyl, from the Watchland to farmers and butchers and the other Eyes and Arms knew her, and they *listened* to her when she explained to them her faith, her mission, and the need for not just her, but *everyone*, to believe in Myrionar. "It has already fulfilled much of Its promise to me," she would say, "and I now *know* that It will somehow fulfill the rest of it, so long as I stay true. And I know It will bless us all if we can all find it in our hearts to keep our faith in the Balanced Sword."

"I think...yes, I think they are," she said finally. "Oh, I'm always going to be nervous that leaving will trigger some catastrophe, but waiting forever will be worse. There's only..."

Somehow he caught on, perhaps from seeing her glance around the room. "Oh, that's right. Your aunt isn't here and so there won't be anyone guarding the family home."

"Is that silly of me? I mean, it's not like the house will fall apart, Vanstell will—"

"It's *not* silly at all," Poplock said emphatically from somewhere near the cheese wheels. She saw him pop up from behind one, chewing on a berry. "The Vantages are a symbol to your people. Even if you aren't here, this place is going to be a symbol, and someone might decide that burning that symbol down, like they did your parents' house, would be a great statement of how weak you and your god are. Someone being the false Justiciars, or their boss." He made a comical face. "Well, okay, hard to *burn* this place down since it's mostly stone, but you get the idea."

She wished she could argue that, but she couldn't. Vantage Fortress *was* a symbol, hundreds, maybe thousands of years old, and if their enemies wrecked it after she left...

She toyed with the seasoned steak in front of her. "You're right, of course. But I can't stay here forever. Your mission and mine...time's not standing still, and we know what's happening elsewhere. But I need *someone* who will be able to keep Vantage Fortress...*alive*, I guess, even if they're not a Vantage. Vanstell—"

Vanstell shook his head and smiled. "My Lady, I am—with no false modesty—an excellent Master of House, and I have been proud to serve you and your family in that capacity for the last twenty-two years. But I am, regrettably, not a person with the dynamic and powerful presence you would need."

Kyri smiled fondly at him. "I was about to say something of the sort, because I know what you like to do, and if you wanted to be that kind of person, we'd already know it. But then...who? Or do I leave anyway?"

"You may have to," Tobimar said with obvious reluctance. "Believe me, I understand your concern—in your position I'd share it—but as you said, the world isn't waiting for us."

"Perhaps *I* might offer a solution," said an impossibly familiar voice from the doorway.

Almost without realizing it, Kyri found herself standing, staring in simultaneous disbelief and joy.

Tall, angular, straight of figure, impassive of expression, Lythos, her invincible, imperturbable Master of Arms, stood framed in the doorway.

And then the *Sho-Ka-Taida* collapsed to his knees.

"Lythos!"

CHAPTER 4

Tobimar hadn't recognized the tall *Artan*, but he knew the name that Kyri gasped as the warrior nearly fell face-first to the polished stone floor. *He taught her entire family, including her parents, her brother, and her sister.*

Kyri reached the *Artan* warrior, whose deep-violet hair pooled slightly on the floor before him as he knelt on all fours, arms and knees supporting him so he looked like a man broken. "Lythos... *Sho-Ka-Taida*, are you all right?"

The head lifted then, and Tobimar could see a tiny smile, a glint of amusement in the eyes that matched the hair. "More exhausted and worn than I have been in many generations, but my injuries are minor. I have...perhaps driven myself too far, too fast, and have so failed to take my own advice, eh, Kyri Vantage?"

"You...you..." To Tobimar's astonishment, Kyri suddenly burst into tears and threw her arms around Lythos; by the *Artan*'s expression, it was at least as great a surprise to him. "Lythos, I thought you might be *dead*! Thank the Balance!"

A great sadness descended upon Lythos, clouding the long, aristocratic features and dimming the smile. "Ah, of course you would have. Nearly I was, as well. It has been a trying time—but no less for you, I think."

Leaning slightly on Kyri's arm, Lythos stood. "If you will allow me to sit at table with you, I can refresh myself some and speak with you a while, before I must rest. But now that I acknowledge my body's warnings, hold them no longer at bay, I will admit that rest must come soon."

Kyri helped him sit. "You said you were *injured*, Lythos." She said the word as though she found the concept impossible to grasp. Then she shook herself and straightened. "I'm sorry, I sound like I'm fourteen again."

Her hands rested on Lythos' shoulders, and the gold-fire glow of the power of Myrionar shone out, the power that Kyri Vantage could wield because she was the one, the true, and only Justiciar of Myrionar. Even though this was far from the first time he had seen that power, the sight still sent a tingle of awe through Tobimar. His own god, Terian, rarely granted such powers to warriors who walked the world, nor did He often intervene directly.

Lythos' head came up, and in his eyes Tobimar saw an echo of the same awe, and, at the same time, something else: vindication. "So it *is* true, Kyri Victoria Vantage. You are now the Phoenix Justiciar, the one to reclaim the honor that was lost and cleanse the stain from Myrionar's name. So I heard rumor as I approached." His voice was stronger, though still exhausted, and the lines that had hinted at pain and injury were gone.

Kyri bowed. "Because you taught me, and I learned, I suppose, enough."

"Enough, yes." He smiled again, and that simple expression made Kyri smile back at him. For a moment Tobimar found himself wondering if there was something else in that smile, then kicked himself, mentally. *If there is, it is no business of mine. Besides, he is* Artan *and ancient; he wouldn't think of . . . and there I go again! It's not my* business! *Stop thinking about it!* Why *am I thinking about it?*

Vanstell himself laid a plate with carefully prepared delicacies before Lythos. "Welcome home, *Sho-Ka-Taida*," he said. "You have been greatly missed."

"Many thanks, Vanstell." Lythos took several bites, sipped at water, and seemed to finally begin to relax. "Milady Kyri Vantage, I bring to you a message from your aunt, your middle namesake Victoria."

Formality; it is an important message, then.

Kyri had clearly caught that implication as well. "May I have the message, then?"

From within a case bound to his armor, Lythos withdrew a

gem and placed it in Kyri's hand. Tobimar saw Poplock rise up in startlement. *Gem of Speaking; haven't seen one of those since I saw one conveyed by linkstone to Toron himself. They're expensive and used only for carrying messages of great import.*

Kyri took the gem and held it tightly. "I am Kyri Vantage. Show me the message," she said.

Tobimar had only seen Victoria Vantage once, from a distance, in front of the Palace of the Dragon, but from that glimpse and the portraits around the house he could instantly recognize the older woman—hair streaked with silver, proud and sculpted features not terribly different from those of Kyri herself—who suddenly appeared in the air before them. She wore a brown and green travel outfit, with a pack perched on her shoulders and a staff in her hand.

"Kyri," Victoria Vantage said, "As you have this message, you already know that—by great good fortune—Lythos has returned to us. I hope this message finds you well and...successful in your quest.

"I had *hoped*," and her voice was wry, "to return to Vantage Fortress relatively soon; I hardly intended to leave you with no support, even if the Dragon King could not aid you, and I was certain I could find someone to watch over Urelle while I returned to assist you.

"However...Urelle took things into her own hands, and has run away."

Kyri gasped in shock. "*Run away*? Oh, Myrionar, no!"

Victoria Vantage shook her head. "Now, don't panic. At least, not terribly much." The apparently apropos comment reminded Tobimar strongly of the message he'd received from Khoros, where every comment he thought to make had already been anticipated and answered by the ancient mage.

"She didn't run away from despair, nor to try and catch up with you," Victoria continued, and Tobimar saw Kyri relax the tiniest bit. *She doesn't want to have that responsibility, of her sister's safety, added to her problems.* "Unfortunately, it is, in a way, your fault. And mine, I admit."

The tension was back, as the recorded message went on. "You of course recall young Ingram and Quester, who helped escort us here to Zarathanton. I also have little doubt that you noticed that Urelle seemed...rather taken with the young man. Which I cannot entirely blame her for, he is formidable, polite, and rather pretty. But a few weeks after you had left...well, obviously I had to inform your sister of what had happened. Keeping such secrets from her would be an insult to one of our family, and she had to know why you had left, and what it meant.

"In any case, she was as you might guess more than a bit annoyed—one might even say quite put out—that we chose to keep her out of the adventure to avenge Rion and the rest. I believe she actually went out one night and tried to get Myrionar to call *her* as well!"

Nervous as she obviously was, Kyri laughed at that. "Oh, she *would*. And I'm half-surprised Myrionar didn't."

"Well, a few weeks after that, Ingram received a courier message from home—from Aegeia itself, one that had been spelled to find him—and it apparently contained dire news of his homeland. I of course gave him leave to return home—we had found a decent household by then—but when he did—"

Kyri finished the line along with her distant Aunt, "—Urelle had gone with him."

"Without warning," her aunt added. "I don't believe this was a *romantic* action—or not entirely. Urelle's a bit more dramatic in that area than you, Kyri, but she's not witless. I believe that she got details out of Ingram of what had happened back home, and decided that if she couldn't help her sister, that she'd help Ingram who'd defended us and guided us. How she convinced *him* to let her come...I have no idea."

Victoria Vantage sighed. "So, Kyri, you understand that I cannot come home now. As you can see, I am leaving—the moment this message is finished—to try to catch up to her. Urelle's not helpless, but you have seen what is happening to the world. I am afraid—I am *very* much afraid—that what is happening in Aegeia is a part of that. I cannot let my youngest niece and that half-grown boy face it alone, or even solely with Quester's help."

She looked momentarily sad and worried. "I pray to the Balanced Sword that you are well, and that you understand, and that—please, Myrionar—you do not need my help now. I know that Lythos will help you in any way he can. May the Balance guide you and support you. I love you, Kyri—and I am as *proud* of you as I would be of my own daughter. Be well, be safe..." and her smile suddenly returned, "and be *victorious*."

The image faded and Kyri stood there for a moment, unmoving. Then she looked down to Lythos, who had continued eating during the message. "So you—"

"—had arrived only a short time after she had discovered Urelle's departure, yes. She begged me to carry this message to you, if you could be found, and I agreed." A shadow passed again over his face. "There is . . . nothing left for me in the Forest Sea, now."

"My sympathies, *Artan*," Tobimar said.

"Thank you. And I forget my manners as well. I am Lythos-Hei-Mandalar, called Lythos by those whom I call friend or ally. As you sit here as a guest, I take you to be at least the latter, if not the former."

"Oh, I'm *sorry*, Lythos!" Kyri looked mortified. "I should have at least done that much before grabbing Auntie's letter. Lythos, this is Tobimar Silverun of Skysand, Seventh of Seven, and one of three reasons I'm still alive after facing false Justiciar Thornfalcon. That little toad poking around through the fruit is Poplock Duckweed of Pondsparkle, the second reason." Poplock waved but said nothing; given that his mouth was bulging, Tobimar suspected he *couldn't* say anything right now.

"It is an honor to meet you both," Lythos said, and rose to give them the wide-armed bow of the *Artan*. "And I suppose that Myrionar's favor is the third reason?"

Kyri's gray eyes twinkled. "Well, okay, *four* reasons. The third I can't introduce to you because he's not here, but his name is Xavier Ross of Zaralandar itself."

The lavender eyebrow quirked upward. "You have indeed found some most interesting allies, Kyri." He leaned back, and his weariness was clear in the way that he sagged slightly in the chair. "You also obviously know what has passed in the Forest Sea and elsewhere, so I will not insist on telling you that dark tale, not now; I have passed through it and survived, and I do not wish to dwell upon it anymore." He nodded to her. "There are some things I must speak of with you alone, even though these are obviously boon companions and Adventurers of much worth. But before that, I will say this: if leave you must, I will take the stewardship of Vantage Fortress, maintaining its name and strength for you. If this will meet with your approval, that is."

"*Meet* my approval? Lythos—this is more than I could possibly have hoped. *Everyone* in Evanwyl knows you, you've been with our family for generations, and even the false Justiciars won't dare go after *you* casually."

That's for sure, Tobimar mused. *A Sho-Ka-Taida of the* Artan, *someone who trained two Justiciars and their parents...and theirs...Doesn't matter if he's not favored by a God, he'd still be open gates of* Hells *to fight.*

"Then it shall be done...as long as you have a clear destination in mind? For I will not approve of just a random wandering to find your answers in this world."

Kyri's smile was now brilliant, a flash of white against skin nearly as brown as Tobimar's own. "Oh, I *do* have a destination, Lythos." She looked to Tobimar and Poplock. "Sorry, but if you...?"

"Of course." Tobimar reached out and plucked Poplock from the table—the little Toad giving him an offended look but hanging onto a small cluster of Pixies' Apples as Tobimar placed Poplock on his shoulder. He bowed to Lythos; Poplock was good at clinging, so he didn't fall off. "We will speak later, then."

"Just as well," Poplock said finally as they exited the room. "I've got something for you. Well, something I *think* will work and I want to test before I gave it to you."

"Something you weren't going to show to Kyri?"

"Well..." The little toad scrunched his face comically. "It's something only *one* of you can use, and honestly, she's got a lot more going for her right now. If it works, it'll be a useful secret that we have as a little backup."

"Okay, what is it?" he asked. They emerged into one of the small side courtyards of Vantage Fortress. "Small" was of course relative; while Vantage Fortress wasn't the size of his home castle, and utterly *dwarfed* by T'Teranahm Chendoron, the Dragon's Palace, it was still a big building and the side courtyards were large enough to fit a good-sized house into. This particular courtyard was a sparring and exercise area, one that Tobimar had used a lot for practice of late.

"Here," Poplock said. From inside the little pack on his back, the toad produced a carved crystal; it was about two inches wide and looked like frosted glass.

"Oh, a summoning crystal? What's it for?"

"That's what I want to test." Poplock bounced off his shoulder and all the way over to the other side of the courtyard, near a notched pell for sword practice. "Okay, now that I'm well away—"

"—are you expecting something dangerous to happen?" Tobimar studied the sphere suspiciously.

"*Trust me*, Tobimar. Now, all you have to do is say 'Come forth!' and throw it down, concentrating on calling something to your aid."

Despite the Toad's occasionally low sense of humor, Poplock was very much his friend and Tobimar would, in fact, trust Poplock Duckweed with his life. "All right," he said. Envisioning a sudden and powerful need for aid, he gripped the gem. "*Come forth!*" he shouted, and threw it down.

The crystal sphere shattered with a brilliant flash, and in its place was . . .

Poplock Duckweed.

Tobimar stared in disbelief, then looked back to where Poplock had been an instant ago. "A *teleport* sphere?"

"No, a *summoning* sphere."

"But . . . you . . . it's summoning *you!*"

"Yeah, pretty darn neat, isn't it?"

"What . . . how do you *do* that? You can't summon yourself!" Tobimar stopped, took a breath. "Okay, wrong, obviously you *are* doing that. But . . . *how?*"

Poplock hopped onto a nearby post, his motion somehow conveying smug satisfaction. "Well, you understand how summoning works, right?"

"Sort of, I guess. I know there's a lot of different types of magic. Summoning . . . you bargain with a being or a spirit, right?"

Poplock waggled back and forth. "Sometimes. Little minor spirits don't have much thinking ability so you can't do much of a bargain, just pull them up, bind them, and let them pop back home when they've done the bound service. Bigger ones you can still bind whether they like it or not, but if you do *that* you'd better be real good at defense, because they'll be really nasty to you if they get a chance. You would too, if someone just dragged you out of your house and stuck you in a crystal, or forced you to promise to come when signaled—even if you were, like, in a bath at the time or something."

"Yeah, I get that." Since he was already here, Tobimar decided to do a little post-dinner exercise. *You can never get too much practice.*

"But a lot of summoning is more . . . contacting the target and working out a deal where you can call on them, and in return you give them something. Sometimes you bind them directly into the summon crystal, but usually it's more a trigger power that just pops open the gate keyed to the target, with their participation helping to draw them to you." The little Toad bounced up to his shoulder. "So I wondered if I could summon, you know, regular people. Sasha thought that was kind of funny; a lot of summoning students ask that question, I guess, and the answer is yes, you can, if they're willing, but there's a catch: the summoning crystal gets really, really big."

Tobimar burst out laughing. "But that's because it's related to the physical size of what you draw through, right?"

Poplock bounced affirmatively. "Quick on the uptake there! Exactly. If you're summoning a spirit—something that's not physical—the crystals top out pretty much at a couple inches or so, but if you're pulling through something solid, mundane, it's gotta be proportional to what you're calling, and that means, for a human being-sized summon, a rock about the size of Kyri's helm."

"Oof. Even with a neverfull pack that's not something you'll carry dozens of." He shook his head, looking down at the little brown Toad. *I think he's smarter than either me or Kyri.* "But for you, it's just a little crystal."

"Right. And it's not hard for me to get in contact with myself and convince myself to agree to work for myself, so the summoning and agreement work out pretty well. Now that we know it works, I'm gonna make another of those, and you get to keep it. Just in case something happens."

Tobimar could imagine a *lot* of scenarios where having that little crystal could come in handy; Poplock Duckweed was *formidable* in a way that even people who recognized that he was, in fact, a full-fledged member of the team often just didn't grasp. "That's a drought-damned good idea." He looked down at the spot where he'd thrown the crystal. "I have to invoke it, trigger it with my own power, link it to me when I use it, right?"

Poplock bounce-nodded in reply. "Right, that's why you have to say 'come forth' and concentrate hard on the calling."

"What happens if *you* invoke it *yourself*?"

The Toad's face scrunched up, one eye practically pulled into the head, the other staring wider in concentration. "Well, it would...hmm, I'd be invoking the magic, but the connection has to go to... But no, wait, that doesn't work, because..." He shook his whole body. "Grrrgg! Gives me a headache! I have *no* idea what would happen, and I am *not* going to try that. No."

Tobimar laughed. "Wouldn't want you to risk it. But it seemed a sort of final conclusion to the whole self-referential idea."

"True enough." The little Toad hopped back onto his shoulder as Tobimar began practicing combat movements. "Training again, *after* dinner?"

"If we're going to be leaving soon, yes. As we so astutely observed before, we're completely outclassed as things stand; we'd better practice whenever we can."

Poplock grunted. "Can't argue that. So just solo practice, or you want to spar?"

"Against you, alone?"

"If you're *afraid*..."

"Maybe I should be," Tobimar admitted. "I've *seen* you in action. But a Prince of Skysand can't back down from *that* kind of challenge." He let the little Toad bounce down and get to the other side of the courtyard. "All right—come at me!"

CHAPTER 5

"A far finer parting, this, than the last time you left us, Kyri," said Jeridan Velion, the Watchland of Evanwyl. The ruler of the little country bowed extravagantly low to Kyri, and took her hand in his.

Poplock felt the tiniest *twitch* from Tobimar at that, and wondered how long it would be before his friend talked to Kyri about what he felt. *I mean, he* can't *be unaware of it...can he?*

"That it is, Jeridan," Kyri said, and her smile held a grateful laugh. There was no sign of the subliminal tension he'd seen in her a couple of times around the Watchland—times in which, she admitted, for some reason she found the man to feel more distant though there was nothing overtly different about his behavior. "I have avenged my brother, we have found the rot at the heart of our country, and have begun the healing. But we can't stay longer; there are still so many questions left unanswered, and we must seek the answers."

The Watchland nodded; he had walked, rather than ridden, to bid Kyri and her friends goodbye, and Poplock could see why. While one of his chosen Arms to guard and assist him today was Torokar Heimdalyn, a Child of Odin in massive armor that was obviously styled something like that of the Justiciars (and thus reminded Poplock of Bolthawk), the other was Gantrista-[unpronounceable], a Shellikaki. Usually called Gan, the gigantic land-crab with his carefully-crafted shell was one of only a few that lived in the forests near the river. Gan obviously wasn't one to ride on any ordinary mount, but was so formidable that accommodating his slowness was generally well worth it.

"So where do you seek?" Gan asked in his sharp, whirring voice. "To the East and the Wanderer? To the North," his massive claws made a shielding gesture, "and the Hollow?"

"Eventually to Moonshade Hollow, I think, yes," Kyri answered, "but first to the Spiritsmith."

"What?" Torokar Heimdalyn spoke up in surprise. "Is your Raiment damaged, then?"

"Oh, it's not for her," Tobimar spoke up. "It's for me." As per their agreement, Tobimar did not draw attention to Poplock. Thus far, the fact that the little Toad was often overlooked, and even if noted discounted as a familiar or a pet, had worked drastically to their advantage. Even here, Poplock tried to mostly maintain a stolid, dumb-toadlike façade and be taken as such. *Whoever the enemy really is, he, she, or it might still have spies here.*

"*My* equipment isn't up to the standards of the Justiciars," Tobimar went on. "So Kyri believes we can get better equipment there."

"You most certainly shall," agreed the Watchland, "if, of course, the Spiritsmith will see you."

"There is that," admitted Kyri, "but I *think* he will not refuse. He implied that I might be able to return without having to run his gauntlet again." She turned and gestured. "And I will not be leaving Vantage Fortress unwarded this time."

The Watchland's face registered genuine surprise and gratification as Lythos came forward. "By the Balance, I had heard rumors, but it is truly a wonderful thing to see for myself. *Sho-Ka-Taida*, I could not hope for better hands to hold the Fortress while its masters are gone."

Good, he's happy. Or he's a really *good actor.* Poplock, honestly, didn't *like* having to be suspicious of everyone, and everything, but after what they'd gone through, it just made sense. The Watchland was trusted by everyone in Evanwyl, which to Poplock's mind made him one of the prime suspects. In theory that was true of Lythos, too, but he and Tobimar had checked the Elf out pretty carefully after his reappearance, and Kyri had no doubts he was who he had been the last time she saw him.

But the Watchland seems to be, well, who he seems to be, too. Poplock studied him carefully through his front webbed feet, held to guide spell-born mystical sight. *General aura's positive, very positive, not dark at all. No sign of shapeshifting. Some traces of magic, but everyone uses some, and he may have quite a few spells around his armor or home. Don't see anything else around him that doesn't belong. That doesn't prove anything, but it's a good indication. Neither of his Arms look suspicious, though that shell of Gan's has got some fairly hefty wards on it!*

"I thank you, Watchland," Lythos was saying, and bowed deeply before Jeridan. "I shall do all in my power to ensure that Phoenix Kyri's work is not undone."

"Then we shall have few fears indeed." Poplock saw Tobimar's distant expression as the Watchland looked down the road that led to the south, and the little Toad recognized that his friend was exercising the strange not-magic disciplines to sense the way of the world about him. *Good, he's double-checking me.*

"You have returned from Zarathanton," the Watchland said. "How was the journey? Can we expect—"

"No, Watchland," Lythos said bluntly. "I was myself sorely beset three times on my journey. Evanwyl is cut off, now; be grateful that the great war keeps the larger powers occupied, with no effort to spare for such a small country as ours. The forces behind these disasters are great, and subtle, and wide-ranging indeed. Evanwyl must rely upon itself alone."

Tobimar moved his shoulder front-and-back—a subtle cue that would just look like a man shrugging or loosening a tight joint, but that they'd agreed meant *All clear.* Obviously Tobimar didn't see anything wrong with the Watchland or his entourage either.

The Watchland nodded. "Alas, I had suspected as much, when no messengers I had sent returned, and no travelers but young Tobimar here. So then I must ask, what of Lady Victoria?"

"My aunt," Kyri said slowly, "has sent, with Lythos, the direction that Vantage Fortress shall pass to me. She does not know when she will return, for she has other duties which have become more pressing." They had decided not to detail those "other duties." After all, Poplock thought, whoever the overarching enemy *was*, it was probably responsible for *all* the disruptions around the world, including Aegeia. No need for there to be any hints as to the family's involvement in *that* mess.

The Watchland looked surprised. "That has a ring of finality about it. Is she well?"

"Last I saw her, excellently well, Jeridan, and so Lythos

confirmed, but she can't return and doesn't know when she will. From her point of view, since I've taken up responsibility for Evanwyl anyway, it's time for me to inherit everything." Kyri looked down. "I'm still going to think of it as hers, though."

Jeridan laughed. "As will every one of us, I am sure. She was mistress of Vantage Fortress in the time of my *father*, let alone in my time. So still I shall hope for her return."

"If she does," Kyri said, "I'll give this right back to her."

There was a chuckle around the small group. "I see you have your traveling pack on; you are leaving this very minute?"

"We are, sir," said Tobimar. "Now that we're assured of the Fortress' safety, we have to move quickly. Kyri's time was well spent here, I think, but we have taken a great deal of time and given our adversaries a chance to recover."

"Then we shall delay you no longer," the Watchland said decisively. "May the Balanced Sword guide and protect you all." He bowed again to Kyri, shook Tobimar's hand—and flickered the very slightest of winks at Poplock.

Hm. So he does *know. Does kind of limit how much I can rely on those results of my vision.* Still, hiding significant facts from those spells took a lot of work.

"Farewell, Jeridan! Goodbye, Gan, Torokar! Goodbye, Lythos!"

The small party turned towards the south and walked onward, towards the distant mountains of Hell's Rim. Poplock, as he often did, watched behind.

And he could see that Jeridan Velion did not move, but kept his eyes on Kyri, until they disappeared into the forest.

CHAPTER 6

"You're *sure* about this, Kyri?" Tobimar said, glancing involuntarily downward. The base of the mountain already seemed a very long way away.

"As sure as I can be about anything which has not yet been proven," the blue-haired Justiciar answered with a smile. With the helm off and the Raiment mostly cloaked, she looked less like the Phoenix Justiciar, deadly avenger of Myrionar, and more like the young woman he'd come to know in the past few weeks. "And even if this doesn't work out, I *am* sure we can get some of the best advice on Zarathan here."

He nodded, following her lead up the mountain. He suspected that he could climb at least as well as she could, though she wasn't bad, but she'd *been* up the mountain before, and he hadn't, so he let her keep the lead. "I can't argue that. Though I don't want to infringe on your honor against these false Justiciars."

She paused as they reached a small ledge and looked over at him, those amazing gray eyes serious. "Tobimar, I guess...I would have been worried about that before Thornfalcon. But if I believe in Myrionar at all—and I do now, with all the faith my heart can hold—then I must believe that It arranged for you, Poplock, and Xavier to be there, either Itself or through Its allies, Terian, Chromaias, the Dragon Gods, even," she flashed another smile, "Blackwart the Great or the Three Beards. And however it was arranged, it is a sign. You came seeking justice and vengeance, and with wisdom you saw past Thornfalcon's lies just in time, and saved me from—oh, very literally—a fate worse than any ordinary death. You are a part of this, and—by the commands of justice—I am now bound to your mission as well. So nothing you gain here *can* infringe on my honor; it *is* my honor."

He blinked. "Kyri, my quest might be a never-ending one, a fool's mission. I may never find the answers, the homeland we left, the Stars or the Sun. There have been dozens of such seekers exiled from my homeland. I would not have you bound to something that may take you from your clear and urgent duty."

She shook her head. "Justice requires balance. Nor can either of us ignore the fact that too many things appear to be happening at the same time. The power behind these false Justiciars may be the same one—or related to the one—that has set all these other plans in motion. And your 'Khoros' already links us. I think, if I'm going to resolve the mystery of the False Justiciars, I will in one way or another *have* to enter the heart of your mystery, as well."

She gazed upward, judging the angles. "And as Sasha determined, that gateway under Thornfalcon's mansion went somewhere into Moonshade Hollow, which you believe—I think rightly—is what's left of your homeland."

"She's right," Poplock said, moving to his other shoulder as they continued the climb. "We'd already come to that conclusion, and it makes more sense the longer I think about it."

Tobimar shrugged. "I can't argue that. But . . . Kyri, while I respect Myrionar—now that I've met you and seen Its power in you, and heard Its tenets, I respect It very much—I'm dedicated to Terian Himself, as are all my family. I can't be one of your Justiciars, so . . ."

"Don't say *can't*," she said with a smile thrown over her shoulder. "I've been thinking about that, and do you know, I can't find a single word in the Teachings that says all the Justiciars have to be dedicated *solely* to Myrionar. The power of the Justiciars is from Myrionar, yes, and obviously you have to conduct yourself in a manner that the Balanced Sword would agree with, but a follower of the Infinite, the Light in Darkness, would hardly do anything that would disappoint a Justiciar."

I hadn't exactly thought of it that way. "You mean a Justiciar could be a follower of another god?"

"I mean I don't see anything that says he or she *couldn't* be such a follower. But don't worry, I'm not trying to force you into that decision."

"But then what..."

"...do I think we can gain from this?" she finished. "The Spiritsmith is one of, if not the, greatest armorers who has ever lived. He's also normally very jealous of his privacy and his knowledge, so much so that he made things work the way I described—such that many who sought him must have died in the attempt. But he did *not* extract from me any promise to keep his secrets, or place on me any of the requirements or commands he did on the nearby villages. If you aren't going to become a Justiciar, I don't know if I can convince him to help you...but I'm very sure he'll at least have some good advice, a name or three of those who *can* help us."

She paused to catch her breath, and so did Tobimar, grateful for the respite. *Where does her family get their stamina? Her strength, her speed, her toughness...they're just stunning. Without Khoros' training, I couldn't keep up at all.*

Once they reached the chimney she had described, Tobimar realized they were now only a short distance from the top...and minutes from a legend. *The Spiritsmith.*

He emerged from the narrow vertical tunnel, breathing hard, and heaved himself upright.

The massive form of an Ancient Sauran loomed over him, scarcely ten feet away and standing over eight feet high, taller than Toron himself, his scales having a patina of depth and iridescence that Tobimar guessed indicated his age far more clearly than any wrinkles could have.

"So you have returned, Phoenix Kyri, and with true blood of false Justiciars upon your sword. It is well. It is very well indeed. Yet you also bring another..." he paused, narrowing his gaze, and then smiling, "*two* others, with you."

"Good eyes," murmured Poplock. Tobimar nodded, impressed; most others didn't even *notice* the Toad, let alone realize Poplock's significance.

"So, Phoenix," the Spiritsmith continued, "is this boy—or this toad—to be the next of your Justiciars?"

Even Kyri, serious though she was, could not keep a straight face as Poplock leapt onto Tobimar's head and struck a grandiose pose. "Indeed, behold the next of the true Justiciars of Myrionar, and my trusty steed!"

The explosive snort of laughter from the Spiritsmith almost blew the little Toad off Tobimar's head. "I see, I see indeed; yet such as yourself are already so mighty that one such as I can do little for you."

"In seriousness, sir," Tobimar began, not without some lingering smile on his face, "I do not intend to become a Justiciar—at least not at this time," he amended. *Why cut off the possibility? Many things may yet happen.* "But various events have made it clear that my path and Kyri's are joined, and thus I may face her enemies, and she mine; and," he drew his blades and presented them, "I have far too clear evidence that my weapons are inadequate to the challenge."

The Spiritsmith looked very interested in his swords—more so than Tobimar had expected. "The twin curved swords... interesting." His gaze traced the blades carefully, visibly pausing when reaching one of the dents or minor cuts on the blade. He then gestured for Tobimar to sheath the swords. "I see indeed your reason for traveling here. And you have done well to have wielded your blades with such skill and power that they sustained such slight damage, overall."

"He helped me slay Thornfalcon," Kyri said simply.

The huge Sauran studied him for several moments, then turned and strode slowly, thoughtfully, across the plateau. Tobimar could see that to the West, other peaks rose, but there seemed to be one clear path—which, if it was truly clear, might actually provide a narrow, straight glimpse at the land called Hell itself. The Spiritsmith was not, however, looking in that direction, but rather pacing with slow, measured strides towards the rocks that surrounded the entryway to his underground forge, his massive tail swinging in time to the steps.

"The intersection of heroes at a battle is not unusual," he said finally. "What other events or circumstances link your two causes?"

Tobimar glanced at Poplock and Kyri, trying to figure out how to go over all of it in the shortest amount of time. It was the little Toad who finally said, "Well... have you ever heard of an old wizard named Khoros?"

The pacing stopped as though the Spiritsmith had run into a stone wall. For a long moment he stood silently, staring seemingly at nothing except a distant peak to the south. At last, he said, "Konstantin Khoros taught me much of my craft, in the days when the world was younger, when Elbon had only the Fifteen and none of the T'Teranahm had betrayed their hearts and souls. And after all had fallen into darkness, he came again, no longer a man of mirth and gentle humor, but grim and fell, and taught me other ways of guiding the powers I was still just beginning to understand. I have forged for him many times, and his designs have guided others; indeed," he nodded to Kyri, "it was he who spoke to me of the designs which became the Raiment of the Justiciars, as well as others. You mean to say, then, that Khoros himself has brought you together?"

Tobimar stared at him, trying to answer while his mind tried to grapple with the implications. *Khoros* taught *the Spiritsmith... in the days before the Fall? But that's...* He could see the same stunned incredulity on Kyri's face, and realized once more how deeply laid were the plans of his old teacher. "I'm not quite sure we can say that exactly... but Khoros taught me to wield these swords—instructed our people in how to forge them, in fact—and he helped Kyri to reach this place originally at a much greater speed than she could have managed otherwise, and even Poplock ran into him once. And there were some others we met who were connected to him."

The huge reptilian creature gave a sigh that sounded almost like a snarl. "Then truly there is a connection. I must think on this. He would have expected you to come here, I believe, and in that he would expect and require that I assist you in some other manner.'"

"You don't have to—"

"ʰ*Grrrk'HA!*" The Draconic obscenity cut Kyri's protest off instantly. "There is nothing to be said against it, Phoenix Kyri. I owe Khoros much. Two worlds owe him much. He, too, owes the worlds, but his debt is not yet due, while mine is, and has been for many millennia past. Come," he gestured, turning back to his caverns, "let us go inside, and you may rest and be refreshed while I consider what I may do."

Tobimar did not object to *that* thought at all. For three days they had been climbing and—training or no—he could use a real sit-down meal, rest, maybe even a bath or shower. A cleansing spell was all well and good, but it simply wasn't the same.

Kyri had mentioned that the Spiritsmith's delvings were extensive, but even so, Tobimar was startled by the size and number of caverns and tunnels. *Of course, if he's been here since the Fall . . . or a little after, since these mountains were created around then! . . . he could have dug only a foot a year and still have honeycombed half the mountain.*

With that much space, it was perhaps not so surprising that he not only offered them guest quarters, but quarters of great size, decoration, and luxury. Even the air, normally thin at over three miles above the lower plains, was heavier and richer here. Tobimar took advantage of the time for a truly marvelous bath; an hour later he emerged, towelling his hair off, to find all his clothes on the bed and Poplock cleaning them off with mutters, gestures, and a bit of bouncing that invoked a mixed-elemental cleaning enchantment.

"Thank you very much, Poplock."

"Well, didn't have that much to do while I waited, and I can use the practice. I'm still learning a lot about magic, and after all the Summoning practice I need to keep up on the elementalist side. So you're welcome."

He watched as a swirl of airy water wove in and out through one of his travel cloaks, a flickering thread of fire somehow encased within. "You may still be learning, but that's pretty impressive. Three-elemental cleaning is a pretty fancy trick, instead of just doing the usual selective displacement."

"Elemental's a lot easier for us Toads, usually, and I figured fire for heating the water, water for the cleaning, air for drying. You already had enough earth in there."

"Ha! Indeed." He picked up one of the finished outfits. "Looks like it worked pretty well to me." He sniffed. "Smells like there might be food waiting outside somewhere, too."

"Then get dressed and let's go!" The little Toad, of course, didn't really have to dress, and even his miniature pack and items tended to conceal themselves magically. You had to look carefully to notice he was carrying anything.

A few minutes later they found their way to a small dining hall; Kyri was just sitting down, her hair and a change of clothing showing that she, too, had taken advantage of their host's amenities. The blue hair cascaded over her brown shoulders in sky-colored waves, with the white flash over her forehead like a cloud drifting in the vault of heaven. *She is gorgeous,* Tobimar thought. *Beautiful and strong as . . .*

At that point it suddenly dawned on him—*really* dawned on him—where his thoughts were leading. *Sand and dust . . . that could be a complication. I don't know what* her *thoughts are on the matter, but we don't have time to follow the path of Learning the Other. Don't know what her people's traditions are, either.*

He shook himself mentally. *This certainly isn't the time. She can't be bothered by my attentions when perhaps the whole world is at risk. Focus! Pay attention to what is* now. Dismissing the distraction—as much as he could, which was far less than he wished he could manage—he returned his attention to the dinner.

The Spiritsmith was at the far end of the table—as was common with Ancient Saurans and Dragons and their kin, his eating area was well separated from the rest, as their diet and manner of eating was often . . . unsettling to others. Tobimar sat down and, after examining the several dishes available, selected a blaze-and-honey style mixed flashfry, one of his favorite types of food. He didn't recognize all the vegetables in this particular recipe, but the meat smelled like hopclaw . . . and there was some sort of seafood in it too. *He seems to live here alone. Must have some very interesting food preparations charms and devices, or he's a very good cook.*

"Sir . . . can you tell me something?"

The Spiritsmith looked up from his platter, and swallowed the ten-pound chunk of meat his teeth had just torn from the boar's leg. "Perhaps. What is it you wish to know?"

He wasn't quite sure how to phrase it. "Well . . . as I said, Khoros taught me—not just how to fight, but how to use this . . . internal power of mine. And a lot of other little things, ranging from philosophy and logic to theory of magic. I always rather liked him, even if he could be pretty maddening in the way he preferred to answer a question with another question and force you to figure it out yourself.

"But . . . everyone else who's known him seems almost, I don't know, afraid of him. They talk about him manipulating people, using them, and then they seem really careful about telling us anything at all. What do you know about him? Is he . . . well, not on our side somehow?"

The Ancient Sauran gave another of the snarling sighs and took another bite from the raw meat. Finally he raised his head again. "It is . . . not that simple a question, and thus the answer you seek is not simple either.

"How much evil must a man do in the name of good before he is, himself, no longer a good man?"

Kyri looked troubled. She said, "You can't do evil deliberately and remain good."

"You are a child of direct faith." The draconic Spiritsmith smiled—in a manner that was probably meant to be tolerant, perhaps even fond, but the sharp teeth covered with fresh blood made it disquieting. "Then how much good must evil achieve before it is no longer evil? Is there no repentance, no salvation for a soul once lost?"

"Well, you can repent...but you can't keep doing evil and actually be good! You have to actually *repent* of your evil, and try to make amends for it, and *stop* doing bad things!" A slight flush touched her cheeks as she seemed to realize how naïve those words made her sound, but she didn't retract them.

"And you, Prince of Skysand? How would you answer this riddle?"

Poplock spoke first. "We all do little evils to achieve good, I think. You killed that boar so you could live. Trees get chopped down to build houses."

Tobimar nodded. "We killed Thornfalcon—and killing people is pretty much one of the absolute wrongs. But by doing that we prevented him from killing who knows how many people, and avenged those who had been killed before." Tobimar shook his head. "But that's a long way from the kind of thing people imply Khoros does."

"Then, Tobimar Silverun, I can say only this: that Konstantin Khoros is, I believe, on 'our side,' as you put it, but that he will manipulate both sides to achieve his goals. It would not be beyond him, for example, to have realized what would happen to the *Artan* in the months past, and to have not only allowed it to happen but even have guided the method of its happening, if that apparent victory of darkness would, in the long run, lead to a greater victory of the forces of light."

Kyri shuddered. "How could anyone live with such choices, if they understood what they chose?"

The Spiritsmith looked at her gravely. "I do not think he *intends* to live with such choices; he simply postpones his death until all such choices are finished, and—I hope and believe—so that never again will any need to make such choices." He stood.

"But he will tell you nothing unless it fits his plans. You will meet him again—of this I am certain. But you will not *find* him, he will find you. This guides my own decision, you see."

Tobimar looked up. "You have made a decision, then?"

"I have." The Ancient Sauran gazed at each of the three in turn. "You have need of new weapons, yes. And those, I believe, I can supply, for I see the design Khoros used, and understand what purpose lay behind that design; so, in his way, he *has* arranged that I do this, by sending his designs in your own equipment—echoes of work done so long ago that the world was a different place, then.

"But more, you must begin to oppose the entirety of this plan that has undermined the power of the Balanced Sword, which has besieged Artania, thrown Aegeia into chaos, and soaked the Forest Sea in blood, and that means preparing to face them in all their guises and in those places where their evil is most ancient and strong, where they began the work of felling the powers of light."

Tobimar looked at Kyri; for a moment both exchanged puzzled gazes, but Kyri's eyes suddenly widened. "You mean—"

"Khoros' commands to you, Tobimar, were clear enough; you simply had not the knowledge to understand them. But the same forces are moving now, and you have met them, and in the end you must face them down, drive them from the lands of your forefathers."

Now he understood, and saw the Phoenix's face pale. "So it's true?"

"I know little of it; Chaoswars have passed, and even this memory was faded from my mind until your presence and urgency made it clear. But there is no doubt. Why else do you find the threads lead here? What importance is there in Evanwyl, what importance was there ever in that small country, save for two and only two things: the first the presence of Myrionar, the highest holding of the Balanced Sword, and the second being that singular gap, the only passage through the Khalal range, through which once flowed riches and heroes, and now is a place of terror and death, Rivendream Pass and, on the other side, Moonshade Hollow, what is left of the lands of the Lords of the Sky, whose name echoed your own, Tobimar Silverun."

As the Spiritsmith spoke these words, so heavy with ancient legend and fear, Tobimar felt as though the cavern swayed with the import.

Then he realized that the cavern *had* swayed. The hanging lights were swinging, and both he and Kyri were suddenly on their feet. "What..."

The earth shuddered again, and this time a wave of nausea and foreboding washed over him, pressing on his spirit. As he fought it off, he saw Kyri stagger and lean against the table. Poplock shivered.

The Spiritsmith looked even sicker; he stumbled, fell to the floor, took long minutes to rise. But he lunged back to his feet and charged for the exit. "Come. Quickly!"

The three raced after the Ancient Sauran, as yet another shockwave of force and *wrongness* passed through the mountain. "What's *happening?*" Kyri asked, nameless dread in her voice.

The Spiritsmith did not answer. Poplock was muttering something that Tobimar couldn't catch.

They burst out of the entranceway onto the plateau. At that moment a final concussion of earthshock and evil knocked them from their feet, and the sky overhead flickered, as though the sun itself had been momentarily stunned.

Tobimar picked himself up slowly, reaching out and helping Kyri, who seemed even more affected. He became aware that the Spiritsmith was staring off to the West, walking almost as though in a dream towards the far side of the plateau. The massive draconian form slowed, then—shockingly—collapsed to its knees, still staring in numb disbelief.

Tobimar followed the Spiritsmith's gaze. Through the narrow gap in the mountains, a thin sliver of land was visible, a cracked and seamed plain interrupted by virulent green tangles of growth, jagged tumbles of stone shards hundreds of feet high, steaming pools of water and mud, flat and empty desert—an impossible and repellent patchwork of terrain that could not possibly exist together...yet did.

But it was not this which the huge creature stared at in mute horror. Beyond the abominable landscape, far away, at the very horizon or even beyond, was...darkness. Tobimar blinked. The bright sky *dimmed* there, dimmed and went to complete blackness, a darkness that rose up in the center to a knife-thin line that seemed to stretch upwards to the roof of heaven, draining the very light from everything around it and turning it to ebon shadow. And despite being so far away, something about the sight pressed in on the Skysand Prince's senses, as though merely to look upon it was enough to weaken life and break hope. The land shuddered again, this time with the groaning motion of an earthquake, and pebbles and rock cascaded down. "What *is* it? What's happening, Spiritsmith?"

The question, spoken so urgently, managed to penetrate the creature's shock; he turned his head slightly, and the deep-set eyes were wide, with a fear that nothing so ancient and powerful should be able to feel. "T'Ameris Kerveria," the Spiritsmith said quietly. And then he translated, and Tobimar understood the true meaning of horror. "The Black City. The Fortress of Kerlamion Blackstar.

"The Gateway and Nexus of all Hells is come once more to Zarathan, and Kerlamion its King sits on his throne and gazes out upon our living world."

CHAPTER 7

Aran stumbled, fell to his knees, remained in that position, unmoving, for long moments, waiting for his head to clear. *I've been... driving myself hard. Far too hard.*

A part of him tried to force himself to lunge back to his feet, but now he knew that much of that was anger at himself, rage and guilt. "Sit still," he told himself, and sat down. He was near his destination, though he saw nothing to indicate that a path to the Hells lay here, in the tangled jungle of the land that was, itself, called Hell; but if there was, he would not be wise to come before Kerlamion exhausted, weary of mind and body both.

He forced himself to sit, to eat of his rations, to drink water. But even sitting still, in the quiet greenery, he was tense, trying to watch everywhere, for he had learned all too well in the last weeks that danger could be anywhere.

This place deserved its name, he felt. He had spent years as a Justiciar of Myrionar—or, as he was now being honest with himself, as a false Justiciar empowered by what was almost certainly a great demon, perhaps drawing power directly from the King of All Hells himself. But though his true nature as a Justiciar had been dark, he had in fact spent much of his life as a defender of Evanwyl, protecting it because Myrionar, the so-called patron of Evanwyl, was too weak, or too uncaring, or both, to do so.

In that time he had faced many enemies—bandits and murderers and other ordinary people turned against their own kind, yes, but also many worse things. The blade-legged doomlock spiders, monstrous creatures which could lash out with cutting forelegs to drag you, slashed and bleeding, to their deadly venomous fangs, or who might first entangle you in paralyzing webs before closing in; graverisen, fearsome shambling undead *things* that seemed slow, clumsy, until they would suddenly scent the living and rush upon them with terrifying speed, rending men limb from limb and feasting on their entrails; flame-ants, dwelling within the earth and carrying the fires of the interior with them, swarming and consuming everything they touched like a conflagration; even, once, something for which he had no name, an armored monstrosity the length of a dozen wagons that came ravening out of Rivendream Pass, with a mouth like a cavern of blades and claws that cut stone like grass, and healing so swiftly that wounds closed even as the blade passed through the flesh.

But such things were the *ordinary* here. All his powers had been needed, every day, as he made his way through the twisted, hideous, contradictory terrain of the Circle of Hell. He could not imagine how the true Hells could be much worse than this place, where he had seen a floating black cloud, like a thunderhead come to earth, turn and pursue a creature, rend it apart with screaming wind and crackling bolt, and leave a shriveled, desiccated, scattered corpse behind; where a great stone had suddenly moved, become a hunger-howling mass of granite which he had to trick into a fall to shatter hundreds of feet below; where a lovely flower had suddenly bent down towards him, opening a maw that dripped corrosive sap upon him that even left a scar on his nigh-invulnerable armor.

He had often thought of turning back, but now, he knew, there was nowhere for him to go back to. The false Justiciars knew he had been sent on a special mission; if he returned without that power he sought, they would know his will and courage had failed, and worse, that he had given up on the oath so fiercely and publicly sworn to their... patron. And before he left he had been told, by that same patron, that Thornfalcon's fall had torn the veil of secrecy, and because of that he knew that Evanwyl itself was now no longer his home. He could never walk the streets again as Condor. There was little he knew of the lands beyond, and he didn't know how he could have made his way through the lands elsewhere, even if their patron allowed him such a simple escape.

And even if he would have, he now held himself in utter contempt, unworthy to return until he truly redeemed himself. Whatever the excuses of rage, of revulsion and terror and denial, he had himself betrayed his father, Shrike. Oh, he had excuses—shock, white-hot anger, unthinking escape from a horror he had never imagined—but the last comment of their patron as he departed had struck deep and reminded him of how Condor was as guilty as the one he sought. "You have little time and a long distance to cover," their patron had said, smiling falsely from beneath blonde hair and blue eyes, "so make haste. Worry not; we shall tend to Shrike's body and hold a funeral in your absence."

I who was so furious at this . . . Phoenix for leaving my father to rot . . . I did the same thing in my anger and need to find vengeance.

There were even brief moments he wondered if he *deserved* to find vengeance. *I've helped murder people. Should I seek vengeance if there are those out there who would seek the same on me?*

The worst of those, of course, would be Kyri Vantage. Condor faced that truth. He'd helped *kill* her parents—even though it had been Shrike who struck the killing blows. And he'd known what was going to happen to her brother, even though—in all honesty—he couldn't have done anything about it. He wondered how she was. *Maybe she's found some peace in faraway Zarathanton. I hope so. As long as she's alive, I know there's a bright spot out there, somewhere.*

He rose and dusted himself off, finally, feeling much more *himself.* Food, drink and rest; a soldier, or a Justiciar, needs these to keep going. He'd neglected himself from shock, pain, guilt, and desperation, and that could have gotten him killed.

I have to be almost there. Their patron's directions had been clear and simple—follow specific landmarks that, despite his fears, had been easy to spot, and even in thick jungle he'd been able to find spots to verify his heading often enough to not get lost.

But he had no idea of what to look for *after* he got there.

Green sunlight gave way to unfiltered gold, and he stepped from the edge of the jungle to see a plain of waving green and rose grasses—with some rippling movement that was not just wind—before him. The plain stretched several miles before him and to either side; towards the horizon, low, jagged, bare mountains rose abruptly, smoking faintly in the lowering sun. On his right, the plain gave way to a dusty, cracked plain with what appeared to be ancient ruins wavering in the distance through the heat of the day. On his left, the plains reached a river, on the other side of which lay a dark-green forest of pines. He shook his head at the warped and contradictory sights. *The monsters are bad enough, but this* place *is insanity incarnate.*

Without warning, shadow seemed to boil up from the ground, flow from the air above, and the ground shuddered. He was suddenly assailed by a feeling of such terrifying foreboding and evil that the darkness he had known all his life seemed light and friendly.

And then there was a concussion, a roar and scream of earth and air rent and crushed, and he was blown from his feet, deafened, battered, cast aside like dust before a storm. He tucked and rolled, but all around him he heard creaks and tearing, rending, ripping sounds as the screaming manic wind blasted the forest flat, sending the boles of mighty trees smashing down around him, shattered limbs battering Condor, trying to crush him even through his Justiciar's Raiment.

The air was cold now and the sunlight gone, and he smelled chill of ice and the scent of decay of eons, and looked up.

He came to his senses slowly, aware by the stiffness in his limbs and dryness of his mouth that he had been gazing in unbelieving horror for minutes with no thought at all, just absolute disbelief and terror.

Before him loomed the Black Wall as told in some of the oldest tales, polished like an obsidian monolith a thousand feet high and more. But even as tall as it was, still beyond it he could see twisted spires, dark buildings, and far beyond, in the center so far off that it would be beyond the horizon, a tower of pure ebony that rose towards the roof of the sky and faded into . . . elsewhere.

Now he understood his patron's knowing smiles, Kerlamion's laugh. There was no passage here to the Hells.

The Hells had come *here*, to Zarathan itself.

The forest was deathly silent now. Even the worst monstrosities he had seen would have fled, be cowering in their burrows or still running, flying, swimming through the ground until they dropped of exhaustion.

And then there came a sound: the sound of an incalculably huge lock opening.

Directly before him a gate began to slide open in the impregnable black wall. Sterile, sharp white light poured from within that gate, a light so cold and dead that its touch seemed to leach away color and life. Silhouetted against that light was a black form, round in outline but with hints of much worse.

As Condor's eyes adjusted to the fell light, he could see the Thing more clearly, and wished he couldn't. An ovoid, leathery-skinned body was supported by four talons like those of a gargantuan bird of prey, and sported night-black wings like a monstrous bat. A long, flexible, wattled neck held a long head that shone like black bone or perhaps the carapace of an insectoid abomination; the dead-white glowing eyes certainly had the pupilless, faceted look of the eyes of most insects, but the mouth was long and jagged, as though the beaked mouth of a snapping turtle had been crossed with that of a wolf, or perhaps a dragon. The long, slender tail included black, bladed spines.

And then it spoke.

The voice was startling. It was pleasant, gentle, sweet, like that of a young girl—though beneath and behind it, almost beyond the range of hearing, was an undertone that sounded like distant screams.

"Condor False-Justiciar, step forward."

It was the last sort of voice he would have expected from that monstrosity, and it added a crowning touch to the horror.

But I long since left my choices behind. Shakily, he walked towards the monster.

It smiled, a flexing of a face that should be incapable of flexure, another horrifying tiny detail. "Well done. You have arrived precisely as directed. The King of All Hells will be pleased indeed, for to cross the land called Hell is a considerable feat." It turned and moved a wing down, an ebony ramp. "I am to bring you to the King immediately."

The wing was frighteningly solid beneath his boots; it did not feel like a leather pinion, but rather a bridge of stone. The creature's back was softer, dry and flexible as the hide of the elephant Condor had seen once; yet there was something repellent about it, perhaps a faint scent of dry decay, as of a house abandoned in the desert for centuries.

Smell of decay or no, the Demon—for such Aran knew it had to be, and a powerful one indeed, to be sent on a personal errand for the ruler of the Black City—leapt up and arrowed into the now-darkened sky with speed and agility a smaller creature would envy.

Now Aran could see the city from above, and knew his horror had not reached its limits. The Black City stretched from horizon to horizon, a ten-mile circle of blackness—black walls, ebony buildings, night-shadowed streets, all arranged in perfect circular arcs. The city rose slowly, a vast cone-shaped arrangement of structures and roads all converging on the gargantuan castle in the center, itself echoing the design of the whole: a ring of walls, a ring of towers, and in the center a great single keep that rose up and somehow faded away; it hurt his eyes and mind to look at how it went from something that *was* to something that *was not*. At intervals along the great outer walls were guard towers, posts with guards and with great engines of destruction that looked like nothing he had ever seen.

Below, demons—monstrous forms of all shapes and sizes—moved busily. Many were marching, drilling—parts of an army so huge that Aran couldn't grasp it—but many others seemed to be going about their business as though they lived in an ordinary city. Yet even there something seemed wrong, *off*, as though even in living daily lives there was something terribly twisted and unnatural about them.

The Demon upon which he rode flew straight up one of the great thoroughfares, a road running true as a sword-stroke to the central tower. The gates of the castle were already open, and nothing challenged his mount as it flew directly up to the door of the central keep itself.

"Here you dismount," it said in its eerily pleasant voice. "None save those granted audience may enter the Tower of the Black Star."

Condor said nothing; he wanted to save his breath and his courage for the coming confrontation.

The doorway to the Tower was open, yet nothing could be seen within; it was deadly black. Aran glanced back, but knew there was no choice. *I made this decision as soon as I demanded I be given the power for my revenge.*

He brought the image of his foster father's face to his mind, drew strength from the anger he felt as he contemplated that face as he had last seen it: glaring open eyes beneath a fragment of Shrike's own axe, plunged lethally into his forehead.

With a deep breath, one scented with old decay and something sharper but no less deadly, Aran strode through the doorway.

The echoes of his footsteps... *changed* as he passed into the

Tower; they whirled upward in pitch, then dropped so low as to be beyond hearing, chasing themselves in a rumbling, squeaking chorus around the interior. Within a few steps, the darkness lightened, slightly, and now he could see the Throne.

It stood in the center of the Tower, and the Tower was but a single titanic room, an empty, unadorned space of pure black polished stone a quarter-mile across. The black Throne was simple, a cone that rose from the floor, carved out so that Someone could sit in it, and then continuing up, up, out of sight into darkness, impossibly fading, blending into the void above.

And in the throne sat Kerlamionahlmbana, the Black Star of Destruction, a figure hewn from the darkness darker than his surroundings, with only blazing, eerie blue-white light showing where his eyes were. The black figure was itself surrounded by a faint blue-violet aura, and a distant wailing howl emanated from Kerlamion, as though the air itself feared his presence.

Aran, the Condor Justiciar, felt his heart hammering faster than ever before in his life, even more than when he was confronted with his patron and Thornfalcon's true power. This was the King of All Hells, and no name had ever been spoken with greater fear, save perhaps only that of the Slayer of Gods, the Hunger without End, the King of Wolves, Virigar—and even he, it was said, would not care to casually offend the one who sat upon the Ebon Throne.

Aran knelt and bowed his head.

"Rise and approach, Condor," the King of All Hells said, and his voice was both rumble and howl, the sound of air or water being sucked into a void, screaming and growling at once.

Aran stood, feeling his knees trembling. *I asked for this. I asked for this. I must move forward. Doomed and damned I may be, but at least I must not fail in following my own course. I will not collapse and be shown a coward here, not now.*

Somehow he found the courage to stride forward as though at a review, steps rhythmic and steady as a drumbeat, ignoring the eeriness of the echoes and the deadly darkness that loomed ever higher before him.

"Stop," commanded the King of All Hells, as Condor had come to within fifty feet of the Throne, and Kerlamion rose to his full height, his nigh-invisible head thirty feet above Condor's own.

Kerlamion looked down upon him, and there was *power* in that gaze; the mere regard of the Ruler of the Hells was enough to feel as though a leaden blanket had fallen over Aran. But Condor held tight to his pride and purpose, and raised his head to meet that terrible, blank, flaming stare.

Kerlamion chuckled suddenly, and that was perhaps the most horrid thing Aran had ever heard, causing a sick sweat to spring out across his brow; it was a laugh that had humor and understanding in it, yet mixed with malice and hatred, all twisted and warped by the distortion of sound around the King. "So, Condor, called Justiciar, you come seeking power, power to match and outmatch your enemy, the slayer of the father of your heart?"

"Yes, your Majesty."

He nodded. "Know, then, that this is a great boon you seek; for you wish a power sufficient to withstand the power of a god, and return against it enough power to break that god's wards on its last champion. Yet," and suddenly a blaze of howling blue-white showed as Kerlamion smiled, "yet, in truth, it is well within my power to grant you this boon; for I am called 'demon,' but I am as much god as Myrionar. Indeed, I am greater by far, and have faced the Light in the Darkness himself, contested power with Elbon Nomicon, and still I hold my throne and none dare oppose me here."

I must not be utterly cowed. He is volatile—this I know—but he will not respect weakness at all. "This is true, Majesty, yet the boon was already asked, and you bid me here to receive it, not to impress me with your power, which is indeed beyond compare."

The deadly blazing eyes narrowed, but the tone showed it was with more amusement than annoyance, and Aran permitted himself to relax the slightest bit. "So. I have devoted some small time to contemplating how best to provide that which you have asked. And seeing you, I now see the best—perhaps the only—true choice. Give me your sword."

Aran's hand was already complying, even before he realized it. *Disobeying him would be almost impossible.* The sensation was itself frightening; he had never found himself so unquestioningly obedient to anyone or anything before. He extended the blade to the King of All Hells, hilt-first.

Kerlamion did not bend down; the Justiciar's blade Skyvault floated up and hung before the burning blue eyes.

Then Kerlamion reached back and drew forth his own Sword. The blade blazed as black as Kerlamion himself, devouring any light that approached. "The Sword of Oblivion, the Consuming Blade," the King of Demons said. "Greatest of all weapons, before which none may stand."

To his astonishment, Aran saw that the outline of the Consuming Blade was nearly identical to his own, merely immensely larger. "There is a kinship between us, Aran of Evanwyl," Kerlamion said, with another touch of that monstrous humor. "We wield similar blades in much the same way, and for much the same purpose of vengeance against those who have wronged us. So to you...I give much the same power."

There was a rending sound as though something had torn sky and stone, and a tiny shard *split* from the Blade of the Demon King and dropped slowly. It shimmered with the terrible blue-white fire, and descended until it touched Skyvault—

And Skyvault *vanished*. In its place was an identical sword, save that the blade was black as night, glinting with the deadly azure-tinted white power. "A piece of my own weapon I give to you. The Demonshard Blade will strengthen you, guide your hand, and deliver absolute force to your blows. Even against the Phoenix Justiciar of Myrionar it will be unstoppable."

The Demonshard drifted down to Aran's upraised hand, and as soon as his fingers touched the hilt he felt a *surge* of strength, of confidence and power such as he could scarcely believe. Even the King of Hell, while still awe-inspiring, seemed less fearsome. Stunned, he raised his head. "I thank you, Majesty. Is there *anything* that can withstand this weapon?"

The eyes narrowed and that terrible smile drew a line of consuming dead fire across the face of night. "Its source and parent, my own blade, of course. But other than that? Aran Condor, even were Terian himself to come before you, he would be cut, yea, and the wound pain him for ages to come. Once you have left my presence, I do not believe you shall find anything to withstand the Demonshard. Wield it well in our service, Condor, and I shall be well content."

Slowly, the King of All Hells seated himself. "You may go."

The confidence of the Demonshard allowed him to bow calmly and turn, striding to the exit.

But inside, he desperately wanted to run. And a part of him thought, perhaps, that he would be much wiser to cast this blade aside, and keep running.

CHAPTER 8

"What, young Prince? You thought my skills suited only to metalwork?" The Spiritsmith was dipping a pearlescent cloth into some liquid that shimmered like moonlight.

Kyri saw Tobimar give a wry smile. "I suppose I *did* assume that, yes. Clearly I was mistaken."

"When making armor, can one neglect the padding, the straps, the parts that make it truly wearable and secure? And if these be weak, will they not define the weakness of the armor?" The Spiritsmith's voice, she noted, was not angry or sarcastic, merely instructive, as he watched closely the way the cloth swirled and coiled without even the slightest touch from his hand. "And many are the forms of armor; I know them all, from woven bamboo and leather to chain and scale, solid plate and metal cloth, all the forms and types that have ever been imagined. These I know, as I know all weapons, forge all weapons, here, whether they be blades of metal or mauls of *kerva* wood, nets woven of shadow and light or a bow to call down the stars."

"And a good thing, too," said Poplock from a different corner of the forge. The little Toad was sitting on an anvil, surrounded by hundreds of tiny gears, springs, levers, and other less identifiable components; he was hammering on some new piece of metal even as he spoke. "If you were always working metal, I wouldn't be able to use your anvil."

"Ha! True enough, my friend. But for one such as yourself, who has already taught himself much of the craft of metal and

the way of machines, I am glad to lend you the use of the forge
and what materials you find; even building your largest creations
will take but little of what I have."

Kyri was glad to hear that cheerful tone in the Spiritsmith's
voice again. For the first few days after the Black City had
arrived, it had seemed he might not emerge from his shock. But
on the fifth day, he had emerged from his private chambers and
slammed his massive fist on the table so hard it had cracked the
solid stone. "Enough!" he had said. "Terrible the days upon us,
and worse to come, but that calls me to action such as I have
not had in ages gone, and you are the first who need me."

She saw Tobimar look to another part of the workshop, where
two new swords sat within a glowing pit that shone with soft golden
radiance; they were nearly ready, according to the Spiritsmith.

"So," she said, "what exactly is that stuff?"

"This?" the massive Sauran said, indicating the swirling material in the vat. "Woven from the webs of the stormsnare, the
great spiders of the Khalals. One of the strongest of cloths, and
capable of holding strongly to great virtues of power."

"Stormsnares? You mean the *Charahil*, the Winds that Walk?"
Tobimar said in surprise. "I've never encountered anyone who
successfully took any of their webs; those who claimed to be
hunting them...never returned."

"*Hunting* them? How barbarous. The *Charahil* are wise and
ancient as a people, and nothing like the Doomlocks and other
monstrous spider-kin. I killed none for these webs; rather, I trade
with them, and gain much from the exchange."

Kyri smiled, remembering a similar question about a vat of
Dragon's blood. "Do you get *all* your materials voluntarily?"

The Spiritsmith bared his immense bladed teeth in a grin. "Not
all, no. Just those that I can. Demon blood and bone and hide,
these are not given willingly, to name three obvious examples.
Many indeed are the monstrous creatures whose bodies yield
materials peculiarly appropriate for my work, and most of them
will not donate of themselves so freely either."

He reached in and pulled the stormsnare fabric from the vat;
the liquid beaded and ran off as though the cloth were waxed...
but there was now a new moonlight sheen to the material. "Excellent. This will be a fine foundation for your new armor, Tobimar."

"I don't want to impose—"

"There is no imposition," the massive scaled smith replied, spreading the cloth wide on a granite table. "Soon enough I will have to travel elsewhere—for surely my King and kinsman Toron will have need of my skills now. But you three will be traveling into the heart of much of this evil, and I will ensure that you are all three well protected." He managed a wry smile. "Khoros knew this would happen, and thus your presence here is as clear a command to me as though he were here to give it."

"Not to pressure you...but how long until the swords and the armor are done?"

"Your swords...another day and a half. Most of that, however, is infusing the various powers and assuring that they are permanently affixed to the blade in their essence. I expect that I shall complete this armor in that time. It is not, of course, nearly able to match the Raiment of a Justiciar in most aspects, but it will protect you far better than your current equipment and will have certain virtues of its own...as well as being exceedingly light and not bulky, so as not to interfere with your style of combat."

Kyri nodded. "You mean unlike my style, which is generally more to hit things harder until they break."

Both Tobimar and the Spiritsmith gave a snort of laughter. "You do yourself something of a disservice, Phoenix Justiciar," the Sauran smith said, "but yes, in essence. You have more need of mighty defenses and slightly less of movement—though as you are already aware your Raiment impedes you very little."

"Yes," Kyri agreed. "For its bulk it is *very* light, yet strong." She remembered other things she'd felt in battle. "And has that peculiar trait of my sword, as well."

"Peculiar...ah, indeed. You mean the fact that its lightness is only perceived by yourself, but that it retains all its mass to resist blows as the metal from which it is forged."

"I'd noticed that," said Tobimar, "though more its opposite, with Thornfalcon."

"Yes, the lighter blades of the Justiciars are forged with the ability to strike and withstand blows as though they were much greater than they are," agreed the Spiritsmith. He began to mark the cloth—delineating a pattern for the armor purely by eye, it seemed to Kyri. There were no templates, nothing to show Tobimar's measurements and ensure its fit, yet she was certain that when the Spiritsmith was done the new armor would fit Tobimar as though it were a second skin.

"So in two days or so, you will be ready to depart," he said, picking up the earlier thread of conversation. "You may make free with my supplies for that journey; I myself will be departing shortly after."

"Departing?" Kyri repeated, bemusedly. "I remember you saying something about that earlier, but honestly I thought you lived here always!"

"In the normal way of things, I do," the huge Sauran agreed, going over and checking the swords sitting in their shining pit. "But the Black City has come to Zarathan, and I know that my King will be mobilizing all he can muster to confront the armies that will—beyond doubt—soon march from those gates. I will go to them, that they can have my aid; perhaps I, who have walked the world far longer even than they, can help them find other allies, even call the Great Dragons themselves to awaken—if they can, for the cycle turns, and not in our favor, I think." He looked distant. "So have I gone to them before, I can sense, even through the faded memories of the Chaoswars past. When the great wars have begun, then I must heed the call of those who need my arms and armor to stave off the darkness that ever threatens to fall."

Tobimar nodded. "Of course, that makes sense. So we'll be heading for Moonshade Hollow while you head for Zarathanton." He shook his head. "I just wish we knew more about the place, but Kyri says no one knows anything about it—that even Rivendream Pass isn't known much past its entrance, and there's a lot of miles of the pass to go through."

Kyri nodded, looking into the nonexistent distance. "Rumors in Evanwyl say that the Hollow's really a pretty big place, ringed with mountains, and in the middle there's supposed to be Darkmoon Lake, but...that's rumor. No one's ever confirmed anything except that there are really dangerous *things* that like to come out of Rivendream Pass."

"There *is* one who may know something of the Hollow, and perhaps even of its past," responded the Spiritsmith, returning to the table with the cloth laid out upon it. "Knowing that you would wish such counsel, yet have little enough time left to waste in travel, I have called to him, in the hope that he will come here, rather than force you to journey thence. And I believe he shall."

To say she was startled was putting it mildly; everyone who had ever journeyed into Rivendream pass had either never returned, or retreated to safety after going no farther than a few miles. And its *past* was before the last Chaoswar, which meant that no one should be able to recall anything of it clearly. "Who, sir?"

"That would be me," said a voice from behind them, at the entrance to the forge.

Kyri whirled.

Standing in the entry, holding a staff nearly covered with glittering runes and bound with black metal, blond hair flowing to his shoulders, with strange blocky armor that reminded her of that which young Ingram had worn and a black cloak slung over his shoulders, was a figure out of legend, a picture from a storybook.

"The Wanderer," Kyri breathed, feeling a thrill of awe through her.

Tobimar was also staring in disbelief, and even the usually relaxed Poplock's eyes were wider.

He bowed low before them. "I suspect that my reputation exceeds me, but I am, indeed, Erik Arisia, the Wanderer."

Kyri found herself opening her mouth, and knew she was about to start absolutely *babbling* questions. *No!* she told herself sternly. *The last thing he needs is someone asking him questions about his old adventures—whether he really had struck down the great dragon Frostreaver with a single blow of his staff, or outwitted one of the Nine Kings of Night by simply accepting his soul within, or whether he and Larani Darkwood had . . .*

"I . . . Sir, I had never expected . . . you came *here?*"

He laughed—a very human and ordinary laugh, and suddenly she didn't see a legend, just a young-appearing man of about twenty-five to thirty, leaning on a staff and amused by her stuttering question. "Relax, Kyri. I know I've got quite a rep, but don't be overawed. And yes, I came here instead of lurking in my stronghold waiting to mess with you on the way in. When the old lizard makes that kind of request I figure he's got a good reason for it."

There was something familiar—yet alien—about the way he spoke. Tobimar's eyes narrowed. "Forgive me, sir . . . but you sound almost like . . ."

". . . like your friend Xavier? Yes, he and I share something of the same background."

"So it *is* true! You came here from the sister world too!"

"Most of what they say about me is true," he agreed. "And most of it is false, and most of it's also exaggeration and confusion. Some of that's my doing, a lot of it's just the way things get repeated."

"How did you know my name?" she asked after a moment, trying to figure out if he was just being obscure or *meant* something by all that. "Oh, wait. The Spiritsmith—"

"Didn't have to tell me. Evanwyl's not very far from the Broken Hills, and once you started raising something of a ruckus I made sure I knew who was who over there."

A thought struck her. "Do you know how to find the Retreat?"

The Wanderer chuckled. "*Know* how? Well, sort of. I could probably do it myself, if I wanted to. But I can't tell *you* how to do it. I have . . . a kind of unique position with respect to godly magics, something I can't lend to you. And I've got some other work to do, now that I've been pulled out of my shell." He tilted his head, then nodded. "But I think—when the time comes, which isn't yet—you'll find a way in yourself."

"What do *you* know about this whole situation?" Poplock asked.

"That's a nice generic question," the Wanderer said with a grin. "I know quite a bit about *parts* of it—a lot of parts you won't care about. But I can tell you something interesting about Moonshade Hollow. Not *details*—I haven't actually been very far inside and that once was a while back—but there *is* something in there—a god, a mystical ward, something—that suppresses or at least affects the operation of various mystical powers. I *think* that applies to godly powers, even."

Tobimar frowned. "So Kyri's powers . . . won't work?"

"I don't think it's quite *that* bad, but my guess is that they'll be more limited. Moonshade Hollow isn't the only place like that—Elyvias, for instance. If Moonshade Hollow is like Elyvias, you probably will find a lot more, oh, gadgetry—magic placed into items in one way or another. Summoners and Gemcallers will be a *lot* more common than your standard wizard like me."

"Ha! You, a standard wizard," said Poplock. "That's funny."

The Wanderer acknowledged that with a laugh. "Okay, fair enough. I use a lot of standard wizardly tricks, though, and those were pretty damped down in both Elyvias and Moonshade Hollow."

"What about Rivendream Pass?"

The Wanderer grimaced as he wandered up and glanced into the pit where Tobimar's swords were sitting. "Oh, that's as nasty as you think it is. Moonshade Hollow's definitely got something of *really* dark nature in it, and the Pass is like a crack in a tank of something nasty; the nasty stuff flows along it until it dries out. And when it dries out it hardens. In this case, that means you keep getting monsters showing up. It's a dangerous route, but about the only one you can take."

"Toron said you might know something of the Hollow's past?" Tobimar asked.

The Wanderer turned and looked at Tobimar quietly for a moment. Kyri was suddenly struck by the intensity of both men's blue eyes, eyes that were as nearly identical as hers and Xavier's. "I am not immune to the effects of the Chaoswars," he said finally. "But I am...more resistant, I suppose you could say, than others. So I do know a bit. I remember Heavenbridge Way, and that it was a green and pleasant place, a fine journey with a great road that ran from one side to the other, to end in the realm of the Lords of the Sky." He nodded to Tobimar. "A land that was called Silavarian, which in the ancient Dragon's tongue means, roughly, the Land of the Eight-Starred Sky." The Spiritsmith repeated the name, as though recognizing something of distant memory. The Wanderer went on, "Or maybe of the Sky of Eight Stars on the Land—it's clearly a contraction of some sort and figuring out the missing pieces isn't easy."

"Silavarian," repeated Poplock. "That could become 'Silverun' very easily."

"Very," agreed Tobimar. "Anything else?"

"Some. Though both Evanwyl and Silavarian were small, they both had power and influence considerably greater than their size. Myrionar was at its peak of power then, worshipped by many across the continent, and Evanwyl was the center of the faith. And the Lords of the Sky..." he grinned again. "There was a good reason for that name. They had either discovered a secret, or developed a technique, which allowed them to make airships that traded across the continent, and by the end were well on their way to helping to unite most of the countries—not under one flag, but in trade and better understanding. Powerful enough to travel without concern of attack by any save a Dragon in the air, swift, much more reliable and less able to be interfered with than teleportation or other such spells, the airships of the Lords were the bedrock of trade and diplomatic communications."

Kyri felt cold and knew Tobimar had the same thoughts. "And *that's* why it was singled out by the Demons in the Chaoswar."

The Wanderer was grave. "I would guess so, yes. With the usual disruption by the forces unleashed in a Chaoswar, only the Lords' ships *could* have maintained any sort of cohesion between countries. They *had* to be taken down. The fact that—according to strong rumor—they were blessed of Terian and held the Seven and the One merely made them a greater target."

Kyri saw Tobimar nod, at once more solemn and more confident. *Of course. This is what he and his people have been searching for, and now the Wanderer's finally confirmed everything he hoped to believe.*

Then Poplock said, "So . . . what are you hiding?"

The Wanderer raised an eyebrow. "How do you mean?"

"You're good at ducking and weaving, but so am I." The little Toad squinted at him narrowly. "You didn't answer my question, really. Just diverted off into talking about what you knew about the *Hollow*, but I didn't ask about that, I asked what you knew about the *situation*. And I think you know a *lot*. You're the guy they say the gods tread lightly around, that's not bound by destiny, that's faced down Dragons and devised weapons against demons, that's tricked one of the Nine Kings with a handful of sand and his own pure will. You're living a hop or two from Evanwyl. I think you know what's going on."

Kyri turned to look at the Wanderer, who was smiling bemusedly at Poplock. "Cogent and well stated, little Toad. I don't know *everything* that's going on. But I do know a lot more about it than you do. And I'm not going to be able to tell you much."

"Why *not*?" Kyri demanded. "Do you like playing games with people? That's not what the stories say!"

Now there was no sign of a smile on the Wanderer's face; instead there were lines of worry, of pain that had not been visible before. "No, I don't. It is not that I don't want to tell you, Kyri, Tobimar . . . Poplock. It's that I cannot. I *dare* not." His gaze caught hers. "Recall the words that Myrionar spoke to you, the night It called you to its aid: '*What I know would be too danger-ous for you now, and there is still much hidden from me,*' yes?"

She was stunned. Only five people other than herself had she ever told of that particular speech: Aunt Victoria, Toron, Tobimar, Poplock, and Xavier Ross. "*How do you know that?*"

"Because Myrionar *told me*," he answered, and his voice was cold iron. "And those words are just as true now. There are truths you cannot—you *must not*—know."

Tobimar's fists clenched. "So. You, like Khoros...perhaps even *with* Khoros...are playing a chessmaster, using us like pieces on your board, pushing us to perform some set of acts you need done."

"Yes...and no," he said quietly. "Your wills are your own. In fact, they *must* be your own. It is just that there are things you must do in your own way, without direction or control. In fact, if I *were* to attempt to direct you, to tell you everything I know, or part of it, I would likely destroy everything we all hope to accomplish. Even though I *know* that there will be points at which *not* knowing something could get you all killed, and that, too, will destroy everything we hope to accomplish."

Kyri stared at him, anger, concern, and confusion making a nauseating mix in her gut. "What do you mean?" She made a leap of intuition. "A prophecy. You have a prophecy."

For a moment, that smile returned, sharp and lopsided, too knowing yet edged with sadness. "Not...precisely. Though, perhaps, close enough for your purposes."

"A prophecy we cannot be *told?*"

He sighed, turned away, looked at the cold fire on the other side of the room. "Telling...can change the actions of others. Sometimes knowing can be worse than not knowing."

"Explain that," Poplock said after a moment.

The Wanderer rubbed his neck. "Hmm. How to put it... All right. Imagine that I had dropped by Pondsparkle a little before you guys hit your panic mode. I come in, let you know what's going on, maybe give you some assistance in getting that group shut down. Then what happens?"

Poplock scratched his head. "Well..."

"Poplock doesn't leave his hometown," Tobimar said slowly. "Or at least he doesn't leave it at the same time. So he's not there in the Temple when I'm cornered."

Kyri felt a dull ache of grim understanding and continued for him. "So the two of them never meet, and aren't there at the murder of the Sauran King. And don't join with Xavier. So nobody's there to distract Thornfalcon..."

The Wanderer nodded slowly. "I don't like the term 'playing' in this circumstance...but at the same time, it's appropriate. We—including you—are playing a game of bluffs, of shadow-moves and strategies and tactics that interact with each other on a thousand layers. Even an apparent disaster may lead to victory, but if someone *knows* about that apparent disaster, they may choose the apparently better path, and lead us to *real* disaster. It's bad enough that *I* know all of this!" The Wanderer slammed his staff down in frustration, an impact that echoed throughout the forge. "Do you think I don't want to just set things *right*? Hell, it's what I came here *for*. It's my *job*." He looked up, into a sky beyond the stone above. "But we don't know everything, especially about our adversary, and one wrong word...could ruin it all."

Kyri closed her eyes. She thought she could—vaguely—understand what the Wanderer was trying to get across, and it was terrifying and frustrating at the same time. But..."Wanderer, can you tell me one thing?"

He looked at her steadily. "I don't know. Depends on the one thing. But ask."

She looked at her two friends, then took a breath. "Did Myrionar tell me truly otherwise? If...we have faith in this, will we come through? Can I truly have full measure of justice and vengeance, can I find the true enemy behind everything and take them down? Can we all survive this?"

He looked at her steadily, his expression now so carefully controlled it gave away nothing. "I can answer that. You *can* come through. You *can* survive. But there is no certainty that you *will*, and much will depend on your choices—all of your choices. We don't *know* all the details; Khoros doesn't tell *anyone* everything—sometimes I wonder if he tells *himself* everything—Myrionar hasn't revealed everything It knows to me, I've got secrets I can't tell them, and of course our opposite numbers do their level best to tell us nothing at all. I can't warn you, even if I wanted to, of many specifics. A lot of this really, truly *is* on your shoulders, not just a set of moves plotted out in advance. I honestly *do not know* exactly what waits for you in Moonshade Hollow...just that you three, and *only* you three, can face it and emerge to victory.

"And that *is* all I can tell you."

Kyri felt for a moment that she might burst from the frustration, but then took a breath. *Let it go.*

Tobimar looked little different, and she saw him do something very similar. "Well...I thank you for what you *could* tell us, sir," he said. "You did, in fact, tell us some things that will be very useful. Being warned that our powers will be limited in the Hollow...it's sure a lot better to know that ahead of time."

The Wanderer nodded, then smiled again. "Another minor correction...I didn't say that *all* your powers would. Unless I miss my guess, *your* abilities should be very little affected, as yours—and your friend Xavier's—are not, precisely, magical in origin, nor from some outside source like the gods."

"But I'd better prep and load up now," Poplock said wryly, looking at his stuff spread out over the anvil, "because I'm starting out behind and now my brand-new magic's going to have a brand-new handicap."

CHAPTER 9

"All went well, then?"

The light-destroying figure in the mirror-scroll smiled. "Exactly as we expected, yes," Kerlamion said in the eerie deep, howling tones of tortured air. "Condor is on his way back to you even now."

It nodded, smiling; despite the human form, anyone watching would have known there was something desperately *wrong* from that smile alone. "Excellent, my King. I will keep an eye out for him. It would *not* do for him to meet up with anyone else along the way who might reveal some unfortunate facts."

"Even so. But enough of your private projects."

"My apologies, Majesty. If I can only be assured of the one other—"

"Yes. I have given the directions. Balinshar is not entirely pleased, but you have assured me of the necessity, and so what you requested you shall have. Now, of the other matters...?"

Very good. Very good indeed. With the Black City now arrived and all wars progressing, Kerlamion had been delegating more of the details of remote operations to it, trusting the humanoid yet inhuman figure with completing the plan which, admittedly, had been more its than Kerlamion's. This did unfortunately demand rather more of its time than it had expected, especially with the promising and extremely capable Thornfalcon now regrettably out of the picture. "Aegeia is in complete chaos now; I expect the endgame of that little farce to play out in, oh, the next few months. The Academy appears to be out of the picture, or so I am assured by Kurildis and, indeed, no communications other than Kuri's have been forthcoming, so I'm reasonably confident that the job has been done."

It gave a sigh and shook its head. "There has unfortunately been some sort of... disruption in Skysand; forces that we were unaware of. Yergoth thinks he can still prevail with the additional resources granted him, but I am, regrettably, dubious. Whenever someone starts in on that 'everything's under control, I just need a *little* help' approach..."

Kerlamion frowned and nodded slowly. "But if they are delayed even a few months..."

"Yes, that's how I view it. Even if Skysand recovers fully, it will take them months to get any of their forces anywhere that matters, and by then the battles should be decided. Same for Balgoltha and his debacle. All he needs to do is keep the *Artan* busy for even the fourth part of a year and his failure need not be fatal." *Though depending on how things are going at that point, it may well be fatal for Balgoltha in any case. That one's been dodging the consequences for failure since the Fall, and I think his time's just about up.*

"So. What of our greatest adversaries?"

"The Empire of the Mountain, I am afraid, cannot be prevented from mobilizing, though they, like the Dragon-King's State, must keep some of their forces busy bottling up our puppets in Dalthunia. News of the emergence of the Black City will reach Zarathanton soon enough. In the Empire, well, it will be heard there as well in very short time, if the Archmage has not sensed it on his own."

"No matter. We have anticipated this, and their armies will be ineffectual by the time they reach us. But—"

"—yes, Majesty, I was just getting to that. Of Khoros... I must candidly say I cannot find him. I did not expect to, honestly; he is... very good at evading detection. The Wanderer is in fact on the move as well, but I cannot say precisely where he is, either; you know how hard he is to track. Nonetheless, he will tend to be both more straightforward and more cautious. I would expect him to choose some group or location to aid and travel there directly. Khoros is undoubtedly playing the puppetmaster as usual, and thus his hand may be felt anywhere, even if his actual location is far distant." He shrugged. "Our plans attempt to take him into account; his, presumably, attempt to do the same for us."

"And the Gods?"

"The Cycle of the Dragon is not in their favor, as we hoped. Elbon Nomicon sleeps now, and will not be easily roused; so, too, for many of the others of the Sixteen, and of those awake, several were not incarnate on Zarathan when your bargains were struck, so they cannot face you directly." He debated momentarily with himself on whether to reveal some details, decided that it was wise to continue to appear as honest as possible. "The Mortal God, on the other hand . . . there are signs of his activity. I have sensed something of his essence in several locations, and you are of course aware of the Skysand Prince."

Kerlamion's eyes narrowed. "Yes. But if he follows the path you expect, that should . . . eliminate the problem entirely, yes?"

"It should indeed. As you have agreed to my one request, I am confident things will proceed according to plan. Myrionar continues to weaken; the other gods will react as we expect, but the pact limits them. Only the Golden-Eyed and the Reclaimed Temple remain unknown factors in those realms, but while they are definitely in opposition to us, they are also not terribly powerful."

"Acceptable. I expect you to continue to direct events outside of the Black City; my attention will be focused here."

"As you direct, so it shall be, Majesty."

The communications scroll went blank, back to silver-on-gold. It leaned back and chuckled quietly. *Ah, the excitement of beginning the real game at last.* It had not—precisely—lied to the King of All Hells, but the *way* in which it had reported certain facts, deductions, and expectations was certainly misleading. For example, while indeed there had been no new communications other than those of Kurildis from the isolated valley of the Academy, it had also been a significant time since Kurildis had communicated at all. *Kurildis always did seem a bit overconfident; when planning an assault on the institution that trains Adventurers, one would be wise to remember what Adventurers are best known for doing.*

The fact was that while the figure did not in any way *oppose* Kerlamion, Its goals were not those of the King of All Hells, and it was important that Kerlamion not grasp exactly what It intended, until it was far too late to change the outcome.

Time to set the rest in motion. It touched the scroll, spoke several words in the demonic tongue with which the scroll had been forged, and saw the silver fade to cloudy gray. *You had best answer, my friend.*

"You interrupt me again? Speak, then, but quickly. I have little time to spare for distractions, and my other patrons demand enough as it is." The voice was sharp, yet despite the annoyance it was also dispassionate, cold and measured in words and timbre in a way that the inhuman figure found extremely comforting. *Here is someone who will be unswayed by any considerations other than his own.*

"My apologies. But I have excellent news. I promised you an assistant, and have found one that I believe will meet even your . . . extremely demanding requirements. One who also has knowledge that touches on your specialty."

The voice was suddenly a touch warmer. "Really? One who could understand *my* work?"

"I believe so. At least as well as I understand it."

"Hmph. Well, you understand it better than any other I have met, vastly more than these idiots I currently work for. If it were not for the challenge and the resources—"

"I understand. But truly, would you give that up?"

"Never!" the voice snapped. "This has brought me close indeed; even with their demands and distractions I have made great progress." A hesitation, then, "And . . . I will thank you for assisting me to find this place. They do, at least, appreciate what I can do for them, even if they place far too much importance on the trivialities." The unseen speaker's tone warmed again. "So when may I expect my new assistant?"

"In a few days. I am arranging the transport. Also . . . you may expect the key you have been seeking soon, perhaps in a month or three. I cannot *control* this, you understand, but I have every reason to believe it to be true."

"Excellent. *Excellent!* I must begin preparations for the unlocking. Thank you for this news."

The scroll cleared abruptly, making the figure laugh and shake its head. *Unable to even bother with the niceties. I doubt he will remember, or care, to mention this to his main employers. Well, he will play his part nonetheless, and I can attend to his minor lapse of courtesy.*

Once more a gesture and a few words and the mirror turned to gray, and then showed the person he had expected.

"Ermirinovas, how kind of you to answer my call."

"How could I refuse, Viedra," she asked, with a brilliant flash of a smile, "given how rarely you have called of late. Besides, Kalshae is currently . . . occupied."

"Our King has given me . . . many assignments in the past centuries. But I have not forgotten you. What news of you and your sisters? How goes your extraction operation? Has my little referral to you given you assistance?"

"He is arrogant and insolent and one day I will likely kill him, but yes, he has achieved much. More power have we gained than I had imagined possible, especially given the circumstances. But there are . . . side effects." She grimaced and gestured at herself.

"Well, yes, a pity—though there are those who would find the effect quite pleasing. Still, given what you are working with, there are many dangers from the . . . waste products, so to speak."

"And not just in appearance. I have lost at least three of our own people to . . . well, you can guess." Her face fell for a moment.

"Sentiment? I hope you are not—"

The face hardened immediately. "Certainly *not*. But the waste and loss of capable labor are extremely regrettable. Unfortunately, the last and greatest source has proven difficult to extract."

"You may expect the key to that extraction soon enough; I informed our mutual friend of it just ere I called you."

"Oh, *wonderful!*" Lit up with such anticipation, she was quite lovely, the humanoid figure thought with wry amusement. "And then—"

"Then I believe you shall achieve what you seek, indeed. I hope you will remember me fondly."

"If we succeed?" She laughed, and though the sound was light and airy, something within and behind that laugh could have sent chills down an ordinary man's spine. "Oh, then, Viedra, I will perhaps have my own offer to you of something even our King cannot give."

"Indeed? Then I wish you all luck, indeed. I am sending a new aide to assist in the project, and he will also carry details of what to expect and my advice on how to handle the matter."

"You really should call more often, Viedra, if all such calls would be so hopeful!"

It chuckled, and the lights about the room flickered. "You are too kind, Ermirinovas. But I must go; much to do, much to arrange."

The scroll blank again, It nodded, a satisfied smile on its face.

Ermirinovas was powerful, even by demonic standards—one of Kerlamion's second-generation children, rumored to be spawn of Kerlamion and one of the Elderwyrm. But like so many demons, she wanted more—enough to carve out her own realm, either within the Hells, or on Zarathan itself. Her current project—if it succeeded, and nothing went terribly amiss—might give her both. That would be amusing, and for other projects It was contemplating, could be useful as well.

To make that happen, of course, required arranging one more thing. It waved and spoke to the scroll once more, and this time the scroll cleared to show a face—one proud and handsome yet twisted, horned and gray, muscled like a warrior but with the wisdom of ages in the hate-filled eyes, one of those that exemplified the word *demon*. "Ah, Balinshar, how good of you to answer."

"Viedraverion." The Demon's voice echoed tightly-leashed anger. "So you have managed to kiss your Father's . . . feet enough to get him to order one of my finest servants into *your* hands, have you?"

"Oh, very good, his Majesty has already told you." It smiled broadly at Balinshar, not rising to the bait in the least. *You, yourself, are of much less account than you wish, Balinshar, and think yourself of greater power than you are. You are not half so interesting as your favorite servant.* "Send the boy through, then. I have many things to do today."

"I look forward to the day when you stumble, Viedra," Balinshar hissed. "On that day many of us will compete for your soul, if the King of All Hells does not take it himself."

"Yes, yes, I'm sure. Send the boy through." It stood and held the scroll up sideways, left it hanging in midair. "Or must I call Father for more . . . encouragement?"

The answer was a rather pedestrian insult, but then Balinshar had never been terribly creative. A major flaw of most demons, really. "Very well."

At Balinshar's gesture a tall, slender figure moved forward hesitantly. "My lord?"

"Do not be afraid, Tashriel," It said. "I have a unique task for you."

Still looking nervous, the figure—appearing to be a human youth in his late teens or very early twenties, with long white hair and a face whose sharp-carven features reminded It strongly of someone else—stepped forward, and in a blaze of light emerged before It.

The being then passed Its hand over the scroll, returning it to inert blankness, and smiled. It saw the young man shiver slightly. At this range, the yellow eyes revealed some inhuman blood within Tashriel, but he still looked mostly like a young man.

How very deceptive. Even the shiver is deceptive; he would be a most formidable opponent if he chose to be. "Tashriel, I have need of your unique knowledge—your most *ancient* unique knowledge."

His eyes went wide. "My lord...I am forbidden to—"

"Tsk, tsk, Tashriel. The King of All Hells himself has assigned you to me, for this very express reason. I assure you, in this case I have pressing need for the talents you learned...in A'Atla'Alandar."

There was still a trace of uncertainty, but much more of excitement and anticipation in the eyes of the boy-who-was-not-a-boy. "Truly, Lord Viedraverion?"

"Truly, Tashriel. I have a...most *fascinating* assignment for you. One that you will carry out as honestly and humbly as if it were truly what you wished, and have to act otherwise only if the enterprise fails. And in *that* case..."

As It explained, the yellow eyes began to dance with excitement, and It knew that success was assured.

Come, Phoenix and your friends. All will be ready when you arrive.

CHAPTER 10

The crumbling path stretched up between slopes dotted with trees that were touched with a stronger, somehow virulent green, and then vanished into shadow cast by the mountains about.

"Rivendream Pass," the Wanderer said quietly. "This is as far as my magic can take us, as close to your mystery as I can go without traveling with you."

"So, will you?" Poplock asked. "Because that would be really useful, even if you're only half of what they say you are."

He felt Tobimar jerk slightly under him at the casual question and could see Kyri shoot an outraged glance at him from beneath her helm. The two still held the Wanderer in some awe, and Poplock *was* being rather informal.

The Wanderer merely chuckled. "Sorry, Poplock. I can't go much farther; I've got other places that need me, and as I said, I can't tell you what's going on. Going with you, with what I know, that would be potentially worse."

He raised the rune-covered staff and pointed. "The only *good* thing about Rivendream is that it's not a tricky maze. It's the one decent, halfway level path through the Khalal range, and if you stick with the reasonably easy pathways, you will most certainly emerge in Moonshade Hollow. No getting lost, as can happen crossing through mountains in other places."

He turned back to the group and looked at them. *Looks more serious than usual.* "I can't even give you much more advice, let alone direct aid. Kyri...just remember, this *is* part of the mission

81

you follow for Myrionar. While this is also Tobimar's quest, much
of what is to come is yours as well, part of your own journey,
and a terribly important one.

"Tobimar, I can only tell you this: you are, indeed, the true
descendant of the Lords of the Sky, of their rulers. That much
have your people remembered and kept true and pure. You were
chosen by the turn of a card that represents Terian himself; I
cannot watch over you . . . but he may."

Finally he looked at Poplock. "I don't underestimate you,
Poplock, but be careful." He reached inside his clothing and
took out a small ivory colored cylinder with strange writing on
it below an outline of a sailing ship. The cylinder—a container
of some sort—rattled. He unscrewed the top and poured many
somethings that glittered into his hand, selected one, and poured
the rest back, putting the container away. "Take this."

Poplock reached out and took the sparkling object. *Ooh, it's
a crystal. Shiny, natural facets . . . not quite so sparkly as diamond,
though. Water-clear, though with a few black inclusions—not perfect. Six-sided, double termination . . .* "Quartz crystal? No offense,
but I've got—"

"—none like *that* one, my amphibious friend. *That* crystal I
mined, with my own hands, and have carried with me ever since
first I came to this world."

Poplock almost dropped the sparkling stone. "You . . . this is
from *Zaralandar*—what you and Xavier call Earth?"

"It is indeed. One such as yourself might do many things
with that. Save it. Think on it. Use it when you are certain. But
it carries with it some of the essence of my world—some of *my*
essence, in fact, for as I said I dug it from the stone by hand,
broke the stone from the earth and split it with hand-forged
steel wedges and a sledgehammer. My sweat—and maybe a little
blood—was shed getting that very nice crystal out of its stone.
It's a part of me. That by itself makes it unique."

The little Toad bowed as deeply as his anatomy permitted.
"I'll be very careful with it. And I'll think real hard on what I
can use it for."

"Good." He bowed to all of them, a dramatic gesture with
a flare of his cloak. "I hope we shall meet again . . . when you
return."

He took three strides . . . and vanished.

Poplock shook his head. "Makes it look so easy. Well, let's get moving, right?"

"Right," Kyri agreed, and Tobimar nodded, hitching his pack up and making sure it was settled properly. "No point in waiting."

For a while, as they moved farther up and into Rivendream pass, Poplock studied the crystal. There *was* something strange about it, an aura that interacted strangely with his attempts to divine something about it. Finally, though, he put it away carefully into his pack. *Figuring that thing out will take more than an hour riding on someone's shoulder. Quartz has its own virtues, but a crystal from the Wanderer? That's gonna be something special.*

Rivendream Pass continued up—a relatively steep incline at first, but one that abated after a mile or so. The air was somewhat cooler here, and Poplock noticed something. "Look at those trees."

"What?" Tobimar paused and looked. "You're right. Different, not what we're used to at all. I think, from something I read in Skysand's library, that this one's an oak."

"It is," agreed Kyri. "Lythos taught me to identify the higher-slopes' trees. That's a maple, over there, and the dark-barked one over by that rock is *santki*." She frowned. "But all of them look..."

"Wrong. Yeah, I noticed," Poplock agreed darkly. "Branches growing at funny angles. Leaves not quite right. Trunks not really straight."

Tobimar stiffened. "And listen."

Poplock sat up and listened—and looked, no point in not looking.

At first he didn't get what Tobimar was pointing out. There were the faint sounds of movement that you hear in any forest—little creatures, occasionally a larger one...

...but...

...but they were somehow not right, as well. Poplock couldn't clear the mud off it, so to speak, but he could just *tell* that nothing in this place was quite the way it should be. Reflexively he let his tongue snap out and snag a passing fly, and suddenly he found himself gagging, spitting the mangled insect back out. "Ack! Uggh! That was *vile*."

"You couldn't eat an *insect*?" Tobimar studied him with growing concern. "I've never seen anything you wouldn't eat."

"You haven't seen enough, then. But that was in a special class all by itself."

"Poisonous?"

"Don't *think* so ... not exactly, anyway. But ... lemme catch another. Without eating it, this time."

He managed to snag another fly, but transferred it to his front paws instead of his mouth. Kyri came over to watch. "Umm ... Not the fat, sleek shape I expect. Narrower. Faster, maybe. But more importantly ..." he mumbled a few words, took a look at the thing. In his eyes, the insect dimmed, a pattern of dark lines rippling around it. "Dark, *dark* magic influencing it. Don't know how eating it would affect me. Not going to try it to find out."

Kyri's face went grim. "That means we don't dare eat anything we catch here. Or we have to find some way to purify it that we can afford to use."

Tobimar nodded slowly. "A good thing we *did* pack a lot of provisions."

"Even so ..." Poplock frowned. "There's a *lot* of Moonshade Hollow on the other side, isn't there?"

"You're right." Concern deepened on both the humans' faces. "If we take too long, we could easily run out."

"Depending on how long it takes to get through the pass, it could be not long after we get there," agreed Poplock.

Tobimar nodded again. "Well ... we can think about possible solutions as we continue. We've got a few more hours until nighttime, I'd like to move on."

"Yes. We've got to get going," agreed Kyri.

But she slid Flamewing from its sheath, and Tobimar drew his new, shining blades as well. Poplock didn't draw Steelthorn, but he did make sure it, his clockwork crossbow, and a few other things were close to hand.

This isn't going to be fun at all.

CHAPTER 11

Kyri shook herself, breaking out of a reverie of remembrance, seeing again the darkness of Rivendream Pass, the serpent's corpse, the burned bush. The memories of how they had come here seeming to have streamed by her in a moment; she shivered anew at the oppressive *wrongness* that now weighed upon her. "We were warned," she repeated. "Warned that even Myrionar's powers would be weakened here."

"True...but the Wanderer had said that was inside Moonshade Hollow. Instead, we're barely halfway through Rivendream, and it's already affecting you." Tobimar looked at where the charred corpse lay. "And these things..."

"Almost familiar, aren't they?" Poplock commented.

"Yes..." The three stood, contemplating the remains for a moment, and then Tobimar snapped his fingers. "I have it. The things we fought in the clearing, after Thornfalcon died."

"Very similar in feel," agreed Kyri. The same feeling of *wrongness* and ancient evil pervaded most of the things in this pass. "But yet..."

"Yeah. Yet," agreed the Toad. "These things are disgusting monsters, but all the ones we've seen have been, well, *normal* twisted disgusting creatures, if you know what I mean?"

Kyri blinked. "Umm...I'm not quite sure I do, actually."

"Well, a *lot* of the things that attacked us in the clearing weren't...well, they weren't *one* thing, if you know what I mean."

That made sense. "You're right. There were those nameless

85

monsters like men crossed with centaurs and something worse, the *bilarel* with a crab's arms, and so on."

"And there were a *lot* of them," Tobimar said. "If that was a gateway, there had to be just an *immense* herd of the things waiting to come through."

"Bad news twice over," observed Poplock. "First, means someone has a heck of a lot of monsters—and probably *made* the things, too, somehow. I've heard of lifestitching of various types, but... that's *hard* magic. Not just dark, though the way those things were made it's definitely dark, but really, really difficult. Playing with life—changing it—that's one of the harder parts of magic. Second, means whoever it is can keep these things from fighting *each other*, or they'd have ripped each other to shreds as soon as they came through."

"By the Light, you're correct. I hadn't thought of that, but it makes sense. And it's ugly."

"This whole *thing* is ugly." Kyri couldn't keep from shivering, and not just from the air which was cooler than she was used to. "Tobimar, if the maps we have are even *close* to correct, Moonshade Hollow is *hundreds* of miles across in all directions. Can we even *survive* in that place, with what we've seen so far?"

"Do you have faith in Myrionar?" he asked her quietly.

"Yes," she answered without hesitation.

"Then believe in it and the Wanderer. They said we *could* get through this, and while the Wanderer said he wasn't going to be able to help us, I'll bet he'd have at least given us a decent *hint* if he thought we were underequipped. Somehow there's a way through this."

Kyri nodded and smiled at him. *He knows how to support me, support my faith, even when it isn't his.* That meant a lot to her... especially now. "You're right. I must have faith, and I *will* have faith. Somehow we will find a way through even the Hollow." She glanced back at the charred area. "Honestly... we've been sort of lucky, I think."

"You've got a *strange* idea of luck!" Poplock muttered.

"No, really. Most of the things we've run into have been, well, *obviously* dangerous, actively hostile. I think that thing was a *voromos* originally, or its ancestors were."

"Voromos... Yes, I think you're right. The poison spitting fits, and the three ridges on the head look close."

Tobimar nodded. "It was bigger, more hostile, and its venom was actively controlling things it touched instead of just making them docile and eventually killing them, but yes. So...?

"Ohhhh, I think I get her point. These things, they're all up-front killers. How'd you like to deal with Rivendream's version of a forestfisher or a, what's the name, *itrichel*?"

Tobimar shuddered, and so did Kyri. "A mindworm? No thank you. Nor the other. You're right. Let's hope we stay that lucky, at least."

Kyri shivered again. Forestfishers, or *jilyesh*, were giant spidery creatures that would use their webs to drop poison onto sleeping victims; *itrichels* were worse—intelligent parasites that used guile and stealth to acquire new hosts. Both were, fortunately extremely rare. But they were, indeed, excellent examples of what she meant. "Yes, let's hope so," she agreed.

They continued along the deceptively green and bright valley; a few flat blocks, here and there, were the only reminder that a great thoroughfare had run from one side to the other of Rivendream Pass, once Heavenbridge Way. Kyri watched ahead of them carefully; she knew that Tobimar was checking the sides, and the little Toad was watching their rear. But the discovery that the Wanderer's warning had been true weighed on her. "Poplock, are you feeling the same resistance to your magic that I was feeling with Myrionar's power?"

"Hm. Haven't tried yet; summoning crystals use mostly power you stored up before, you know. And they're sorta aided by the use of the crystal medium. Not as much as gemcallers, though. Let's see..." He mumbled some words, sketched a symbol in the air; shimmering light twined in mist, touched with fire, descended over both her and Tobimar, cleansing them of the mess from the last battle. "*Whooof!* Yes, that was *tough*. Normally that'd be really easy to do, but that felt more like it was a spell twice, maybe three times that complex." The brown Toad rubbed his broad chin thoughtfully, looking back behind them. "No, that's not quite it. It didn't feel more complicated, but like I was having to... *drag* the magic out of the world, instead of it just flowing. Like walking up a flowing stream, how the very nature of it fights you. Right?"

That described the feeling she'd gotten very well. "I think you've got it. Perhaps also like trying to draw a breath underwater through a long tube." She glanced to Tobimar before returning her gaze forward. "Your abilities are unhindered?"

"They seem to be so far. This fits with what we were told."

At least one *of us will be at full strength.* She knew that even with this handicap, her sheer power would probably exceed that of Tobimar—weakened or not, Myrionar *was* still a god, and she was Myrionar's last, final hope, to which all power might be directed in extremity. And she still had the Vantage strength; nothing could take that from her unless it were something like poison. *And anyone else trying to use magic in here will be handicapped as well.*

The real problem, she thought, still remained food and drink. Purifying what they found here to be safe wasn't easy, and now it would be even harder. Moonshade Hollow was supposed to be *worse* than Rivendream Pass—the source from which this stuff at the edges *came* from.

She honestly wasn't sure she *wanted* to know what could be worse.

Then she saw what was ahead. "Oh, Myrionar's *Balance*."

Here, near or perhaps just past the crest of the pass, halfway to their destination, the mountains had lost part of their great battle with the elements, and unleashed their fury on the valley below. The pass was filled with jumbled, sharp-edged rock and earth to a depth of seventy to a hundred feet—a recent, massive landslide, probably no more than a few weeks, maybe less; in the relative stillness of the area, she could still hear muffled but definite sounds of shifting, settling rock.

It was clear there was no going around the slide; they had no choice except to go over it or through it. Briefly she thought of the unstoppable power she had unleashed in the final strike against the army of abominations on Thornfalcon's estate, but shook her head; that had been a truly justified action, one of vengeance finally attained. Using that level of power just to clear the road—even if she could *reach* that level of power here—would not be looked upon kindly.

"Sand and grit," muttered Tobimar. "That's going to be an absolute *gem* of a climb, let me tell you. We'll be lucky to get over it with only one of us crippled."

"Might not be so bad for *me*," Poplock said, eyeing the massive tumbled wall of fractured stone. "It's settled enough that a

little Toad of my weight probably won't bother it. But you guys...
that's not going to be a fun climb."

What had she just been thinking? *Go over it.*

"I've got an idea," she said. "I haven't tried this before, but
I *think* it should work."

"What? Remember the power—"

"I know. It's probably going to be pretty hard to do here,
if I can. But if I can it'll save us time, and potentially injury.
Honestly," she looked again at the unstable mass, "I can see too
many ways this wall of shifting rock could *kill* us outright." She
looked up and took a deep breath. "So let's see if I can *fly* us over."

Tobimar looked at her and his eyes suddenly showed a child's
wonder. "Fly? You can *fly?*" He looked suddenly embarrassed.
"I mean, I'd heard the stories, but Thornfalcon didn't fly, so I
wasn't sure..."

"I *think* I can. It's one of the powers of most if not all of the
Justiciars; Thornfalcon knew I was right there with him, so he
probably didn't think it was worth the risk to become an aerial
target." She felt her own heart starting to beat in anticipation, not
just in tension for success or failure, or in fear of what might be
waiting. *Flying.* Wasn't this one of the greatest dreams? And by
his expression, one that Tobimar shared. "Let me try, anyway."

She closed her eyes and concentrated. "Myrionar, God of Justice and Vengeance, hear me. Give me the Wings of the Phoenix,
wings strong and true enough to carry me and my friends over
this barrier, carry us into the sky and to the lands beyond the
wall before us."

A shiver of anticipation washed down her back, and then suddenly it was *more* than anticipation; between her shoulderblades
a warmth, a tingling fire that energized her, even as she felt the
effort of drawing the power through, and threw her own will into
dragging the energy through the interference of Rivendream Pass.
And as the power slowly yielded, the sensation became warmer,
spread, and she saw a golden glow beginning to illumine the
world through her eyelids. She let her eyes open slowly, but still
did not look behind her, only focusing on her need, seeing only
what was before her, cast into brilliant relief and sharp shadow.

Tobimar was staring in awe, and even Poplock turned to take
his time to stare.

With a final effort she felt the blessing complete, and looked.

Gold-flaming wings stretched glittering, shimmering pinions fifteen feet on either side of her, and she could feel...she *knew*... how to use them. She laughed, even as she felt a little trembling in her knees from the effort she'd just expended. "It *worked*."

"It would certainly appear so," Tobimar said, still staring. "Can you carry me? Poplock, obviously, will not be a problem."

"I'm sure I can. But let me just test the wings first..."

With a spring she leapt from the ground and found herself arrowing upward, wings both beating and simply *lifting* with a marvelous lightness that made flight simplicity itself. She glanced down, seeing that behind her she left a trail of auric light that only slowly faded.

The height, without anything below her, was a bit dizzying, but she focused on direction, on motion, on understanding how to *move* in the air. It was something like swimming, something like running, something like swinging by a rope, but at the same time nothing like any of them, a glorious speeding through the air that was as natural as breathing and as wondrous as dawn.

She alighted in front of Tobimar, and wondered if her eyes were shining like his, and suddenly laughed. *We're still young. I can laugh for joy if I want, and here, in this place? It's* needed.

Tobimar echoed her laugh, his voice joining hers and sending echoes of pure wonder chasing through Rivendream Pass. "You're amazing, Kyri!"

"Me? It's Myrionar, not me."

"Myrionar may have the *power*, but this is *you*," he said firmly. "So...can you lift us?"

"I'm sure I can. That felt no harder than walking or running, and I could carry you easily enough for quite a distance." She held out her arms. "Let's try it."

She was surprised to see his already-dark skin flush darker, but Tobimar stepped forward and let her pick him up. "Hold on—I don't know how my balance will be affected when I do this," she said.

"Hold...on? Um... Oh, of course."

His right arm slid easily behind her neck. She found her heart beating faster. *What am I...*

Oh, by Myrionar, *I'm not...*

But as she felt his other arm come up to clasp his hands together, forming a strong, solid loop around her neck, pulling his head in to rest against her shoulder, she realized that *she* must be blushing too. *Oh, I think I am. Of course I am. How stupid of me not to have noticed before.*

"Ready?" she asked.

He looked up at her, and their gazes met.

It was at least several seconds before he blinked, and shook his head. "Oh, yes, I'm ready. Sure." He muttered something that she couldn't quite catch.

"Oh, for Blackwart's *SAKE*, what's *WRONG* with you two?" burst out Poplock, who bounced on her head and then dropped back down to Tobimar's chest. "*Kiss* already!"

Kyri dropped Tobimar in startled mortification; fortunately his reflexes kept that from being total disaster. Poplock, of course, landed perfectly. "Don't tell me neither of you noticed it. *I* have watched the two of you since you met. *No*, don't you even start arguing, Tobimar, I know your people have all sorts of formal stuff there but this isn't the time or place. I'm *not* going to have you hopping around the bushes avoiding it for the next few months! Now get up and go kiss her. Unless you want to tell me you don't want to do that?"

"Tell you I...no, of course I...*Shiderich!* You...*toad!*"

Kyri just stared at Poplock, unsure as to whether she wanted to laugh, cry, or...or *what* she wanted to do. "I...but I didn't know if..."

"Stop the *stuttering!*" The little Toad's voice was startlingly loud and yet completely in control. "By the *Helpers*, I have no idea how your people manage to breed as fast as you do. Kyri, you tell me if I'm wrong when I say you find Tobimar exactly your type?"

"Well...no. I mean, yes." She could feel enough heat on her cheeks that she was certain water would *vaporize* on them, like on a hot griddle. "*Balance!* I mean, you are not wrong!" She found herself feeling almost *defiant* as she stared at Tobimar, who had picked himself off the ground; his hair had come unbound from its usual restraint and fell in an ebony waterfall around his face.

"And Tobimar, you've been *staring* at her practically constantly ever since you met her—whenever you didn't think she'd notice. But I *had* to notice. So?"

She couldn't believe this...and yet, she *could*. This was... exactly how Poplock handled everything, so directly that no one ever saw it coming. "You're *ordering* us to...?"

"To understand that *both* of you feel the same way, yes," Poplock said, and there was a twinkle in the golden eyes. "So you don't have any doubts about what you feel."

Tobimar looked at her. "I wish I'd had the courage to do this *myself*...but I didn't want to intrude on your mission with my feelings."

Kyri giggled suddenly. "I didn't want to intrude on *your* mission!"

The dark-skinned young man took a hesitant step forward, but his brilliant blue eyes were locked on hers...and she saw no hesitation there. "So...?"

"So I think we'd better do as the Toad tells us," she said, and before she could change her mind, stepped forward and bent down.

It wasn't maybe the *best* kiss—in technique—because, well, she wasn't sure *how* you did this. But his arms did go around her neck, twining in her hair, and hers did the same to his, and even if they didn't know exactly what they were doing...that didn't matter nearly so much as the fact that they *were* doing it.

Finally they separated, and she looked down into blue eyes that were a thousand times brighter than she'd remembered, and wondered how they could *shine* like that.

"*Terian*, you have beautiful eyes," he said. "The way they shine..."

I suppose we look the same to each other, she thought, and realized then just what that meant he was seeing in her, and paused for a moment in wonder. *I...never thought of this before. Not really. There was Aran, for a short time, and Jeridan's occasional hints...but those chances never became anything. But this...*

"Kyri," Tobimar said softly, breaking into her thoughts, "I'd like—I think we'd *both* like—to continue this...but we've got things to do, and this isn't the safest place. So...if you could...?"

She laughed suddenly, and felt a fierce joy. *No more uncertainty. Just the surety that he's with me, and I'm with him.* She reached out to him again, even as the little Toad bounced back up to Tobimar's shoulder. "Hold on, then!"

Together, they blazed a trail of light into the sky.

CHAPTER 12

Poplock tasted the air. *Definitely* more humid. "I think we're nearly down. Look at the mountains."

Tobimar's gaze flicked to both sides, then he paused. "He's right, Kyri. This canyon's coming to an end, and the warmth, the feel of the air... I think we're almost there."

Almost in Moonshade Hollow.

It hadn't been—quite—a nonstop series of battles from one side of the pass to the other, but there had sure been more than their share of ambushes by things that might *look* ordinary but would be more savage, malevolent, or lethal than their ordinary equivalents, and sometimes by things that weren't in any sense ordinary. One out of every three nights was disrupted by some *thing* that couldn't let people get a decent night's sleep.

Poplock shook his head slightly (which was about as much as a Toad's anatomy allowed). Even though he could often take naps on Tobimar's shoulder, he was still exhausted; he couldn't imagine what it must be like for the two humans. Kyri was constantly called upon to heal any of them—though Tobimar could heal himself to a limited extent—and Tobimar had to keep his unique senses constantly attuned.

How in Blackwart's Name are we going to get through this place alive, let alone in any shape to deal with, well, whatever things are hiding here, and find the key to Tobimar's quest?

He knew *Kyri's* answer to that, and—to a certain degree—he understood and agreed with it. Her mission was based on

maintaining faith in her god Myrionar and that if she maintained said faith, somehow things would work out. And it was
true that if you couldn't rely on the gods to carry through with
their promises, they weren't much good to anyone.

There was, however, the fact that Myrionar had been systematically weakened by some truly monstrous enemy that managed
to corrupt Myrionar's own order, and either did this without
Myrionar *realizing* it until too late, or under some kind of circumstance that prevented Myrionar from telling anyone. Either of
these possibilities was pretty shocking...and caused Poplock to
privately doubt that Myrionar could *absolutely* guarantee anything.

Which meant they had to make their own luck. Which seemed
pretty challenging in this place.

It was warmer here, as Tobimar had noted, but the comfort
to which they were accustomed didn't do much to make the little
Toad relax. The very *atmosphere* made him feel prickly all over,
as though he'd rolled in a bed of groundthorns.

He caught movement from above, ducked aside. A tendril
from the tree nearly caught him—and was neatly bisected by a
blow from Tobimar's blue-green glittering blade. The entire tree
shuddered, then started to reach forward, a low, wood-tearing
rumbling issuing from it.

The clearing was suddenly lit by golden light as Kyri drew
Flamewing, and not only that tree, but several others, suddenly
leaned back, away, moaning. *Yeah, you're a tree, and that's a
flaming sword seven feet long. A* holy *flaming sword.*

"Stay back, corrupted forest," Kyri said, tense but sure. "Touch
my companions, touch me, and fire will cleanse this place from
one side to the other."

It was something of a bluff—if Myrionar had the power to
cleanse entire valleys with fire it probably wouldn't have its current problems—but Poplock saw with great satisfaction that none
of the trees wanted to call her bluff. They drew aside, fell into
inaction, and moved no more than ordinary trees as the three
continued their journey.

After a few moments, Kyri sheathed her greatsword. "Myrionar's *Balance*, the forest itself is against us."

"I know. And...I must speak honestly, Kyri—I have no clear
idea of where we must go from here," Tobimar confessed. "We
only knew the homeland must exist somewhere, but I need proof

that I have found it. From what the Wanderer said, the Seven and One were held by my people, and we do not have them, so they must still be here. But all the Seven could have been held in two cupped hands, and the Sun itself in two more, so they are small enough clues to search for here."

Kyri nodded. "I know. But there can't be *just* monsters and jungle here. We already know that—Thornfalcon arranged for that gateway. Someone lives here and creates monsters even worse than the ones we've met thus far. I can't believe they're completely alone. So there must be people here, good or bad, and if we can find anyone native to this place, they'll be able to guide us."

"I hope you're right," Tobimar said, impaling a black and gray scorpion, about the same size as Poplock, as he spoke.

They continued on; Poplock's ears suddenly caught a hint of a new sound. "Hold up." He turned slightly on Tobimar's shoulder. "Over there. I hear a river or big stream."

"That could be good," Tobimar said as they shifted their course somewhat. "Almost all cities and villages are built close to water sources. Follow this one down and we should meet up with someone."

"Probably," Poplock agreed, "but you'd better watch your step closely, because with what we've seen so far, what do you think's living in the rivers and streams?"

Kyri grimaced. "An excellent point. Let's not get too close to the water, then."

It *was* a small river—fifty yards across at the point they emerged from the jungle and found themselves on the banks. "Whoops. That's too close."

On a sandbar a few hundred yards away, Poplock spotted a very large reptilian shape, ridged and sharp with a long, blunt head and lots of teeth. "*Way* too close."

The others agreed and quickly backed away from the shimmering, poison-green waters. Based on sound and occasional sights through the trees, the little group followed the river at a distance of twenty or thirty yards from the edge.

For several hours they followed faint game trails through the jungle, and were mostly unbothered; given that some of the trees seemed not only to be able to move but made sounds, Poplock suspected that word had spread through the forest that the three newcomers were not easy prey. The sun was becoming low, as shown by slanting beams of light through the canopy, and Poplock began to think about camping and how to keep themselves safe during the night in this place.

Without warning, Kyri and Tobimar pushed through the next line of greenery to find themselves standing at the edge of a clearing about two hundred yards across. Looming up not far away was a monstrous thing, an armored grub with wide mandibles, gleaming red eyes, and hissing breath, large as a house, glowering down at a tiny figure—Poplock guessed no more than five feet high—in delicate blues and greens, seeming frozen before it, scarcely fifty feet from them. The creature gathered itself and screeched.

But it never had a chance to complete the lunge. Kyri and Tobimar had reflexively sprinted forward, and the creature balked as it found itself face-to-face with two armed opponents, one holding a blade seven feet from pommel to tip, the other with two swords gleaming cold and bitter. Glancing backwards, Poplock saw a dumbfounded expression on the green-blue clad girl, a look of disbelieving shock that told clearly how very little she had expected any intervention.

But the creature was only momentarily taken aback; it gave vent to a rippling roar and flowed forward, extending its body as grubs do. The great mandibles rebounded from Kyri's armor but sent her tumbling; Tobimar, however, leapt *up*, bounding from the mandibles to the top of the creature, and then spun, bringing both swords down at the juncture of head and abdomen.

The roar turned to an ear-piercing shriek of agony, and the thing began to whip its body back and forth, Tobimar barely maintaining his grip (and Poplock hard-pressed to keep a grip on Tobimar). Black blood oozed from the sword-wounds, as the creature turned to writhe on its back; Tobimar barely yanked his swords out and rolled clear in time, with Poplock almost getting squished beneath the Skysand Prince's body.

Their attack had been more than enough distraction, however, and before the monstrous grub-thing could do more than turn towards them, the golden fire lit up the clearing with promise and peril. "Myrionar's *FLAME!*" Phoenix Kyri shouted, and the flaming blade impaled the creature, detonating fire throughout its body; it stiffened and fell limp.

Tobimar immediately turned to the little figure. "Are you all right, Milady...?"

Poplock now realized that the figure wasn't a little girl, but a young woman, just a very diminutive one. Her blue and green outfit was a strange combination of diaphanous clothing and what appeared to be crystalline armor. She had short golden hair, a bow tied in it to one side of her head, and no weapons in evidence unless something was concealed in a few small pouches at her waist, or, possibly, the wand or tube by her side that glittered with multicolored gems.

Her expression was startling—somehow both annoyed, amused, and impressed. "I am *perfectly* fine." Her voice was a sweet soprano, even more startling for its purity and beauty in this distorted forest. "I *am* surprised *you* and your companion are unharmed, and I am *quite* unaccustomed to being interrupted in my hunt."

Teeth as bright as sunlight on flowers flashed as she gave a sudden smile. "But I see the interruption was well meant, and you had no idea of what you did, so I thank you for the thought." Her brow furrowed. "Yet...which of the *Sha* do you come from? Your speech is strange, an accent I do not know, and your clothing the same; yet I thought I knew them all."

Of all the things he'd expected, *this* wasn't one of them. Poplock, as usual, kept his mouth shut; best to let the others talk.

Tobimar shook his head in bemusement, then bowed deeply. "My apologies for what I now see to have been a crude interruption in your own quest. I am Tobimar, and this is my companion, Phoenix." They had agreed that there was no immediate reason to reveal any possible connection between Tobimar and the past; it might be dangerous to do so, given the fact that demons were hunting his people and trying to prevent him from completing this mission. And, of course, when on duty as a Justiciar, Kyri was not Kyri Vantage, but merely the Phoenix.

"We come from beyond the pass in the mountains," Tobimar continued.

Now her eyes widened. "From...*there*? But we are taught that none live beyond any of the Mountains, not from the North to the South nor East nor West. Do you speak truly, Tobimar?" Before he could answer, she shook her head. "Yet it *must* be true, for how could you be so strange to the world that you did

not recognize one of the Lights themselves? And I am remiss!"
She bowed to them, a gesture with one arm across her body, the
other gracefully held more aloft. "I am Miri, Light of the Unity. I
thank you for your aid, needed or not." She glanced about. "This
is not a place for talk or questions. Come, let us go to the city."

"So there *is* a city?" Phoenix asked, a relieved tone in her
voice. "We had begun to fear there was nothing here but monsters and evil."

Miri laughed. "A city? Say, rather, the greatest of cities, and
her children. Follow, and you will see."

Inwardly, Poplock had to smile. Perhaps these people had
somehow survived and built themselves a civilization, but as the
three of them had been to Zarathanton, it would be rather hard
to top *that* as the "greatest of cities."

Following Miri, it took only a relatively short time—perhaps
fifteen minutes—to arrive in front of a startling wall of shining
green-gray stone, fifty feet high. A wide, solid gate was set in
that wall, of solid steel, or so Poplock thought. *That would be
quite a challenge for most things to get through*, he had to admit.

Miri stepped up to the gate and put her hand to it; Poplock,
watching her carefully, could see that she was inserting a ring
on her middle finger face-first into an aperture in the gate. It
instantly *clicked* and the gateway swung open. A wide corridor
led through the wall a short distance, and the three humans'
footsteps echoed sharply on the polished stone as they walked
to the ending of the corridor; the gateway at that end swung
open as they reached it, and a haze of golden light greeted them.

Poplock blinked his eyes in disbelief.

They stood atop a ridge, looking down on a sprawling town
dotted with great trees amidst a sweep of pure, green grass
that stretched down to the blue-green of the river that passed
through the middle of the town. Great white, fluffy clouds drifted
through a sky bluer and more pure than he remembered even
from Evanwyl; in the distance were tilled fields, and a winding
road extending to the horizon. Birds flew, trilling, and he could
smell the purity in the air, in the land.

A buzzing insect flew near, and he snapped out his tongue.
Even the taste of the creature was like something new, something
born pure and unique into the world for the first time, and
Poplock could see the stunned surprise on his friends' faces too

as they gazed on the world about them, smelled the fresh and untainted breeze, looked upon even stones and earth that seemed more *right* than anything they had ever seen. The setting sun cast a glow over the clouds and everything else that touched all with the wealth of the heavens.

"Welcome," Miri said. "Welcome, travelers from afar, to the Unity of the Seven Lights; welcome to Kaizatenzei."

CHAPTER 13

"You are tense this morning, Lord."

It raised an eyebrow and smiled. With the false Justiciars no longer free to roam Evanwyl, it no longer cared about the use of words that might reveal its secret guise; the Justiciars could no longer accidentally reveal anything.

What *was* surprising and amusing was Bolthawk's observation, and the fact that it was true. "You see clearly, Bolthawk. How did you know?"

The Child of Odin gave a tight grin, even as he whirled his axe around in a quick cut that necessitated an immediate dodge. "Seen it before, truth be told. Usually you're fluid as water, clean as air. This morning, though... your movements are just a touch jerky, your glances stray wider, as though seeking something." He barely blocked its return stroke, but continued, "I see it only in mornings, so I think... a dream, yes?"

Perceptive indeed. The true irony is that each and every one of these people... with the exception of Thornfalcon... could have been excellent Justiciars in truth. "Yes."

"Would you care to speak it? Or is this a different dream each time?"

The creature considered as the two of them had a few more passes at arms during their practice. *I have never told this to a mortal before, and indeed only to select few others. Yet... why not? They have much fear of me, yes, but fear is not the best or only way to control. And he shows considerable courage in daring to ask such personal information, as a dream can give hints of weakness.*

Finally he decided and disengaged. "No, you guess aright, friend Bolthawk. It is the same dream, always the same dream, that causes me a few hours of . . . tension, every so often." It leaned on its sword and looked off into the distance. "The preliminaries may vary, but always the true . . . nightmare, if you will . . . begins with the same realization:

"I am being *followed*."

It placed so much emphasis on that phrase that Bolthawk raised his own thick eyebrow. "Is that so unusual, then?"

"Oh, indeed. A most novel sensation, actually. No one *ever* follows *me* . . . not unless I *want* them to, of course . . . and in the dream, I cannot remember inviting any pursuit.

"So I look about, extending all of my senses—my *true* senses, you understand—and yet I find . . . *nothing*."

It found to its surprise and amusement that *gooseflesh* had risen on its arms. *This body's reactions still can go beyond expectations.*

Yet the reaction was not, in fact, entirely inappropriate, for the dream itself was emphatic and clear, and it could feel the certainty waiting in that memory: despite the failure of its senses, *something* was following, out there in the darkness that was darker than any night.

"I quicken my pace; whatever follows me, the proper course is to meet my adversary on more advantageous ground. And it is then that it strikes me: I do not know *where* I am going! I am unclear as to my goal." It smiled one of Its least-comforting smiles, and was rewarded with Bolthawk swallowing nervously. "You understand, of course, that I *always* know my goal, and have for . . . well, much, much longer than you or any of your people have been alive."

Bolthawk nodded, and it continued, "I carve my way through the forest I now find myself in, a trackless jungle that I travel with ease yet with no clear path or destination. And then I hear . . . a noise.

"Something *is* there. Something is coming. Behind me." It closed its eyes, remembering. "I whirl, looking, gazing with all my intensity. My other senses say there is still nothing, nothing there at all, but then I see something. A flash of eyes.

"But not just any eyes, oh no. Gray eyes, eyes like storm-clouds and steel, cold and grim yet transcendently certain, with not a trace of doubt or fear or hesitation, eyes that penetrate all my deceptions, and I know that my pursuer *sees* me, knows me for what and who I truly am, and yet does *not* turn back, does not recoil, does not pause, but comes *on*, ever closer." It drew a breath, one that actually held the faintest tremor of excitement or even, perhaps, fear. "And I feel a shock through my very soul, for I know—*know*—the truth. That *these are the eyes that could end me.*"

It smiled and shrugged. "And then—always—I awaken."

Bolthawk considered. "So, you've never seen the person *with* those eyes?"

"I have never seen my pursuer's face," it admitted candidly. "Never descried the hands or body, never even sensed the nature of the soul that must accompany that body. For all my life—and that has been, you realize, a very long life indeed—whenever the dream or vision comes I see only the eyes, that wide, gray, unwavering gaze."

The false Justiciar hesitated momentarily, then shrugged. "You know, Kyri Vantage has eyes just as you describe."

It laughed. "Oh, not *quite*, my friend. Or, to be fair . . . not quite *yet*. I have met many, many with gray eyes before, but never *those* eyes. Sometimes the wrong shade; other times the wrong gaze, too gentle, too uncontrolled . . . never quite the same. Phoenix Kyri's eyes are too heated in their vengeance, too passionate. These eyes are those of one who has contemplated my destruction not for mere months, but for uncounted years, and who knows precisely my nature, and yet feels neither fear nor uncertainty; he, or she, or it, *knows* that they will make an end of me. This does not describe her. Yet." It smiled. "But on the positive side, Bolthawk, the dream—which I believe fully, mind you—gives me much comfort. For I then need fear neither demon nor dragon nor god, but only that unknown pursuer. On the day I see those eyes in life, on that day—and no other—I will discover if I can ever die."

It raised its blade again, seeing the understanding on Bolthawk's face. *Yes, my friend, this confidence also reminds you that any plans you and yours have for turning against me are futile.* "Shall we continue?"

A few minutes later, It smiled inwardly. It sensed Condor's approach long before he reached the clearing in which the Justiciar's Retreat lay, but allowed him to come nearer without giving any sign of awareness, continuing its sword practice against Bolthawk's axe. It was therefore Bolthawk's sudden glance of startlement that apparently alerted it to the new arrival.

"Condor! What a triumph, you have returned from Hell." The creature allowed his voice just that edge of derision that he knew would be most galling.

But Aran's expression was... *changed*; there was a confidence and a narrow-eyed appraisal, so extremely different from that which he had worn prior to departure, that it found itself studying him with a more attentive eye.

"Returned from Hell twice, yes—as you must have known."

Bolthawk stared from one to the other, then said to it: "So the rumors... they're *true*?"

"Ask your brother in arms, Bolthawk," It said. "For he has been there, it seems."

"Rumors?" Condor laughed, but the sound was cold, cold. "What rumors? Do they say that the sky darkened and the land called Hell shuddered at a horror to make that very land seem a refuge of sanity and safety? Do they say that Kerlamion Blackstar has found a way to violate the very boundaries of life and death and the gods? Do they say that the Black City rests here, its gates opening onto Zarathan itself? Then what they say is true, Bolthawk, for I crossed into the center of the land of Hell, and thence walked straight through the Gates of the Black City."

Bolthawk blanched at these words, spoken both with a casual venom that was too matter-of-fact to be doubted... and too cold and mocking for Condor.

But It merely cocked its head slightly. "And did you find what you sought?"

So swiftly that mortal eye could never have followed it, Condor's sword sprang from its sheath and was there, in his hand, the point barely a hairsbreadth from the creature's throat.

But *not* Condor's sword, in fact. The blade pointed at it was dark as night, shimmering faintly with blue-white and accompanied by a dim moaning as of air falling to its doom. "Ah. I see."

"I think you do, yes."

It looked into Aran's green eyes but let its smile return. "A mighty blade indeed. But are you going to waste your time and energy killing me, or will you seek your vengeance?"

For a moment, It thought that Aran, the Condor Justiciar, might actually *do* it—kill the true source of his pain, the corruption of Myrionar's chosen, the one who had pulled all the strings and brought him to this point. But to *truly* do that, Condor would have to admit, fully, that both he and his foster father had no right to complain against any act by the defenders of Evanwyl or, indeed, the rest of Zarathan.

The black blade returned to its sheath in an instant. "Not yet. You still have answers I want, and information." Unspoken was also the fact that the creature before Condor was also the source of his false Justiciar power, power he would still need in his mission.

It gestured, and Bolthawk bowed and left immediately; It could sense the other Justiciar's fear and relief at not being involved in this. "I know what information you seek. The Phoenix has departed Evanwyl. I did, in fact, lose Phoenix's track for a short time, but by good fortune only a day or so ago I found that Phoenix's party had taken the path I had expected, given what they found at Thornfalcon's mansion."

As a native of Evanwyl, Aran could not repress a shudder as he realized what it was saying. "You mean...Rivendream Pass?"

"It is the obvious and, even, inevitable path. They know that they cannot yet find the Retreat; they know that Thornfalcon had some sort of connection to the other side of the Pass; they know, too, that Evanwyl's fortunes were tied to that which once lay beyond the Pass, and Myrionar is no doubt guiding them."

"When did they enter the Pass?"

"Two, three weeks ago, I believe."

Condor cursed. "Then they are far ahead of me. Reaching the Pass from here will take most of a week as it is."

It smiled, and was pleased to see that Condor still found that expression disquieting. *As well you should, little Justiciar. As well you should.* "That, at least, I can assist you with."

Condor's eyebrows rose visibly. "How?"

"Within this realm, I have gained...considerable power—as one might suspect. Go, replenish your supplies from our reserves, and meet me in my chambers and I will be prepared."

It did not, in fact, take much preparation, but it was best for Condor and the others to have mistaken ideas about Its powers, Its nature, Its goals, and effectively everything else. So Condor entered to find an elaborate mystical circle laid out in the center of the huge dark room. "You can teleport me to them?"

"Not to *them*, no. I have hardly had any direct contact with Phoenix or any companions the true Justiciar of Myrionar may have—that would be... unwise, at the least. But I *can* cut your travel time, by sending you directly to Rivendream Pass." This would also have the absolutely *vital* effect of keeping Aran Condor from discovering the actual nature and identity of the Phoenix Justiciar of Myrionar. It had to get Condor well away not merely from Evanwyl, but from his fellow false Justiciars, since *they* knew the truth and would certainly tell him as soon as the topic came up.

Aran *would* learn the truth, of course... but that had to happen only at the precisely correct moment.

Aran stepped carefully into the circle, making sure to neither rub out or smear any of the symbols; experienced as he was around things mystical, he was not going to take chances on such a ritual being disrupted. "I'm ready."

"Then I wish you... good hunting, Condor."

There was a flash of light, and Condor was gone—on his way to a rendezvous he desperately wanted... and would undoubtedly regret, once it occurred.

If he was even *Condor* anymore, by the time he found his quarry. A gift from the King of All Hells was not, exactly, a safe thing to receive. Especially not for a young man who thought he still wanted to be a hero.

It laughed and gestured, cleansing the floor of the ritual circle. There were other amusing things to attend to. It wasn't *quite* time to talk with the King again; It was still deciding how, exactly, the next sequence of events must be played. The grandiose overarching plan was, of course, going to start coming apart; while Aegeia still *seemed* well enough in hand, there were a few points that indicated things might start turning around soon—even though the agent It had in place claimed all was proceeding as planned.

But that would still be some time yet. The real key decision was when, *precisely*, It would have to admit failure and be cast on its own by Kerlamion as the King of All Hells sought to finish by sheer brute power what could not be completed by manipulation. Too early, and It might lose support that would be useful for its own endgame. Too late, and Kerlamion might realize that he was the one being played and throw all plans off. While It thought that even Kerlamion could be dealt with, having the King of All Hells as a direct and immediate threat while trying to complete its own plans would be a serious problem to properly executing the last stages of the plan.

Oh, It knew the King *would* eventually discover the truth. It looked forward to that moment, properly staged; the right *denouement* of the play was the key to its enjoyment, after all. But it was a challenge to make sure all the cast played their parts when most of them didn't know they were part of the performance, and when the few that did, such as Khoros, would do their best to ruin the final act.

Unfortunately, there were so *many* elements to be balanced here—and elsewhere, and "elsewhere" required just as much attention as its plans did here; that was, naturally, one reason that It was often unavailable for the Justiciars and other allies—sometimes it simply wasn't *there*.

After another quick check with all Its agents—especially Kalshae and Ermirinovas, who should be having new visitors soon—the creature felt that it would have to make another trip and hope that everything continued on course. It could not neglect the *other* game, already in progress, on a far more distant playing field.

But time enough for *that* game when said time came; the last skirmish had been surprisingly painful, if instructive, and thus well worth continuing. For now, however, It had plenty of things to do here. It sat down and placed the golden scroll in its holder, and smiled.

So *very* many things to do here.

CHAPTER 14

Kyri forced herself to step forward, belatedly following Miri as the much smaller woman strode quickly in the direction of the beautiful city below them. She exchanged a disbelieving glance with Tobimar, and could see even Poplock's eyes wider than usual.

This... makes no sense at all. Yet I can sense nothing dark. My powers may be reduced here, but they are not gone, *and the only darkness I can sense at all is the forest that lies behind us, barricaded on the other side of that wall.*

It was more than that, she admitted. It was not merely the absence of darkness; *that* was the way of the world on the other side of the mountains, of Evanwyl and most parts of Zarathan not immediately under the sway of something demonic or otherwise corruptive. This "Kaizatenzei," or at least the part of it they were now in, *shone* to her senses. Everything—from the armor on Miri's shoulders to the grasses bordering the pathway down which they walked to the great trees that grew like sentinels throughout the city—glittered with promise and strength, a *rightness* that she had only felt in moments before, when Myrionar Itself touched upon her, as though this entire *city* was holy ground, infused with the essence of the divine.

As they approached the town, a tall young man with a long yet handsome face, dark brown skin, and ebony hair, in armor which seemed as ceremonially delicate as Miri's but less brightly colored, in muted shades of green and brown rather than Miri's brilliantly shining sapphire and emerald, stepped forward and waved, performing a perfunctory bow which Miri returned. "Light Miri, welcome back! We had not expected your hunt to end so soon!" His voice was strong and clear, reminding Kyri somehow of Rion's when he had become a Justiciar.

"No more had I," Miri said with a laugh. "But that is the least of surprises today. Shade Danrall, allow me to present Tobimar and Phoenix, who saw me facing a *nalloshoth* and thought me endangered, and so came magnificently to my rescue."

"Truly?" Danrall looked curiously at them. "Well, courageously done, even if unneeded. From which *Sha* do you hail?"

"Ah, there is the true wonder," Miri answered. "For they say they come from beyond the mountains, and I believe them."

Kyri saw Danrall's jaw drop, stretching his already-long face into comic disbelief. "From the—"

"Yes," Kyri said, unable to keep from smiling herself. "And allow me to say that for us, this is just as much a surprise. We thought all of this great valley was like the forest outside your walls."

Danrall recovered quickly. "Then I am doubly surprised that you dared even enter!" he said with a smile.

"Truly said," Miri agreed. "Now, Shade, I want you to keep this quiet. I cannot avoid some attention, of course, but I don't want our newcomers bothered until they have had an opportunity to rest; they have traveled through the Pass of Night and the belt of corrupted forest twixt there and here, and surely they need some time to recover and refresh themselves."

Kyri couldn't argue, though a part of her was still concerned about just what the whole impossible situation *meant*.

"I understand, Light. What would you have me do?"

"Tell the current Color—it is still Kerrim, is it not? Yes, I thought so. Tell Kerrim that we have two visitors, heroes I think, from beyond the mountains, and that we should have a proper welcome and council with them upon the morrow; I expect he'll have you notify his Hues and the other Shades of the city. I will inform the Lady of Lights myself, once I am done here."

"As you will, Light."

Miri turned to them as Danrall jogged off. "I hope I am correct in thinking you need some rest—and perhaps time to readjust your expectations and thoughts, yes?"

Tobimar laughed. "You are certainly correct, Miri. This is

completely opposite to our expectations, and we have indeed been exhausted by our journey through what you call the Pass of Night and what we call Rivendream Pass. If you have only sent scouts up that place before, I do not wonder that you believe nothing good exists outside."

"Good. Then I'll guide you to the Sunlight Rest—the best lodging house here—and you may take your ease until the meeting is arranged, probably tomorrow at this same time." She turned and led them past the small, open shelter that Danrall had been sitting in—obviously a guard post—and down the path which was now becoming a paved street running straight into the center of the wooded city.

"So your title is that of Light, and from what I heard you have your other... what, military ranks?... of Colors, Hues, and Shades, yes?" Kyri asked.

"Military is a bit grandiose," Miri answered with another smile. "The *Tenzeitalacor* are more guardians of the *Sha*, or cities. We resolve any arguments, investigate crimes, deal with monsters and such problems."

That at least provided an opening. "More police than soldiers then. But crimes and monsters? Those seem hardly imaginable here, from what I see," Kyri said. They were now passing one of the great trees, a massive red-brown trunk wider across than two wagons placed end-to-end, holding aloft branches that stretched hundreds of feet wide and high. Beneath, multiple buildings—houses and shops—were arranged along the streets that branched off from the main roadway they walked along. Multiple people—mostly human, though Kyri saw at least one or two that appeared to be *Artan* and possibly one Child of Odin—waved or nodded to Miri, who returned their greetings cheerfully but showed no tendency to pause or talk, leaving the various people to stare curiously at the two figures walking just behind the Light.

Miri shook her head. "Kaizatenzei is beautiful and peaceful, but people are still people. And in the regions between the seven great cities and the Unity, there are wilder areas, not nearly so hideous as that jungle we met within, but still not places without danger."

Tobimar pointed to some other figures Kyri had noticed, ones that had not waved, bowed, or even stared. "Who are those?" he asked. "I notice they are doing the more menial tasks." The nearest of the figures, clad in a simple gray tunic and apparently bald of head, was sweeping up dust from the street; that explained, at least partially, the cleanliness of the city.

Miri looked where he pointed. "Oh, now, say not who, but *what*," she said with a laugh. "Come, I will show you."

The diminutive warrior quickened her steps to bring her in front of the working figure, which straightened up as it noticed her. At this range, Kyri could see that it was indeed not a living creature. The body appeared to be made of something like fine pottery, with glints of metal at the joints; there was a face, but mostly just painted or inlaid, with only bright green crystal eyes and a mouth that could move. It bowed to Miri. "I recognize you, Light," it said, in a calm, even voice. "Do you require a service?"

"Merely that you tell these strangers of yourself, then you may return to work."

It repeated the bow; Kyri found it somewhat eerie to watch, because unlike a living being, the repetition was absolutely exact, yet the fluidity of the thing's movement was nearly equal to that of a human being; even its hands were detailed and fine enough for the most delicate operations, while their material hinted at the potential for immense strength. "I am an Eternal Servant, number fifty-seven of those assigned to *Sha Murnitenzei*, named Patina for my finish." It held out an arm, so they could see the patina of fine cracks in the glaze of its body. "I was created one hundred twenty-two years ago by Master Wieran and assigned to this city one year following. My primary duties in the time since have been maintaining the cleanliness of the streets and building exteriors."

Having completed this description, Patina returned to sweeping up the dust of the street.

Kyri noticed Poplock's tense posture, the pose that generally showed that he was bursting with the desire to ask questions but knew he couldn't. Still, she'd studied enough basic magical theory to guess what he wanted to ask. "Hundreds of automata, all running for hundreds of years? How? Building such things is extremely difficult, as I understand it. Where we come from, people still do most such work."

Miri shrugged. "*How* is a question for Master Wieran, for he was the one who designed them and produces the Servants for us, a few every year, but over the years he has dwelt with us that has added up to considerable numbers indeed; I think there are about one hundred and eighty in each of the seven cities, and somewhat more than that in Valatar itself."

She looked up. "Ah, here we are."

Sunlight Rest was an imposing building, stone-fronted with support beams of deep reddish-brown wood and a large double door in front made of a lighter, amber wood, carven with a complex pattern of twining vines across a setting sun; currently both doors stood open, splitting the carved sun down the center, half on each. Miri led them inside, ignoring the curious stares of the various patrons within and walking straight up to a white-haired older woman who was just finishing giving instructions to two youths and one of the Servants.

The woman glanced up as the small group approached her, and rose from her desk smoothly. "Light Miri, a pleasure as always."

"Oh, you don't have to be so formal."

"Miri, then," she said with a smile. "What can I do for you?"

"Something simple enough, Dania," Miri said. Gesturing to Kyri and Tobimar, she continued, "These two are to be guests of the Lady of the Lights herself."

"And does the Lady know this yet?"

Miri laughed, a cheerful ringing sound that brightened the shaded interior of the inn. "You know me awfully well, I see. She *will* know. But true, for now, they are my guests."

"Well enough," Dania said. "Two rooms, then?"

"Adjoining, if you can," Tobimar said quickly.

"Of course," the older woman said. "You can leave it to me, Miri."

"I knew I could," Miri said with another bow that caused the ribbon in her hair to bounce. "Phoenix, Tobimar, I have other duties now, but you'll be as comfortable here as anywhere in the city, and I'll send word later when the meeting is all arranged."

"Just a moment, Miri," Kyri said. "We're still trying to understand exactly where we are. Do you have anything about these seven cities, your Unity, and so on?"

Ignoring Dania's sharp, startled glance, Miri nodded and dug into a tiny pouch at her side—a pouch that allowed her to insert at least half her arm inside. *Neverfull pouch*, at least. "Umm... here! This is a simple map we make...oh, there are a few notations on the back.... Ah yes, I don't need those, so it's fine, you can have it." She handed the folded paper to Kyri.

"What about tomorrow?" Tobimar asked. "Do we stay in our rooms until—"

"Oh, no, no, you don't have to do that!" Miri said, an apologetic look on her face. "I didn't want us all bothered on the way here, but you don't *have* to be some kind of a secret! If you want to, by all means, look around, see whatever you wish. Just check back here every so often so you will get my message."

"All right, then," Kyri said. "Please don't let us detain you any longer; sorry for the trouble."

"Oh, it was no trouble at all," Miri said, and then with a rather girlish squeal said "Oh, this is going to be so *exciting!*"

She recovered her poise instantly, looking slightly embarrassed, and bowed with the uplifted arm again. They returned the bow as best they could, and Miri left with a wave and a spring in her step.

Dania, studying them more intensely than before, led them upstairs, where two doors at the end of the hall opened into a pair of high, clean, fresh-smelling rooms.

Now ... we need to talk!

CHAPTER 15

"I have absolutely *no* idea what is going on now," Tobimar said bluntly. He rubbed his temples, in the vain hope that the pressure might force the ridiculous situation to align into something he could understand.

Poplock, who had finished checking the rooms to make sure there were neither magical nor mundane spies, bounced his agreement. "This makes *no* sense."

Kyri sank into a chair as her Raiment flowed off, leaving her clad in simple pants and shirt. "I wish I could explain it. Your people were *driven* out of here, by demons that hounded you all the way across the continent, right?"

"And whose curse *still* follows us; Xavier, Poplock and I found that out the hard way, yes. So you're sensing the same thing I am?"

Kyri nodded in disbelief. "This . . . place. It practically *sings*. You don't think it's the effect of getting out of that vileness that was in the forest into a place that isn't vile?"

"You mean, like stepping out of a cave into sunlight? The way it dazzles you for a bit, seems brighter than normal sunlight?" Poplock said. "No, don't think so. I think it'd be almost as shocking going just from Evanwyl to here. This place . . . it even *tastes* different."

"I agree," Tobimar said, and forced his brain to start working on the problem. "There's a purity here, something way beyond the ordinary."

Kyri reached into her pack, sitting next to the chair where

she was sitting, and got out a bottle of water. "Let's test that, anyway. This is perfectly good water, in a preservation bottle I bought in Zarathanton; filled it just before we left Evanwyl, and it should be just as good now as the day I left. They have running water here, yes?"

Poplock bounced into the bathroom which adjoined both rooms. "Hmmm...there's a spigot with red and blue gems on the sides...yep, I touch them and get water at different temperatures."

"All right, come back out and I'll do a little test."

Kyri came out a moment later carrying two of their water cups, both filled with water. "Here, Tobimar. Taste them."

He reached out and took the cups. "Which is which?"

"Not telling you. That's the point. I want to know if you can tell the difference."

"Right." He took a sip of the lefthand cup. Cool, sweet water, very nice, just as he remembered from the Vantage estate. He swallowed that, then took a sip of the righthand cup.

The cool flow danced through his mouth, invigorating, replenishing, as though he had gone half a week without drinking and now, finally, was given the chance. The water washed away some of the tiredness of the road, the fear and tension of their journey through the savage jungles of Rivendream Pass and the exterior of Moonshade Hollow, and lifted his spirits as though he knew his homeland lay just outside the window. He stood stock-still, astounded, then put both cups down. "It was the one in my right hand."

"Yes. So it isn't an illusion of our perceptions."

"Most definitely not," Tobimar said emphatically, then considered. "I suppose it *could* be an illusion of a more sinister sort. We have heard of spirits and monsters—and especially demons—which can construct a pleasing illusion, even a seeming paradise, for unwary travelers, and as they think they're sitting down to a great feast or bedding down in a fine inn for the night, they're actually approaching their own destruction."

The little Toad gave a bounce-shrug. "Well, we weren't exactly unwary. But a powerful illusion can catch even the wary. Still, I haven't noticed anything that tells me this is illusion."

"How could we tell?" Kyri asked reasonably. "If the illusion's good enough..."

That's a scary thought. How can *we tell?*

"Creepy," Poplock said, almost as though reading his mind. "And while I've got magic, it's...well, *mundane* magic, if you know what I mean. It's not something unique and special."

Tobimar caught the hint. "Meaning that the two of us *do* have something unusual. You're right. Kyri should see if Myrionar will grant her the Eyes of Truth, and I will see if the High Center will reveal anything to me."

"Fooling a god should be pretty hard," Kyri agreed. She began a quiet prayer.

Tobimar closed his eyes and took a deep breath. *Even if it is illusion, the illusion leaves me my* self, *and it is the* self *that gives me the power of my skill, the martial art that Xavier and Khoros call* Tor. *If I can meditate, it matters not where my body truly is; my mind will find the truth of it.*

What Khoros—and his friend Xavier—called "High Center" was the key. It was challenging to reach in combat, but here—surrounded by friends and, at least as far as he could tell, safety—there was no threat to distract him, nothing to interrupt his inner peace. He rose through the Centers and Visions until he stood above himself, feeling the web of probability, the possibility and certainty of the universe's connection to him, his connection to it.

Tobimar opened his eyes, and he could *see*. The room fairly *blazed* in his sight, a solidity of essence that was almost as tangible as steel, as warm as sunlight, as certain as his mother's love—and almost, almost *familiar* in a way. He couldn't be certain, but there was indeed something about this feeling that tugged faintly but insistently on threads of memory.

But more; the song of the world stretched beyond. He could sense the possibility of danger away to the south, beyond the wall, but nothing here. There might—possibly—be a hint of danger to the north or east, but he could not be sure.

Most important was the absolute conviction of solidity. This was no trick or illusion. He was as certain of this as he could be of anything. If this *was* an illusion, it would be something so powerful that he could do nothing at all against it, so he would assume it was, in fact, real. He released High Center and leaned back. "Real. Exactly as we perceive. As far as I could sense, everything is as it seems to be. If there is anything dark here, it is hiding itself behind a very real cloak of light."

Kyri opened her eyes and nodded. "I feel the same thing, Tobimar. This is *Truth*. Enemies could be here—*must* be here, I think—but they are well-hidden."

"Hm," Poplock grunted. "Maybe even using the light of this place almost literally, like shining a light in someone's eyes so they can't see what's behind it."

Tobimar didn't like that thought, but it fit all too well with the situation. "You're probably right, Poplock. We'll have to be even more on our guard. On the positive side, at least we don't need to worry about the local environment killing us."

"I suppose—to be just," Kyri said, with a smile, "I should look at the other side. Aside from what we *assumed* coming here, do we have any reason to believe there *is* something…wrong here?"

Tobimar was taken somewhat aback by the question, but he thought about it. Instead of assuming, based on what they knew coming through the pass, that there *had* to be something wrong, did he have any actual *evidence* for that?

"Yep, we do," Poplock said after a few minutes.

Tobimar felt there *was* something, but he couldn't quite figure this out, either, so he shrugged. "All right, Poplock, what have you got for us?"

"They can *talk* to us."

Kyri looked askance at the little Toad. "And? I can and have talked to people from Evanwyl all the way along the Great Road and off it, and so have you."

"Ahh," Poplock said, lifting a finger in such a scholarly way that Tobimar couldn't repress a small snort of laughter, "but *those* places are all connected. Remember that Miri said that as far as they knew, nowhere outside of this 'Kaizatenzei' was habitable. The Chaoswar was about twelve *thousand* years ago."

Now the Prince of Skysand understood, and he could see that Kyri was starting to grasp it. "Language *changes*," Tobimar said slowly. "It's said that after the Chaoswar, when the peoples emerged from the catastrophe and started to find their neighbors, the farther they went, the harder it was to understand them. It took centuries for language to re-stabilize. There's enough contact all through the Empire of the Mountain and the State of the Dragon King so that we all keep roughly the same language…but there's no *way* these people just happened to keep the same language. All I hear from Miri is an accent, no worse than Kyri's or yours."

"Or yours," Kyri pointed out, "from our point of view." She nodded. "So they *should* have developed their own language—"

"They *did*," Poplock said. "Let's look at that map, shall we?"

Kyri spread the map out on the table and Poplock hopped up to get a better look.

"Sure, look at this. Name of this country is 'Kaizatenzei,' and they asked what *Sha* we were from. These things are all labeled *Sha*, so I'm guessing that means 'city,' or something like that. And the city names... Murnitenzei, Vomatenzei, Alatenzei, Ruratenzei... all with a theme. Not sure what 'tenzei' means, though... she said *Kaizatenzei* meant, um, Unity of the Seven Lights, so Tenzei could be Unity or Light, or even Seven I guess."

"Seven? That wouldn't make sense."

Tobimar snorted again. "Wouldn't it? It would make sense for *us*, you know. That is, Skysand. Now if—"

Suddenly he broke off, staring, thinking. *Can't be... but it fits. It fits so well.*

He became aware that Kyri was poking him. "Tobimar? Tobimar, what *is* it?"

Tobimar Silverun felt dizzy, lightheaded at the thoughts chasing through his mind, but the thoughts didn't just make sense, they felt *right*. "Seven, Kyri, Poplock. Seven Stars and a Single Sun."

"What... Oh. You mean there's seven cities plus the big one—"

"More! More than that! By Terian Himself, it's right here! The Stars were lost! But look on this map! *Seven Stars and a Single Sun hold the Starlight that I do own.* What if the Stars are *here*, somewhere? What would a place be like, where the artifacts of the Light in the Darkness were left to themselves? Like this place, maybe?" He reached out and touched the cities marked on the map. "And look. Four cities here. Three here. The capital, Sha Kaizatenzei Valatar, here, between the groups." His finger traced a slow curve, going around the four, passing through the capital, then around the other three, back through the capital. "*These Eight combine and form the One... form the Sign by which I'm known...*"

Kyri gasped. "It is. It's Terian's symbol!"

"The symbol of the Infinite. They're *here*, Kyri! The lost treasures of the Silverun, of the Lords of the Sky! The Seven Stars, and the Sun itself, are *here!*"

CHAPTER 16

"Come in," Tobimar's voice said cheerfully in response to her knock.

Entering, she saw her friend's hair completely unbound, a flowing waterfall of smooth ebony startling in its length and black-shining perfection. "*Balance*, I know a lot of women—and a few men—who'd *kill* for hair like yours."

"Why, thank you!" Tobimar bowed, the hair following in a smooth flow that he cast back from his face with a practiced gesture as he rose again. *By Myrionar, he is handsome. And now I can let myself recognize it.*

He raised an eyebrow as she didn't say anything, then grinned happily. "Are you *staring* at me?"

She didn't try to conceal the blush. "I am. You're worth staring at, Tobimar Silverun of Skysand."

"As are you, Kyri Vantage, Phoenix Justiciar!" He stepped forward swiftly and kissed her; it turned into something longer than the quick peck it had started as; the world faded away for the several seconds his lips lingered on hers.

Finally they separated, and both laughed, just a bit, and she knew he laughed for the same reason—for the joy of seeing their own joy reflected in another.

"Keep that up, and I'm going to have to go to that party by myself," Poplock commented from the nearby table, where he was packing away an astonishing assortment of crystals, springs, gears, gadgets of various types, and other supplies. "And they're not even supposed to *know* about me."

"I'm tempted," Kyri admitted candidly.

Tobimar's dark cheeks darkened further. "I...well, we've only just started...and..."

She laughed. "Your people really do have rituals around this kind of thing, don't you?"

He shrugged, but smiled in response to her laugh. "Yes. I suppose much of it came out of the desperate years where we were trying to survive, and as the Silverun family we're much more subject to etiquette than the average person. Aren't there any...traditions around dating in Evanwyl?"

"A few, yes, but not that would apply to adventurers. It's not like we're children without any awareness of responsibility."

She could see he was thinking that over as he got that magnificent mane under control and tied it back. Knowing how much simple magic she used on hers, she was impressed that he was apparently doing it all by hand.

Finally he finished tightening the silvery ribbon with a fancy flourish. "Done!" He looked up to her. "I'll...think about how I want to approach this, Kyri. The...Way of Sacred Waters, as we call it, is something very unique and precious to us. I lived in Zarathanton long enough to come to understand that for some it's...no more important than any other form of pleasure that involves other people, but it's very special to me and I don't think—"

She held up her hand. "Tobimar. I'm...somewhere in between; sex is a special thing, but not the sacred thing your people make it. So I can understand both sides. But believe me, I appreciate your hesitation. And it's fine. Besides, as Poplock pointed out, we're trying to keep him a secret, and in any case I don't want to risk the damage Poplock could do on his own."

"I beg to point out," the Toad said dryly, "that it wasn't *me* who incinerated two hundred yards of tunnel and forest in one blast."

"True enough. So, o cautious and non-destructive Toad, any new observations before we go?"

"A few. I was thinking about those Eternal Servant things, and how hard they should be to make, and then I remembered that the Wanderer said something about that."

"He did? I don't remember him saying anything about golems or automata," Tobimar said, strapping on his swords.

Poplock was almost done replacing his equipment in his pack. "Not in so many words, no. But he said something about magic placed into items being more common."

Kyri nodded, making sure her Raiment was as spotless as possible by surveying herself in the full-length mirror. "You're right, he said it was like that in Elyvias as well. So maybe it's easier to make such things here than it would be in our part of the world."

"Could be," Poplock confirmed. "What little tests I've been able to do *have* seemed to show that making *physical* things with magic—alchemical tricks and such—are easier than just calling up the magic and letting fly with no physical channel. Even so," he continued, hopping to his accustomed place on Tobimar's shoulder, "that kind of thing's not going to be *easy*, and to have made *hundreds*... I want to meet this 'Master Wieran' of theirs."

"I can't blame you," Tobimar said. "For my part, we were able to show that there *used* to be an ancient tower near the center of town, in that park with the huge tree in the middle, but given that they're trying to keep some of the facts about us quiet we couldn't ask about it in more detail. I'm hoping we can get some of that settled tonight."

Kyri knew just how important that was now. If Tobimar was right, one of the Seven Stars might be *here*—buried under the ruins of the tower, perhaps. The thought was enough to send a chill down *her* spine; she followed Myrionar, she respected many gods, but Terian was the shining beacon that even other deities looked to. What must it mean to Tobimar, whose family—whose entire *country*—followed Terian's guidance?

"Are we ready?" Poplock asked.

"I think so," Kyri said. "Remember, I am simply Phoenix, or Justiciar Phoenix. I see no reason to reveal other names, and since I'm on duty..."

"Oh, none of us are arguing," Tobimar said. "We're hiding Poplock's existence as our equal, and in my case we're going to say nothing of my family name or background unless we have to. There's *something* wrong here, behind all the perfection, and this means we'd better be doubly careful."

"Then... let's go!"

Miri was waiting at the bottom of the stairs, bouncing from foot to foot with energetic excitement. "Oh, *there* you are!" she said.

"Good thing you came down now," Dania said, and looked fondly at the diminutive Light. "Miri was about to wear a hole in the floor pacing."

A slight rose tint touched Miri's startlingly fair cheeks—lighter than almost any skin Kyri had seen—and she gave an embarrassed laugh. "Well, it's so . . . exciting!" she said, repeating herself from the prior night. "Come on, I've got a coach for us!"

Kyri found herself smiling as well. There was something infectiously cheerful about Miri's boundless enthusiasm. "Lead on, then!"

The coach was, like everything they'd seen in Kaizatenzei thus far, beautiful in every aspect: wood polished to a mirror gloss, ornamented with carven vines outside and lit within by a soft, forest-green luminance that emanated from the roof of the coach. One of the Eternal Servants drove the coach, which was drawn by four sithigorns, of a breed Kyri had never seen—black with gold-edged tailfeathers. The overall effect was striking.

Miri insisted on them getting in first, then bounded in and sat across from them. "To the Manse, Quickhand," she called up to the driver.

"Yes, Light Miri," the Servant said, and the team of giant birds immediately began pulling the coach along.

"So the 'Manse' is the local ruler's home?" Kyri asked. "Would that be the Color you mentioned, Kerrim?"

"Oh, no, Kerrim isn't the *ruler* here. That would be Reflect Haldengen."

"Reflect?" repeated Tobimar. "That's a title?"

"Yes. You of course can't help but notice that we've built our whole country around the theme of light—something you'll understand more, I think, as you stay here—and the city . . . ruler, head, whatever you might call it, is called a 'Reflect' because something that reflects returns light to those it is directed upon."

That made sense to Kyri; symbolically it meant that the ruler was reminded that their job was to make the world better for those being ruled. "An inherited position?"

"Oh, no. We have almost no inherited positions in Kaizatenzei, at least not in government!" Miri's voice held a note of pique, as though the very idea was an offense. "Reflects are elected by a general vote of the population, once every five years. It's of course not uncommon for a Reflect to maintain that position for a long time, if he or she does a good job, and in fact Haldengen has been Reflect of Murnitenzei for seventy-three years as of today."

That *was* a long time. "With such time of service, I venture to guess that he's either extremely old, or not entirely human."

"Oh, very good. Haldengen Baldersedge is his full name."

The significance of the name did not escape her. "An Odinsyrnen, then. So he has ruled to the approval of the population for that long? I look forward to meeting him."

"No more than he's looking forward to meeting you. I'm *hoping* that the Lady herself will be able to come. She said she'd let me know if she could."

Tobimar raised an eyebrow and leaned forward. "Your own ruler? The Lady of Light, you called her? But wouldn't she be in your capital?"

Miri smiled, this time with that particular narrowing of eyes that says *I have a secret!* "Oh, yes. But still she may tell me she will come, and then you shall see indeed."

Kyri saw a tiny movement from Poplock—one of the trivial-seeming movements they'd agreed upon for various signaling purposes. Tobimar acknowledged Miri's secretiveness with a chuckle. "I see there's something you want to show off later. I notice a lot of magic—the lights along the road, the Eternal Servants of course, the clean stoves within the inn we stayed at, and so on. You must have many powerful wizards here."

"Well, of *wizards* we have relatively few—if by that you mean those who cast spells freestanding, so to speak. Many alchemists, gemcallers, summoners, a few symbolists and chosen of various religions, that sort of thing. You'll be meeting one of the best in the magical arts tonight—I'm sure that Hiriista will be there."

Kyri kept her face neutral, but she could see the satisfaction in Tobimar's eyes. That fit exactly with what they had deduced. Magical activity connected to material media—alchemical products and devices, the spirit housings of summoners, and so on—was highly functional here, making up for the difficulty of direct application of mystical or deific power. "That's very different from home," she said. "There, impressing magical energies into any object is a more difficult project, and while I've heard the term *gemcaller*, I've never met one, and I'm honestly not even sure what it means."

Poplock's mouth tightened with heroic resolve, preventing him from entering a conversation obviously dear to his heart. She wondered if he'd explode sometime during this party from sheer frustration. But they all agreed that Poplock had demonstrated just how deadly he could be when his presence, or capabilities, were unknown, and even under these conditions Poplock had himself insisted he remain an apparently stupid, harmless toad as long as possible.

Miri shrugged. "Actually, I'm not *terribly* well versed in that either, but you can ask old Hiriista if he's there." She looked out the window. "Oh, we're almost there!"

The Manse was a lovely home, much of it carved out of and into the stump of some gargantuan tree, fifty feet high and seventy feet across, showing that something awe-inspiring had once stood here. Flowing out from the wooden bulwark that formed its central pillar, the remainder of the Manse was constructed in harmony with that source; even in the fading light of sunset she could see that the wood had been carefully matched, the polished stone facings chosen for their complementary color and patterns.

Golden light shone from the windows, and she could hear music faintly echoing through the air as they drew nearer, accompanied by the susurration of distant conversation and laughter. A pang of memory struck her heart as she remembered the so-similar sounds and lights of another party, the one in which her brother celebrated his selection as a Justiciar. There was the same air of joy, of wonder and faith, that had been in the air that day, too.

Once more she was struck by the *rightness* of everything in Kaizatenzei; even their construction was of a piece with everything else they had seen. Yet by the Wanderer's warnings, and by those of Myrionar, she knew there had to be something else, something darker, waiting somewhere near. *What is hidden here? How is it hidden? Will we get our answers here?*

"Here we are!" Miri said, and bounced from the coach before it had even quite stopped. "Come on, I can't *wait* to introduce you!"

"Coming, Light Miri," Tobimar said with exaggerated formality. As they alighted, they exchanged glances.

All eyes open. All senses alert.

Let's see what mystery awaits here!

CHAPTER 17

One major advantage of being thought a dumb animal was that you could look at pretty much everything whenever, and however, you wanted, and no one would even *notice*, let alone wonder why you were looking; at most they'd pick you up and throw you out, or return you to your apparent owner. Poplock smiled to himself. He'd spent almost four years in Zarathanton honing that skill, disappearing underfoot or being ignored sitting on a low table or wagon.

It *did* require a lot of patience and restraint, of course, and even with the signals they'd worked out, there were going to be plenty of times he had to just *hope* the others did the right things. But on the other hand, he might be able to learn things no one else could.

The three humans alighted from the coach and walked up a curving, gently illuminated pathway to the double doors at the front of the Manse. The doors stood open on this warm, pleasant evening, the light spilling from them to guide visitors inward. Poplock caught a passing darterfly and was reminded anew of the perfection of the place. *Which keeps me suspicious. Nothing's perfect, not without gods meddling. And when gods meddle, little mortals get hurt.*

As the three paused in the entryway, adjusting to the brightness, Poplock surveyed the room. He was impressed; Sha Murnitenzei wasn't a *huge* city, not compared to Zarathanton, but even so there was quite a turnout for this shindig, as his distant cousin Lormok might have put it. He guessed there must be over a hundred people in the brightly lit hall. *And you'd think this would be a pretty select party. But maybe not, they seem to act as though everyone's basically equal.*

"We're *here*, everybody!" Miri announced to the room at large as they entered. Heads turned, and a ripple of laughter chased around the hallway. *Everyone's smiling—kind of smile you give to someone you like. She's popular here, and this informality's almost certainly part of it.*

That happened to put Light Miri right up at the top of Poplock's *suspicious* list. He didn't have any *evidence*, of course, but it made sense. If the baddies could use this overpowering goodness as a cloak, then the best disguise would be as the nicest person you could find—and as someone with enough power and authority to go anywhere and do anything, which seemed to be what a Light did.

Of course, she *could* just be as nice as she appeared, in which case she might be in more danger than anyone else once the real baddies showed up.

Many of the partygoers immediately gravitated towards them, but the mass parted in the center to let through the short but impeccably dressed form of a Child of Odin. He was clean-shaven, which was rather what Poplock had expected—his name implied a follower of Balder, who was depicted by the Odinsyrnen as clean-shaven—but his silver-and-gold hair was very long, reaching almost to his knees, and while styled was not restrained in any way.

"Haldengen Baldersedge," Miri said, a touch more formally, "allow me to present to you a Justiciar of Myrionar, called the Phoenix, and an Adventurer of—Zarathanton, was it?—yes, Zarathanton, named Tobimar. They have crossed the mountains themselves to come here." She turned to Kyri and Tobimar. "Phoenix, Tobimar, allow me to present to you Halgenden Baldersedge, Reflect of Sha Murnitenzei."

"An honor to meet you, sir," Tobimar said, with Kyri making a similar greeting.

"Not at all, not at all," Halgenden said. "Far more an honor to meet *you*. Crossed over through the Pass of Night? By the Light in Darkness, *that's* a feat I never thought I'd hear of, let alone done by some coming from the *other* side. Decidedly impressive, I must say."

The phrase *Light in Darkness* got Poplock's attention, especially since he could feel Tobimar's shoulder tense on hearing it. They'd seen no temples that appeared dedicated to Terian, but "The Light in the Darkness" was one of the most common of his titles. *Interesting.*

"Thank you, sir," Kyri began, and Halgenden shook his head.

"None of this 'sir' business, or 'Reflect' or any of that dustballery! You call me Halgen, like everyone else who's not mad at me, and I'll call you Phoenix and him Tobimar, yes?"

Kyri laughed. "All right, Halgen."

"Agreed, Halgen," Tobimar said with his own smile.

"Let me introduce you around, here." He gestured to another Odinsyrnen, a very pretty woman (at least as far as Poplock's admittedly limited judgment of humanoid beauty was concerned) of about Halgen's apparent age and as solid has he. "This is Freldena Baldersedge; I'm her husband, and a lucky one as well, given that her family's been—"

"Frigga's *name*, Halgen, you needn't bring all that up!" Freldena said in a mildly exasperated tone. Her fond smile took the edge from the rebuke. "Honored to meet you both, Phoenix, Tobimar."

After they exchanged greetings, Halgen continued introducing them—two dozen introductions in the space of a few minutes, which Poplock knew would lead to Kyri and Tobimar having to ask most of them their names again shortly. He was pretty sure the one that *would* stick was that of Hulda, Freldena and Halgen's daughter, who looked to be an adorable six years old and knew how to play on that—clearly the darling of the party.

"So, I hope you're enjoying your visit to Murnitenzei, Phoenix, Tobimar," Halgen said, leading them over to a table laden with mostly-unfamiliar foods—though Poplock could see parallels to some of the cuisines he'd seen in Zarathanton.

"Very much so, Halgen," Tobimar said, starting to load up a plate at Halgen's gesture inviting him to do so. "Not something we expected, I'll tell you!"

Most of those around laughed. "No, I wouldn't think so!" Freldena said. "So on the other side of the mountains, it's like this, then, not like the forest outside our walls?"

"Not *exactly* like this," Kyri said. "But not monstrous like that, no, definitely not."

"Then what in the name of the *Seven Lights* brought you here?"

Halgen demanded mildly. "Even one like Miri, here, wouldn't assay *that* crossing without an *exceedingly* good reason!"

Poplock hid his grin. This was another area they'd had to discuss and plan out; they *needed* someone to ask that question and bring up the subject so that they could turn the questions around and find out things about this place. *And we had to know what story we wanted to tell, to keep from revealing things we don't want told.*

"We had a few reasons, actually," Tobimar answered. "In Phoenix's country—which is just the other side of the Pass—we found evidence of a particularly vile conspiracy, and some of that evidence seemed to show that they had support from something on the other side of Rivendream Pass. Seeing *this* place rather throws doubt on that, though."

"Do not go *quite* so fast, Tobimar," Miri said, looking more grave than usual. "While it would seem almost beyond belief that anyone in Kaizatenzei proper could be involved in anything dark—and even less so in anything that contacts people we did not know existed—I would not exclude the possibility that something in the surrounding forest has had such contact and influence. Despite all our efforts of the centuries, the forest still surrounds us, presses against us, and yields only grudgingly to us; I would be unsurprised to find there is something more than mere dumb malice lurking there."

She's able to be serious and focused. Not surprising, but she sure works that bouncing, laughing girl business a lot.

"But you said a few reasons," Halgen said, a question in his eyes.

"Well," Tobimar said slowly, "the main other reason is that I'm chasing a legend."

"Oooh! A legend! I love legends!" said Hulda brightly.

"So do I!" Miri agreed. "Can you tell us this one?"

"Well, it's not the most *happy* story..."

"It's okay," Hulda said. "Some of the ones Father has told me aren't always happy. Just let me know when you're coming to really sad parts."

"I'll do that," Tobimar promised.

The story Tobimar told was—pretty much—the one he'd told Poplock and, later, Xavier and Kyri, of the lost homeland, the flight to safety, and the unique curse that his ancestor had discovered and that now had fallen on him.

"But I had a few clues, and one of them was the way the oldest stories of my people began: 'Long ago, when justice and vengeance lay just beyond the mountains.' We'd known we were looking for some place on the other side of, and protected by, mountains, but when I remembered that old saying, it stuck with me. And then I realized that the country on the other side of the Pass from here—a country called Evanwyl—had as its patron deity a god called Myrionar, the god of Justice and Vengeance—I suddenly realized that I might have found my answer."

"A fascinating story," said a quiet voice with just the hint of a hiss in it. "You may well be correct."

Poplock found himself nearly face-to-face with a *mazakh* standing over six feet tall; it took no acting at all to jump in startlement and scuttle around behind Tobimar's neck; Tobimar himself twitched a bit, as might be expected given the two encounters he'd had with the so-called snake men.

"Ahh, Hiriista, good to see you could make it!" Halgen said warmly. "Tobimar, Phoenix, this is Hiriista Twice-Hatched, one of the finest magewrights in all the Seven. Hiriista, Tobimar, Adventurer of Zarathanton, and the Phoenix, Justiciar of Myrionar."

"An honor," Hiriista said, bowing fluidly with a pose similar to that which Miri had used. Viewed when not attacking, Poplock could appreciate the severe beauty of the creatures; not really snakelike, they were more like very tall hopclaws—bipedal reptilian creatures with colorfully patterned scales, a long balancing tail, and two arms with powerful hands; Xavier had said they reminded him of something called 'velociraptors.'

"And comfort your pet," Hiriista went on, "I am not in the habit of eating toads."

"Duckweed will appreciate that," Tobimar said, reaching up and giving Poplock a reassuring pat. Poplock relaxed visibly, and gave an inward smile. Using his original given name made him sound a lot less suspicious than 'Poplock,' if anyone guessed what that meant. "So you think I may be on the right track?"

"In some of the few ancient writings unearthed," Hiriista said, "I have seen a very similar phrase, something like 'Justice and Vengeance were as near as the other side of the mountain.' And your story mentions your interest in the number seven, which is surely of interest here."

"But was there a 'seven' before Kaizatenzei itself?" Kyri asked.

"Because I get the impression that Kaizatenzei as you know it is much more recent than the last Chaoswar."

Hiriista hiss-shrugged. "I do not know your 'Chaoswars,' but it is true that Kaizatenzei is not ancient. And yes, there are ruins of towers, from which it was said that light used to shine and protect all about them, found in the cities of the Seven Lights, and only in those seven cities—aside of course from the Unfallen Tower in *Sha Kaizatenzei Valatar*, the capital. Indeed, those cities were *founded* around these ancient towers, and there is reason to believe that there is, or was, some special virtue associated with them."

He restrained himself from exchanging glances with the others, but he knew Kyri and Tobimar did so; that confirmed their suspicious about the Seven Stars almost completely. "You mentioned ancient records?"

"All the most ancient records are kept in Sha Kaizatenzei Valatar. If you would learn more on these subjects, I would suggest you travel there."

"We had already expected to do that, but you give us even more reason to do so," Kyri said. "If I might ask, what exactly is a 'magewright'?"

"You know not the term? A magewright is one skilled in all the arts of magical creation and use—alchemy, gemcalling matrices, summoning arrays, mystical constructs, symbological circles, and so on. Halgen may exaggerate—"

"He does not," Miri put in.

The *mazakh* bowed. "I shall argue not with one of the Lights. Then I am indeed quite adept in these areas."

"You're a gemcaller?" Tobimar said, asking one of the questions Poplock *really* wanted to ask. "I've *heard* of it, vaguely, but apparently it's hard to make it work where we come from. I've generally only heard it mentioned in connection with Elyvias, which is itself if anything harder to reach than Kaizatenzei."

"In truth? I am surprised. It is one of the most useful and formidable arts, for those who can master it, but it does require considerable preparation initially. I would demonstrate, but not here; it is not something to do casually."

"Then perhaps another time?"

"Certainly; are you a student of things magical?"

"I dabble a bit," Tobimar said honestly. "Mostly I just like to see everything I can, as does Phoenix."

Miri suddenly stood up. "Ohh! The Lady of Lights says she will come!"

All eyes were focused on the diminutive Light. "*Now?*" said Reflect Helgen, eyes wide. "Oh, Miri, I'm hardly prepared to—"

"Piffle. She knows perfectly well what the situation is, but people from *outside?* She's not going to wait until they can make it all the way to Valatar!" With a "shoo" gesture, Miri waved others back until she had a clear space twenty feet across. "All right!" From one of the little tubes or arrays of crystals on her belt she took a large, water-clear gem. "*TO ME!*"

She threw the crystal on the ground and it exploded in brilliant, multicolored light that dazzled everyone, Poplock included. When the light faded, Poplock saw to his startlement a tall woman, as tall or taller than Kyri with hair red as bright coals, in gold-trimmed crystal and cloth armor similar in style, if not details, to Miri's. She held a staff of crystal as well, a staff that shimmered through the hues of the rainbow, and there was a great sword slung over her back. She had none of Miri's bubbliness, but instead had the same serious demeanor and appearance of quiet strength that characterized Phoenix Kyri.

Summoned by a crystal that *size? I'd say it's impossible, but I just saw it!*

Things are really starting to get interesting!

CHAPTER 18

Tobimar didn't have to look at Poplock to know the little Toad's eyes were even wider than normal. *It has to be that thing about it being easier to focus magic into solid objects; they can use much smaller crystals for summoning living beings.*

The red-haired woman immediately bowed deeply to Kyri and Tobimar, again in the same way as Miri. Tobimar imitated her and saw Kyri do the same.

"Welcome to Kaizatenzei, Phoenix, Tobimar," the woman said in a warm, rich contralto. "As I am sure my Miri has told you, I am Shae, Lady of the Seven Lights."

"Lady Shae, it is an honor, and I admit to also finding it astonishing—your arrival, that is."

She laughed. "Oh, we had rather *hoped* it would be. Especially Miri, she loves her surprises." She reached down and took a crystal, this one a lovely shade of blue, from her own belt. At this range, Tobimar could see that the crystal came from a slanted cylinder with multiple slots in it, each slot just the right size to hold one of the crystals; Shae and Miri each had several of these devices. "The summoning crystals are somewhat complex to make—alas, we cannot make them for ordinary travel, any more than we can use our singing arrays to allow everyone to speak with each other across the miles—but they allow my Lights, myself, and a few select others to be able to travel where we are needed swiftly, to aid each other as we can."

Since she held it out to him, Tobimar reached out and gingerly took the shining crystal in his hand. "This one is for Miri, I would guess."

She raised an eyebrow. "A guess, or a deduction?"

"A bit of both, I suppose. I don't know enough to be *sure*, but you have so much emphasis on lights and colors—I saw that your armor is essentially clear crystal," *though*, Tobimar noted to himself with some relief, *not clear beneath, or I might find it extremely distracting*, "while hers is mostly pale blue, so I would guess that the other Lights have similar armor in shades of red, orange, yellow, green, and violet."

"Well and correctly reasoned," Lady Shae said with a nod. "And from her expression I think the Phoenix had made a similar deduction. But I suppose quick wits would be a requirement to survive the Pass of Night."

"It certainly doesn't hurt," Kyri said wryly. "Though some might say it also takes a lack of wisdom and self-preservation."

Tobimar was still studying the gem, trying to think of things Poplock would ask. "So, can just anyone use these, or only you and the Lights?"

"Oh, anyone can," Miri answered. "If you threw that on the ground and said 'To Me!' I'd appear right there. Please *don't* do that, it'd be such a waste."

"Of course not," Tobimar agreed. "I was just wondering. And you *have* to come? You can't choose *not* to come?"

"Actually, you *can* choose not to accept the summons," Lady Shae said. "In that case, the crystal will not break. However, I would be *very* loath to refuse such a summons; after all, I have to presume that these would never be used without either prior agreement, or a true emergency. However, if I was in the midst of something I could not leave, I could—and at least once, I did—refuse a summons."

"Amazing," Tobimar said, handing the summoning crystal back to Shae. "Where we come from, such tricks of teleportation are severely constrained, and to do this...I think it would take crystals larger than your head."

"Truly?" Shae looked astonished. "So even magic is not the same everywhere? There is so *much* we do not know, and so much we are just now starting to rediscover." She glanced aside and smiled. "Hello, Reflect Halgen. My apologies, I was so interested in our new arrivals that I have neglected to greet you."

"Quite understandable, my Lady. Will you be staying the night?"

"I wish I could. Unfortunately, there are so many things left to do, and in fact I'll be working for some time tonight."

Kyri raised her own eyebrow. "Ruling Kaizatenzei is that demanding?"

Both Miri and Shae burst out laughing. "Oh, now, I am terribly sorry for that impression! No, no, the Seven Lights demands far less of my time than you might think. I am also a researcher, somewhat along the lines of Hiriista there, and much of the research throughout our land comes in the end to me. So much to read, to test, to experiment on, to understand."

So their leader is also a . . . magewright? Sage at least. Don't want to pry too much, though; if they're not what they seem, we want to also seem less than we are. "Tell me, if you would—what *are* the Seven Lights? I mean, I have seen their names on the map, but I don't know what they mean."

"Ah, of course you would not. Just as light itself can be shattered by crystal into separate hues, which the sages number at seven, so there are seven great sources or types of light: sunlight, starlight, moonlight, stormlight, forestlight, firelight, and earthlight—or, respectively, ruratenzei, kalatenzei, syratenzei, vomatenzei, murnitenzei, hishitenzei, and alatenzei."

"I understand most of those, but what are stormlight, forestlight, and earthlight?"

She nodded. "Perhaps the less obvious, yes. Stormlight is lightning and other similar illumination seen during great storms; some have also said the rainbow is part of this, but others argue against it. Forestlight is the radiance of the firefly, the log-lantern, the glowing fire that is cold and eerie of hue that can be found in the depths of woods and sometimes the marshes. Earthlight," she smiled, "well, that is the light of the interior, the fire that wells up from the Earth itself."

"Many, such as my people, also consider the light of molten iron and other metals being worked to be part of the earthlight," Hargen said.

Poplock had been right. Those names showed at least three separate language influences, none of them pure; the rhythm of most of the words and names reflected the classic *Artan*, which constructed almost all concepts into triads—the most familiar being Nya-Sharee-Hilya, Surviving the Storm of Ages, or their homeland Ar-Tan-Nya, The People Who Survive, sometimes just translated as We Survive. He could easily hear the other words dividing that way—Kaiza-Ten-Zei, Voma-Ten-Zei, for instance.

Then there were language roots, like the ancient Sauran for thunder and lightning, *vomat*, found in *vomatenzei* or stormlight, and the Odinsyrnen word *ruri* meaning *sun* and echoed strongly in *ruratenzei*.

There *had* been a unique language spoken here, and somehow—he'd bet in the last thousand years or so—it had been slowly replaced with the language that most of Zarathan spoke. And as they'd already discussed, that couldn't happen by accident. Someone—or something—had quite deliberately guided the language to dovetail with something that the other inhabitants didn't even know *existed*.

He realized he'd missed something in his reverie, snapped back to the present. "Pardon me, Lady Shae; I was thinking about your concept of lights, as light is also terribly important to my people, and became distracted."

She smiled. "Forgiven. I understand you believe that here, in this very valley, may be your own people's ancient homeland?"

"Yes, Lady Shae. I hope to be able to verify that."

"If it can be verified, that will be at Sha Kaizatenzei Valatar, and now that I have seen and sensed the two of you myself—"

"Sensed?"

The big woman laughed again, the sound echoing through the hall, and suddenly stopped, her eyes twinkling yet dangerously sharp and narrow. "Oh, yes, my friend. Do you think I would bid my Miri to use a crystal simply to satisfy my curiosity and greet a few travelers? No, no; it was far more than that. I have the safety of my people foremost in my mind. I knew that Miri is excellent in judging these things, but the idea of someone reaching us through the Pass of Night? That was utterly unprecedented, Tobimar of Zarathanton. I could take no chances; I had to see you, bend all my senses upon you and see if you were, indeed, what you appeared, or something foul with a fair seeming atop, if you catch my meaning."

Dangerous indeed. And is she *what she appears to be, or not?* "And?"

"And as I was saying, now that I have sensed you, I know you for who you claim to be; adventurers with hearts of light, not of darkness. You, in particular, are surrounded by an aura of light, Tobimar, but your companion as well; even your little pet shines strongly, and by this I know your mission is not one of ill. So I say to you, come—come to Sha Kaizatenzei Valatar, and I will welcome you there, and I shall command the vaults of the past be opened to you to search."

Kyri bowed to Lady Shae, Tobimar mirroring her. "We thank you for this generous invitation. I don't suppose we could use those crystals to get there, though."

"Oh, that would be convenient, yes. But no, I am afraid not. Master Wieran would have to calculate your matrix, manufacture the crystals. Perhaps when you arrive, you can ask him, if he has the time."

"We have heard his name several times; it sounds like he can work miracles."

Miri nodded, the bow in her hair bobbing. "Miracles is close enough! Though he's a bit...difficult."

"But men of genius—as he is often wont to remind us—are often a bit difficult," Lady Shae said. There was a note of... exasperated affection in her voice. "Still, without him we would not have accomplished a tenth of what we have." She glanced at a shimmering sphere across the room, which Tobimar realized must be a clock of some sort. "I must bid you farewell. It will be some time before we meet again—for the journey will not be a short one, no matter the route you take."

Lady Shae hesitated, then made a decision. From another of the cylinders she produced two perfectly clear crystals. "Miri, here—to replace that which you used," she said, giving one to the blue-crystal-armored Light.

Then she turned to Tobimar and, to his astonishment, placed the other in his hand. "For you, Tobimar, and your companions. You are unique, and the light in your spirits has brought hope and joy at the knowledge that the world beyond the mountains is not all as that forest which surrounds us. I give this to you as a symbol and shield—a symbol of trust, and a shield to protect you in case anything dark pursues you even here."

"I...Lady of Lights, I don't know what to say."

She smiled. "Your reaction confirms my impulse. Keep it well. I can see you will not use it frivolously."

He bowed again and placed the precious crystal immediately into a small pouch at his side. "I do have to wonder what would happen if you were summoned at a more...delicate moment."

Hargen coughed, Miri looked shocked, and a gasp ran about the room. For a moment, Lady Shae just stared, but then she threw that magnificent head of red hair back and *roared* with laughter. "Oh! Oh, Tobimar, if all Adventurers are like you, we have been sorely deprived!" She went into another fit of chuckles, and Tobimar could see everyone else relaxing slowly. "You mean, perhaps, if I were in my bath? Then I must regret to inform you that the summoning includes the clothing and equipment of your matrix, with only certain variations, so even were I to begin clad in nothing but mist, I would arrive full-clothed as you see me here."

Tobimar felt his face red-hot, but he had asked the question quite deliberately; not only had he gained some knowledge of how the devices worked, he'd also gained insight into the Lady's character, and that of those around her. *They weren't afraid of her, they were afraid for me, by their expressions, which means that she has some reputation for temper but none for cruelty.*

Still not a sign of the rot that must *be somewhere at the center of this place.*

Lady Shae stepped back, and a space cleared about her. "Miri, I know you will have other errands to attend to, but I make them your responsibility; make sure they arrive safely at Valatar."

Miri bowed low. "It shall be done, Lady of the Lights."

Shae returned the bow, then raised another crystalline device, something like a small net of colored diamond, to her lips. "Pertrelli, now," she said; a moment later, she vanished in a fountain of light.

Everyone was left staring for a few moments; Tobimar felt a small weight slide down and off him, and knew that Poplock had taken advantage of the distraction to move off. *I somehow doubt he'll find much here, but it's worth at least looking around.*

Miri turned to them and nodded. "You heard Lady Shae—I'm responsible for your safety all the way to Valatar now!"

"Does that mean you'll be traveling with us all the way?"

She sighed and shook her head. "No, there will be other things I have to do at times. But I'll make sure I know where you plan on going and that you at least have a good idea of what to expect." She smiled. "It's not like I have to worry about whether you'll be in danger in the wilder lands between; I've *seen* you in action, after all."

Tobimar grinned back. "True enough."

"Would it be an imposition if I were to accompany you?" Hiriista asked.

Kyri glanced at him, and he shrugged. "I see no problem, Hiriista," she said. "You know the way?"

"There is a road that follows the grand circuit, yes, and I can tell when you are reaching branches or following the true course."

"As long as you're not needed—"

"I am," Hiriista admitted, "but I also require some resupply of various materials which are nearly impossible to get except at Valatar; without them my usefulness here will be significantly reduced." He looked over at Hargen.

The Child of Odin frowned, but then sighed. "If you feel you must, then you must."

"Well, I *must* eventually, and I cannot argue that such unique arrivals provide an impetus to make the matter more urgent than otherwise."

"It's settled, then. But that's a matter for the morrow, and for this evening, I insist we talk more about *your* homes, Phoenix, Tobimar." Hargen gestured them towards a large table. "Eat, drink—and talk—are very strongly indicated. As you can see," he gestured, and Tobimar could see that most of the crowd were following along, "you will have a *most* attentive audience!"

CHAPTER 19

Finally starting to wind down, Poplock thought to himself. He'd managed to wander around most of the huge house of the Reflect while the others were in conversation; as he'd expected, in most cases people didn't even *notice* him if he was at all cautious, and at most they picked him up and moved him somewhere they felt he belonged.

There wasn't a *single thing* he'd found that was indicative of anything wrong here; it was, he admitted, perhaps a bit contrarian that this made him *more* suspicious than he had been. But while there were prison cells—and not many of them—they were comfortable, and mostly not in use, nor with much *sign* of use. He couldn't find any secret passages, heavily warded locations—aside from basic defensive wards around the perimeter of the grounds—and the armory was about what he expected in a good-sized town, allowing for the fact that they didn't have spellslingers but did have these "magewrights" to provide them with good equipment.

Even the conversation had been interesting but absolutely *harmless.* Mostly of course they'd been asking questions about the world beyond their mountains, and been riveted by Tobimar and Phoenix's descriptions of Zarathan's other countries and cities, but now that things were starting to break up, the newcomers were finally getting their turn to ask questions. From his current location on a mantelpiece, Poplock could hear Phoenix talking to one of the local Hues, Zelliri. ". . . you are all trained at Valatar?"

"Yes," Zelliri nodded, her medium brown hair moving little because it was tightly braided around her head. "Every few years there's a competition among all the children of the right ages—between thirteen and sixteen, for humans—and the ones that show the best talent, dedication and focus in the needed arts are selected as candidates to replace any of the *Tenzeitalacor* who may have been lost or chosen to retire."

"Is that common? Members of your Unity Guard being lost?"

Zelliri shrugged. "Common . . . no, but it happens. I think it's probably one or two a year across all of Kaizatenzei. We don't often lose a Light—if you ever see Light Miri in action, you'll know why—but you've also seen what's in the forest . . . outside. And sometimes there are still things inside, between the cities."

That was at least fairly similar to home; get far away from the cities, things got less safe. But here, Poplock was pretty sure, it had to do at least partially with the magic that surrounded the city itself. *I'm betting that the pure perfection we're sensing here will be less in the in-between lands.*

"What's the training like to become a Hue?"

Zelliri got a faraway look in her eyes. "What's it like? I'm not sure I could describe it to someone who wasn't there. Oh, some of it's just exercises, weapons training, and so on . . . but there's techniques we're taught . . ." She shook her head emphatically. "Really, I can't tell you. Secret, honestly."

"I understand. There's things I guess we couldn't tell you about our skills and training, too."

Poplock scuttled along, moving behind vases and bowls and other things that dwarfed him. This was a typical conversation; a few interesting tidbits, nothing to hang anything *real* from.

Looking around, he noticed Hiriista was no longer immediately visible. *That surprises me. He was obviously trying to pump us for information on magic, and could tell that there was more to learn.*

Poplock slid down from the mantel and scuttled around, sniffing. There was a particular scent to *mazakh* and he was familiar enough with it to get a good trail if the traces were recent.

The trail led outside; easing out into the darkness, Poplock let his eyes adjust to the night before moving farther along.

It didn't take very long to find Hiriista; he was standing in a small grove of bushes, laid out like a five-pointed star, to one side of the house entrance. The reptilian creature was squatting on its tail and looking up at the stars.

As Poplock stopped, the head swiveled. "Ah. The third and most interesting of our visitors arrives."

Does he know, *or is he guessing?* Poplock just sat still and blinked stupidly at the *mazakh*.

"Naturally you're too smart to speak. Or perhaps I am wrong and you are, indeed, no more than a pet, or a familiar, with a touch more than the wild gives you but not an intellect on a par with your companions. Yet, I think otherwise." Hiriista looked back up at the stars. "Here we are in private; no others are here to observe. So—as you move not away—I will indulge myself with the speculations, and see if you agree with my conclusions, little toad.

"First, it is your pose, your way of moving and sitting; the body has a language of its own, and while often yours says 'I am nothing but a foolish toad,' at other times—often when others seemed not to be looking—it said other things to me. I saw your attention focused strongly on those speaking of certain things; I noted you kicking or nudging your companion Tobimar subtly, and shortly afterward he would ask certain types of questions. I am, you see, somewhat adept at reading the words of the body, as my people are rare in Kaizatenzei, and to live with humans well means to understand their meaning in movement as well as words."

Hiriista reached slowly into a pouch at his side—a movement clearly intended not to frighten either dumb Toad or intelligent Adventurer—and brought out a metal and wood something which he put into his mouth. Scent rose from it, which Hiriista inhaled. "Still, this is mere circumstantial evidence, and a matter of interpretation. More telling, I think, is your face. A casual observer might not understand what they see, but I do. You are *not* an ordinary toad such as might be found in local swamps and ponds. Your eyes are set more forward, looking more as a human does, able to focus both eyes on targets. Your legs—fore and rear—seem jointed just *slightly* differently, and your forefeet appear more dextrous than ordinary. Your head, too, is some what higher and broader—perhaps to hold more of a brain to think with?" He gave an amused sigh, and a puff of the scent was faintly visible in the air. "Still, these *may* just be signs of a different variety of toad, one more suited to being a pet or familiar."

Well, he's doing very well so far. Wonder what else he has? Poplock mused. He wasn't going to decide what he would *do* about the *mazakh's* observations yet, and might as well hear everything he had to say.

"Third...ahh, that has to do with tactics. The Phoenix and Tobimar are both clearly warriors. They have some powers of their own, implied in their stories and the way in which they move, but the conversations on things magical clearly say to me that neither of them is well-versed in the ways of magic—whether that of your home locale, or of this. Yet does it make sense, I ask myself, for a party to set out to solve such a mystery as Tobimar describes, without at least *someone* who can, if not *use* magic, at least *understand* it well enough to address magical barriers and opponents? I would say not. And that, my friend, leaves *you* as the only possible candidate. Unless you happen, of course, to have another ally who is invisible and undetectable." The magewright gave a hissing chuckle.

Ironic that in theory we could *have just such an ally. Xavier would scare the scales right off you.*

"Now, I have no intention of telling anyone else my deductions. I understand *perfectly* why this would be your tactic, Duckweed. Tiny, unnoticed, and potentially deadly; what a wonderful resource you must be, especially if your adversaries do not suspect your presence."

Poplock grinned and gave his own shrug. "It's proved useful a time or two," he said.

The sharp *hiss* of startlement showed that despite his deductions, Hiriista had been uncertain. "So it *is* true! I thank you for speaking, little one. You *are* their magician, are you not?"

"Oh, I dabble—more than Tobimar or Phoenix, that's true. But yeah, I'm the one they'll be asking whenever things get magical."

"So it was on *your* behalf that Tobimar was asking about gemcalling?"

"Basically. Sure, he was curious too, but I'm the guy actually interested in *learning* it, if I can."

Hiriista spun and squatted again, now facing Poplock directly. "Well, since we shall be traveling together, I think I may be able to enlighten you on this. There are certain...limitations of the art which may make it generally more difficult for you to practice, but we shall see."

"I can teach you about magic from our side of the mountains, too. What I know, anyway, which isn't a *huge* amount but probably is enough to give you an idea of how we work."

"I would be extremely interested to learn such techniques. Now that we are aware of the world beyond, I feel certain I will travel there one day, as you have traveled here."

"Don't try *that* alone. Rivendream Pass is just as nasty as you think."

"Indeed, indeed. I have ventured outside of the wall...not far, you understand...and I know well what sort of monstrosities I might face." A hiss-click of pride. "But they know not what *they* might be facing, either."

Poplock figured the *mazakh* was probably right. Light Miri respected Hiriista, and given what she'd seemed perfectly happy to take on by herself...that made Hiriista pretty darn dangerous. "You say there aren't many of your people around?"

The magewright's head bobbed from side to side in a negative. "Indeed, not many. In all honesty, not enough for us to maintain our population; we reduce in numbers and I fear it will be not too many generations at all before we are gone."

"Well...there's lots of *mazakh* on the other side of the mountains, but most of them aren't very nice people."

The crested head tilted. "What do you mean?"

Poplock gave him the same tilt. "You want the water-pure truth?"

"I do."

"Okay, then. Most *mazakh*—and I mean something like ninety-nine out of a hundred—are demon-worshipers, following their own demons called the *Mazolishta*. Ran into one once, not very friendly at *all*."

Even with his minimal experience with *mazakh*, Poplock could see the shock and disappointment in Hiriista's pose and movements. "I...see. Then I apologize in the stead of all my misled brethren."

"Hey, not your fault," Poplock said cheerfully. "On my side... I'm guessing there aren't any Toads here at all."

"None I have ever heard of, no. Are all your people so small?"

Poplock gave a croaking laugh. "Ha! No, I am a runt by

their standards too. Most of them are at least the size of one of those flagstones on the path to the house, and some weigh more than you do."

"So, even in your home lands, you are oft ignored. I see. Well, as I said, I shall not betray your most interesting secret. Do you intend to keep yourself hidden from Light Miri—assuming she has not already guessed?"

"I think so. She doesn't *need* to know my abilities right now, and having an unknown resource can be a lifesaver. I've saved lives before with that."

"I do not doubt it—and I now guess there are parts of your friends' tales that might be told a bit differently if they were to include your role in affairs." Hiriista stood, putting away his scent-device. "I believe the festivities are nearly over. Is that your friend?"

Faintly, from the door, he heard Tobimar calling "Duckweed? *Duckweed!*"

"Whoops! Gotta go. Thanks for a really interesting talk." They exchanged bows. "Once we start traveling, I guess we'll have a *lot* to talk about."

"I think we will, yes." Hiriista agreed.

A few moments' hopping took him to Tobimar, who relaxed as he felt Poplock's familiar weight clambering up to his shoulder. "Thank goodness," he said, in the tone of someone chiding a pet, "I was worried. Don't go wandering off like that!"

Poplock maintained his own silence until they returned to the inn—and until he'd managed to verify that there were still no spy charms, scrying, or other means of observing them without being detected. "Whew! So, you guys find out anything?"

Kyri made a face. "I found out that everyone's curious about Evanwyl and the rest of Zarathan, that I'm already being compared to Lady Shae because we're both very tall and built like warriors, and that I can't sense a single thing worse than petty jealousy and human anger anywhere."

"Pretty much the same here," admitted Tobimar. "Not a trace of darkness that I could sense anywhere. Their Colors and Hues all were given secret-secret training that they remember fondly but can't talk about, that's about the only interesting thing I found out."

"Yes, I had similar conversations," Kyri said. "They're very proud of it—reminds me a bit of the Justiciars, but mostly just because it's a tight-knit group with strong spirit of unity." She glanced to Poplock. "Same with you?"

"Well, mostly. I poked around everywhere I could reach in the mansion and found nothing. But there *was* one interesting event. I got caught." He summarized his conversation with Hiriista.

Tobimar exchanged an impressed glance with Kyri. "By the sands, he's good. We were trying to hide you but he still saw through it. Do you think he'll actually keep you a secret?"

Poplock thought about it. "I think he *wants* to. What I *don't* know is whether he's got obligations to, say, the Lady of Light or Miri that might require him to let them in on the secret whether he wants to or not." At their expressions, he snorted. "Hey, *someone* here has to be the cautious one!"

"No, you're right," Kyri said slowly. "We *know* there's something wrong here, and that means we can't take anything at face value."

"On the positive side, it means that you'll actually be able to work with him on the various talents that work here and don't back home—and, I guess, vice-versa."

"Exactly," Poplock said, catching a passing fly. "And I *really* need that information. If they do all their major magic by this gemcalling and summoning and alchemy and such, I have to get a grip on how that stuff really works here, and how I can deal with those if things turn ugly."

He noted the yawns of his companions. "But you guys are tired—and so am I, I just don't yawn like you. Tomorrow we choose which way to go and get going, right?"

"Right," agreed Kyri. Tobimar snagged her for a kiss before they went to their rooms—a kiss that went on long enough that Poplock was tempted to set up a timer; instead, he just hopped to his place in a corner of Tobimar's room.

Tomorrow we stop hanging around and get to moving again!

CHAPTER 20

She skipped her way along the hallway, then bounded down the three hundred forty-three steps, taking them three or four at a time, to finally burst through the massive double doors that opened easily for her—and only a very few others.

The room on the other side never failed to impress her—and, in the moments she was honest with herself, sent a tingle of apprehension through her as well. Arranged like a gigantic amphitheater with circular levels descending in ranked order, forty-nine levels each with its own corresponding complex symbology intagliated in silver and gold and crystal on the great domed roof above, the room was both immense and hollowly imposing. Even her light footsteps sent sharp echoes chasing themselves around the room, past the polished metal and glass and shimmering gemstone retorts spaced about the levels and the spaces awaiting other chambers, retorts, tubes, or crystals to be inset, in their turn, beneath the *T'Terakhorwin*, the Great Array.

In the center of the huge room, beneath the core of the Great Array, was a flat space nearly a hundred yards across, with a floor of polished obsidian inset with platinum and *krellin* runes so closely spaced that there was nearly as much soft-silver shining as deep black glint. Despite the size of that area, not terribly much of the floor was visible, for arranged all about, in concentric seven-sided patterns, were ranks of alchemical and mystical equipment of more complex and diverse designs than she had ever seen anywhere else.

The master and designer of all of this glanced up as she entered. "You interrupt my work." His white hair cascaded across his shoulders, his pale eyes stared at her from deep-set, shadowed sockets in a narrow, ascetic face that showed lines of concentration but none of smiles. The only other person present made himself unobtrusive, obviously wanting to avoid being involved in any major discussion.

She flashed Tashriel a quick smile, then turned to Wieran with a sigh. *He hasn't the faintest* trace *of courtesy. I shudder every time I have to have him come up and interact with other people, for fear he'll forget his instructions.* "I wouldn't do so without reason, and I think you'll find *this* reason more than adequate."

She reached up to one of her armor's shoulderpads and, with some effort, detached a section which had made the one a bit thicker than the other. Beneath the false surface could now be seen a multiplicity of runes and symbols, engraved in a way that strongly mirrored that of the ground below her.

The blue eyes narrowed, and a hint of a smile appeared—a smile which was not, in any way, comforting. "The data gathering is *complete*?"

"I spent several hours in the company of the target. That should be enough, right?"

"If it *is* the correct target, yes." Without request or preamble, long, spidery fingers snatched the former coverplate of her shoulderpad away from her; Wieran crossed with metronome-precise strides to a complicated piece of equipment a short distance away and fitted the thin plate into a holder.

An entire portion of the array above and below suddenly hummed into life, and a blue-white fire burned for a moment above the plate, a fire whose light both excited and pained her. "Yes, yes, *yes!* That *is* the key we have sought!" Weiran said, with the most animation she had ever heard in his voice. "Have it brought here *immediately!*"

The joy she felt at knowing victory was at last within their reach was tempered by the sudden demand. "Master Wieran," she said carefully, "they are currently in Murnitenzei, and the key is not alone. We must take care not to alert any of the party to anything untoward, and really, we haven't anything with a foolproof method to transport someone so far."

Wieran's mouth tightened, but then he took a breath and relaxed. "Very well, Miri. I suppose I can take the time to finalize preparations for the unlocking in the meantime; it has not been a priority until now."

The ground beneath them suddenly quivered—a tiny amount, but more than enough for both Miri and Wieran to notice. Miri glanced involuntarily at the wall she knew lay to the West, and thus beneath Enneisolaten, the great lake. "Is...it...secure?"

Weiran's reply was matter-of-fact, holding none of her uncertainty or—to be perfectly frank with herself—fear of what lay beyond. "The Array holds him, yes. And once the key has arrived, *that* will no longer be a concern for any of us."

"You can keep it restrained for that long? When the cycle is turning in their favor?"

A short, humorless laugh. "Your desperate bindings held it for millennia before I came; with the perfection of *my* designs? Not even the Dragon King himself could break free! But I understand your fear; if break free it does, *I* will not be the one it comes for first, but rather those who asked its aid and then betrayed it. Now," Weiran turned away, "leave me, Miri. I have work to do and need none of your distractions."

"You're welcome," she muttered under her breath as she ran back up the stairs. *Even his most polite behavior would get him killed in some places.*

But that was only a minor annoyance today. The singing, painful brilliance she had seen stayed with her and erased her resentment at Wieran's arrogance. Once past the wards at the top, she concentrated and in a flash stepped straight to the hallway outside her own chambers.

Inside, she quickly set up the mirror-scroll and invoked its power. For several minutes the gold-shining surface remained blank, showing only her own face, but then, without warning, it darkened, and a cheerful, blond-haired man—or rather, something that had the outward appearance of a man—looked out; his boyish grin widened further as he saw his caller. "Why, Miri! What a pleasure, as usual. How are you?"

"Well enough, Viedra. I have called to thank you; the key we sought has indeed arrived. Master Wieran verified that this morning."

"You doubted me? I'm almost wounded, Ermirinovas."

"Say rather I was not going to celebrate until I was sure," she responded with a smile of her own. "But now it is certain. In a month or two, once he has arrived, the entire work will be completed."

"A month? Oh, I imagine the old man is a bit put out by that."

"He'll have to accept it. We need to understand both the key and his companion; we don't want unexpected events undermining the final seal and release."

He nodded. "Oh, certainly not. His companion . . . yes, she is quite interesting. Please keep me informed—especially as to her ultimate fate. I've been following her myself for a project of my own."

Miri raised an eyebrow. "You did not say she was important to any of your projects! I thought we had full operative authority here!" Her jaw tightened. *If he puts restrictions on how we can deal with them—!*

Instead, Viedra laughed. "Oh, but of course you do. Take whatever approach you require, just tell me of the outcome, yes?"

Mollified, she nodded. "As you wish. Do you have any use for Wieran afterwards?"

"After?" The smile was not quite human, the teeth suddenly a hair too sharp, too shiny. "Oh, I think by then Master Wieran will have outlived his usefulness. Don't you agree?"

She giggled, a sound a listener would have found distressingly incongruous with her thoughts. "Oh, I think both Kalshae and I would agree on *that*." She smiled in anticipation. "The real question will be whether *I* get to kill him . . . or *she* does."

Viedra's laugh was as human as his appearance usually was, big and cheerful and warm. She appreciated *that* incongruity herself. "Well, then, I wish you all the success possible, and that sounds like a *wonderful* thing to look forward to. I thank you for confirming things with me. Now, I must be going—" he broke off. "Oh, dear. Yes, there *is* one more thing."

There always is. "What?"

"There's another young man following that delightful Phoenix. It's *very* important to me that he *not* catch up to her. Can you make sure of that?"

"Do you want him killed?"

Viedra shook his head. "Oh, no, no! I want him to keep *following* her, just not *reaching* her, until you are all done, that is.

Preferably not even have much contact with those who have seen her. Can you arrange that for me?"

She was relieved; this would be both simple and amusing. "Oh, I think so. I'll lay a false trail for him in the opposite direction around the lake from the one they select and periodically check on him. Good enough?"

"That will be *splendid*, Miri. Oh, yes—Phoenix doesn't know she's being followed, and she shouldn't be allowed to know."

"Of course."

"Excellent. Then I will leave you to it—our Father has tasks for me today."

Miri waved and the scroll went blank. Glancing at the time-crystal, she bounced up and headed to the Valatar Throne.

Lady Shae saw her come in and waved absently. Miri, seeing she was busy hearing the grievances of the people and making decisions, went to one side of the Throne and waited patiently. Even small details like this were crucial to the overall plan.

Finally the last of the morning's petitioners left and the doors shut behind. "Kerlamion's *breath*," Kalshae muttered venomously, "I grow so *weary* of this charade at times. Such *petty* issues they have. Hardly even a decent bout of hate or killing rage or spite."

Miri laughed. "Oh, if you take the border areas you can get a lot of that!"

Shae looked at her askance. "*You* have the option to patrol; that's rather limited for me."

"The price you pay as the Lady of Light."

"Ugh. I feel so *contaminated*." Kalshae shuddered and for a moment her form wavered, becoming less human, darker.

"Oh, I don't mind; I can switch back and forth between the self I'm being for the game and who I am; it's become almost its own reality."

Kalshae looked at her sharply. "Be careful, Ermirinovas! Dalurshinsu and Yurugin said similar things before..."

"I know perfectly well what they said. I also haven't been playing around with the Stars and Sun directly like they were."

"Still, you should come down and sit next to our prisoner more often. His darkness is a welcome antidote to that agonizing light."

"I'll try. But unlike you, I have a lot of places I have to travel to. You can always go downstairs in between duties."

"Just watch yourself. I'm not sure how either of us could handle all this by ourselves."

Miri nodded, but smiled confidently. "Oh, I will. But really, it's only another few months." The smile sharpened. "I've directed this plan for thousands of years; what could possibly break me *now*?"

CHAPTER 21

Kyri took a deep breath of the morning air, which once more brought that *sparkling* feeling into her, something beyond the freshness of an ordinary dawn. *I wonder how I'll manage to adapt to the ordinary world when we go back,* she mused. *Evanwyl will seem dull and grimy by comparison. Even Zarathanton may pall.*

The three of them stood at the eastern gate of Sha Murnitenzei, looking at the rolling hills that led off into the golden haze of dawn, Poplock sitting comfortably on Tobimar's shoulder. Next to them, Hiriista was adjusting a large backpack, jeweled bracelets and necklaces chiming as he did so.

Shade Danrall stood nearby, straight as a column; he was to escort them a short distance as he was going on patrol in that direction. Kyri gave him a narrow glance as he looked away. *Something about him's . . . different.* She remembered their first encounter with the Shade; he had been stunned by their arrival, a bit nervous, instantly ordered away by Miri to run an errand. He'd shown up at the party, too, and been similarly nervous and diffident.

He *seemed* the same today. Even now, he was being a bit wide-eyed and nervous about escorting them when they'd already shown how formidable they were. *Yet I can't shake the feeling that he's not nervous at all. That he's completely focused on the situation and not in any way affected by it.*

What was *really* maddening was that this whole situation rang a faint bell of memory and her brain was refusing to come up with the connection. *Let it go. The connection will come in time, when you're not trying to force it. And you may be imagining things.*

"You're not coming with us, Miri?" she asked. "I thought—"

"Yes, I'd *planned* on at least starting the journey with you, but last night, *just* as I was going to bed, I got a message that there's something wrong near Sha Vomatenzei; sounds to me like something got over the wall and is skulking around the farms there."

"Yes," Tobimar said thoughtfully, "I suppose that the wall can't do much to stop things that fly or are really good at climbing or jumping from surrounding trees."

"Do not underestimate the *Tenzei Kendron*," Hiriista said. "Powers are woven into it which prevent easy contact even by the denizens of the surrounding forest, and which discourage and confuse those which attempt to pass above or below it. It takes something of considerable power or skill, or both, to pass it."

"Which unfortunately means that if something *does* make it over—or under—the Wall, it's very dangerous," Miri said regretfully. "So I'm heading off in the opposite direction. I'll catch up to you as I can."

They exchanged bows and Miri impulsively embraced them both. Kyri was startled but returned the hug; there was something inherently lovable about the little Light, and the strength in her arms reminded Kyri that she was no more delicate than Tobimar. "You be careful, Miri," she said.

Miri looked startled, then smiled brilliantly. "I'm not used to people *worrying* about me! But I guess if anyone's got a right to worry about me, it's the people who crossed the Pass of Night. Okay, I'll be careful. You too, Phoenix! And Tobimar! I don't want to have to explain to Lady Shae how we lost our special visitors."

"*And* a significant magewright," Hiriista said dryly.

"*And* a *most* significant and beloved magewright," she agreed with a laugh. "Goodbye!"

Miri skipped away, a casual-appearing gait that still somehow took her down the road back into town so quickly that it was only moments before she vanished from sight.

Hiriista gave a sigh and rattled the feathery spines on his neck; the sound gave Kyri the impression of exasperated fondness. "And there she goes, bouncing like a hatchling. Sometimes I cannot *grasp* how she can manage her duties half as well as she does."

"*Magewright* Hiriista!" Danrall said, a shocked tone in his voice. *Yet... it still seems a bit off to me.* "How—"

"Oh, pissh!" The *mazakh* dismissed the comment with a wave. "She's hardly unaware of my opinion. Don't worry yourself with the reputation of your superiors, they can well ward themselves."

"O-of course, sir." He bowed to them. "Are you ready to begin?"

"Lead on," Kyri said.

"So," Tobimar said as they began walking east along the road, "when exactly are we parting ways?"

"I would expect sometime after noon," Danrall answered. "My patrol's going to take me out to a particular crossroad that leads south to the Wall, then west along it to the Gate-Post where I'll spend the night, then continue west about an equal distance until I turn north and join up with the road.

"Shade Ammini," he continued, mentioning one of the other Shades, a broad dark-skinned young woman Kyri remembered from the Party, "will be leaving about now and going in the opposite direction, but she'll turn north, then after she reaches Nightshine Rock she'll go east and spend the night at Rimestump, then patrol east to Sentry Hill and return to the road at about the point where I'll be leaving it."

Kyri could envision the described paths easily in general terms—two rectangular loops, one to the south and one to the north of Murnitenzei. "So each patrol takes two days. You do this how often?"

"Dual patrol's done at least once a week and sometimes twice. The Hues roll dice to determine which day, and sometimes whether it'll be night or day patrols. That keeps anything from being able to be *sure* of our patrol timing. And of course the timing shifts if we run into something."

"Does that happen often? Running into something inside the Wall?"

Danrall spread his hands uncertainly. "Well, it *happens*. Not very often, but... maybe two or three times a year here. I'd guess it's about that often in the other cities. Twice a year we send a big patrol—all three Hues and four Shades—along the Necklace—"

"Necklace?"

Hiriista laughed, a hissing sound like a boiling kettle. "Yes, you did not hear that name before? That is the name many people use for the main road that circles Kaizatenzei, through all the Seven and to the One, because it is like a necklace with jewels spaced along it."

Kyri smiled. "That *does* make sense. A nice image. So you send patrols along the Necklace twice a year—all the cities do this?"

"Yes. That way there's a force to clean up anything that's gotten through and is hiding in the parts between cities, bothering outlying villages but not rooted out by the normal patrols, that kind of thing."

It sounded like they had a pretty good system in place to maintain the safety and peace. She presumed even the outlying villages had their own ordinary defenders, but the things outside the Wall would require something out of the ordinary. "That still seems like a fairly small force, having seen what lies outside your Wall—each city has one Color, three Hues, and seven Shades, right? So that would be for all seven—no, eight—cities, eighty-eight plus the seven Lights, ninety-five for the whole country?"

"It may seem small, but given our training and abilities, it is enough," Danrall said with some pride.

"That must be *impressive* training," Tobimar said.

"Oh, it is. We are taught..." He shook his head as though catching himself. "But no, I can't tell you. Secret, honestly. It is not safe, though." He looked down, sadness clear on his face.

"You lose candidates in the training?"

Danrall hesitated, then nodded. "Over half...do not make it."

Myrionar's Name! Half *of their carefully selected candidates* die *from the training?* "You lost a friend or two, I guess."

"Two. One of them was my best friend since I was three, so long that I couldn't remember *not* being her friend. We were all so excited to be chosen, but I was scared too. Khasye kept my spirits up, gave me the confidence...and then..." He trailed off, and for a few moments they walked in silence.

"I'm sorry," she said finally.

"Thank you. It was a couple of years ago...but it still hurts to remember it."

"I don't know that it ever *stops* hurting," she said honestly, thinking of her parents and her brother and feeling anew the stab of loss and anger, "but I can tell you it does get better as time goes on."

Danrall looked at her with new understanding. "You...?"

"My father, mother, and older brother. Yes." *And a lot of other people, not as close... but just as important.*

They walked in silence for a while, and when conversation resumed it was about more mundane things—the types of animals and plants found in this region of Kaizatenzei, what they could expect along the road ahead, and so on. Finally, shortly after lunch, Danrall bowed to them and began walking south along a less well-maintained, but still clear and reasonably level, path to the south.

"*Finally!*" Poplock said as the Shade disappeared from sight.

The rest of them laughed. "Ahh," Hiriista said, rattling his crest in amusement, "it must truly be a challenge for you to be so silent at all times, Master Toad."

"Sure ain't easy, I'll say that." He looked over at the *mazakh*. "So, are people going to think we're one of these patrols?"

Hiriista tilted his head quizzically. "In truth, I had not thought of that. But indeed they might; Tobimar and Phoenix are of a reasonable age to be Hues or Shades, and I have been known to accompany such patrols."

"Does it matter?" Kyri asked. "My sworn duty is to protect and aid any in trouble anyway; even if we aren't your Shades and Hues, we'll still be willing to help anyone who needs our assistance."

"My duties are much the same, as a magewright instructed by Lady Shae herself," Hiriista admitted. "Then we may consider ourselves just such a patrol, in spirit if not in fact."

"I'm betting that troubles are most common at the midpoints between the main cities," Tobimar said. "Given what you've all mentioned about the way in which the cities grew and all."

"You are correct, of course. And sometimes the problems are purely... internal. While none of us like to think of other people being capable of evil, it does still happen on occasion, especially farther away from the great cities."

"Well," Poplock said, "We'll hear about it if we hear about it, I guess. In the meantime, I've got a lot of questions that I haven't been able to ask!"

They all laughed. "I am sure you do, Master Toad," Hiriista said, still chuckling like a clockwork whistle running down. "But the ones I think you are most interested in must wait until this evening." He took in Kyri and Tobimar with his glance as well. "We will have much to discuss, I think."

Was there something else in his voice...a warning?

"I'm sure we will," she answered, feeling a new hint of caution and disquiet rising within her. "I'm sure we will."

CHAPTER 22

"Gemcalling," Hiriista began, "is a combination of one's personal magic, alchemy, symbolism, and the channeling of power outside oneself."

"Whoo. Sounds complicated," Poplock said. The four of them were seated near the cookfire; Tobimar and Kyri were taking turns watching the food as it cooked, but they were old hands at this sort of thing and clearly didn't need to focus much attention on it.

"Complicated in concept, yes, and challenging if you do not understand the methods and requirements, but not terribly complicated in practice if you have the requisite tools. First, you need to have the basic talent for magic; I understand this is true of you, perhaps less so for your friends."

Poplock glanced up at Kyri and Tobimar, who nodded. "I was told I could be a...mediocre wizard, depending on what path I chose," Kyri said. "A decent summoner, maybe. Tobimar?"

"My...master," Tobimar said, "told me that I had considerable magical potential but my best course did not lie in that direction. I guess I use some of that in the practice of my other skills, the combat arts he taught me."

Poplock knew that Tobimar was talking about the manipulative magician Konstantin Khoros; given reactions to that name elsewhere, he didn't blame Tobimar for evading that potential pitfall. "So yeah, I've got pretty good magical talent and I've been learning a lot about it," he said. "What would I have to learn to be a Gemcaller?"

"You will need a *Tai Syrowin*, a Calling Array, first," the *mazakh* answered, with a teeth-baring smile that seemed a challenge.

With that hint, plus the name of the discipline, Poplock understood. "Ha!" He bounced over and pulled on the various pieces of jewelry Hiriista wore. "Can I borrow one of them, then?"

"Excellent. You grasp the meaning instantly. Not *all* of these are Calling Arrays, but many are. Yes, I in fact have thought about this and I do have one Array that I may give you." From a pouch Hiriista took a bright silver-and-gold ring with an empty setting for a large gem—Poplock guessed it would hold a gem between ten and fifteen carats—and handed it to the Toad.

Studying the ring up close, Poplock could see several unusual features. The setting itself was complex, with magic he could easily sense; by pushing at the prongs with his various tools and concentrating his own magic into the tools, he quickly realized that the setting was designed to accommodate gems of virtually any shape meeting the size limitations. The prongs themselves had tiny lines of a brilliant blue tinged with gold—a color that made him blink, then bounce over to check out Kyri's Raiment. He glanced up. "Thyrium. There are thyrium channels through that ring."

The crest drooped and rose in appreciation. "A *very* good eye you have, Poplock. Yes, the thyrium channels are an integral part of the Calling Array, providing a link and channel between your own power and that of the selected gem."

"Ooo, so you need magical gems to do this?"

"Yes. I am not sure I have—"

"Maybe *we* do. Tobimar?"

"What am I, a bank vault?" his friend said humorously. From its usual place under his outer clothing, Tobimar produced his secure pouch of gems that he had brought with him from Skysand—a country with a widespread reputation for the variety and quality of gemstones it produced. He poured the contents onto one of the plates they already had out.

Hiriista gave an appreciative hiss that approximated a whistle. "I was unaware you carried such wealth on you."

Tobimar gave a wry grin. "I don't advertise it. Unwise in most places. So, would any of these do?"

The *mazakh* magewright bent over the sparkling mound. "For beauty, these would be nigh-unmatched. For power..." He dug through the gems carefully for a few moments, then bobbed in decision. "This. An Ocean's Tear, I think?"

The large, teardrop-cut gemstone was a beautiful blue-green and shimmered with light of the same shade, rippling like the ocean on a sunlight day. "Yes, one of the best I've seen," Tobimar said.

"This will be ideal."

"Hey," Poplock said. "How do you know what an ocean is? I mean, all you've got is that big lake there."

Hiriista's hiss was a laugh. "Do not discount Enneisolaten so swiftly; it is an inland sea, in a way. And while it is true we have never seen such a thing as an ocean, some ancient stories and tales remain which speak of such things... and the names for these stones echo those legends, I think. Now, to our business again. As one might expect, this stone's power will be related to water. Can you fit it into your Array?"

It took Poplock several minutes—he was unfamiliar with the exact mechanism, and it was obviously intended for use by people with larger, stronger fingers—but eventually he was rewarded with a *snap!* sound and the blue-green gem was securely set in the ring. Immediately he could see a faint shimmer of ocean-colored light rippling along the thyrium traces and even glimmering on the inside surface of the ring.

Hiriista picked it up and noted the same phenomena approvingly. "Well set, and the Array has already synchronized to it nicely."

"So, how do I use it?" Poplock slid the ring onto his upper arm, where it fit fairly well. He could feel a tingling sensation, a ripple of mystical force.

"Not *that* simple, no, my friend. We will have to teach you to become attuned to the Array, and then to the stone itself. We will work on this, and I am sure it will not take overly long, but it will not be done this evening."

Kyri looked at the ring and then at the multiple other gem-inset objects Hiriista carried. "So once attuned, what can you *do* with gemcalling?"

"Many things—perhaps not as many as a... free-standing spellcaster could do, if such were able to explore their full capabilities, but many. Here, allow me to demonstrate with a gem similar to that which your friend has."

Hiriista stood and raised one clawed arm; a green stone on

his bracelet suddenly blazed with emerald fire, which rose up and became a wave of deep sea-green that thundered outward, raging through the forest, toppling smaller trees and stripping larger ones of their bark, scouring the ground bare, an unstoppable raging torrent that ended as abruptly as it had begun.

Oh, ouch! That would have hurt! "That's impressive!"

Hiriista bowed; his own body language indicated slight embarrassment. "Well, yes, but I have practiced for many years indeed, and I have been attuned to that gem for over a decade; we are old friends, one might say. In addition to such crude offensive capabilities, different gems may protect, enhance, or heal. That was what we call an Essential Call—it calls forth a force based on the essence of the gem. If I attuned myself differently to that or a similar gem, I could use an Essential Call to bring it forth as an enhancement to let me travel unimpeded through water, or to heal and rejuvenate those who are tired or injured."

"And what are the other kind of calls?" Poplock asked.

"Summoning Calls. Not the same as the work practiced by actual summoners, who bargain with various beings and spirits—you understand?" At Poplock's nod, Hiriista went on, "Good. A Summoning Call is in a sense similar to an Essential, but the gemcaller is not trying to call out the essence of, oh, the *overt* elemental or magical force, but a *personification* of the force within, and usually for that you need something that *has* a connection to the personification. You are familiar with suncore?"

"Mystical amber," Tobimar said promptly. "Either formed from the sap of some extremely rare trees, or from ordinary resin exposed to extraordinary magical forces. It's rare and hard to work."

"Precisely so. It turns out that, just as ordinary amber may trap objects and even insects within it, suncore can trap a mystical... trace, or echo, or remnant, of a power that manifests nearby. This may be a representation of a powerful animal, a nature spirit, or something more powerful. You can call forth that echo and have it assist you for a short time."

"Wow. So if you had a piece of suncore that was at, oh, a battle between two gods..."

"It is possible, yes, that you would then have something from which you could call an echo of a god to your service. Summoning gems such as that are, of course, rare—"

"I would think so!"

"—but the more valuable and sought after for all that." He tapped a necklace, on which was a large golden drop of glowing amber. "This is one of the few I have ever seen, and I am privileged to be allowed to carry it with me; it is one of the strategic treasures of Kaizatenzei, for within this drop slumbers a fragment of the essence of Shargamor."

Poplock dropped the tools he was putting back into their case, and he heard Kyri gasp. Tobimar, who had just been testing one of the dishes he was preparing, managed to gasp part of a spoonful into his lungs and spent the next minute coughing it back out. "A piece of a *GOD?*"

"An *echo* of the great power, yes. Not his equal in any way, but nonetheless a tremendous force to have at hand. I have very rarely had cause to use it; I hope I shall never have such cause again."

Poplock looked with new respect at the assortment of jewelry. *Would never have thought it was so powerful.* "Well, I have to say, I'm that much more excited about learning this!"

"And I cannot blame you. We shall work on it over the next few weeks, and I am sure you will come to grasp it quickly." He turned his gaze to Kyri. "But I have my own questions as well, and now that we are alone, it is important that we talk."

His eyes were narrow and focused, and held very much the essence of the hunter that was the nature of a *mazakh*. "So tell me, Phoenix: why were you so wary, this morning, of Shade Danrall?"

CHAPTER 23

Tobimar saw Kyri freeze, and her posture alone showed that Hiriista's question had struck home. For his part, Tobimar was mystified. He hadn't noticed anything to be wary of—although, to be fair, he hadn't been looking hard this morning. They had been pretty sure that whatever they were looking for wasn't in the immediate area.

A quick glance at Poplock, and the little Toad gave a whole-body shrug. *He didn't notice anything either.*

Finally Kyri took a deep breath. "I suppose it would be useless to pretend I don't know what you're talking about."

A faint hiss of amusement. "I am afraid that you are not terribly good at hiding your surprise, no. Perhaps you can dissemble well when prepared—I know several such—but without warning, no." The hunting look was back. "So, Phoenix, will you answer my question?"

The embarrassed tone when she answered told Tobimar that even without the firelight Kyri's already dark cheeks would have been touched with rose. "It was just a ... stupid impression. Probably nothing."

"Then it does not matter if you tell me."

She looked around, then smiled sheepishly. "I suppose not. There really isn't much more to it, to be honest. I just felt there was something ... *off* about him." She paused, lips pursed, and he could almost see her mind working.

"All his words and overt actions were exactly what I would

169

have expected from my brief contact with him," she said finally, "and my prior contacts—when we first arrived, and later at the party—didn't have this funny feel to them. But this morning... it felt almost as though he was *playing* himself, an extremely good actor, but one who was really much more competent and controlled, not confused or innocent or overawed or any of those things."

Hiriista let out a long, satisfied hiss and bobbed his head. "Precisely so. You have the instinct, young Phoenix; you just have no training that tells you *why* your instinct says what it does." He glanced down to Poplock. "Do you comprehend what I am saying?"

Poplock closed one eye, wrinkling his face, and then the eye snapped open. "Ohhh. What we talked about before. The language of the body."

"Correct. I have never met anyone else who noticed—or, to be more precise, who would *admit* to noticing this... anomaly; I believe that there are a few others who have, but they, like myself, have been afraid to speak of it, for it seems so impossible that there *could* be something wrong with these, our protectors. Yet I have seen it many times, a subtle—a *terribly* subtle—shift in posture, in facing, in the way an arm is held, a spine straightened, a head tilted, and suddenly one of the Colors seems not himself at all to me, even though not a single word or action is obviously out of place. And often this happens shortly before they go on a patrol or mission."

"You said one of the *Colors*," Tobimar said. Hiriista bared some of his teeth in a humorless grin as Tobimar went on, "but Danrall is a *Shade*. Are you implying..."

"I imply nothing. I have seen this behavior in Colors, Hues, and Shades. Not—so far—in the Lights, but in honesty I will say that my contact with the Lights other than Miri has been limited."

Kyri looked more carefully at their companion. "Why do you bring this up? Why tell us, rather than Miri, for example?"

"Well, first," the *mazakh* said with a note of grim relief in his voice, "because until now I had found no confirmation of my senses. I am, perhaps, by far the most sensitive person in Kaizatenzei to such things, but that meant I had no one to compare my impressions with—at least, no one who would dare speak to me of these impressions. You, as independent forces with no knowledge of anything here, were perfect subjects. The fact that you instantly picked up on the same anomaly...that is tremendously important.

"Secondly, the mystery appears to touch upon most of our guardian forces. If it has not affected the Lights, I cannot discount the possibility that it *will* affect them—whatever it is. Yet who could I possibly find that would be formidable enough to survive the investigation—if there indeed *is* something wrong—and not already a part of the potential problem? Few other people of such skill and power are found here in Kaizatenzei who are not part of these forces." He gestured around the camp. "But you three... ahh, you are outsiders, unique, unknown, but—I now know from both my own observations and those of Lady Shae—of good heart and will. Thus I trust you, and hope you will trust me."

"Not to be a complete cynic," Poplock said, "but how do you know you can trust Lady Shae's judgment?"

Hiriista looked momentarily offended, then laughed, a hiss that echoed through the forest. "I suppose I should consider even *that* possibility...but no. In this case her judgment merely affirmed my own, and she had no way of knowing what I was looking for. I have my own ways of judging people, as you know. If she herself is the source, or a victim, she was not subject to it at that moment, and so I trust her senses; you are not agents of destruction but protectors."

Tobimar had been thinking while they spoke, and he didn't like where his thoughts were taking him. "If you've seen this on three of the four levels of your..."

"...*Tenzeitalacor*, or Unity Guard," Hiriista supplied helpfully.

"...Unity Guard, yes. If you've seen this on three of the four levels, is it your assumption that it affects most, if not all, of the people *on* those three levels—that is, most or all of the Colors, Hues, and Shades?"

"It is. I have seen it frequently enough that if I make some basic assumptions—drawn from my experiences—about how often the situations occur that cause this shift, then at least eighty percent of the *Tenzeitalacor* below the Lights are affected."

Tobimar nodded slowly. "I guess the next question is...do you have any reason to believe this is actually a *problem*?"

Hiriista opened his mouth to reply, and then stopped, his mouth still hanging open for several seconds before he slowly closed it, hissed, and then bobbed his head in a rocking motion before finally speaking. "I...confess that I do not, in fact, have any *evidence* that this is a problem. It *feels* wrong. I have no explanation for this that makes sense and is innocuous. Yet... no, I do not have any actual *reason* to believe that this anomaly is a problem, save only my own instincts." He hissed again, a whistling chuckle, and his own posture was turned inward, embarrassed. "I find myself most discomfited by this realization."

"You've never confronted any of them when you felt this... difference." It was a statement, not a question, and Kyri's voice was deadly serious.

"No...no, I have not. Both uncertainty and caution stayed me from that course of action."

"Instinct isn't something to be disregarded," Tobimar said. "If Phoenix sensed the same thing, and it made *her* uncomfortable too...?"

"It did," Kyri said emphatically. "I felt almost as though someone...or, even, some*thing*...much, much more aware and intelligent was watching me through Danrall." She frowned. "It was...familiar, almost. *Balance*, I can almost get it, but it's dancing just out of reach."

Hiriista cocked his head, more alert. "What? You have had this feeling before?"

"I think so. I think so." Kyri rapped her forehead as though to loosen something stuck there.

"It'll come to you," Tobimar said. "As I was saying—if she felt the same thing, and it worried *her*, then I think you're right to be cautious. We knew something was wrong in this place when we came here. I'd *hoped* it was something in the forest outside—"

"No," Hiriista said decisively. "No, I do not think so. Lady Shae believes so, but—in honesty—she almost *has* to believe that. She watches for threats *outside*; I think she does not believe, nor *want* to believe, that within Kaizatenzei itself there could be true evil. I myself do not *want* to believe it, but even the rather...edited version of events you have told us implies that your adversary Thornfalcon had an actual *contact* here, one who could supply him with the monsters you fought. No such organized power has ever been sensed, or even suspected, outside our walls. The only organization we know of...is here."

"Then seems to me that we have to assume the weirdness in

your Unity Guards is probably linked to what we're looking for," Poplock said. "And that it's not a good thing. So, if you've got that far, you *must* have some suspicion. It's either something working its way *up* through the ranks, bottom up, and nearing the top, or something sitting at the top running things. Which, I hate to say it, puts Lady Shae and Light Miri *right* at the top of my suspect list."

"I think you are only half right," Hiriista said, obviously restraining himself from further outrage on behalf of his ruler. "My suspicions are of something much worse, in a sense. Although having our most trusted ruler—"

"*THAT'S IT!*" Kyri shouted.

"What?"

"Trusted ruler, that's what. I used to feel *exactly* this kind of thing around one other person. I even *told* you about it, remember?"

A chill went down Tobimar's spine. "The *Watchland*."

"The Watchland. Watchland Jeridan Velion, the ruler of Evanwyl, most trusted man in the realm, a man I trusted almost without reservation...except on the days that I didn't feel I could trust him at all."

"Fascinating," Hiriista said. "The same feeling?"

"Almost identical, I would say." She shuddered suddenly, and Tobimar touched her arm in support. "Every so often I would feel that he was saying the same words, offering the same help, the same advice, and yet there was nothing true or real behind those words, just something else, cold and watching."

"And your Thornfalcon had a portal that led somewhere to here, from which came monsters. A definite connection between the countries." Hiriista looked out into the darkness, and despite his inhuman face Tobimar could plainly read his discomfort and fear.

"Master Wieran," Tobimar said.

Hiriista nodded with another hiss. "The aloof power neither above nor below. The creator of our Servants. The one—it is said—who helped devise the training of our Unity Guards. *That* is who I suspect—the one I *must* suspect—of whatever has been done to our people. He is in the perfect position, with the perfect knowledge, to tamper with people in such a fashion, and..."

Poplock tilted his body. "...and...?"

Hiriista looked down, then up. "And I have met him, twice. Both times he seemed reasonably courteous and attentive...but his body language radiated impatience, a complete lack of interest in the political and social interactions about him. It was very much as though he was given a script—or, more likely, had given *himself* a script—to appear the wise elder statesman, but had no more *understanding* of what such a person would really be like than would a *nalloshoth*."

He said no more immediately, and he didn't have to. If the ancient genius whose works were spread throughout Kaizatenzei—whose Servants performed half the work of the cities or more, whose training guided its defenders, whose other works commanded the respect of its rulers—was actually a monster who would work with Thornfalcon...

...then it wasn't just Kyri and Tobimar who were in danger. Not just Evanwyl.

It was all of Kaizatenzei, too.

CHAPTER 24

The misshapen creature—a deformed, monstrous hopclaw, he thought—shrank back as the moaning blade cut through the air. But Condor leapt completely over it, cutting off its escape. One clawed arm flew off, trailing blood. The other. The creature was screaming in terror and pain now, but Condor merely grinned and continued. *Try to ambush me? Learn what you pay in pain!*

Finally it was over—too soon, Condor thought. This unending trek through Rivendream seemed like a nightmare, no rest, nothing safe, even the *insects* more vicious than anything he'd ever encountered. So he'd become harder in return. *Take your amusement as you can. It's for sure nothing else will amuse me here!*

It dawned on him that the forest rising up before him was warmer, with more scent of wet and growth. A spurt of triumph went through him. "I *made* it!" he heard himself say. "I'm in Moonshade Hollow!"

The words, however, reminded him that no one had ever *returned* from this trip. And he was following someone who undoubtedly had gone *deeper* into the Hollow.

Phoenix.

He had only a vague idea of what Phoenix looked like—basically a description of the Raiment the Phoenix wore. But it didn't matter. A shivery, hot hatred and joy rose in him at the thought of what he would do to the unsuspecting Justiciar when he caught up. His hand caressed the hilt of the Demonshard and he thought he heard a second laugh echoing his own.

Was that a *tree* reaching towards him? Even as the laugh trailed off he drew the Demonshard and swung in a single motion; the black blade carved through reaching branch and yard-thick trunk as though they were barely there at all, and he stepped aside as the twitching, roaring forest giant crashed to the ground. "Any *others* wish a taste of my blade?" he demanded. The rustling was one of fear, of things that would flee if they could. He smiled. "I thought not."

The power of the Demonshard never ceased to amaze him. The sword supported him when he grew weary, gave him strength in battle, even guided his actions. Now he *knew* that he could defeat the Phoenix, even if they had been able to kill Thornfalcon. Why, once he'd *mastered* this blade...perhaps Thornfalcon's old patron could be removed as well...

He made his way through the forest, and the news seemed to have traveled before him; creatures slunk from his path, the trees themselves leaned away.

The problem was *finding* Phoenix. Being even a few days behind the rogue Justiciar and any allies Phoenix might have meant that any trail they left was effectively gone, erased by weather and growth and other creatures. But there *had* to be more here than just jungle; if he could just find someone, or something, to *talk* to...

Suddenly, in the slowly-falling gloom of night, something huge loomed up before him. He paused, squinting, then as his eyes adjusted realized that it was a *wall*—an immense barrier, smooth and hard, stretching as far as he could see to right and left.

"Well, now, *that* is certainly promising!" he said to himself. Anyone who could build a wall like *that* would know a lot about the region...and, just maybe, would have seen someone else passing by...

The problem was going to be getting *in*. There was probably a gate somewhere along the wall, but no telling how far away— or what guards might be there. He didn't want to necessarily announce his presence; if Phoenix had made contact, well, there was a good chance that he or she had also made a good impression. Might even, possibly, have told people about the Justiciars.

Better to get in secretly, scout things out first. Try not to kill anyone he didn't have to; that could be inconvenient.

The wall was small by some standards, he supposed, but fifty feet of greenish stone was more than enough of a barrier to daunt most people or monsters.

But most people were not Justiciars—real or false, both had vast power. And as Condor...

He felt a great...weight, a *pressure* that impeded his ability to draw on the power of his station. He gripped Demonshard and power flowed through it, into him, and he felt himself rising into the air. *This place actually fights against the power our patron gives us. What is Moonshade Hollow, and how is this possible?*

Still, he was rising into the air now, rising to the top of the wall. *Not too high. Just above, dart over and drop down. Be as hard to spot and track as possible.*

Level with the wall, he gathered himself, glanced to both sides to make sure there was no sign of an observer atop the wall, and then concentrated. *Full speed ahead—*

The impact with empty air was a shattering, tearing thing, something *clawing* at him with disorienting, vertiginous might that nearly sent him weaving away. Confused, unable to understand what was happening, he simply *drove* forward, trying to overpower this intangible, inescapable barrier of whirling, dizzying nausea and battering, insubstantial resistance.

With a sensation like tearing through a bramble hedge and a whirlpool simultaneously, he hurtled through, out of control, spiraling towards the ground; he was vaguely aware of smoke streaming from him, of agony burning through his entire body and soul. The ground rose and smashed into him like a bludgeon and he rolled over and over, trying clumsily to absorb the force of the fall and, mostly, failing.

He lay still for long moments, feeling the pain of burning and bruises and cracked or broken limbs. For a few breaths it felt to him as though he had come down in some vile swamp, a place filled with such foulness that it nearly choked him. He cried out and struggled vaguely, as though he could somehow push the air away from him.

Then something *snapped* within him, and abruptly—despite the very real pain of his fall—he felt himself more clearheaded than he'd been in...was it *weeks*?

The air about him was not foul; no, it was fresh, fresher than any he'd breathed in memory. Just the taste of the air in his lungs, the feel of the soft, warm breeze lifted his spirits, made the pain recede. He reached into his pack, found a healing draught, drank it down. As his injuries receded into memory, he took stock of his situation. *On the ground, surrounded by ruined greenery, that's not a surprise. Stars visible overhead. No sign of hostiles . . . and none of the feeling of menace I had in Rivendream Pass or that forest outside the wall.*

Condor stood slowly. Night birds sang softly, and the trees nearby did not move; they were stately and massive, radiating a feeling of stability and safety. It was a change as sharp as though he had stepped through a door from an icy mountain peak to the welcoming warmth of home, and he couldn't imagine how this was possible.

At the same time, it made him feel . . .

Suddenly a recent memory flashed through his mind: the cowering hopclaw, being carved apart . . . a laugh . . .

Aran, the Condor, found himself on hands and knees, the sharp, repellent stench of vomit rising from the ground before him. *What in the name of the Balance . . . ? What was I doing? What was I thinking?*

The strain of traveling through the monstrous Rivendream Pass had been great, but he'd walked through *Hell*—and then through the gates of the actual Black City itself. He hadn't turned into someone who would torture helpless creatures *then*, so . . .

He reached up, and realized the scabbard over his shoulder was empty. *Of course. I had the Demonshard in my hand when I came over, and then I crashed.*

It took only a few moments to find the great black sword, point-down in the ground about twenty yards off. Nearby, the grasses were black, and the night-noises went silent. He could feel the malevolence radiating from the ebon-glowing blade, and understood.

"You were *changing* me," he murmured angrily, and reached out, yanking the Demonshard from the ground.

Instantly a cold, hostile presence entered his mind—as, he now realized, it had been doing all along, for all the time he'd held it. But here, in this place of incredible purity, he could sense it clearly for the first time.

No, he said to the Demonshard.

It raged at him, then pleaded and bribed, reminding him of its strength, its powers, everything it could do for him.

"You will give me your powers. On *my* terms."

Now it cast aside any pretense, and Aran found he could not release the sword's hilt as dark, malevolent power trickled into him, oozing into his mind, seeking to surround and crush his will and make him back into the monster it had designed—that *Kerlamion*, he now realized, had designed him to be.

The fury at being used was a cleansing fire, and he drove back the Demonshard's insidious attack. "I am *not* your tool. I am not a pawn in anyone's game anymore! This is *my* vengeance, this is *my* mission, and you are here to serve *me!*"

The Demonshard did not, exactly, speak, but he could understand its outrage and contempt. "No, I'm not going to destroy my homeland, or anyone else's. I'm after the Phoenix, and that's *all* I'm after. When I go back to the Justiciars, I'll do it as *myself*, and if I decide I want to clean *that* house up, you'll help me do that, too!"

The Demonshard bent all its will against Aran's, and it was like bearing up the weight of an entire world, crushing down on Aran Condor as though there was no possibility of resistance.

But he remembered Shrike, the hidden gentle smile now gone to dust; he remembered his own anger and hatred of himself when he dared not act; he remembered the devastated face of Kyri Vantage and his own regrets that he had never spoken to her as he wished, and grabbed regret and anger and beauty and pulled it into himself, made himself greater and stronger with the oath to never yield, never give in, never compromise again.

"I gave up *everything*," he growled through gritted teeth. "I let them lead me on until I was a mockery of what I knew should be. So be it. But I was still *myself*, and I am still *myself*, and I will *remain* myself, no matter if you or your own dread maker and master were to try to undo me."

Slowly, one finger rose, loosening its grip on the hilt of the Demonshard.

"You are a *weapon*. You are *my* weapon and you will serve *me*, Demonshard! *I am no one's tool!*"

Two fingers, and the weight of the great blade made it tremble, near release. Desperate, the fragment of the sword of the King of All Hells exerted its full strength, trying to take control of Aran's body directly.

But that, too, would not work; Condor met that attempt with contemptuous anger and venom at being tricked, lashed it with his driving will until, without warning, his hand opened and the Demonshard fell back to the ground.

He glared down at the weapon, his mind now entirely free. "I am the master here. *Acknowledge me!*"

The Demonshard shimmered and the distant howl of obliterated air filled the space all about. But the anger of the sword faded before Condor's unwavering fury. "I need *a* weapon. But a weapon that thinks to wield *me* I do not need. Choose swiftly, or I shall leave you here and take my chances alone."

Slowly the Demonshard went quiet. Then it rose up and presented its hilt to him in silence. This time when he grasped the sword, he felt no hostility; only a grudging respect and concession.

"Good," he said. "Remember this well, Demonshard. For this *is* your last chance. If *ever* I suspect you are attempting to play me again, I shall dispose of you forever. There will be no more chances. Am I understood?"

The sensation was now more cowed and cautious.

"Good."

He sheathed the great bastard blade and looked around. The question now was... where to go?

After a moment's thought he shrugged. Without any other indication, why not just head straight away from the wall? The wall had to surround something, so heading towards the center should bring him towards at least some part of whatever the wall protected.

Even though the jungle here was little less dense than outside the wall, or on the other side of the mountains, it *felt* far different. Making his way through this wild tangle somehow did not drain him as it normally would; he felt as though he were taking a walk in a stunningly huge garden. The very idea of "danger" seemed distant indeed, and he wondered what kind of a place this was.

After almost an hour of walking, he saw the undergrowth thickening, but with signs of opening up beyond—the usual pattern near a clearing of some sort. Shoving his way through the dense border, Condor popped out of the jungle and found himself at the edge of a broad roadway, of carefully maintained stone, that ran roughly East-West, if he read the stars right.

Even as he made that judgment, he became aware that there was *movement* approaching him.

The moonlight made colors hard to make out, but he could see clearly that it was a small woman, a girl really, almost skipping along the road. Her hair was fair, probably golden blonde, and she wore peculiar-looking armor of crystal with other garments of a light and translucent material. She suddenly halted, staring, and then...well, *bounced* was the only description for it, she bounced forward, smiling broadly.

"Well met," she called out, and gave a strange, sweeping salute that caused the bow in her hair to bob. "Light Miri of the Unity greets you!"

CHAPTER 25

"Magewright Hiriista," the *Artan* said, his delicate features taut with concern, "I implore you and your companions to give us aid."

Hiriista cocked his head, and Tobimar thought there was a miniscule smile implied. "Perhaps if you were to state your problem, my companions Tobimar and Phoenix, and I, might be able to say if we *can* be of any assistance. Your face is somewhat familiar, but I regret to say I do not quite recall..."

"*Atcha!*" The sound was an explosive one of distress and self-reproach. "Many apologies, Magewright. I have been searching the Necklace for assistance and my mind is not focused or calm. I am Cirnala of Jenten's Mill."

"I recall Jenten's Mill—a village quite some miles north of here, approaching the shores of Enneisolaten—on a narrow inlet from the lake. You are one of Jenten's—the third of the name, I believe—hunters and warriors at need. Yes?"

"Exactly so!" Cirnala looked much relieved that Hiriista recalled so much already. "We are not large, only a few hundred people, but we have always done well and had no unexpected troubles..."

"Until now," Tobimar finished. "What is the problem?"

"Children," the *Artan* said quietly. "Children have been disappearing."

That was enough for all of them; Hiriista simply glanced at their expressions and nodded. "Lead on, Cirnala. Tell us the rest as we travel; it will be a few days to reach Jenten's Mill, and if children are at risk we should waste no time at all."

Tobimar could hear a particular emphasis in the *mazakh*'s voice, and suspected the reason. Hiriista had said that there were so few of his people in Kaizatenzei that they probably would eventually die out; it was likely, then, that their hatchlings were prized even more highly than they were normally. Anything threatening children...

"How did it start?" Kyri asked.

Cirnala's story was mysterious and chilling. A few months before, his cousin's son Tirleren had disappeared while playing in the forest near the inlet. A few weeks later, another child, this time a human girl named Demmi, vanished, also while playing. It emerged that Tirleren had claimed to have been playing with Demmi in the days before his disappearance, while Demmi said she hadn't seen him much beforehand, and that Demmi had claimed she was going off to play with an *Odinsyrnen* child named Hamule—who hadn't seen her on that day, or several other days Demmi had said she and Hamule were playing. This was verified by Jenten, the Reflect and grandson of the founder, who had seen Demmi go into the woods on her own, and Hamule's father, who had been fishing with her all day.

The town had of course immediately tried to keep an eye on all the children, making sure they were always escorted, and searched for any clue as to what could have lured the lost children away and misled them into thinking they were meeting with children that were elsewhere. No traces were found, however, except for a few personal possessions—Tirleren's fishing rod on the shore of a stream, Demmi's dagger in the middle of the woods. Tirleren's mother had descended into complete apathy, having lost her lifemate Siltanji only a few weeks before her son, and the entire village was in a state of near panic.

But panic can't be maintained forever, and in small villages even children have tasks to complete, so while they kept trying to maintain escort, it was inevitable that at some point they would be out of sight of someone. And a couple of weeks later, Hamule disappeared, between her front door and the Reflect's own home.

"And you have no clues? No monsters or creatures spotted in the area, no blood or trails, no one acting strangely?" Kyri asked carefully.

"No, we..." Cirnala trailed off. "Well... there is one thing."

"Don't hold us in suspense!" Tobimar said, as the *Artan* paused again.

"There is one person. His home is in the woods, outside of town, and not that far from where Tirleren and Demmi disappeared. He's refused to come into town during the emergency, and when we sent a delegation to talk to them, he *threatened* them. But..."

"These hesitations are useless," Hiriista said sharply. "What *is* it? Who is this person?"

"Zogen Josan," Cirnala said reluctantly.

Hiriista stumbled to a halt. "What? What did you say?"

"Zogen Josan," Cirnala repeated.

Hiriista stared. Tobimar finally nudged him. "What is it, Hiriista?"

"Zogen Josan was once the Color of Sha Alatenzei," Hiriista answered finally. "It is rare for any of the Unity Guard to retire in any manner than via funeral, but when he reached the age of forty-five years he did so. I remember the occasion well, it was quite an event in the capital—he was thanked for his service and he even gave a short speech, in which he said something like 'I'm quitting now while I'm still beating the odds, instead of the odds beating me. I hope you don't hold it against me.' That was only ten years ago. Always cheerful, like most Colors, a magnificent warrior, spent more than twenty years as the protector of the Earthlight City..." The *mazakh* shook his head. "That he would not be helping, and instead refusing contact..."

"If you knew him, did you ever notice anything...unusual about him?" Tobimar asked carefully. They didn't want to reveal their particular concerns, but in this context the question shouldn't be revealing.

Hiriista glanced at him with a neutral expression, and only said, "Not that I can recall; he was as most others of the Unity Guard in that regard."

And by his estimation "most others" of the Unity Guard have shown the behavior that he and Kyri noted. So I can take that as a "yes."

"Now you comprehend our problems, sir. Do you think you can help?"

"I think I *must* help," Hiriista said flatly. "My companions—"

"—feel the same way. And if this *does* somehow involve a former Color, I presume he would be extremely formidable."

"Undoubtedly why they sent Cirnala looking for help. Alas

that the farcallers are so difficult to make; it would be useful to
have them in all towns and villages as well as the major cities."
Cirnala nodded.

"Did Zogen Josan only begin acting oddly after these disappearances began?" Kyri asked. "After all, I suppose that if mysterious disappearances started happening, some people might
get nervous."

"A former *Color*, become nervous over such things? That
seems unlikely," Hiriista said skeptically. "What would you say
to a similar statement about one of your Justiciars, Phoenix?"

"A point. Cirnala?"

The *Artan* hesitated again, then shook his head. "No, Phoenix. I am afraid not." He looked to the north, as though hoping
impossibly to see his village ahead of them. "At first, we were
overjoyed at the thought that a former Color would be retiring
to Jenten's Mill. And for the first...oh, year, he was everything
we hoped—helpful, multitalented, hard-working. But then..."

He shook his head helplessly. "He just slowly seemed to...
fade. Or retreat. Sometimes he'd still come out to help when
needed, and he didn't seem any less capable, but he'd be quiet,
not joking or laughing or staying any longer than he had to.
Zogen would just go back to his home in the woods and stay
there. He didn't even trade in town much anymore—just hunted
and fished alone. The children—" his breath caught, then he
continued, "the younger children, the ones who hadn't seen him
early on...they called him 'Shadowman' because he would come
and go through the woods like a shadow. He was...their scary
story, I guess. Though not scary enough to keep them out of the
woods, and several of them said that if they actually *met* him
in the woods he was quite kind—helped them find berries, gave
back toys they lost, things like that."

"Did he get any worse?" Tobimar asked, guessing what that
poke from Poplock meant.

"Recently, yes. Jenten went by to see how he was after we'd
had one nasty incursion, just a few weeks before all this started,
and he reported that Zogen *threatened* him—even loosed fire at
him—to keep him away from the cabin."

The three exchanged glances. It sounded like a case of mental deterioration—someone who started out reasonably sane but
something went wrong and then they steadily and unstoppably

degenerated until they were completely insane. In the State of the Dragon King or even in Skysand there were usually ways to stop or even reverse this, especially with the help of the priests or mages, but here that didn't seem likely.

Especially—now that he noticed—that the supernal *rightness* of Kaizatenzei was fading. *We're between cities, where their influence is weakest, where the Seven Stars did not reach.*

Where there can truly be monsters.

"Were there any more disappearances?" Kyri asked after a moment.

"Another little boy—one that, as you might guess, Hamule had said she was playing with, disappeared the day before I left. He was with his parents visiting with the Reflect and his family, and vanished while he was playing *inside* the mansion. A side door was found open and running footprints going into the forest could be distinguished on the ground. There *were* some other marks on the ground farther in but they could not be distinguished clearly enough to make any sense of them." Cirnala sighed. "And since it will have been more than a week since I've been gone, I suppose another child may have been taken."

"Tell me truly; they were already speaking before you left of Zogen being the one responsible, yes?" Hiriista asked.

"Yes, Magewright."

A long hiss escaped the *mazakh*'s lips. "Then it will not be long before they overcome their fear of the strength of a Color and decide to use sheer numbers to put a stop to this. If they are wrong and, somehow, Zogen Josan is not to blame, an innocent man will be killed, and if they are right, Zogen will kill many of them...perhaps *all* of them...before it is over."

"*All* of them?" Kyri repeated incredulously.

"It is...possible. If he has fortified his home and is prepared..." Hiriista shook his head and his whole body followed suit.

"Then we'd better hurry," Tobimar said, and picked up the pace.

"We *will* hurry," Kyri said, and her voice was chilled steel. "And we will put an *end* to this, before any more innocents are killed."

CHAPTER 26

The echoing, many-layered murmur ahead of them was unmistakable; they had heard something similar on the day they had—with Xavier—confronted Bolthawk and Skyharrier. It was a crowd, perhaps a mob.

Hiriista broke into a trotting run, his tail held high, head maintaining a steady level to guide him. Kyri sprinted alongside of him. *Please, Myrionar, let us be in time!*

The forest opened up ahead, and they found a cluster of buildings—a moderate-sized mansion to the far right on a rise, houses and small shops a bit below it, docks and boathouses and other buildings at the edge of a rippling sheet of water that extended and widened to the north, where more forest closed in beyond the town.

Filling the main intersection, a sort of rough rectangle, was a mass of people; Kyri guessed it at over a hundred, and all of them were armed. As they approached, she could hear murmurs and shouts in which Zogen Josan's name was recognizable, and not in a good way.

Cirnala stumbled up behind them, pushed past as the two slowed. "Let me . . . tell them you are here . . ."

The *Artan* took a deep breath and shouted, "*LISTEN!*"

His voice was startlingly powerful for his slender frame, and heads immediately turned in their direction. A murmur went up, and, gratefully, Kyri heard the angry rumblings subsiding, giving way to surprise and curiosity.

"Cirnala! You're just in time!" The speaker was a tall, very handsome human who appeared to be in his late fifties, with his graying black hair and sharp black eyes that glanced in the direction of the other travelers before returning to the exhausted *Artan*. "We were just about to go confront Zogen."

"I've brought . . . help," Cirnala said, still catching his breath. "To solve the mystery."

"No need to solve it anymore," said a woman with dark brown hair, hefting an axe that looked almost as large as Shrike's had been. "Saw him, Nimelly did—Zogen Josan, running into the woods with Abiti under his arm!"

"Abiti! Oh, Light, no." Cirnala was mometarily stunned.

"That's why we can't wait any longer," the older man said. "But we'll be glad of any help."

Hiriista bowed to him. "Magewright Hiriista of Sha Murnitenzei."

"I have heard your name, Magewright. Reflect Namuhan Jenten; I welcome you to my small village."

Kyri had suspected this was the Reflect from the way the others had instantly parted to let him through. He seemed naturally in charge. She thought his bow was a trifle stiff and hurried, but given the circumstances that wasn't surprising.

Hiriista gestured to them. "My companions are guests and welcomed as equals by Light Miri and the Lady Shae herself, for they have come to us through the Pass of Night from the world beyond." Eyes widened and breaths caught at that statement, as the *mazakh* magewright continued, "Warrior of Justice and Vengeance, the Phoenix, and her companion, Tobimar. They are here to assist as well."

"As I said, welcome indeed. I will not pretend that the thought of assaulting a former Color of the Unity is less than tragedy . . . or less than terrifying." The others were getting restless, but the Reflect held up a hand. "And justice and vengeance surely is what we need here."

An opening. "Then allow me to go first, sir. I am the Phoenix Justiciar of Myrionar, and my god's first directive and highest duty is to apply wisdom and mercy to arrive at justice, and when justice demands, to deliver the vengeance of the gods. I have seen the things your Unity Guard face, and I have survived the forest that surrounds Kaizatenzei; my friends and I may survive a confrontation with this Zogen Josan far more easily than would your people, who are—if I see aright—mostly unused to such combat."

The head tilted slightly, but then nodded. "You see truly. We have a few warriors...but none trained with the Unity Guard, and what little we know of Zogen is fearsome. Very well; if Cirnala has come so far, so fast, to bring you here, and you are vouched for by the Magewright and the Lady herself, I yield gladly the forefront. But I hope you are ready—"

Kyri was already striding in the direction of the forest; she could tell that Tobimar and Hiriista were right behind her. "Children are missing; of course I am ready." Cirnala had told them roughly where the retired Color's cabin was, and as she expected the *Artan* quickly jogged up to guide them.

The villagers—*not so much a mob now, thank the Balance!*—trailed close behind, with the Reflect leading them. "This Abiti—boy or girl?" she asked.

Cirnala closed his eyes as if in pain briefly. "Daughter of Genata and Ivilit—they run the local tavern, great favorites of everyone as you might guess, and Abiti was... *is* a charmer. Fearless girl, helped track the depthshade just a few weeks before this happened."

The "depthshade," Kyri remembered, was the local name for a crocodilian monstrosity which was equally at home in water or on land, with legs suited for running as well as swimming. It had been lurking around Jenten's Mill for weeks, apparently, ambushing sithigorn chicks, young forest antelope, and herd calves until someone noticed the reduction in livestock and a hunt was organized—a hunt that cost more than just the life of the monster.

One more reason for us to go first. If hunting even a local predator is dangerous enough that some of the locals get killed, fighting a trained warrior of this Unity Guard would be much worse.

She remembered that Hiriista had said Zogen might kill *all* of those who came after him. *That puts him up on our level, maybe better. And I am weaker here.*

She concentrated, *dragging* the power down through whatever monstrous resistance it was that nearly blocked her connection to Myrionar. But drag it she did, and she felt the strength building up within her. *I'll be prepared as well as I can by the time we get there.*

"Zogen will be expecting some kind of assault from the village by now," Tobimar said quietly. "Wouldn't you say so, Cirnala?"

A reluctant nod. "Probably, yes."

Kyri understood what he was getting at. "Then can you and the others stay back? Not only will it be safer...but if anyone can somehow talk to him, get some sense out of him, won't it be someone he doesn't think is pre-judging him?"

Cirnala's face wrinkled in surprise. "Well...I hadn't thought of that. But—"

"I can understand reluctance—and obviously the Reflect and the rest of you have a feeling of responsibility. But if you're right, he has at least one child now, perhaps *still* has the others. If it begins with an assault, might he not use the children as a defense?"

The Reflect had overheard them. "A grim thought, but true enough. But if you take too long, he might do more."

"If we can keep him talking, he will be less able to do anything else, I think. Especially if he is trying to understand who we are and what we're doing here," Tobimar said.

The Reflect hesitated, then took a pained breath. "My heart screams out that I must run forward...but your words ring true." His dark eyes measured both of them. "Very well. We shall wait at the gray stump—it is well out of sight of the cabin, but if battle is joined we can hasten to your aid in moments. I cannot guarantee how *long* I can hold my people back, you understand."

Kyri grasped his hand impulsively and bowed over it. "*Thank* you, Reflect. I understand entirely. Honestly, if we cannot reach him, or find some advantage, in a relatively few minutes...I think there will be no need to hold any back."

His startled face creased in a momentary smile, and his returning grip was powerful. "Then I wish you luck; I hope for a way out of this horror."

The three of them—four, counting the generally-unnoticed Toad—moved forward past the stump; while there were some murmured protests, Kyri felt great relief as the crowd stopped, many of them looking relieved themselves that their confrontation with an ex-Color was postponed. *Myrionar, show me the way. Let us find a way to prevent any more deaths. Let us find a way to save that child, or all the children if they still live.*

"So, want me to do some scouting?" Poplock said as soon as they were out of earshot.

Hiriista blinked, even as both Kyri and Tobimar grinned savagely. "I did not fully comprehend the other advantage of your size, little Toad, but now I do. While we confront Zogen, you will gain entrance and find out the truth within."

"If that's Phoenix's plan."

"It is *exactly* Phoenix's plan, Poplock. If we can get his attention, get in, find out what you can, and get back fast. We'll keep him talking."

"Got it."

She turned to the *mazakh*. "Does Zogen know you?"

"Oh, certainly. We weren't *close* friends, but casual friends, good acquaintances and colleagues in a way; I have been one of the major consultants for the Unity Guard as they traveled through Sha Murnitenzei for the last, oh, twenty-five years, and often travel with them for various missions."

"Good. Good. That might just give us an opening." They could see the retired Color's cabin now—a large construction of logs with multiple sections, obviously several rooms. *Pretty good-sized house.*

"How do you mean that?"

Kyri felt her face going cold. "I was thinking on the way here. What could make a man like Zogen Josan, the one you described at his retirement and evidently the one they saw here for a while, change, retreat like that? And after our other conversations, the first thing I thought of was...what if he felt there was something *wrong* with him?"

A slow hiss. "You mean...what if he somehow sensed or acknowledged whatever it is that we have noticed in the others. He is retired, no longer active. Perhaps in the slow passing of peaceful days, with no activities to distract him...yes."

"A good thought, Phoenix," Tobimar said. "And you have a plan?"

"Sort of. I'm playing this by heart, not head. Just...follow my lead."

He touched her arm and smiled. "Always."

She smiled back, then turned to the silent cabin. "Zogen! Zogen Josan, once-Color of the Unity Guard, I would speak with you!"

Her voice echoed through the forest, more powerful than any ordinary human voice, and forest-sounds momentarily quieted in its wake.

A moment went by. Two. Then, as she was about to call again, a voice answered from the cabin, a deep but weary voice. "You are not from the Mill. Surprising. But perhaps no less enemies, for that. Who are you?"

"I am the Phoenix, Justiciar of the god Myrionar, patron of Justice and Vengeance." As she spoke, she saw a tiny flicker of motion, a scuffle of leaves; Poplock was on his way.

"Myrionar...I have not heard that name. And a strange title you have. As to justice, alas, I fear no justice can be found here."

She beckoned to Hiriista, who stepped fully into view, saying, "Zogen, do you know *me*?"

"Magewright? Magewright *Hiriista*? Could that be...?" The incredulous voice suddenly hardened. "But no. It would be too glad a coincidence, too fine a chance." The voice wavered, hope and fear evident. "But if you are... If you truly be Hiriista, then tell me, what words did I speak to you in Sha Alatenzei, when we stepped from a particular drinking establishment?"

Hiriista tilted his head, then suddenly gave vent to a steam-kettle laugh. "You opened your mouth, yes, but it was not words that came out! And then you fell nigh-senseless and I had to carry you to your room in the Steamvent Inn."

There was a faint sound, as of a man dropping heavily into a chair. "*Light*...it *is* you, isn't it? But..." the suspicion was back. "Those with you...they must be Unity Guard, then."

"Do we *look* like Unity Guards?" Tobimar asked quietly.

"No...no, you do not. There is something strange indeed about you. I know not the workmanship on your armor, Phoenix, nor the pattern of your clothing, young man."

Kyri shook her head, trying to make sense of this. *His voice is tense, exhausted...near the edge of a breakdown. Yet he does not speak as a madman. At the same time, there was a witness to him actually abducting a child.*

"That," Hiriista said, "is because you see before you far travelers indeed: Phoenix and her friend Tobimar hail from beyond the great mountains, through the Pass of Night; Lady Shae herself has looked into them and seen their truth."

Truth. That's it! I've never tried it...but I know it can be done. She concentrated, let the power she had been gathering flow into her. *Myrionar, give me your eyes and ears. Let me see what truly* is, *not what others desire I see, nor what my own beliefs would like to see. Let me hear the truth, and be deaf to falsehoods.*

She sagged as though a massive weight had landed on her; the power she had gathered before was suddenly all needed merely to *support* her as she was forced to reach out, grasp the distant power, yank it towards her, an effort like dragging granite boulders. *Myrionar, I had never realized... the* POWER *needed for the truth-sight.* Only the mighty prayer and miracle she had called forth on the night of her defeat of Thornfalcon, when she shattered a mystic Gateway and evaporated an almost uncounted host of foes, had demanded more focus and power from both her and Myrionar. And it was *harder* here, even harder than it had been in Rivendream Pass, harder even than her sensing for hidden evil in Sha Murnitenzei, for truth-telling meant discerning the secrets hidden in another soul without injury—in short, seeing into that strange place beyond the living realm where the real and the possible intersected and tracing those threads, rather than seeking to break the target's will. *That suppressing power is stronger, much stronger here. And it is darker here, not even merely less good. This is a dangerous place.*

Zogen Josan had recovered from the expected surprise. "This is truth? Do you swear it, Hiriista? Swear by the Light that these are no Unity Guards nor any of their servants, but new-come heroes from beyond the Pass?"

Hiriista's voice was puzzled, but at the same time Kyri heard relief in it—relief that his old acquaintance seemed willing to talk, might be able to be reached. "I swear it, in the name of the Light in the Darkness, the Seven Lights and the One Light, by my Oath and by my Family."

"Then... then I believe you. I have to believe someone can be trusted. But... but I think it is too late, far too late."

"Maybe not, Zogen Josan," Kyri said, the power finally come into her. She saw the world now as though it was both brighter and darker than before, flickering with strange fire, whispering hints of words. "But I must ask you. Did you kill any of the children that have disappeared?"

"No!" The voice was emphatic. "I have killed no children! I would *never* do anything like that!"

The first part was true; she could *hear* the truth in it, the rightness in the statement like the beauty of a pitch perfect note.

But the second part sounded a hair off, the glow was dimmed, grayish. *Why would he say he has killed none of them, yet be less sure of what he would do? Does he doubt himself?*

"But you were seen *taking* a child today."

"To *protect* them!" Zogen said emphatically. He had come forward, and she could now see him, a tall black-haired man with a haggard, drawn face that must normally be quite handsome. "Though I fear there is nothing I can do to save them."

And the truth, twice more. She knew she could not keep this power up much longer.

"What are you afraid of, Zogen Josan?" she asked finally. "What makes you fear to trust your comrades, your Reflect... and yourself?"

The former Color's breath caught; the gasp was audible from where they stood. There was a long, long pause. Then, finally, he spoke, in a voice so low she could barely hear it.

"Sometimes I would look in the mirror and not know, exactly, where I had gotten the bruises I saw. And then I would forget them, and not wonder. And other times, I would remember doing something, yet the memory did not always ring true, as though I had seen it, but was as though I had stood outside myself, watching."

Ice trailed down her spine, for she recalled the Watchland's own words: "...for many of the last few days I have felt almost outside myself, watching what I have been doing..." And the Truth of Zogen's words was undeniable.

"And," he continued, "and sometimes I have seen my friends, and for a moment... wondered about them. Wondered if they were as they seemed. And as I thought of these things, I was more and more sure that many of my deeds were just shadows of truth, and I have had nightmares of *other* things. Places of terror I have never seen in waking, things that hide behind faces I trust, but are not what they seem. And I know now that one of them is *here*."

The Sight was gone now, but she was sure that he was telling the truth as he knew it. "How do you know, Zogen?"

"I knew there was something wrong, even before Tirleren vanished, so I started watching the children in the woods. Watching, making sure they were safe, I thought... but I didn't understand, not then. Only after he disappeared did I guess... but I could not be sure, for I found him too late."

"Found him?" she repeated, even as she felt something small scuttle up her armor.

"Yes. In the wood, near the town. But I still didn't *know*..."

"Five children," Poplock's voice said softly in her ear. "Tied up downstairs and secured in cages. But something's funny about a couple of them, I think. Didn't dare poke around long—there were all kinds of weird crystals and things that might have been wards and such."

"What didn't you know? Zogen, why did you take the children?"

"I found out what was trying to take them. All of them were being brought to him."

She suddenly connected little pieces of Cirnala's story and with a sinking feeling in her gut knew what Zogen was going to say... and who it was coming just now up behind her, emerging from the forest...

"They were being brought to the Reflect," Zogen said, and his breath suddenly caught.

Kyri looked back.

Reflect Jenten stood there, the entire mob just behind him.

CHAPTER 27

Tobimar tensed, and began to bring up the High Center. *If things go bad, we will need all my skill. I don't know exactly what Kyri was doing there, but I could tell she just pushed herself a long ways.*

Poplock scuttled up his leg, even as Reflect Jenten spoke. "You imply that *I—*"

Kyri stepped between the house and the Reflect. "Both of you, pause a moment, before accusations and fear drive you to actions that will end in tragedy. Please—let me see if I can untangle this, for I think the truth is more strange than any of us know."

As Kyri continued, Poplock relayed his information about the children. *Locked up* and *restrained? What possible reason could this man have for such actions?*

The crowd murmured, and there was a dark tone to their words. A faint sound from the cabin, perhaps inaudible to any save Tobimar as his senses extended, told him that the ex-Color had drawn a large blade. Then he saw the Reflect's eyes narrow, but the man left his hand on the hilt of his weapon, and did not draw it, as he studied the three figures before him.

"As you will, Phoenix," he said finally. "But bring your light to this swiftly, for I have no patience for those who would accuse me of atrocity, and none of us have any for those who harm children."

"I thank you, Reflect, and I understand," Kyri said. Her voice was respectful and cautious, the tone of someone walking on eggshells. *This isn't like Evanwyl, where everyone had known her*

199

since she was a child, would give her any benefit of the doubt, and she knows it. "First, while I wish to be clear that I do not suspect you, I think you should realize that even in the scant evidence the three of us have heard, there is some just reason to wonder. May I present those points to you, understanding that I mean only to point out the potential for such a perception?"

The Reflect's eyebrows rose. "Truly? You think you have heard evidence that could be taken against *me*? Very well, speak."

Kyri stood taller, and her demeanor was now more of a judge reviewing evidence and measuring the accused. "For the initial disappearance none could give evidence as to exactly when or where it occurred. But of the other four, what can we say? If I believe the testimony I have heard, there is this: the last one to have claimed to have seen Demmi alive was you, Reflect Jenten, who said that you had seen her go into the woods alone; Hamule was said to have disappeared between her home and your home, Reflect; the fourth child, whose name I have not yet been told—"

"Minnu," Cirnala said, looking thoughtful.

"—Minnu, then, disappeared from within your house; I do not know if there is a connection to you with the last child, Abiti—"

Now a few of the crowd were looking at the Reflect, and Jenten's own face was less confident and sure. "Yes," said the woman with the huge axe. "Nimelly—the one who told us that Zogen had taken Abiti—is Jenten's Head of House."

Now pale, Jenten glared at Kyri, and Tobimar's grip tightened on his swords, even as the Skysand prince started to see the entirety of the pattern. "You said you would not accuse me, yet your words seem woven to do precisely that!"

"Hold, sir," Tobimar raised one hand. "She simply wished to show that it would be easy for someone looking at the pattern to come to the conclusion that you *were* to blame. But there is more to it—much more to it—than that. Especially in the first few instances, the children were off with others—who specifically denied being there, later. Yes?"

Jenten and the crowd shifted, realizing that Kyri had meant her words and that there was no immediate accusation of their leader. "Yes," Cirnala said.

"And is it possible that Jenten was with the children during those times? Or is it not the case that Reflect Jenten has far too many responsibilities to be able to be absent from view so often?"

Startlingly, Zogen replied from within his cabin. "That…that is exactly the case. The Reflect would have been often busy, with many people around him, on the days that the children were playing in the woods."

"Yessss," Hiriista said, nodding. "And consider: at least three of our victims spoke of meeting someone else, several times. A *different* 'someone else,' for each child, over a period of time. Even the other disappearances did not happen instantly, but over a period of time." He looked sharply at Cirnala. "Tell me, the depthshade that was killed—had it taken any adult creatures— aged, crippled, otherwise easy prey?"

The others blinked at this sudden shift of questioning, but Cirnala simply looked up and away, thinking.

The connection was suddenly clear to Tobimar, and he felt Poplock's grip on his shoulder tighten. Kyri's expression became marble-cold.

"No," Cirnala said finally. "No, Magewright; only young animals."

"And each separated by at least a week of time."

"Yes," the Reflect said, understanding coming into his voice. "Are you saying what I believe you are, Magewright?"

"That this is a continuation of the same problem? Yes, I think so. Creatures such as the depthshade are like many other such creatures; they wait in ambush and take the unwary, the unprotected, the alone. They do not choose only one sort of creature, it matters not to them. And while sithigorn chicks are often numerous enough in a brood that they are likely to be caught alone, both forest antelope and your usual herd animals keep the young and mothers to the *center* of a herd. The opportunities to take such young prey are very limited unless…unless you had the ability to convince your prey that you were not a predator."

"But it *was* the depthshade!" burst out another man, tall and gaunt. "We set the watches, *caught* it as the little calf came down to the water." Then he paused. "Came down to the water…alone. Without its mother, without any others of the herd."

Exactly. "Then what we are dealing with," Tobimar said with growing conviction, that feeling of *rightness* that his *Tor* training provided emphasizing his words, "is a creature that targets the young, that can trick others into perceiving them as one of their own kind, that requires some level of time and preparation of the victim—at least by preference—and that uses other creatures as its agents. The depthshade was such an agent or, in truth, a victim, as is whoever the thing is using now."

"But why just the young?" the Reflect asked. "And how is it that this thing was using the depthshade?"

"What happened to the depthshade's corpse?" Kyri asked, cutting short a desperate poking of Tobimar's neck by Poplock. *I guess she's asking the question the Toad wanted asked.*

"Brought to my home to be prepared for mounting as a trophy for the village," the Reflect said, "Immediately after the kill."

"And was there anything unusual about the corpse when it was being prepared?"

The Reflect shrugged, then looked into the crowd. "Nostag, you were preparing it for display."

The tall, dark, broad-shouldered man nodded emphatically. "Indeed I was, sir, once the immediate prep had been done by your household. There *was* one oddity. Rear of the skull, remember?"

"Ahh, yes. We thought it had been injured there not long before, explaining why it decided to stay here and try for easy prey." He looked back to their party. "There were three small holes at the base of the skull, and some a bit lower down on the spine."

Exactly. "We are dealing with something like an *itrichel*, as my people call them—I've heard them called mindworms and brain-riders, too," Kyri said, echoing Tobimar's own realization. "But this one's worse, with abilities I've never heard of. I can't imagine why—"

"*Enneisolaten,*" Hiriista said bluntly. "The great lake is not named 'Sounding of Shadows' for no reason; there is great beauty about its shores, and nearby, but it seems great darkness lurks somewhere in its depths. Abominations sometimes crawl from below, and indeed they are often versions of other monsters made worse. Finding a way to cleanse the shadows from the lake is one of Lady Shae's great quests."

"It doesn't matter," Kyri said. "Not now, anyway. The important thing is that someone in your household, Reflect, ended up the next host of the *itrichel*. I don't *think* it can be you—it would most likely be one of those involved in the handling of the depthshade immediately after it was captured and killed. But if what I've heard of these monsters is right, we know why it went after young animals and children."

"*Incubators,*" Hiriista said, the last *s* trailing off in a hiss.

"It uses the young's strength and growing spirit to provide the perfect environment to grow its brood."

"By the Light," Cirnala said, and the faces around showed their horror. "That means that the children—"

"You have it!" Zogen shouted, and the door swung open. "They've been sick, all of them, but they've been getting violent—"

"You *have* the children and you never *told* us?!" the Reflect's hand went to his sword-hilt.

"I didn't know if I could trust *anyone!*" Zogen snapped back.

"Come on!" Kyri said, striding towards Zogen. "Enough time for recriminations later! We have to help those children now, before it's too late!"

Hiriista and Tobimar followed, but Hiriista's tense walk and muttered words gave Tobimar a cold feeling. "For some, it has been many weeks. If the brain-rider has had so long to grow and be established..."

"I will *not* let children die," Kyri's voice was cold iron. "If they still live now, then I say that Myrionar will *forbid* them from dying. It would be *unjust* for us to have solved the riddle and still fail to save them."

Beneath Zogen Josan's cabin was a surprisingly large basement, hewn by impressive effort from the rock and earth and well furnished. The furnishings, however, had been hastily rearranged, and five cages were set along the far wall. They were well-made cages, and cushioned, not rudely fashioned or uncomfortable, but Tobimar could see they were strong and secured on the outside by locked steel clips.

Kyri glanced grimly at the children restrained within them, and suddenly went pale. "*Ur-Urelle?*"

The far right cage had a young *Artan* boy in it...but at the same time, Tobimar felt a...*pressure* that had no physical source, a *push* inside his head that came up hard against the discipline of High Center. But though there was a momentary blurring, a hint of other features, he saw only the young boy. At the same time, Kyri's expression showed that she saw someone she recognized. Which was of course impossible.

"Unless your 'Urelle' is an *Artan* child, she's not there," Tobimar said quietly.

Kyri shook her head, then glared at the end cage. "So. The last evidence we needed."

"That's new," Zogan said. "Tirleren was the worst off, but projecting a different seeming? No."

"If it can do that, it is nearing maturity," Hiriista said bluntly. "I am afraid the host is ... unsalvageable." His voice was cold, filled with anger and helplessness.

"We are not separate," Tirleren said. "We are one, now. If I leave him, he will die." The smile that suddenly appeared was more a rictus, something aping the expression but not quite familiar with how it was done. "Of course I will leave soon anyway."

"Soon," agreed a little human girl in the third cage. *That must be the second victim, Demmi.*

A third child, a Child of Odin, looked vaguely puzzled, as though there was some thought or idea that was just coming to him, while the other two were horrified. "No, no, I don't want to have something in my head!" the little boy—*Minnu?*—said tremulously.

"Don't worry," Kyri said, taking off her helm and putting it down. "I'll take care of it. It's going to be all right. Even for you, Tirleren."

For an instant, Tirleren's face showed a flash of horror and hope, and then went back to cold watchfulness. "Separate us and he dies. I will not."

"Whether or not he *does* die," Reflect Jenten said, "I assure you, you *will* die, no matter what tricks you might have to escape. Correct, Zogen?"

The ex-Color straightened. "Correct, Namuhan," he said, using the Reflect's first name in return.

"Hiriista, do you have anything that could help?"

The *mazakh* swayed his head doubtfully, but pulled out a red vial of liquid, and fished a particular green-glittering amulet from within his assortment of jewelry. "This may suffice for the least-affected. But I very gravely doubt that anything can be done for Demmi and Tirleren, save to ... end this."

Cirnala turned away at those words.

"*Try,*" Kyri said. "Try, and I will do the rest."

"What can you do, if even the Magewright believes it is impossible?" Cirnala said, his quiet voice filled with hopelessness.

Kyri's head came up, and Tobimar saw a faint golden glow about her. "All I can do is have faith. But what I have faith *in* is Myrionar, and I do not believe It will allow such injustice this day."

Hiriista gazed at her, then sighed and nodded. "I will require each of them to drink a portion of this restorative. To get at least those two to drink will require force."

Tirleren's eyes narrowed, and his eyes momentarily showed a yellowish cast, even a faint glow. "Oh, yes, try that."

"Don't let him intimidate you," Kyri said. "The *itrichel* isn't yet full-grown. If we hadn't forced the issue, it would not have revealed itself—just used its powers to get Zogen to release it and the other four once it *was* full-grown."

Cautiously, Zogen opened Tirleren's cage.

As the door came fully open, Tirleren's arms tore free of their bindings and whipped out, sending Zogen tumbling away. Tirleren leapt from the cage, shredding the bindings on his legs, straight for Kyri.

Kyri's gauntleted hand caught the mindworm-possessed *Artan* in midair and held him high, with scarcely a sign of effort as he hammered uselessly at Phoenix's hand and forearm. *I'd forgotten how* strong *she is. That's the legendary Vantage strength they talk about in Evanwyl—and if he can't break her arm through the Raiment, he's got nothing to give him leverage.* "Now."

Tobimar had already increased his own strength and speed, and saw both Zogen and the Reflect stepping up to help. Between the three of them, they were able to use leverage of their own to restrain Tirleren and force his mouth open. Hiriista poured a small portion of liquid from the vial into Tirleren's mouth and poked the throat in a fashion that forced a reflexive swallow.

Instantly Tirleren went nearly limp, twitching. Hiriista looked grave, but had them repeat the maneuver for Demmi. Hamule, the little Child of Odin, was able to force herself to sit still for the dosing, and while she looked to be in terrible pain didn't seem in as much distress as the other two; both Minnu and Abiti took their doses easily.

Then Hiriista took up the green-stone amulet. "By Ocean and Forest, let impurity be banished!"

Emerald light blazed from the stone and exploded into the five children. Hiriista held the stone in a deathgrip, scales standing up around his hand from the tension, and *drove* the power forward.

All five screamed, but those of Demmi and Tirleren were shrieks of tearing agony. *Something* rose up in that forest-green light, five *somethings* struggling and scrabbling with multiple pairs of legs to hold on as they were rejected by the bodies they had inhabited, creatures not entirely solid nor entirely immaterial being ripped from the napes of the childrens' necks. Tirleren's was the largest, the length of Tobimar's forearm and giving vent to its own high-pitched keening of pain and fury; Demmi's was only slightly smaller.

Shades paler than normal, Zogen Josan and the Reflect stepped forward as one, and blades leapt from their scabbards; the floating creatures were sundered instantly in a pair of mirrored strokes.

Hiriista's light faded. Minnu and Abiti lay crying, Hamule was barely conscious, but the other two were sagging down as though nothing was left.

Kyri caught the two before their heads hit the floor, gazed at them, and put her hands on the two. "Myrionar, hear me. Heal these children, innocent victims of monsters who sought more than their mere deaths."

The golden, singing light of Myrionar answered her, and Tobimar once more felt the rush of awe that power inspired. He had seen it more than once, but there was something *different* about it that made even great magics less impressive by comparison. You *knew* that you saw the power of a god in action.

But in his current state, seeing with the High Center through his trained senses, he saw something else; Kyri's power poured into the two bodies, and most of it was pouring out again. "Phoenix! Something's wrong!"

Kyri's shoulders tightened. "I . . . see it. These monsters . . . wove into their souls, not just their bodies. These are soul wounds, their very essences ripped apart. I should have suspected it."

"Then . . ."

"Then I have to do something else."

The auric aura flared higher, filled the entire room with the tingling power of Myrionar, and he could see something else happening; a weave of golden energy, extending from Kyri, twining about the shining but tattered spirits of the children. *By Terian, what's she doing? How can she be pulling that much power from Myrionar here, when—*

No. Oh, by the Light in the Darkness, she's not getting it from Myrionar . . .

"Stop, Phoenix!" he shouted, barely keeping himself from using her real name. "Stop! You can't tear your own soul apart to—"

"I *swore* I would not let this happen! And it *can* work, I know it can! I saw the Arbiter—"

He remembered her story—and that the Arbiter was still, a year later, hurt and weakened by the attempt that ultimately had failed.

No. She's going to kill herself doing this! Maybe they're not as hurt as her brother was, but one soul can't possibly bind—

One soul?

He reached out and put both of his hands atop hers, resting on the heads of Tirleren and Demmi. "Let me help, then. Take from me."

A blink, a hesitation...and then a rush of understanding and gratitude.

Tobimar could not restrain a grunt of agony as the tearing began, ripping delicate strands of his very soul carefully away from the edges, sewing up the ruptured spirits of the children they were saving.

And then there was another presence. "I cannot allow you to take all of the risks for my own people," the Reflect said.

And another. "We are comrades, are we not? Let a Magewright support you as well!"

And a third, touching hesitantly, then clamping down with decision. "And can I do less who was once a Color?" asked the voice of Zogen Josan.

And even Poplock bounced to her shoulder—wordless, of course, so as not to give himself away—but Tobimar knew she would understand the offer as clearly as if it were spoken.

Kyri looked up and her smile lit the room more than her own power.

Myrionar's power mingled with their own and stripped pieces from all of them—but among so many, six souls to heal two children, Tobimar could tell that the damage was so much less that Kyri would not die, would not even be crippled from this attempt, because they were supporting her, giving her the strength that she could never have survived tearing from her own soul alone.

Even as he became aware of another commotion behind them, the blazing gold-fire detonated around the six of them, all flowing and channeled by the power of Kyri Victoria Vantage, the Phoenix Justiciar of Myrionar. A towering, shining sword-balance burned in the air, visible above and through the cabin as though the walls were made of clearest crystal. "Myrionar, by the sacrifice of the willing and bindings of pure soul, by the power of mercy and of justice, and by my will and your wisdom seal these wounds, heal these souls and let these children live again!"

The concussion of power scattered them across the floor like pebbles, yet Tobimar felt no more pain, only tired exaltation. He blinked, clearing fiery afterimages from his eyes.

Tirleren and Demmi lay still in the middle of the floor, Kyri collapsed beside them. And then Tirleren slowly raised his head, Demmi as well, and suddenly began to cry—tears of pain and fear, yes, but also clear tears of relief and joy.

From the floor, Kyri opened her eyes and looked at them all, a smile on her face. She looked past him and her exhausted smile widened.

Crowded around the bottom of the stairs, mostly fallen from the same final shock of the ritual that had felled the five involved in it, were half a dozen of the villagers—and, still standing but staring with impossibly wide blue eyes, was Miri, Light of Kaizatenzei.

CHAPTER 28

Miri stepped into her guestroom at the Reflect's mansion and closed the door, leaning against it heavily. *I'm* shaking*! Shaking like a terrified human!*

Her current body *was* human, in a way... but in all the centuries she'd been in such bodies, she'd *never* had such a reaction. Miri held her arm up in front of her, watched the trembling of the delicate hand, the imprecision of its movements, with stunned fascination; it took twice as long as normal to set the wards and seals of privacy.

In a way, she could understand it. So many shocks, one after another. First, stepping into that cabin and seeing the true power of a god unleashed—through the constant oppressive interference of Moonshade Hollow which impeded even her kind—and the incredible, heart-wrenching beauty of that power and the Phoenix, tearing her own soul and the voluntarily offered souls of the others so she could patch together the shredded, dying spirits of two children, and beyond. Though Phoenix had not realized it, her power had flowed even beyond the two most wounded, touched upon Hamule and bound her wounded spirit just a touch, eased the pain and memories for all five.

Miri found a wondering smile on her face at the thought, then banished that expression with shock and panic.

It didn't hurt. Why didn't it hurt?

But that question hadn't occurred to her right away. She had been uplifted, confident, and helped Phoenix to rise. It was agreed

209

by all three—herself, Phoenix, and Tobimar—that the master *itrichel* had to be dealt with immediately, and that it had to be in the Reflect's household.

And they'd been right; Nimelly, his Head of House, had been the host of the creature. Once she realized she was cornered, she had fled, with the three of them in close pursuit. Tobimar had outdistanced them for a few moments and brought the *itrichel* to bay . . .

And that was the second terrible shock.

Tobimar had faced the *itrichel*-Nimelly with a serene face, a transcendent look in his eyes, twin swords held parallel before him, and she *knew* that pose, that stance, remembered the terrible gray-eyed calm that had advanced through the armies of Kerlamion as though the demons were blades of grass before his vengeful hurricane, in the days after the Fall. *That Art is not lost, and does that mean that . . . He . . . is returning?*

She had stumbled, but somehow—though the terror was nigh-overwhelming—caught herself, regained control, only for yet *another* shock to overtake her.

For the *itrichel* had snarled, "How do you *resist?*" as her blade rang against Tobimar's.

"Yield and you may learn. Fight and you will die," Tobimar had said bluntly. "For my companions are here."

Nimelly then leapt back, with an agility far beyond human, and came on guard, watching all three. She smiled. "But are they companions you can *trust?*" she had asked . . . and for a moment the narrowed eyes had flickered yellow-green, looking directly at Miri.

It knows what I am! It could betray everything!

She had launched herself into the air, even before her course of action was clear; by the time she reached the apex of the leap, she had known what she must do. The two companions *must* believe she was their ally and friend, which meant she must somehow save Nimelly—and absolutely, permanently silence the *itrichel* before it could reveal the truth.

She unleashed a Shardstorm, impaling Nimelly in multiple yet non-vital points with the glittering blue-ice fragments. The *itrichel*, realizing it was trapped, had abandoned the body, tried to flee, but in doing so gave Miri a clear opportunity, and the Hammer of Thunder obliterated every trace.

And even *then* there was no respite from the tension; for what if Nimelly remembered what the *itrichel* knew? She hadn't . . . but there were also other *itrichel* out there by now, matured from the sithigorn and other young animals. If *they* knew the truth...

She sat down on the bed, trying to clear the confusion and panic and elation and fury, to get some kind of idea of what she actually *felt*, to make *sense* of it all. I *cannot* have felt joy at the Phoenix's ritual. I *cannot!* That would mean...

She drove *that* thought out with sheer terror and denial. For if *that* was true, then somehow the thing she had resisted for millennia, that had been trying to eat away at her *self* for all the time they had been here, was finally overcoming her, now, just when complete victory was in her grasp. It wasn't happening. It *couldn't* be happening. It was the *persona* she had adopted, that was all. "Miri" would of course be awed and overjoyed, fascinated even, by such a miracle. And miracle it was; not all the magic of Kaizatenzei could have saved those children, but the Phoenix of Myrionar had made it look easy—though as Miri had seen, it was certainly not.

In a sense, that was good; attention was entirely on the emissary of the God of Justice and Vengeance, and for once that meant that people downstairs *weren't* all crowded around Miri, so she had been able to get away without drawing attention to herself. And she *needed* this time alone.

And there were people she needed to talk to. Oh, yes, immediately.

The golden scroll was instantly out of her pack and set up. Miri found herself bouncing her knee in nervousness as she waited for the other person to answer. *Stop that! I must* not *show any such weakness in front of* him.

But that was easier said than done. The problem was that she was feeling entirely too many things right now, some good, some bad, and some just *confusing*, and that made her twitchy and annoyed. Which wasn't at *all* a good thing to be in conversation with *Him*.

Even as she drew a breath and tried to focus on calming herself, on dealing with the mission, the golden scroll darkened and cleared to show the ever-pleasant features of Viedraverion's current form. "Ermirinovas! Always a pleasure."

She decided that his infuriating cheer needed to be dealt a bit of a blow, and that would also help cheer *her* up. "You treacherous little *nyetakh*."

Instead of looking taken aback, the smile widened. "And as always I can rely on your unswerving politeness! What is it that—"

"The so-called 'key' is a *Tor master!*" she snapped, feeling again the chill and shock that had nearly overcome her.

"*What?*" The surprise on the face was genuine. A moment later, the smile returned, this one of chagrin. "Ah. Of course, I should have guessed, given his instructor."

She felt the blood leave her face and dizziness assailed her. *Curse this human body!* "Are . . . no, you cannot be saying that *He* has returned, is instructing—"

"Oh, no, no, not *him*. I have not seen him, nor sign that he . . ." Viedraverion paused. "Or perhaps I have. I must think on this. But in your particular case, no. But that is little comfort, I think, because his instructor was Konstantin Khoros."

"*Khoros!*" She spat the name out like a curse—which, indeed, it was. "And you did not see fit to *warn* us?"

The infuriating smile was back. "You asked for me to watch for certain things. I watched for them. I think you would still want your key even *with* this complication, yes?"

Calm. Calm. It was hard, much harder with the turbulent confused emotions within her, but she forced herself to clarity and some measure of calm. "Yes. Yes, we would. So . . . enough of that. However, there *is* the matter of his companion."

"Oh?"

"She is the channel of a *god!*" Anew she saw the towering golden Sword-Balance, blazing up and through the cabin, rising above the trees, and felt again that strange chill and warmth, the *power* of a deity manifest in the girl who was sacrificing part of her *own* soul, as well as those of others, to save two children she had never before met. "A full channel, not some random priest! I have never felt such a thing, not even from the Stars and Sun!"

The blond-haired form leaned back in his chair and smiled. "Well, yes. You have dealt less with the gods and their powers than I, so you do not understand the difference. In the Stars and Sun of Terian, you have a vast *power*, yes, but they are, in the end analysis, merely containers for power, not the Light in the Darkness himself. That does not of course mean they are *safe*, as you well know, but they are not themselves the Will of the Deity made manifest." He gazed into a distance she could not see. "Even if they *were*—say if Terian had been called forth to activate them—there would be a difference. Terian has immensely many shrines, temples, priests, worshipers—scattered across the entire continent, some even within your own valley. He is many places at once, always.

"Myrionar, however...has only the Phoenix. Oh, there is one priest, but even he looks to *her* as the example and symbol. You felt the power of a focused, even desperate god providing what it could to its one remaining champion, and that, I have no doubt, was a magnificent sight indeed to one of our perceptions."

"Oh, it *was* magnificent!" She caught herself before she went any farther. *This part I play is becoming too real. I must remember it is only a* seeming, *not an actuality...or it might* become *actuality.* "But also dangerous."

Viedraverion shrugged. "If you make too many mistakes, yes. She is a very formidable young woman. But you have the power, you have the allies, you have the advantages. I trust you will be able to handle her and your key."

"As long as Khoros isn't directly intervening." She didn't even want to *think* about that. Ermirinovas was powerful, yes, but she knew that going up against a Spirit Mage of Khoros' age and power would be a foregone conclusion, and not one in her favor.

"No, of that I can be sure. My...sources tell me that he has actually been seen serving as advisor to the new Sauran King as they prepare for the counterassault against our beloved father."

That was something of a relief. But..."Does Father know?"

"I presume he does. He has his own spies."

She studied him. "You don't seem concerned. I thought you had an interest in this Phoenix."

"I have an interest in how her journey ends—in victory or in failure. I won't tell you you cannot deal with her in any fashion that suits your needs."

"Indeed?" He nodded. "Well...all right. Also, I did intercept your other visitor, Aran Condor, and sent him the *other* way around the Necklace. I'm arranging for sightings and rumors of the Phoenix along the way, so he'll stick to the trail and never wonder about it all the way there."

"Really? Well done, little sister. I commend you. Exactly as I would have asked." He looked off to the side. "I must be going; other responsibilities call, and I believe we have...cleared up our misunderstanding?"

"Sufficiently. Farewell, Viedraverion."

"And you, Ermirinovas."

She put the scroll away, checked the seals and wards again. Not that she expected anyone to try to spy on her—the Phoenix certainly would never even think of such a thing and she doubted Tobimar would either, and none of the others in Jenten's Mill would dare—but only a fool trusts unreservedly.

Once she was sure that things were still secure, she removed the farcaller from her pouch and placed it on the table. "Lady Shae," she said.

The image of Kalshae's human form materialized almost instantly; she was in her own chambers, so there was no need to delay. "Miri. What is it?"

Now she had someone to *really* vent her tension on. "I would ask rather what is *this?*" She held up one of the *itrichel* corpses.

Kalshae blinked in startlement. "Where did you—"

"Jenten's Mill. An infestation that came up out of the *lake*—how very surprising," she let sarcasm fill the last words for a second or two before continuing, "and then when the townsfolk stopped depredations on their young livestock the thing took over one of the townsfolk and started abducting *children!*"

"Well, that's unfortunate, but—"

"Unfortunate? You *fool*, Kalshae! You and Wieran play with all these clever little inventions but you never see the way the game has to be played, and you have too little respect for the danger! They sent for help and found our key and his party—and naturally they came right away."

Finally Kalshae was giving her undivided attention to Miri, and Miri began to feel—slightly—better. "Now it was bad enough that it was hurting the town; as long as we're running a kingdom we *need* stability, not fear and uncertainty. But far *worse* was the fact that it was one of *yours*."

"How do you—"

"How do I know? How do I *know*?" She leaned forward, glaring so fiercely that Kalshae actually stepped back a pace. "Because the Father-damned thing almost *gave me away*! The *only* thing that kept the whole situation from going straight to the Light was that the master *itrichel* got fancy and instead of just telling them what I was, hinted and looked at me in a way I couldn't possibly mistake. I could tell it expected I would betray them at that point. I finished it instead.

"*Fortunately,*" she continued, overriding Kalshae's attempt to speak, "they thought that it was simply planning on mind-controlling us—it couldn't affect Tobimar—and that was why we wouldn't be able to be trusted. And while they *had* wanted to capture it and question it about its other nest, they understood my need to act."

"I see." Kalshae gazed at her, then finally—unwillingly—bowed. "I...am sorry. It was thoughtless and incompetent of us to allow such a thing free, and I will make no such mistakes again."

"See that you don't. You may have more raw *power* than I do, Kalshae—although not as much as you think—but *never* forget that I planned this entire thing. You will *not* ruin it for me."

"Understood, Miri. Understood." Kalshae waited to see if Miri accepted her contrition, then, "Now...how many people were killed? The master-*itrichel*'s host, of course, but how many others?"

"None, actually. I was careful with the Shardstorm."

"Wait, now. There is no way that you can cure a child ridden by an *itrichel* for longer than—"

"Oh, yes there is. If you happen to be the chosen representative of a *god*. Phoenix's story is one hundred percent true; she was able to pull enough power from her god to heal all five children, including two with nearly full-grown mindworms."

Even as she said that, Miri regarded herself with confusion and disbelief. *Tell Kalshae about the soul-tearing! About how Phoenix had to use her own soul and those of others to heal the children! That's* vital *information! It tells us that Phoenix—and perhaps Tobimar and Hiriista!—will be weakened for some time! It also tells us about how far they will go to save others!*

Tell her!

But somehow she found herself silent, adding no more details, and held her face so controlled that not a hint of additional information was shown on her face. Even as she let that moment pass, she felt that strangeness within her growing, as though the decision had strengthened it. With frozen panic she shoved that very awareness from her mind and focused on the woman before her.

"By the Throne! That's...frightening," Kalshae said slowly. "Especially doing it *here*, where even we cannot pull in more than a fraction of the power that is normally ours. But there is no suspicion of us?"

"None. Especially after our successful hunt. Though there are more *itrichel* out there to hunt, since not all the missing livestock from the first attacks have been found."

"Still, if they have not conferred with the master *itrichel*, they will know nothing."

"Let us hope so. But I will have to stay here and *complete* the hunt for all of the things to make sure. Do you understand how much time this will make me waste? If just *one* person hears the wrong thing and I'm not there to kill them or wipe their minds—"

"Yes, yes, I *do* understand. My apologies, again." She tilted her head. "Wait a moment. You said that the master *itrichel could not* affect Tobimar Silverun. Why?"

Miri couldn't restrain a nasty grin. "Because he is a *Tor* master."

The reaction was everything she could have hoped for. Kalshae shrank back in horror, her foot ran against some object fallen to the floor, and she stumbled. "*Impossible*! They were eradicated from—"

"I *saw* him. Just as I remember seeing the Eternal King himself from the walls. I cannot mistake those moves, those stances. And Viedraverion tells me that our key was trained by Khoros."

Kalshae vented an obscenity that momentarily darkened the crystal. "Are we against *Khoros*? If so, we must simply abandon this plan entirely."

"I would not be so hasty...but no. Viedra says that the old mage is advising the Sauran King and will probably be on the front lines."

"Bad for Father, good for us. All right. Will the key be continuing on tomorrow?"

"I think so. Perhaps the day after; the townspeople are very grateful. I will then catch up with them once the hunting of the other *itrichel* is finished."

"I think you should stick with them as much as possible... just to make sure they don't see or learn anything...dangerous."

"I'll do so as much as possible," Miri said with a smile. *Smile? Suddenly I feel so much...lighter! What in the world could be causing that?*

"All right. I'll go deal with Wieran over this...unauthorized release."

"Better you than me. Good luck."

"Thanks. I'll need it."

Miri put the crystal away and stood. *It's getting towards dinner time; Phoenix will be wondering where I am!*

She set out from her room, a bounce in her step again.

CHAPTER 29

"You will always be welcomed in Jenten's Mill," the Reflect said, bowing deeply to Kyri; the assembled crowd also bowed. Poplock could see the slight darkening of the already-dark cheeks that told him the Phoenix Justiciar was embarrassed. "And we shall not forget your teachings."

Kyri's smile was still a trifle disbelieving, but very happy. "I cannot thank you enough—"

"No," Zogen Josan said, cutting her off emphatically. Nimelly and the five children echoed the word, and the rest of the crowd nodded. "It is we who cannot thank you enough. You cut through fear and illusion and mistrust; together you found the truth. But you, Phoenix, then drove forth the darkness and healed those who were beyond help, brought children from the grip of death back to us, at the risk of your own soul. Even as a Color I have never seen such power, or felt such . . . *blessing* as came from the power of Myrionar." He held up the handwritten sheets that Kyri had spent the last day and a half writing. "These shall be studied and learned by heart, and know that the word of the the God of Justice and Vengeance shall never be forgotten here."

Kyri's gray eyes were filled with tears; all she seemed capable of doing then was to bow almost to the ground and then clasp Zogen's hands.

The rest of the goodbyes took, as Poplock had expected, something close to an hour of repetition of goodbyes, good-lucks, thank-yous, and other expected sentiments. He glanced sideways

to Hiriista, who gave an ironic shrug. But at last the houses of
Jenten's Mill had vanished to view and the quiet of the forest
had once more fallen upon them.

"*Finally!*" Poplock burst out. "Away, and alone for a while,
so I can *talk!*"

Tobimar looked at him sympathetically. "This hiding your
existence isn't easy, is it?"

"Mud-sucking *hard* is what it is. But we've got to keep doing
it, so I'm going to be doing a lot of talking until Miri catches
up with us."

"Why stop then?" Kyri asked. "Miri's really—"

"—a Light of Kaizatenzei," Hiriista said bluntly. "And after
what we learned from Zogen, I feel even more strongly that we
must be cautious about the Unity Guard."

"No two ways about that," Poplock said. "In between other
conversations, he mentioned recurring images that were really
pretty darn creepy—dreams of lying down, unable to move, as
though he were in some sort of coffin—but a coffin with a window, through which he saw what seemed rows of other coffins,
ranks upon ranks of them."

"I'm not sure what it means." Hiriista took out his scent-pipe
and filled it. "But he says he occasionally had this dream or vision
throughout his tenure as a Color, has never had it since retiring,
and that he heard similar tales among others of the Guard. If
Miri is unaffected, that may mean that she simply has not yet
been targeted, or she has been fortunate... or that she is part
of the problem."

Kyri sighed. "I know. You're right, of course. Thornfalcon fooled
everyone until he decided he no longer needed to trick them. I
have to presume that this is even easier here in Kaizatenzei."

"Precisely," Hiriista said. "Why do you think we questioned
Zogen when Miri was elsewhere? She works far too closely with
Lady Shae and Master Wieran for us to rule that possibility out."
The Toad could tell by the tension in the walk, the stiffer lashing
of the tail, that thinking such terrible—probably treasonous—
thoughts hurt his scaly friend badly.

"I understand."

"You'll have to be especially on your guard," Poplock pointed
out. "Once Miri gets back you're going to have a hard time getting away."

Tobimar chuckled. "Yes, you've got quite an admirer in her now."

"Well, she *is* very nice, and we've got a lot to talk about. She's an incredible fighter—I still am amazed by the way she finished off that master *itrichel* without killing Nimelly."

"Oh, yeah, about that—Hiriista, what does..." Poplock concentrated on trying to recall what he'd heard, "um, '*Vomatenzei Borok—cho!*' mean?"

"Ahhh, yes, you don't speak the old tongue."

"Well, I know 'Vomatenzei,' that's 'Stormlight,' right?"

"Precisely. What you heard was an invocation of one of Miri's particular powers—all the Guard have some of their own. That translates, roughly, to 'Stormlight Hammer—strike.'"

"Makes sense; that sent what looked like a ball of pure lightning down on the *itrichel*, left a crater fifteen feet across. I would've thought her powers would be more water-based."

"Storms are merely water and air, are they not?" Hiriista pointed out.

Kyri smiled, then took a deep breath. "Mmm. That...lightness of the world is starting to become stronger, I think."

"Yes. As we progress closer to the Necklace it will return." The *mazakh* looked down at Poplock. "Now, my apprentice, how are you doing in your studies?"

"Kinda interrupted by having to pretend to be *stupid* all the time. But I was planning on practicing calling a defense, a sort of ice shield. At my size, defense is what I really need. I could always start practicing offense later."

"In a sense, yes, but remember, your attunement to a gem is dependent on a specific Calling. You cannot switch back and forth between different...modes of operation for a given gem. For example, if you invoke your Ocean's Tear to provide the defense you have envisioned, that is all you can call upon that gem to do unless you reset its individual matrix, which will negate all of the work you have done to develop your connection to the gem. The Summoning Calls are somewhat different—it is difficult to impossible to somehow repurpose such a stone—but for most gemcalling, a stone's path can be reset but the progress along that path will be lost."

"Does that mean I can't switch in another gem without losing all the progress I made with the other?" That would really be annoying; he wasn't *big* enough to wear the wide assortment of bangles, bracelets, and necklaces that Hiriista displayed.

A hiss of amusement. "Oh, no, no. The gem and you retain your link even if the gem is not in a calling matrix. I apologize; the terminology is clear to an expert, but I admit it is confusing to a layman. A Calling Matrix is one of these particular pieces of equipment that has a setting for a calling gem. But each individual gem has its own internal matrix—for lack of a better word—which is established by its usage by an individual gemcaller.

"This matrix exists simultaneously in both the gem and the gemcaller, and thus while the same gem could be used for different purposes by two different gemcallers, for the same gemcaller to use the gem for a different purpose involves erasing that prior relationship between the two; since the increasing connection over time makes a gemcall more powerful, easier, and faster to invoke, most gemcallers are very reluctant to, shall we say, repurpose a gem with which they have any significant experience."

"But I *could* have several gems and swap them out of the socket without losing my connection with any of them?"

"Precisely."

Have to get myself a little collection, and practice swapping, then, Poplock thought to himself. "Well, I'm not very big, so I can't have your big bracelets and such with several matrices, but do you think I could get a few more in Alatenzei?"

Hiriista's back scales rippled in an uncertain way. "In Alatenzei...perhaps. Though that would depend on if any magewrights had some to sell, or had sold off any to the stores for various reasons. In Kaizatenzei Valatar, of course, it would be easy."

"Yeah, but I'd *really* rather get them well before that."

"Seconded," Tobimar agreed.

"Indeed?" Hiriista tilted his head. "Why so?"

"Think about it," Poplock said, hopping up on Tobimar's head so he could see farther away. "If there *is* something wrong with the Unity Guards, it could go all the way to the top. And we're already *pretty* suspicious of this Master Wieran. Well, we don't want to be still trying to learn our new weapons if we start poking around and the mud starts sliding."

"Your metaphor is unfamiliar, but I take your point, indeed. But how do you intend—"

"To practice if we end up with Miri or someone else following?

Make sure people know that Tobimar's little pet always goes off foraging at night when we're traveling. Not like anyone can contradict him, right?"

"So you can go as far away as you need and practice," Kyri said. "Makes sense. And we can even do something else, like combat practice or whatever, that will keep attention focused on us during the evenings, so that no one really wonders too much about you."

"Good idea," Poplock agreed. He caught a beetle flying by, chewed reflectively. "Problem is we still have too many questions and not enough answers. Even if this Master Weiran is the baddie that Thornfalcon contacted, we don't know if he's the *real* bad guy here, or if it's Lady Shae, or someone else that we haven't thought of. And there's one thing that's *really* got me worried."

Now the others were all focused on him. "What is it, Poplock?" asked Tobimar tensely.

"We haven't been attacked *once* since we got here," Poplock said gravely.

His two main companions frowned, looking confused, but in a moment he saw Hiriista's head bob. "Yes, I see."

"Okay, I *don't* quite get it, Poplock. Want to explain that?"

"Look. Thorny managed to arrange one hell of a gateway to provide him with monsters on demand, right? Had to be something that his ally worked with him on. So he *had* to be communicating with said ally. Stands to reason *someone* here knew perfectly well about the other side—the language business shows that, too—but specifically they were working with the False Justiciars.

"But we also know that Thornfalcon *wasn't* the real top of the chain."

He saw Kyri's eyes narrow in understanding even as Tobimar grunted. "Got you. We have to assume the person running this whole thing knew what Thornfalcon was up to, or at least was able to find out. And so *someone* on this side has to know about our mission."

"Yet they haven't done a single thing to try to stop us," Kyri finished slowly. "Not even arranging an accident here or there. The incident in Jenten's Mill doesn't qualify; we might not even have *heard* of the place if we'd come by just a day earlier or later, or gone the other direction around the lake."

"It *could* just be that whoever or whatever it is didn't learn about our arrival until later—though with those farcallers they use I'm not sure I'd want to bet that way—but it *does* make me wonder."

"And your instincts have been pretty good so far," Kyri said, giving him a quick pat. "So... I wonder, too."

"Doesn't matter," Tobimar said after a moment.

Poplock looked over at his friend's face, about six inches away. "What do you mean?"

"If we're even close to right, the real source of trouble here is somewhere in Sha Kaizatenzei Valatar, the capital. So if your suspicions are correct, they're trying to lull our suspicions while they bring us to where they're strongest."

"Okay, yeah, but so?"

Tobimar's grin was as sharp as his blades. "So that's where we'd want to go anyway... except they're not wearing us down along the way. They may just find that by luring us to their head-quarters, they've managed to get us right where we want them."

CHAPTER 30

"Look out!"

Kyri barely brought her sword around in time to catch the impact of the crystal staff. *Myrionar's* Balance! *He's hitting as hard as a Justiciar!*

It had all happened so fast. Asked by the residents of Windtree, a small town a little down the road from Sha Alatenzei, to investigate a series of abductions and murders, the small group had put together multiple little clues that had meant nothing in isolation and followed them to an area outside of town where only a few people lived. And then Govi Zergul, a few moments ago a quiet, colorless man answering a few questions, had let slip a detail about one of the victims that they knew only the murderer should have known.

Seeing the expressions on their faces, Zergul had leapt back with surprising agility and suddenly beautiful ruby crystal armor had streamed from a nearby case onto his body, ending with a matching staff landing in his hand—all in the time it took them to realize what was happening.

Now Govi Zergul whirled the staff around in a fluid motion, the dark-stained wine-red crystal armor he wore flickering with a lurid bloody glow. Miri was just coming to her feet, blood flowing freely from her scalp, and Kyri's fury rose higher at the sight of the delicate Light wounded and dizzy.

Still, anger wasn't going to be enough; Zergul's speed and skill were preternatural—better than she had even imagined possible for someone living on the outskirts of this, the third little town they'd encountered after passing Sha Alatenzei. She actually found herself *backing up* before his furious assault, his face still eerily calm, with the same half-smile he'd worn when he'd answered the door.

Then her foot caught on a projection of rock and she stumbled— only slightly, but she knew that was enough.

But the expected blows never landed; with a ringing chime, twin blue-green blades caught the red crystal staff.

Kyri recovered as Tobimar took up the battle, and for a moment she found herself staring. The Prince of Skysand was a whirlwind of blades, each blow precise yet delivered with vicious force, and now it was Govi who retreated, one step, two, trying to disengage from the ice-blue eyes that were reading his every move, and in a blur Kyri could barely follow Tobimar's right boot caught his taller opponent on the chin. Govi Zergul staggered back—

And froze, Miri's blue crystal dagger appearing at Govi's throat from behind and a taloned, scaled hand lashing out to seize the man's upraised arm. Hiriista tore the staff from Govi's grasp and kicked his knees out from under him. Miri's dagger followed his throat down. "Well, I think we can take your guilt as proven, Govi Zergul. In possession of a Color's armor—of Bryall of Hishitenzei, who vanished around here fifteen years ago, I think—assaulting a Light and other allies of Kaizatenzei, the trail of suspicion that led us here... If you are *lucky* you might live. I'm almost sorry you surrendered, though."

Govi's half-smile was barely dimmed. He chuckled, a dry, reedy sound. "Guilty? Yes, I killed them. The Color was a fortunate accident; he thought I was *helping* an injured child, not *killing* her, so he came close enough to get my blade in his neck. Then, oh, how wonderful a gift it was..."

Kyri felt nauseated. The tone of his voice reminded her forcibly of Thornfalcon. *I'd hoped in this shining place such things would not happen. But then, we are now at the place between cities, where it weakens.*

Gray dust drifted down over them, bringing the odor of sulfur; Tozak's Cauldron, one of several active volcanic cones around Sha Alatenzei, was sending a plume of fine ash even this far away.

Kyri saw Gozi subtly tensing, preparing for escape. Miri spat. "Gift? Then I take from you this gift!"

One of the crystals on her armor—on her delicate hairpiece-like helm, located directly over her forehead—shone with blue radiance, and the red crystal armor abruptly *shattered*.

No, Kyri corrected herself. It hadn't shattered; it just came apart into individual pieces, which now fell away from the wide-eyed Gozi like scattered leaves.

"What..."

"Did you think that we gave so powerful a set of weapons to our people, yet had no way to control them? If rogue they have gone, or—in this case—if a rogue has stolen their equipment, there is and has always been a way to tell the Armor of Kaizatenzei that it is no longer being wielded as it should be."

Miri yanked Gozi to his feet. "You are our prisoner. Struggle and I shall render you unconscious and drag you. If you doubt I can...remember my companions will be with us."

After a glance at Kyri, Tobimar, and Hiriista, Gozi was silent and did not resist when Miri bound his hands and began dragging him back to the village.

It did not take long to turn the multiple murderer over to the local Reflect and his guards. "I'll send word to Alatenzei to send someone to pick him up," Miri said, after she checked the security of their prison. "This should hold him for a day or three, at least, and that's all it needs to do."

"We *could* just execute him," Reflect Iesa said, her eyes narrow.

"He murdered a Color as well as your people. He'll either be truthsworn in Hishitenzei or in Kaizatenzei Valatar itself. Yes, he has admitted it, but we will follow the law. If we do not follow the law, can we expect any to respect the law?"

Iesa bit her lip, then bowed and nodded. "As always, you speak wisdom...even if it is sometimes not the wisdom I wished to hear, Light Miri. We will keep him secure, but safe, until others of the Unity Guard come."

"That's all I ask. Thank you, Iesa. I know it's hard for you, and your people, to let him go."

Kyri breathed a sigh of relief once they finally were back on the road, an hour or so later. "I know they would have let us stay, but they're not happy about having to leave Gozi's punishment up to another city or the capital."

"You're right," Miri said sadly. "It will be much less uncomfortable to camp out again. But," she said, brightening and looking up at Kyri with brilliant blue eyes, "thank you so much for helping. This may not have been as tangled a mystery as the other, but your help was still invaluable. I still can't believe he got away with killing so many in so small a town."

"I wish I couldn't believe it, but I've met someone who got away with killing more people in a smaller town. He mostly preyed on those he knew were passing through, of course." On the other hand, Thornfalcon had been unique. She hoped.

Miri's gaze was uncomfortably perceptive. "Something close to your heart, I see. You lost someone...?"

"He had arranged the deaths of my mother and father, and later my brother. Almost killed me, too, if Tobimar hadn't arrived just in time." *And Poplock,* she added to herself; neither of them ever forgot the debt they owed the resourceful Toad.

"Light and Shadow, that's terrible. Was that your... whole family?" Miri's eyes were wide with sympathy.

The sympathy made it easier to talk about. "Not quite. I still have my little sister Urelle, and Aunt Victoria. A couple other cousins off across the country, too, but I didn't see them much."

"Still... what a terrible loss. But the two of you finished—" She halted in sudden understanding. "Oh! You're talking about that monster, what was his name, Thornfalcon! He had killed *that* many?"

Tobimar nodded, grimacing. "They were *still* finding new remains when we left."

A brief silence fell at that; Kyri still found herself chilled, remembering the moment that Thornfalcon, the gentle clownish would-be troubadour of the Justiciars, had turned to face her and dropped his mask, revealing the utterly corrupt and evil truth within that human shell. "Yes," she said finally, "he was that monstrous. And, like Gozi, he was using the armor of a noble order for evil. I wonder how many other parallels we will see."

Miri reached out tentatively and touched Kyri's arm, gave it a gentle squeeze. "I'm sorry. Didn't mean to bring up something so painful."

"No, it's fine." She smiled down at the tiny Unity Guard.

"Well, enough of that kind of subject anyway!" Miri said after a quick smile. "I think there's a good clearing just up ahead for us to camp in. Then I think we should do something more fun!"

"Fun?" Hiriista said doubtfully. "We've just defeated an enemy far more formidable than we'd expected, and spent more time traveling today. How—"

"Oh, piff!" Miri tossed her head cheerfully. "You old faker, you're no more tired than the rest of us are. That was a tough fight, but it was *fast*, and all of us can keep up, can't we?"

Hiriista's scales puffed up with indignation . . . then dropped flat and he gave a rueful hiss. "You have known me far too long and far too well for me to hide, I suppose."

"Exactly!"

"Let me guess," said Kyri. "Sparring."

"Partly, yes, but more teaching. We all fight differently and must have things to teach each other." She looked over to Tobimar. "I hadn't had the chance to ask you, but what *is* that combat style you use? I've never seen anything like it, and it's amazing—that flowing, precise timing."

Tobimar looked pleased and embarrassed at the same time. "Well, yours is just as impressive. But I actually didn't find out the *name* of that style until a few months ago, from a friend of ours who used it, Xavier. It's called *Tor*."

Miri was startled. "Another person with that particular art?"

"Yeah, and better at it than me, too."

"Don't underestimate yourself, Tobimar," Kyri said. "There were *parts* of it that Xavier knew that you didn't, but he said you knew other parts that his master hadn't gotten around to teaching him." She remembered some of the conversations they'd had, and knew that Tobimar had had many more during his travels.

The Skysand Prince grinned and spread his hands, then bowed. "As you say, Lady Phoenix. Xavier said he'd been trained with a specific focus to give him some very particular skills, and his master had said something to the effect that it meant he wasn't going to have some of the other capabilities of *Tor* unless he kept studying and practicing for years afterwards. I think Ma—" He caught himself, continued, "—my master was teaching me more systematically and from the beginning onward. Certainly the notes he gave me on the teachings progress in the same direction."

"Well, I look forward to learning more of this . . . *Tor*, Tobimar," Miri said, obviously fascinated. "And what of you, Phoenix? From what tradition or trainer did you learn your skills?"

Kyri couldn't restrain a fond smile. "From our *Sho-Ka-Taida*, Master of Arms, Lythos, an *Artan* warrior of centuries-old skill and tradition. I guess that some of his techniques are unique to his people. And of course I learned other tricks from the Justiciars before I found out they were corrupt. What about you?"

"Oh, look, here's the clearing!" Miri dropped her pack to one side of the Necklace and began checking for good, flat spaces to pitch tents. "My style is a combination of several taught to the Unity Guard, but mostly *Rurital*, short for—if I remember correctly—*Ruritenzei sarite Althami*, which means something like *Sunlight Dancing on Water.*"

Kyri laughed. "Oh my, that's such a *perfect* description of how you fight—like a pretty sunbeam flicking from point to point on the water, never staying, never pausing."

Unlike Tobimar and Kyri herself, Miri had such fair skin that even a very *slight* blush was easily distinguished—and this wasn't a slight blush. "Oh, well, I think of it more as just jumping almost randomly across opponents and their expectations. Random throws most off, you know."

"As random as my swordarm, yes," Kyri said, looking at her pointedly.

"Oh, fair enough. We shall observe and test each other's skills..."

"... *after*," Hiriista interjected emphatically, "we have our camp set up."

"Of course, *after*," agreed Miri with a laugh.

"Then," Kyri said, dropping her own pack, "let's get to it!"

CHAPTER 31

"We've *got* to be getting close now," Poplock observed. "And about time. We seem to keep getting distracted."

"For good reason," Kyri said, a defensive tone in her voice. "I can't ignore a—"

"Calm down, Phoenix," Tobimar said. *She's been under even more pressure lately than usual. Have to take that into account.* "Poplock was just making an observation. Any of us would have turned aside to help. Even if Hiriista hadn't made us do so."

The *mazakh* bobbed agreement. "Even the mystery of the vanishing dinners in Sha Kalatenzei, though it turned out well, was something sufficiently unsettling that I could hardly have ignored it, and the others were far worse."

"You're right, of course," Kyri said. She bit her lip, then bowed in Poplock's direction. "Sorry, o mighty Toad. I shouldn't have gotten upset."

The little Toad waved one paw dismissively. "Don't worry about it. Tobimar and I know what you've been going through."

Tobimar nodded. "Somehow in just about every instance you've managed to end up in the forefront. Which means you're having to be the 'Phoenix Justiciar of Myrionar' almost all the time—in Jenten's Mill, that bar brawl in Alatenzei before we left, helping Miri catch Govi Zergul in Windtree, the risen dead in Felaffi's Rest, and this latest problem..." He smiled sympathetically and took her hand gently. "Honestly, you just haven't gotten much of a break. Being the representative of a god...it's hard, isn't it?"

She squeezed back, still looking depressed, then sighed. "It is, sometimes. Especially when people are looking at me like I know all the answers, like I'm something...holy, when I know I'm not really any different from them."

"You sometimes ride a fine line between humility and self-denial," Hiriista said dryly. "But yes, I see the pressure, and it is understandable."

"Plus all of us having to watch ourselves around Miri—whenever she isn't out somewhere else—just puts more strain on everyone," Poplock pointed out. "Especially since we have to act like we're *not* watching ourselves."

"I *hate* doing that," Kyri muttered. "She's such a..."

"I know. There seems to be nothing to *suspect* in her, yet we can't ignore the possibility."

"After all," Hiriista said, "you're perfectly nice people and you're fooling *her* into thinking you have no possible suspicion. It would be exceedingly unwise of us to assume that she is incapable of equal or greater duplicity, especially since she *is* one of the Lights, and by all accounts the favorite of Lady Shae herself. If anyone in Kaizatenzei is capable of playing a part to perfection, it would be Miri."

"Or *you*," Poplock said.

"Or me, yes," agreed the reptilian magewright.

"I suppose," Tobimar said, thoughtfully, "that *if* there were several factions of what we would consider enemies, then you could be an agent of one faction and the Unity Guard mostly on the side of another. But that's pretty far-fetched, especially with what we've seen and heard in the main cities. That kind of infighting would cause other problems, and it really seemed that problems of any significant kind were rare."

"It is," agreed Hiriista. "In fact, I find it quite astonishing that we have seen so many problems—and serious ones—along the way."

Poplock squinted at him. "And do you think there's a reason?"

Hiriista was silent in thought for a few moments. Tobimar took the opportunity to look around at the lush forest. The marshlands that had surrounded the Necklace all the way past the "V" intersection with the other branch of the Necklace had finally faded into solid forest and the feel of *rightness* was strengthening; the trees were arrow-straight, their bark unblemished, the leaves brilliant green, with flowers of a thousand hues scattered about the foliage below. The calming hum of bees at work pervaded the air. For those few moments, he simply enjoyed walking with Kyri, holding her hand, as though they were merely out to enjoy the view.

"I do," Hiriista said after a moment. "Coincidence can only be taken so far, and in a normal patrol along the Necklace I would expect only one such incident, not the half-dozen we have dealt with. Yet...I cannot think of what purpose this would serve, or how so many diverse challenges could be prepared in such a manner as to raise no suspicion among the people most involved, and timed so perfectly that our small party alone was the only group to be called in to resolve the issue."

Tobimar glanced at Poplock, who shrugged. "We can't figure it out, either. But at least it's worth thinking about."

"Oh, I assure you I am thinking about it, and will continue to think about it until I have resolved the problem. I do not like unsolved mysteries."

"Helloooooo!"

The call was distant, but there was no mistaking the high, clear voice or the glittering blue-crystal armor on the figure that was fast approaching—from, to Tobimar's surprise, in *front* of them.

"Oh, *drought*," Poplock cursed. "Back to the silent stupid Toad. And she'll be *babytalking* me! And want to keep me on *her* shoulder!"

"Ahh, the torments you must suffer," muttered Tobimar, perhaps *not* with a terribly sympathetic tone in his voice.

"*You* try it sometime!"

"I can't fit on her shoulder."

The Toad gave him a wrinkle-faced glare. "Bah. Talk to you all later."

The little Light covered the distance in mere moments and *threw* herself onto Kyri, who looked startled but not distressed; after that moment of surprise, Kyri returned Miri's hug, and then Miri bounced over and gave a quicker but still emphatic hug to Tobimar, grabbing up Poplock and giving him a kiss between his golden eyes and setting him on her shoulder—as the Toad had predicted—before clasping hands with Hiriista. "Oh, you're all here so soon! I mean, I knew you would make good time, but I never thought you'd have already gotten this far from Kalatenzei."

"We were trying to make up some lost time," Kyri said, and

Tobimar saw she couldn't keep a fond smile from her face. *If Miri* does *turn out to be an enemy, it's going to hurt Kyri most of all.* "I guess we were doing pretty well."

"Pretty well? *Amazing.* I'm glad that I got out when I did."

"Got out?"

She grinned, blue eyes dancing. "Oh, yes. Just in time, too. You're closer to the end of your journey than you think."

Tobimar had been wondering if he should start looking for camping spots; at that remark, his attention was riveted back on Miri. "We're that close?"

She pointed. "See the hill a ways off there? Reach that hill, and from the top you shall first see Sha Kaizatenzei Valatar, greatest city of the world."

Remembering Zarathanton, with its five hundred foot eternal walls, towers stretching a mile and more into the heavens, and a thousand species of people living, working, and playing within those walls, Tobimar had to be a bit doubtful. Still, the idea of reaching the end of this part of their journey was exciting in and of itself. "Then let's go!"

They all hastened their pace (except of course Poplock, who simply held on). "Are we expected, then?" Kyri asked.

"You've been vaguely expected for weeks, but specific preparations aren't yet finalized. You'll be brought to the Valatar Throne directly, of course—Lady Shae's directives were very clear on that—but as to other proper welcoming for such unique guests, well, that will take a bit more time."

Tobimar caught Kyri's eye-roll towards the heavens. *Yes, it does sound like we're going to be caught in more formality and speechmaking. Poor Kyri. At least I was raised with the idea that I'd be a governor of one of the cities of Skysand, possibly even the Lord of Waters, so diplomacy and meetings and formality are pretty much in my blood. Kyri never had that much of it, even though her people were Eyes of the Watchland; Evanwyl's too small to really support that much formality.*

"But our friends have their own urgent reason for their journey," Hiriista said. "I hope there is no plan to waste overmuch of their time on empty formalities."

"I'll try to keep Lady Shae reminded of that. But if I understand correctly, Phoenix, you are indeed a representative of your own country? And Tobimar as well?"

Tobimar felt a small shock in his gut. *We'd tried to hide that aspect...* But even as he thought it, he realized that side comments in their story would have revealed that he had considerable rank and station, even if they had managed to avoid revealing exactly *where* that rank and station came from.

"Er... I suppose I could be called that, yes," Kyri said after a pause. "The Watchland's Eyes have served as emissaries and ambassadors on occasion."

Can't contradict what we've already said. But that doesn't mean I can't do a bit of dodging. "Technically I am in exile," said Tobimar, "but not a dishonorable one, and certainly that makes me a representative of my country by blood and tradition, even if one who cannot at this time escort you or your own representatives to my homeland."

Miri laughed and gave an apologetic shrug. "Then I am sorry, but there will be only so much I can do. Remember, we've had *no* contact with anyone beyond what you call Moonshade Hollow since our records began. You're all too important as symbols and contacts for us to *not* formally welcome and try to establish relations with."

Tobimar shook his head and looked sympathetically at Kyri. "Sorry, Phoenix."

Inside he was more tense. *We know for a fact that Miri's wrong; there's been contact with* something *in our part of the world for a long, long time; leaving aside Thornfalcon's secret weapon, the language proves it. And it's pretty much guaranteed that whoever or whatever it is has to be somewhere in their capital city.*

Then they crested the hill; even before then, Tobimar realized he was seeing *something* in the sky, but only as they reached the top did it dawn on him what that something *was*.

For long moments Tobimar was only conscious of staring, his mouth half open.

Sha Kaizatenzei Valatar lay before them, less than five miles distant. The city walls were pure white, fifty feet or more in height, surrounding a perfect circle two miles in diameter. But those walls looked tiny, a mere line of snow-brightness around an assembly of delicate, shining constructs that *soared* into the air, floating, held down—or supported?—by spiraling crystalline threads.

In the center, a Tower stretched into the sky so high that the wisps of cloud in the blue were drifting *below* the Tower's apex, which shone with a spark of polychromatic brilliance, a Tower shimmering like a tracery of frost and a dusting of rainbow against the endless blue of the heights and the deeper blue of the great Lake behind, a Tower so slender that it looked like a single stalk of wheat thousands of feet high, growing from a building like a closed flower, with arching traceries of gold and silver surrounding crystal and marble curves dotted with windows.

Bridges as thin as dreams connected the high buildings across the city, bridges with no supports that arched half a mile and more across the sky. Below, Sha Kaizatenzei Valatar sparkled, a thousand handfuls of gem-dust sprinkled in a perfectly arranged wheel, radiating out from that central Tower.

Tobimar finally closed his mouth, then bowed low to Miri. "I must beg your pardon, Light Miri," he said.

She blinked in surprise, though her smile at their astonishment could not be hidden. "My pardon? For what?"

"For our doubts," Kyri replied, bowing herself.

"We have seen many cities," Tobimar said, unable to keep his eyes from the shining city before him, "including *Fanalam' T' ameris' a' u' Zahr-a-Thana T'ikon*, Zarathanton as we mortals have called it, and we were agreed that there was no possible way in which any city in this small and hidden country could rival the majesty or beauty or power we saw there."

"And we were wrong," Kyri said, an awed tone in her voice. "For I cannot say for sure which city looks greater to me."

"Nor can I," Tobimar said. "So we beg your pardon for having doubted you. If Sha Kaizatenzei Valatar is not the greatest city in the world, it is surely a close-run race indeed."

Miri laughed and clapped her hands. "You are forgiven! For really, I rather *thought* you'd believe that, and hoped to astound you once more." She grabbed Kyri's hand. "Come *on*, then! If we hasten, we can take our supper at the table of Lady Shae herself!"

CHAPTER 32

Kyri couldn't keep herself from gawking as they finally entered Sha Kaizatenzei Valatar. The sun was setting, casting long, pink-tinted shadows across the city, and the softening light made the buildings with their impossible delicacy look even more ethereal. The bridges they had seen, bridges which in some cases spanned half the city, were made of polished slabs of shining metal, stone, and wood that simply *sat* on thin air, with exquisitely slender traceries forming railings on either side. Aside from the railings, nothing linked the slabs together or supported them.

Pointing with her one free hand (Miri having the other currently), Kyri said, "Miri, how is that *possible*? I know that in theory magic can do almost anything, but that's..."

Miri laughed. "Oh, we can't do that by ourselves. Not yet, anyway."

"Not yet," agreed Hiriista. "I had forgotten how this must look to one who had never seen such things. The civilization that was here before us... they had solved many riddles that elude others, and one was obviously how to conquer the rule of air and weight. Within buried wreckage and ruins across Kaizatenzei there are pieces of what seem to have been ships and buildings which, freed of their entombment, could soar of their own accord into the sky, needing neither power nor ritual to do so."

"Amazing," she said. *One more confirmation of the legend of the Lords of the Sky. Even now, twelve thousand years later, parts of their ships are still ready to soar.* "So you built all of this?"

"Almost all," Miri said. "The Tower of Light was here before any of us, and holds the Great Light within it. Its delicacy and beauty inspired us, however, and thus we have tried, as much as we can, to make our city complement and reflect the loveliness of the Tower."

The Great Light. Tobimar's glance was lightning-quick, but she knew what he was thinking. *Unless our deductions are entirely wrong, then up there is the Sun of Terian, probably the most sacred relic of Tobimar's religion.*

"The Great Light?" Tobimar asked, even as she thought that.

"Our symbol and support," Miri said, pointing to the shining multicolored brilliance at the very top of the Valatar Tower. "The Great Light and its Tower were here in the beginning, and have endured even when the other towers across the land finally fell."

A perfect opening. "I remember someone mentioning towers standing in the other cities. So were there lights of some sort in those, as well?"

"According to the old records, yes; lights very like the Great Light, but they faded or vanished eventually, and when they did, their towers crumbled." Miri anticipated their next question. "And we don't know why they faded; some think that their light was merged with the Great Light, others that it was used defending us from the darkness surrounding Kaizatenzei.

"But the Great Light has never flickered or faded, and we believe it is eternal."

"I would truly love to see it. Is that possible?" Kyri was impressed by how controlled Tobimar's apparently casual question was.

"You will have to ask Lady Shae—but, honestly? I can't see that she'd say *no*! Not only are you unique visitors, but also you've done so much for us simply on your way here that I can't imagine her denying you much of anything."

Even the houses within Valatar were beautiful, though Kyri realized that part of that was the singing *rightness* which was more intense and pure here than ever before. To her eyes, everything was touched with a hint of light, from the older gentleman who bowed and stepped aside to let them pass to the little girl chasing a feathered lizard—obviously a pet—around her yard, to the houses and even the birds that fluttered by. *What must it be like to* live *here?*

The base of the Valatar Tower was even more beautiful at close range than it had been from afar. Kyri was entranced by the filigree of crystal and metal—gold, platinum, and others—worked through the polished stone of the folded-petal walls. *It even seems... no, it does shimmer with light of its own.* She could feel, now, a faint *Presence* far above, a power that was not that of Myrionar but echoed the purity and majesty that she had felt from the god when it had manifested to her. *It must be the Sun, then. What else could it be?*

But as she concentrated on that sense, for a moment—a splintered instant—she felt *another* Presence—no, at least *two* other Presences, in a flash as though a door had abruptly opened and shut, or she had walked past a wall with a tiny hole through which light could pass in only one direction. But *these* Presences were neither light nor comforting. One was immense, black, brooding, hungry, filled with fire and resentment. The other was cold, calm, calculating, but with dark amusement waiting just beneath and a vast well of power waiting to be drawn upon.

At the same moment the ground shook beneath them, a faint but emphatic shudder that jingled crystal, set the Tower swaying for a moment, and made everyone stumble just a bit.

That gave her enough time to hide her reaction. She managed to keep any expression from her face, caught herself and kept moving forward without more than the slightest hitch in her stride. Her heart sank, and Kyri realized that part of her had really started to believe that Kaizatenzei was as pure as it looked.

But it's not, and there are dark, dark enemies waiting for us, perhaps within the castle itself.

At the same time, that didn't mean that most people here were not exactly what they appeared to be. She believed... she *had* to believe... that most of what she saw was real.

"Are earthquakes common here?" Tobimar was asking.

Kyri thought that there was a fractional pause before Miri answered, as though she were distracted. But if there was, it was extremely short. "Not *common*, but not unheard of."

She pointed to the shore of the great lake, which was visible down one of the streets; Kyri could see small, disturbed waves lapping chaotically at the beach. "The source appears to be somewhere out in Enneisolaten. You remember there are volcanoes near Alatenzei; if such are somewhere beneath the great Lake, it is unsurprising we'd have these occasional shakes."

The door to the Tower flowered open before them, and she saw the entrance hall was as light and airy as the exterior, with arching filigrees of silver and pearl outlining and emphasizing the curves of the almost translucently delicate walls, and marble of many subtle shades—rose, white, violet, shading to aqua and azure below.

Within were two guards—a somewhat-overbroad man, dark-skinned with a great black bushy beard, and a slender waifish woman with startlingly pale blonde hair—both wearing armor similar in design to Miri's. The man's armor was deep violet and indigo overall, while the woman's was amber and citrine with hints of orange.

The man straightened up instantly—he had been leaning nonchalantly against the wall—and raised an eyebrow. "Back so soon, Miri? Why, you left only this morning!" His voice had the rumbling timbre of a man who, if he chose to shout, could probably be heard a mile away.

The other guard had looked more at the newcomers. "I think she completed her mission, Tanvol."

"What? Oh, marvelous! Are these—"

"They are! Phoenix, Tobimar, this is Tanvol Davrys, Seventh Light, and Anora Lal, Third Light of Kaizatenzei."

The two Lights bowed in the same manner as Miri, and Kyri strove to match them. "May your days be ever bright. Welcome to the Valatar Tower, Phoenix and Tobimar." Tanvol glanced a bit farther back. "And of course you as well, old lizard."

"I thank you, naked mammal," Hiriista said with a steamkettle laugh. "Greetings to you, Anora."

"And you, Hiriista. I see you've been making sure our visitors stayed out of trouble."

A hiss of amusement. "Oh, I think I might describe things differently."

"Come *on*," Miri said. "We can talk later, right now I have to bring them to—"

"Yes, yes, go on, Lady Shae's mentioned multiple times that she wanted these visitors brought in straightaway," laughed Tanvol.

The next door flowered inward, rather than outward, and led to an intersection, with a corridor that obviously proceeded around the entire building, and another short corridor directly ahead, ending in a large set of double doors that looked as delicate and ethereal as the rest of the Tower. Despite that, Kyri had a feeling that she would find it impossible to break those portals unless she called upon the power of Myrionar—and maybe not even then. "Miri, is there any particular tradition or ritual we should observe when greeting Lady Shae here?"

Miri hesitated. "Well...no, not really. I mean, there's a normal bow and greeting that citizens do if they're coming to ask her help or have her hear a case, but you're not citizens and don't fit in any other category. You're *unique!*"

With that, she bounced (there was no other way to describe it) to the doors and flung them open. "Shae, they're *here!*"

Tobimar failed to restrain a snort of laughter. "No ritual indeed."

Kyri couldn't keep a grin off her face. "But that *is* Miri."

As they entered, they could see a similar tolerant, fond smile on Lady Shae's face. "Yes, I see they are. You might have announced them properly...but all right, I see you couldn't possibly have done so." Shae stood and bowed, which they returned. "Phoenix of Myrionar, Tobimar of Zarathanton, I bid you welcome." The smile took on a hint of Miri's mischief. "And what do you think of our little town?"

Kyri found herself laughing along with Tobimar. "Was it so terribly obvious, Lady Shae?" she finally managed.

"That you thought we were a quaint, small country which was probably not terribly advanced? Not *obvious*, perhaps, but certainly easy enough to derive from your conversations."

"Well, as we said to Light Miri," Kyri said, now serious, "we apologize for misjudging you...and for doubting the beauty and majesty of this, your capital."

"Apology accepted, and thank you." Lady Shae strode down her steps to face them. As Kyri had remembered, Shae was even taller than she was, towering at least a half-head above her, huge yet beautiful; she moved like a gloomcat or other big predator, lazily yet with confident power. "I had not expected you for another several days, at least, but it will not take long to arrange a proper welcome."

"You mean a large and complex banquet which will include many political pit-traps for me to evade."

Miri giggled and then caught herself, but Shae also smiled. "Perhaps that is a bit *too* accurate, but yes. Miri, take them to the guestrooms we set aside, and let them prepare. Dinner will be in...an hour and a half, shall we say?"

Miri bowed and then turned to the others. "This way!"

No rest yet. But I think I don't have much choice.

And with what I sensed...now I know we're at the right place.

CHAPTER 33

"There were some crystals that seemed suspicious," Poplock told his three friends, "but I was able to blind them, if they're watchstones, and a few wards made sure they're not listening through those. Otherwise, nothing."

"Watchstones? Really?" The *mazakh* looked worried.

"Like I said, I'm not sure—but they just didn't quite seem to fit with everything around them, and this place looks like it was built with no expense considered too big, you know?"

Hiriista went to the indicated locations and studied the small crystals, now covered with what appeared to be dull mud. After a few minutes he sighed. "I believe you are correct, my friend. A *most* disquieting thing to discover here."

"You sure they weren't here all along?"

"Of course they..." Hiriista trailed off. "No," he said finally, "no, I am not sure. I have never been in this *particular* set of rooms before, to begin with, but to be completely honest with you, I have never *suspected* such a thing, so upon reflection I find I cannot say that there were not any such things where I have stayed in the past. Still," he said with a sighing hiss, "it is, as I said, most disquieting."

"I find it almost comforting," Kyri said from where she was brushing her hair, getting it back under control after the shower she had taken; Poplock always found that drying brush of hers fascinating, as it was such a delicately adjusted magical item of such utterly mundane utility. It also had the apparent side effect of drying clothing underneath the hair, preventing the white-and-green, elaborate dress Kyri had selected from her neverfull pack from being streaked and spotted with water.

"*Comforting?*" repeated Tobimar with incredulity, as he also tended to his hair; he was avoiding the trouble of water spotting by leaving his fancy jacket and shirt off, only his singlet still covering his upper body. "What in the name of the Light do you find comforting in the idea that our hosts are, or could be, spying on us?"

Kyri smiled, though Poplock thought he saw a very sad edge to the smile. "Two reasons, really. First . . . honestly, put yourself in *their* position, and especially the Lady Shae's. Here come these people through a pass that, as far as you know, leads to something as close to Hell as the world could hold. They *seem* to be all good people, they *appear* to be heroes that you could trust, but *are* they?"

"True," Poplock said with a bounce. "And really, that's the way *we're* looking at *them*, right?"

"Given what we were expecting when we came here . . . yes, I guess so," Tobimar conceded. "So you're saying that doing so indicates that they aren't being stupidly trusting."

"Right, or at least that's one big possibility. The other is that Lady Shae or someone else here that's running the show suspects that we're a danger, and they're spying on us specifically to find out what we are and what we know."

"Which is almost comforting because it means that your deductions were correct and the evil you seek is, indeed, here in Valatar," Hiriista said.

"Right."

Tobimar glanced warily at the blackened crystals. "But if they're trying to spy on us to see what we know, and they see that their watchstones and other scrying aren't working, I'm wondering if we're in danger right now."

Poplock gave a deliberate shrug. "If they're that focused on finding out our secrets and ready to move? Yep, I'd expect they'll be pounding on our doors any minute now. But I'm betting not. If they're not routinely used, no one will notice what we've done, at least not soon. If they *are* routinely used, they probably still don't want to call *attention* to it, and if *we* are polite enough not to mention it, they probably will let the subject be passed over. It becomes a signal—'I know that you know that I know,' if you know what I mean?"

Tobimar laughed. "I guess I do know. Yes, if Mother for some reason *was* spying on one of our guests back home, and the guest found out, neither of them would ever actually *comment* on it unless they felt the confrontation would itself be worth the effort. You're right."

"So if we aren't suddenly attacked in the next few minutes, we can figure that we're safe for the moment, anyway," Kyri said. "All right. We've only got a half hour before we have to go downstairs, so I have to tell you now: I sensed something dark, just when we were arriving."

Poplock found himself leaning forward in anticipation. *Well, dust and mud! I'm actually* glad *we're finding something! No wonder people back home though I was a little dried in the head.*

"Sensed what?" Tobimar asked.

"Two things, actually. Both very strong. One of them was... angry. Hungry. I got an impression of fire and night at the same time. The other one was much more focused... felt very dark but controlled, amused, considered, and had an incredible mass of power associated with it."

Hiriista narrowed his eyes. "Did you get a direction? A distance?"

Kyri screwed up her face, thinking, then shook her head. "I have to *guess* that it's close—maybe in the Tower itself somewhere—but that's just a guess, based on the fact that it was only here that I sensed it. But I suppose the Tower, with the Great Light above, could also be focusing powers like mine. Myrionar and Terian are closely allied, after all."

Tobimar frowned, shaking his head. "That's what worries me most. The Stars and Sun were... *are* artifacts of Terian himself; it was said that Terian constructed them with his own hand and infused them with his power, and Terian is acknowledged even by the other gods as one of the three or four most powerful beings of all. How in the name of the Light could evil *live* in proximity to that power, let alone hide from it?"

"Yeah, that's sure been buzzing just out of reach for me, too," Poplock said. "What I've heard is that anything really evil—the kind of darkness Phoenix senses and all—that even *touches* one of Terian's artifacts goes *poof* in a big flash of light like the core of a lightning bolt, nothing left, just ashes. You'd think Demons and whatever would stay away from that like giant ants avoid Pondsparkle."

"You would, yes," Hiriista said thoughtfully. "Yet do not underestimate our opposition. If—as the Phoenix's senses indicate, and the logical progression of your quest would require—somewhere here is hidden a vastly powerful portion of a demonic conspiracy, then it is not in fact so badly affected." He pulled out his scentpipe, which Poplock noticed Hiriista did whenever thinking hard.

"Still," Hiriista continued slowly, "we can take it as a given that nothing of true evil would *choose* to stay near such powerful artifacts of a deity of the light unless there was some very, very strong motivation, some huge benefit to be gained from it."

"Well, it camouflages them, right?" Poplock pointed out.

"Hmm, yes, I think we can take that as a given at this point. The radiance of the Lights literally dazzles the senses, to the point that even those of lesser gods cannot penetrate the light around them to see the darkness just a short distance away.

"Yet..." Hiriista inhaled scent, contemplated for a moment; Kyri and Tobimar were still finishing their hair, but were otherwise silent and attentive. Poplock waited.

The *mazakh* magewright shook his head with a hiss. "Yet there is more...much more...behind this. If what the stories Miri recounted say is true, then your Seven Stars are *gone*. Something has destroyed artifacts of one of the most powerful gods. Yet the *effects* of their presence remain; we can sense this in every one of the major cities that had one of the towers of the ancient days. Why? Surely the *objective* of destroying such an artifact would be to neutralize its effect, wipe out its power."

"Unless," Poplock suggested, "they wanted to *use* its power?"

"But using it would..." He paused again. "You may have something there, my little friend. I am utterly unsure how it could be accomplished, but the idea of *taking* the power of one of the gods would be tremendously attractive to any demon, if they could figure out some method to avoid said power-theft from being fatal." He breathed out a few more scent-clouds. "I must think on this...and observe what is said and done. I trust you will all do the same."

"Oh, trust me, my eyes will be watching *everywhere*," Poplock said emphatically.

"Count on it," Tobimar said, taking Kyri's hand and giving it an emphatic squeeze. "So this dinner might be useful."

"Almost certainly," Hiriista agreed.

At that moment there was a soft knock on the door. "Lady Phoenix and company, dinner is served," said the voice on the other side—a man's voice, which Poplock thought belonged to a gray-haired man in severely-cut robes who had been just to one side of Lady Shae's throne. This memory was confirmed when Tobimar opened the door and the man bowed low. "If you will all accompany me . . . ?"

"Certainly, Pelda," Hiriista said, putting his pipe away.

Pelda led them down one of the flights of stairs they had taken to get there, but from there turned down a smaller hallway that curved around the interior of the Palace and through a doorway on one side. As they entered, Poplock felt Tobimar relax slightly and similar relief become visible on Kyri's face as they saw that the room, while large, was no great dining hall or ballroom, and the long table in the center was adequate for ten but not for a hundred.

"Welcome, Phoenix of Evanwyl, Tobimar of Zarathanton, and of course Hiriista!" said Lady Shae, rising as they entered. "Come, sit here to my side, that I may speak with you easily." She gestured to three seats that were at her left hand, as Lady Shae was seated at one end of the table.

"Thank you, Lady Shae," Kyri said, taking her indicated place directly next to the ruler of Kaizatenzei; Tobimar (with Poplock on his shoulder) sat next to her, and Hiriista took the third seat. Directly across from Kyri was Miri, with her fellow Lights Tanvol and Anora in the next corresponding seats. "I had thought from your words that there would be a great banquet—"

"Yes, that *was* my first thought, but Miri and the others pointed out that there was hardly time to properly arrange it, and undoubtedly many of the guests I would wish to attend would already have other plans this night. Time enough for that later." Shae smiled. "And besides, I suspect you could do without such pomp for this night, am I correct?"

"*Quite* correct, Lady Shae!" Kyri answered emphatically, something Tobimar echoed.

A door on the other side of the room opened, and Shae rose with a delighted expression. "But here is one guest I had *hoped* to introduce you to. Welcome, Master Wieran!"

At *that* name Poplock focused all of his attention on the

newcomer—without, of course, being obvious about it, which was something hard to do. Fortunately, he'd had a lot of practice over the past months of looking cluelessly stupid and gazing seemingly at nothing while actually studying something carefully.

The first thing that struck him was *precision*. The figure of Master Wieran was tall, angular, sharp, wearing an immaculate white outfit that covered him almost like a gown, yet was set in creases as clear as the cut of a formal suit, emphasizing the man's height and spare figure. A single row of black buttons ran straight up the center of the sculpted gown or coat he wore, and small instruments of some sort projected from an exterior breast pocket. Wieran's face was long, narrow, with a high forehead; his hair was moderately long and arrow-straight, white as the snow of the mountain heights.

Black, glittering eyes peered sharply from deeply sunken sockets beneath snow-white brows and scanned the entire room with a penetrating gaze as intense as any Poplock had ever seen; that gaze seemed to linger for an instant longer on Poplock than the little Toad was comfortable with.

Then Master Wieran's thin-lipped mouth turned up in a smile and he spoke—in a startlingly low and gentle tone. "Thank you, Lady Shae. It was fortunate that my experiments are all in a condition to be left to themselves for a few hours." He gave a bow that was as precise and unnaturally abrupt as the opening and closing of a fine pair of scissors. "And the chance to meet people who claim to have come from beyond the mountains, through the Pass of Night? Hardly to be missed."

Wieran strode—with a quick, unvarying rhythm that reinforced Poplock's impression—and took his seat at the very end of the table, opposite Lady Shae.

Fascinating, Poplock thought. *Symbolically that makes them near-equals, facing each other, each dominating one end of the table, making him possibly outrank even the Lights in importance.*

"We've heard much about you, Master Wieran," Kyri said. "It's good to finally meet you. I am called the Phoenix of Evanwyl, and this is Tobimar of Zarathanton and elsewhere. I understand you already know—"

"—Hiriista, yes, of course." That gaze flicked—the merest blink of light from beneath the brows—to Poplock again before returning to Kyri. Poplock kept still, but he had a feeling that

Wieran already suspected something. *And if so, he's* really *danger-ous. Even Hiriista had to think for a while about whether I was worth suspecting or not.* "*The* Phoenix—a title, then. Your armor was described to me. Symbolic?"

"Yes; I am a representative of the god Myrionar, and when becoming one of Its Justiciars, I relinquished my birth name for the symbol."

"Representative of a god? Most intriguing," Wieran said, as servants came in with floating trays of food. *Well, now, that's just showing off this stuff they have. If they can do* this *with it, I'd think they'd have used some of it in the other cities.* Poplock could think of a *lot* of uses for a material that could float like that. "There are only a few gods worshipped significantly in Kai-zatenzei, and I have not heard yours named before."

Kyri gave a wry shrug. "Honestly, there aren't that many outside of my hometown who *have* anymore." She looked at the tall white-haired man. "You said 'people who claim to come from beyond the mountains'; does that means you doubt our claim?"

"It means I am *exact* in my wording, Phoenix." The smile that took the edge off the wording was, to Poplock's eyes, just a fractional second too late and too mechanical, a quick afterthought added by rote. "As I do not have *proof* that you have indeed accomplished that which was previously considered impossible, I cannot simply accept it without reservation. I therefore view your statements as claims and will continue to do so unless and until I have been presented with adequate proof."

"I see," Tobimar said. "A wise policy for an...alchemist, as I understand it?"

"Alchemy is one of the disciplines I have studied and con-tinue to study, yes," Wieran answered, as he used a two-tined fork to convey a slice of some brown root to his mouth; Poplock noticed that even Wieran's *plate* reflected his precision, with the food divided up very evenly between three separate locations on the plate, separated by ruler-straight empty spaces. "But I am no more a simple alchemist than you, by your appearance, are merely a swordsman. I am a student of all things that lie beyond the merely physical, and their interactions with the world; alchemy, gemcalling, symbolic enchantment, elemental magic, essential wizardry, the powers of the gods, all of these and more are my field of study."

"And if we continue down this path," Shae said with a chuckle, "he will talk about all of them, in detail, for the entirety of our dinner, which I think might prove tedious for the rest of us."

Wieran responded with a quick, sharp snort that showed annoyance at being interrupted, but it was a momentary thing only; in the next moment he gave a smooth shrug and smiled at Lady Shae. "As you say; I have a habit of discussing my work at length whenever opportunity presents itself."

"I don't mind," Tobimar said. "I'm sure it would be a fascinating lecture—"

"—but there is time for that later," Miri said, instantly cutting off the possibility that Wieran might mistake that for an invitation. "I think Lady Shae—and most of the rest of us—would like to hear more about where Phoenix and Tobimar come from! That would be more evidence for you, wouldn't it?"

Despite his narrow construction, Wieran gave a momentary impression of bristling and puffing out like an agitated blowsnake. "What? That's merely hearsay, it could be nothing but tall tales and fantasy..." He trailed off, then resumed. "Yet, yes, perhaps. Even the most elaborate tale eventually must show its nature; it is not possible for mortal minds to create a world that remains consistent under all scrutiny. So perhaps, yes, it could be evidence." He glanced at Tobimar and Kyri—and for the briefest instant, again, it seemed his gaze touched upon Poplock.

"Well, then, Phoenix, could you tell us something of Evanwyl? Adventures, sights, tales?" Lady Shae asked.

"Well...of course I can," Kyri answered. After a moment, she began, "I guess I'll start by telling you how we came to be here..."

As the story unfolded, Poplock watched, and every so often, those black, deep-set eyes seemed to meet his.

CHAPTER 34

"Do not *ever*," Master Wieran said coldly, "drag me into such an utter waste of time again. Sitting there listening to that... Phoenix, and our key, drone on about their adventures—which are utterly irrelevant—"

"*Not* irrelevant!" Miri said, cutting him off, anger building in her at the man's dismissive tone. "What she did and her companion did—"

"Compani*ons*, you mean," Wieran said.

"I was referring mostly to the time they spent *outside* of Kaizatenzei, though there are some very interesting and instructive events that have taken place on their way here. And there are indications that they had a third member of their group on occasion, but for the most part—"

Wieran's contemptuous gaze halted her in mid-sentence. "And *you* are one of the greater Demons?" he said, in a tone similar to someone discovering that a much-anticipated present is a cheap and shoddy imitation. "You have spent *weeks* in their company, and you *still* have not the faintest understanding that you were traveling, not with three other people, but with *four*?"

"Four? But—" she froze. *It can't be. That stupid little creature—*

"You *are* utterly blind, and nigh lackwit, as near as I can tell. If you and Shae did not have resources necessary to my research..." Weiran controlled himself with a visible effort. "Yes, *four*. The Toad that accompanies Tobimar is intelligent, perhaps the *most* intelligent of their party. He is the observer, their secret weapon, and—I suspect—their party's magician."

249

Wieran turned away, adjusted a valve and gestured, causing another valve a distance away to open. "Were you *completely* unaware of the fact that they have gaps in their stories, that there were clear areas where events did not quite match up correctly—where even a very minor bit of thought would reveal there was a missing factor—a third companion who was being excluded from the descriptions consistently?"

"I..."

"Pah. Leaving that aside, you are clearly unable to use those blankly gazing orbs that you call 'eyes' for anything useful. That creature's anatomy differs—in easily observable particulars—from that of any nonintelligent Toad in at least four ways."

She found her fists clenching, felt power starting to crackle around them, glaring at the back of the alchemist-sage. *Just one strike, just one, and he will never speak again!*

However, she knew they still *needed* Wieran. "Well, then, my apologies for this failure. Will it delay the final opening?"

Wieran opened one of the sealed tubes, looked in, shook his head, and called Tashriel over. "This subject is no longer functional. Clean this out and we will find another."

He turned back to her, by which time she had managed to force herself to relax back to her normal harmless self; by the quick glance Tashriel gave her as he began removing a desiccated mummy from the tube, her momentary lapse might not have completely escaped notice.

Wieran showed no sign of being aware of how close he had come to being cut down, however. He merely nodded. "A minor delay, perhaps, to evaluate the effect and impact of this Toad's presence. But the major delay will simply be the final preparations for the opening. For that I do need to characterize Tobimar Silverun in detail, and—"

An ice-cold shock overwhelmed her. "Wait. *What did you call him?*"

"Tobimar Silverun. Seventh of Seven of Skysand." He looked at her pale face in chill amusement. "So even *that* you did not know?"

"He...he is one of the *Lords of the Sky*?"

"The Lords of the Sky are dead, Ermirinovas. He is a descendant of their line, yes. What did you believe the key *was* that I needed?"

"You said it had to be someone of particular characteristics—magical characteristics you enumerated, and you had me send that information to my contacts, but I never imagined that you were talking about—"

"Who *else*?" Wieran snapped, clearly out of what little patience he had. "What other being on Zarathan—save only Terian himself, the creator of the artifact—would be able to unlock that power? Only a rightful descendant, by blood, of those to whom the Seven Stars and Single Sun were *given* in the beginning, or, perhaps, one whom Terian selected to replace them, had they died out entirely."

"And you never thought to tell me this directly?" she asked, feeling an unnatural calm settle on her, a calm backed by a towering rage that rose in the background like a tsunami approaching the shore.

"I had thought you had the wit to—"

"*ENOUGH!*" She felt her form expand, talons extending from her hands as she backhanded the white-haired alchemist, sending him tumbling across the dark, rune covered stone. "Your arrogance and belittling of my capabilities is bad enough, but you use that arrogance and your disregard for others' ability as an *excuse* for every single failure of communication! I have had enough of it, *Master* Wieran!"

As he began a gesture, calculating anger on his own face, she pointed a finger at him, with red-black fire seething about it. "*No.* Do not try it, or I swear I will bring down this entire *room* on you, ruining every experiment you have set in motion." Weiran froze. "Good. Yes, that would cost us dearly as well, but I am now beyond any patience with this.

"We were *hunting them down, you idiot!*" she thundered, and crystal chimed in sympathy all around the great array. "If you'd *bothered* to make sure I understood *what* you were looking for, I might have been able to get such a key *myself*, and at the least I would have called in the demons who were busy hunting down any of the line that left their homeland!"

Wieran looked at her expressionlessly for a long moment, then sighed and slowly—unthreateningly—rose from the floor. He ignored the trickle of blood flowing from his mouth—a trickle which was already slowing. He bowed with more emphasis than his usual automatic salute. "I accept your . . . critique of my performance, Ermirinovas," he said, and his voice held a small but audible note of apology. "Your capabilities and knowledge in my specialty are of necessity going to be less than my own—otherwise you would have no need of me—and I should have made sure you understand the nature of the key in all its aspects. I should also endeavor to be less...judgmental of you in our interactions."

She suspected he was not nearly so contrite as he wished her to believe, but even this was a major concession, and she knew they couldn't afford to kill Wieran. Her real regret was that by not being told the true nature of the key, several of her best agents had been left following a course of action that was exactly the opposite of what was needed, and at least one of them—Lady Misuuma—had ceased to report, presumably killed, quite some months back.

Now that she thought on that, and the location and timing of the reports, she realized that Misuuma's death must have been one of the "various adventures" which Tobimar had skipped over in their retelling. *They've been successfully hiding details of who and what they are, even from me.* "What about the Phoenix?" she asked. "What do you know about her that I don't?"

"She is hardly relevant. I know nothing more of her than you do; the only important point was that she is an emissary of a god, and I will characterize that as well during the next week or three."

"Not relevant?"

"Not for our goal, no." He looked at her with mild surprise. "After all, you will kill her prior to the event, yes?"

"Of course," Miri heard herself say, but within her was suddenly a strange, deep ache, a pain that sapped her of the joy and anticipation such a wonderful opportunity would normally offer. "Well...I have other preparations to make. Will you be able to gather your information without the monitors in their rooms?" It now occurred to her that the little Toad's intelligence explained the minor mystery of how and why those monitors had gone dark, without any apparent actions by Phoenix, Tobimar, or Hiriista. She had *thought* it might be Hiriista doing something extremely sneaky, which would have been worrisome; Hiriista going rogue would be a problem.

"Yes; that was an anticipated setback. I will take them on a tour of my secondary laboratory, and during that time I believe I can gather all the remaining key information."

"Then I will leave you to your work."

By the time she made it up the stairs, Miri had managed to banish the pain from within her. It might not, after all, be necessary to *kill* Phoenix, or she might force the issue.

But why was the idea even worth *worrying* about?

What's wrong with me?

The unsettling feeling made her angry and nervous, but fortunately there was an obvious outlet for that, and she headed for her own room and a certain shining scroll.

"Ermirinovas? What a pleasant surprise," Viedra said, smiling his usual urbane, infuriatingly calm smile.

"It would have been much more pleasant for *me* if you had mentioned that Phoenix had *two* companions rather than *one!*"

The smile broadened. "I *wondered* when you would realize that. Yes, that little Toad is a *most* formidable opponent. I would strongly recommend you do not underestimate him, because—"

"Why didn't you *tell* me?"

Now the smile narrowed, and the glint of teeth sharpened. "Because it amused me *not* to, Ermirinovas. It wasn't relevant to your questions, and you didn't ask the questions to which it *would* have been relevant."

"He has had nearly a *day* here without anyone knowing to keep an *eye* on him. I don't *think* he's discovered anything crucial, but it could have been devastating—"

"Yes, it could have been, and I was wondering when and how you would discover it." The smile returned to its bland form, but the teeth still glittered with death. "I have given you much assistance, Ermirinovas, my dear; that does not mean you are yourself of terribly great importance to *me.*"

"I could tell Father of your—"

"Oh, tish! I assure you, Father has far bigger things to worry about than our little maneuverings."

"The Black City...?"

"Is under siege as we speak, yes. And to my considerable surprise, two of the Sixteen have joined the forces."

"What?" Miri was stunned. "But I thought—"

"Yes, indeed, the cycle currently favors the Elderwyrm, and I had rather hoped that this would cause all of the T'Teranahm of any note to retreat to their great slumber for a few centuries or millennia, but someone—probably the old Spiritsmith, though perhaps the Wanderer en route to something else—kicked both

S'her and Valorkhlmba hard enough to keep them awake. So Father's going to be rather well entertained. Besides," he continued, leaning back and grinning, "he's going to have *so* many more reasons to be unhappy with me shortly."

What? He sounds completely relaxed *with that idea! Making the Lord of All Hells unhappy with you*—"What do you mean?"

"Oh, it will be mostly a matter of the plan coming apart here and there—I suspect Aegeia isn't *quite* as neutralized as reports would have had it, the Academy's probably managed to prevent its utter destruction, and something appears to be giving Balgoltha a truly difficult time finishing off Nya-Sharee-Hilya. Oh, and those forces sent to try and actually make a real assault on Skysand, well, I'm not expecting good news from that quarter, either. That old soul-wizard's been a busy man, I must say. Yes, Father will want me putting out fires and patching the plans, I think, at least until he's sure that he can crush all the major opponents to his rule in one battle. And that will be...five months from now, more or less, if I read things right."

She recognized the warning tone in his voice. If she brought up the minor maneuverings Viedra had done that might annoy Father *now*, they might prove a distraction to Kerlamion's *main* plans...and anything that distracted him from that goal would trigger his wrath. In other words, even if Viedra suffered, so would she.

"I see you understand. Now that you've figured out the last surprise of our traveling band of heroes, I'm sure you can address the problem. Yes?"

She ground her teeth. "Yes."

"Excellent. How is little Condor doing?"

"Oddly."

"How so?"

"He's carrying a weapon that I can *smell* Father on—I swear it's almost like a piece of his sword—"

"It is, in fact, a shard of that blade," Viedra said cheerfully.

"By the Dark! How...never mind. But that just makes it stranger. He's carrying something as black of essence as anything I've seen, yet all he's doing is heroic work. I can distract and slow him by making sure he hears about any trouble in the vicinity, and he may be annoyed at the delay, but he always seems willing to help those in need."

"*Really?*" Viedra broke into peals of hearty laughter. "Well I *must* say that's a surprise—a pleasant one, in some ways, but very much a surprise. I rather expected he'd be something more a monster than you or I in some ways by now."

"Well, he's not. And why a *pleasant* surprise?"

Viedra's smile shifted hardly at all, but suddenly she was seized with the conviction that what she saw was not what she had thought it was, but something far worse; there was a momentary flash of deathly yellow in the eyes, the expression showed a vast and ancient amusement that seemed that of a being very different from even Viedraverion. "Oh, now, that's part of *my* plan, Miri. If you complete *your* little project, now...if you do that, I may even explain that plan to you. But not yet."

That alien, terrifying sensation was gone, even in the moment she had felt it, but the effect of it was not. She had no desire to continue to speak with Viedra at all. "Very well. We will speak again."

She cut off even before his usual jaunty farewell and sat in the quiet comfort of her room, alone and silent, for long minutes. Finally, she took a deep breath and forced thoughts of doubt and confusion from her mind.

I'll go let Shae know about our extra visitor, and then I'll find out what Phoenix is up to!

The thought gave lightness to her heart, and she found herself once more bouncing along, anticipating the next sight of the tall Justiciar, while a part of her wondered *why.*

CHAPTER 35

"Draw your sword, little human. Draw your sword and let me kill you fairly." The distorted face of the *bilarel* grinned broadly, showing huge yellow teeth that looked even worse contrasted with the clay-gray skin, and matched the dull yellow eyes.

Condor's lips tightened as he evaluated the rest of the creature. It wasn't, really, a *bilarel*, but something that used to be, or could have been, one of the giant humanoids; the thing must have come over the Wall here at Evening Dawn, midway between Hishitenzei and Ruratenzei, and it showed all the hideousness of the other things from that twisted forest. *Bilarel* normally looked like gigantic gray strongmen, all smooth, impossibly huge muscles bulging on a frame that simply exaggerated the ideal.

This thing's skin was covered with rough patches like stone, some of the patches growing sharp spines. It wore a swaying shirt of mail that reached nearly to the knees, a shirt whose looseness still failed to conceal the warped shape of the torso beneath, and held a huge axe in one hand; the other hand gripped a large shield. Worse, the forearms had naturally-growing *blades* running from wrist to elbow, and he had already seen that these were poisoned; Mallan Helbert lay twitching on the ground, his daughter trying desperately to administer some form of antidote.

No more time to waste; other people are hurt or in danger. "I'm not wasting my sword on something like you; you'd just get it dirty."

The thing's grin vanished, but it did not charge in anger, as

Condor had hoped. *Tilted* Balance, *the thing's a lot smarter than it looks.* The yellow eyes were studying *Condor* now, recognizing that only someone insane would make that speech...unless they had something to back it up with.

"Is that so?" it finally growled. "Well, I'll do my best to relieve you of that worry...forever." Instead of charging, it closed in slowly, cautiously, shield raised, knees bent so most of its body was protected, eyes watching the False Justiciar's every move as it moved forward, passing the large gray boulder that marked the border of Helbert's front yard.

Condor found himself tempted to draw the Demonshard. This thing was dangerous. But he knew full well that every contact with the sentient blade was a risk; yes, it was now cautious and recognized he was stronger-willed, but Condor knew it would never entirely give up; it was made as a tool of corruption. *As I should have expected from the King of All Hells; a part of me did, but didn't care, not then. And now...a little late.*

The axe screamed down and Condor leapt back, evading the strike, then tumbled sideways to force the creature to turn. This confirmed what he'd noticed when the thing first appeared; it was demon-quick with its arms, but the misshapen torso and perhaps other parts lower down hampered it slightly on the turns. *Which means...*

Condor sprinted sideways, forcing the thing to turn again. Then reversed, barely evading another strike of the axe, and reversed again, then reversed a *third* time. By this point the creature had realized the pattern and settled itself, readying for the next evading reverse.

Which never came, as Condor continued around, now almost *behind* the distorted *bilarel*, and then launched himself into the air, pushing off from the boulder he'd noted earlier. He somersaulted in midair and used the spinning motion to *drive* his heel down and around.

The Condor Raiment's black-forged boot smashed into the *bilarel*'s head like a sledgehammer; Condor could feel the crunching, squashing sensation of bone and flesh being crushed. He rebounded from the impact and completed a flip backwards, landing on his feet, and even as the monster roared in pain and stunned confusion, drove a gauntleted fist into the thing's side, ducked under a wild swing of the axe, and then caught the other arm, gauntlets protecting him from the bladed edge, levering down and around, and the creature teetered, then went *down* with an earthshaking crash.

That won't finish it, Aran, he told himself. But the impact had knocked the axe from the thing's grasp, and Condor dove for it, calling on the power that might be false as the Justiciars, but was still strong, strong, and he felt the massive weapon grow light in his hands; even as the creature shook itself, trying to rise, Condor brought the axe up and then down, as hard as he could. The meaty *thud* was met with an agonized grunt... and then silence.

He turned immediately to Mallan Helbert, whose breath was coming fast and irregular. "Please, let me," he said to Istiri Helbert. The young woman glanced at him helplessly and moved aside.

Using the power to heal was difficult—and these days Aran, the Condor Justiciar, appreciated the irony far less than he used to. But he forced the power to flow *just* so, and blue-gold light shimmered around the darkwood-skinned farmer; Istiri's eyes were wide as she saw the blood-wet cut across her father's chest closing up, a wound in reverse. Mallan's eyes slowly opened, showing his own wonder.

"Son... I don't know who you are, or how you came here at the right time, and I don't know how to thank you, either. But I'd surely like to know all three of those answers," he said after a moment.

Condor chuckled. "You can call me Condor." He gestured at his armor. "As for my timing, I'd heard about your troubles with disappearing livestock and such in town, and thought I'd come check it out. Apparently it decided there was no more need to be cautious just about the time I arrived."

"Are there... more of them, do you think?" Istiri was clearly afraid, but not terrified. Her father being wounded had frightened her more than the monster itself, Condor thought. *Strong woman. Though you'd expect that out here.* In some ways she sort of reminded him of Kyri—Istiri was tall, with long, straight black hair, though her eyes were dark and her face more heart-shaped.

"I doubt it; regular *bilarel* travel alone or in pairs, but this thing was a freak; it's almost certainly alone. If you really want to make sure, get some of the guards from town to check the area."

"You didn't answer the third question," the farmer said, slowly getting to his feet.

Condor shook his head. "No need to thank me with anything more than words. I've got a journey ahead of me and no time to stop...though I've got little choice if people are in danger."

"You're *sure*?" Istiri's voice echoed her father's incredulity. "You just risked—"

"Nothing terribly much, I assure you. Fighting things like that...it's my profession as a Justiciar of Myrionar." *Well, what else am I going to call myself? Not a False Justiciar. I'm not following anything else.*

"Then please accept our most deep and heartfelt thanks, Condor, Justiciar of Myrionar," Mallan said emphatically. "If journey you must, do so, and go safely. But you'll be welcome here for a day or a year, if ever you pass this way again."

"Then I thank you and accept your own thanks." He bowed and, hearing them call farewells after him, strode towards the south, hoping to regain the Necklace and get in at least a few more hours of travel before night fell.

Events like this one...they gave him *hope*. He knew that was a terribly, terribly dangerous thing to have, when you were using surely accursed power and engaged in a mission of vengeance that might well leave you dead or worse. Yet...for the first time he was entirely on his own, possibly beyond the reach of the creature that controlled the Justiciars, and he was helping people not as part of a masquerade but because *he* wanted to, *he* was making the decision to find people in trouble and solve their problems.

The only problem was that it was *slowing* him, and he had been falling behind for a while. Phoenix and her party were like phantoms, passing through towns, leaving a few words and accounts of their presence, an occasional trace along the road, but for the most part seemed to be traveling without pause or comment. *They've got a goal and they intend to make that goal. What? What is Phoenix after* here?

That question was *really* nagging at him. The fact was that— during the times he was honest with himself—he *knew* Phoenix was a hero. He or she—based on the latest reports, probably she—*had* to be; she was the final choice of the true Myrionar, and there was no way she was less than the best the god could find in Evanwyl or immediately surrounding states. Yet it seemed that she was ignoring people in distress, or so blinkered by her mission that she actually wasn't noticing them.

What could be driving her—or him—so hard that they're not performing missions of Mercy, Justice, and Vengeance, so that I— the False Justiciar—have been trying to make up for their failures?

Try as he might, he couldn't come up with a satisfactory answer to this question, and that bothered him a lot. But on the positive side, he was sure of her destination; it *had* to be the capital, Sha Kaizatenzei Valatar. Which meant that if he pushed himself a bit more, it wouldn't be very long before he could catch up with her...and finally settle the matter of his murdered friend.

"Don't worry," he said to the Demonshard, and touched it, feeling the questioning, dark eagerness. "You'll have someone to kill soon enough."

And what then? a part of him asked.

And for that, he was not sure he had an answer.

CHAPTER 36

"I think I'm going to have to hop out of the bushes and admit I'm here," Poplock said.

"What?" Tobimar was startled, and by their expressions so were Hiriista and Kyri. "Why? I thought we'd agreed—"

"We had, but ... Tobimar, I'm good at watching people without watching them, you know. And sure as water's wet, that Master Wieran's guessed our game. Hiriista could do it, I can't pretend he couldn't. Right?"

Hiriista bobbed his head. "Indeed. You have expressed appreciation of my intellect and talents, all of you; understand then that in my honest estimation I am nothing at *all* special when compared to Weiran. Poplock is almost certainly right. Now, that does not mean he will *communicate* his perceptions to the others; he is the sort to keep secrets, whether he is the enemy we suspect or the savior others believe."

"What do we gain by doing this, though?" Kyri asked sensibly.

"Blunt their stroke and perhaps return it upon them," Tobimar said slowly, and leaned back in the chair, causing the front legs to tip up slightly. "Consider: at the moment no one has said anything to us about Poplock; as far as most of them know, he's a dumb animal. Even if Wieran has said something to them, as far as *they* know, we still believe we have carried off this deception, right?"

"Ooooo, I see the way you're swimming, and that's clever," Poplock said. "We confess to the deception ... hmmm, how would be the best—"

"Tell them most of the truth," Kyri said with a quick smile at both of them. "Truth is a lie's best weapon, wasn't that something you told me?"

"It certainly sounds like my brand of wisdom," the Toad agreed with a bounce. "So . . . we tell them that I was kept secret as a sort of backup weapon, until . . ."

"Until," Hiriista finished, enthusiasm rising in his tone, "you became convinced that the enemies you sought either were not here, or were at least not among the highest in the land, so by being open with them you will make them your allies to hunt down these enemies. Yes, yes, that is well thought of. It also allows *you* to define the parameters of the, how should we say, *reveal*." He glanced at the others. "But this, of course, will *only* work if we do it before any of them indicate the slightest suspicion."

Tobimar leaned forward, the chair-legs dropped down with a *thump*, and he rose. "Then let's not waste more time. We were talking about meeting with Lady Shae and the others at the Valatar Throne this morning. Are we ready?"

Phoenix nodded, looking relieved. Tobimar thought he understood; duplicity was one of the harder things for her to manage, and hiding Poplock had been a strain on the Phoenix Justiciar. *Plus the idea of having to wait for the reveal, as Hiriista calls it, would just make it worse.*

"I certainly am," Hiriista said. "And I look forward to seeing what we may learn here. You are a destabilizing influence, which may allow me to observe and deduce from events things which I would otherwise not have seen."

"Happy to be of service," Tobimar said with a grin. *I'm pretty sure he's got to be on our side now; if he wasn't, he's had more than a few chances to stab us in the back or hand us over to whoever wants us.*

Admittedly, the depth to which some beings were apparently playing these games implied that there could be a reason for Hiriista to continue the masquerade even now, but Tobimar really doubted it. And Phoenix hadn't shown any doubts of him, which Tobimar found comforting.

The four of them made their way to the Valatar Throne, where Lady Shae was standing with Miri, Pelda, and a couple of Hues whom Tobimar had not yet met. As they entered, Shae smiled and nodded; Miri, predictably, skipped her way over, grabbed

Tobimar's hands and said "Good morning," bowed to Hiriista, and then gave Kyri a huge hug. *She's affectionate to everyone, but she seems even more so with Kyri.*

"So good to see you all up and ready now!" she said. As she turned to lead them over, Shae finished her conversation and the two Hues bowed and left, glancing curiously at the newcomers. Pelda also bowed and excused himself.

"A welcome to you this good morning," Shae said. "If you are hungry, I would invite you to join me; I was about to have my own breakfast when I was interrupted by an urgent matter."

"Nothing too bad, I hope," Kyri said with concern.

"Oh, not a disaster; more something that could not move forward without my blessing. Never mind that, are you joining me?"

"We had expected to eat either with you, or perhaps later this morning, so yes," Tobimar said, seeing that Lady Shae was already walking towards the smaller side room they had eaten in the prior night.

"Good, good. I expect you'll want to have a good look around, and that Miri will want to avoid her duties for another day while guiding you—"

"*Shae!*"

Lady Shae laughed. "Oh, by the Light, Miri, you're so worried about other people's opinions. Of *course* I want you to make sure our unique guests aren't left to fend for themselves."

No time like the present. "About that, Lady Shae, I'm afraid we have a bit of a...confession to make."

Shae raised an eyebrow, and though her expression was still relaxed, merely curious, Tobimar could tell from the shift in the tall, graceful frame that she was suddenly braced and ready for action. "A confession, you say?"

"Yes," Kyri said. "We've hidden something from all of you since we arrived. Well, actually, it's more accurate to say we've hidden some*one*."

Poplock bounced onto Tobimar's head and waved. "Hello!"

Shae's eyes widened and she gaped momentarily. Miri spat out the tea she had just taken a sip of. "*What?*"

"Lady Shae, Miri, this is Poplock Duckweed...our *other* companion."

Shae had recovered, as had Miri after she wiped her face off. "So your party was three, not two. You know...now that I think of it, some of your stories would have sounded a bit better if there was a third. You changed them, then?"

"Yes," Kyri said. "I'm sorry."

"Well, whether I accept your apology rather depends on the explanation." Lady Shae was no longer smiling, but she did not—quite—look angry, either. "Why did you conceal his existence from us for all this time?"

"And," Miri added, "why did you suddenly decide to reveal it?"

"Holdout weapon," Poplock said simply. "That's what I've been for them before, and it just made sense to try to keep me that way, especially when we came to this place expecting something monstrous."

"As he says," Phoenix affirmed. "Lady Shae, we *know* that our enemy had at least some connection here, somewhere. The worst possibility was that the connection went *here*, to the center of Kaizatenzei. Having Poplock as a backup just in case was so very important. But having arrived here and met you..." she shrugged and smiled. "Our enemy must be *somewhere* around, but I know that you aren't what we're seeking; I'd have sensed it, I'm sure, even through all this light around me.

"And we've gotten to know Miri really well; she's become..." Kyri's expression suddenly was surprised as she went on, "well, one of my best friends, even in these few weeks or months, and I just can't imagine that someone she regards so highly as you would be any less trustworthy. So now we need your help to search for what must be hidden somewhere in Kaizatenzei, and if we're going to do that, we can't be hiding secrets from you anymore."

Lady Shae studied them for a few moments longer, then suddenly threw back her head and laughed the big, hearty laugh Tobimar remembered from the party. "How can I resent something so cleverly done, and with such real and powerful reasons, especially when it is revealed with such flattery? Very well, you are forgiven!"

She stepped forward and extended a finger. "A pleasure to meet you, Poplock Duckweed."

The little Toad took her finger and bowed over it. "I'm honored to finally speak with you." He then bounced off Tobimar's shoulder and landed on Miri's head. Looking down into her eyes, he said, "And sorry to have tricked you for so long!"

Miri stared up at him—somewhat crosseyed, giving Tobimar

an idea of how *he* must sometimes look when talking to Poplock—and suddenly grabbed him off her head. "You're *adorable!*"

Poplock gave a startled croak but was utterly unable to get free from the sudden hug. The helpless, pop-eyed look was just too much; Tobimar suddenly burst out laughing, and so did everyone else, even Hiriista with his hissing shriek of amusement. "I guess you can take that as an acceptance of your apology, Poplock," he said finally.

Finally released, the little Toad made it back to his shoulder. "Or I could take it as my punishment," he muttered.

Lady Shae was regarding Hiriista. "You showed little surprise, Hiriista. Did you know this already?"

"I had *deduced* it earlier," Hiriista said, "though I did not know for sure until they told me, which they did before coming down this morning."

Well, there's *a masterful evasion. He's just not saying* how much earlier *he deduced it, or just how* long *before coming down this morning he was told about Poplock. What was it that Xavier called that? "Telling the truth like a Jedi," that was it.*

Lady Shae smiled and sighed. "Well, all right then." Looking back at the Toad she raised an eyebrow. "'Poplock,' hm? A master of accessing that which is hidden, are you?"

"Well, actually, there's quite a story behind that."

"I *love* stories," Miri said. "Tell us while we have breakfast!"

Tobimar winced inwardly, though he kept it off his face. *But telling them stories about you will reveal . . .*

He stopped that line of thought. *It will show that he's formidable when his presence isn't suspected. But it tells them nothing of any of the skills he's picked up since, and allows us to tell the story of who he's become in whatever way we like.*

Of course, he should have assumed Poplock knew what he was doing; the Toad usually did, after all. And as the tale of the lone Toad against the cult of Voorith unfolded, Tobimar had to smile. *They know he's a menace . . . but they haven't a clue about just how* much *of a menace. And maybe that will be enough.*

CHAPTER 37

"Welcome to my laboratory," Master Wieran said, with a dramatic gesture as he flung the doors wide.

Poplock bounced up on Kyri's head for a better look. "Wow!"

The "laboratory" occupied an entire floor of the Valatar Tower, two levels above the entrance level; it was a ring-shaped room, its interior wall formed by the exterior wall of the *original* Tower, the one that had apparently housed the Great Light since before the founding of the country. But while that made the room impressively large, it was what *filled* the room that really caused everyone to stop and stare.

Laid out in geometric precision around the entire room was an incredible array of glass and crystal and metal equipment—retorts and beakers, distillation assemblies of tremendous complexity, crystalline enchantment matrices, summoning wardstones placed in precise arrays designed to be easily varied, an entire rack of objects that Poplock was *sure* were gemcalling matrices—with carefully sorted stones in divided trays beneath—shelves of books and scrolls and notebooks arranged just so, wide lab benches and experimental slabs adjustable to any angle and height. *Some of those slabs*, Poplock thought, *look like they're for living creatures.*

There were small forges and fires, carefully set in broad workspaces with lots of safety margin; all manner of tools for cutting, grinding, mixing, and otherwise treating ingredients and materials for mystical experimentation; other things that looked like shrines to unknown gods, a workbench with neatly assorted and labeled components for clockwork mechanisms; magical designs worked into sections of the floor; and other things Poplock didn't even have a good name for, except they looked really complicated. Faint scents drifted from various parts of the room—sharp, astringent smells, sweeter notes from herbs and dried flowers, pungent stenches of less-savory materials, all blending in a strange and unsettling mix.

"Wow," he repeated. "I thought I'd seen some fancy workrooms before, but this makes 'em all look like the beginner's kit."

"Truly," agreed Phoenix. "The Spiritsmith's forge was great and held many amazing things, but this goes far beyond anything I have seen, as well."

Master Wieran's face showed a flicker of pride. *Yet something...something about the way he stands still looks funny.* "I have spent many years working on it; I would hope it would be as advanced and comprehensive as possible."

"May we...look around, sir?" Tobimar asked.

"Certainly. Touch *nothing*, however, without my direct and express permission," Wieran said warningly. "Some devices may appear inert, yet be functional; other experiments may seem robust yet be delicate. Disaster is easy to invite into a laboratory, and far more difficult to convince to leave."

As they walked slowly around Weiran's lab, more of it became visible—just as comprehensively complex as the rest. But one thing particularly caught Poplock's eye. Lying on one of the adjustable tables was a very humanoid figure, but there was something... wrong with it, visible even at this distance. "Hey, what's *that*?"

Wieran gave a thin smile. "Ah, I rather expected your eye would be drawn to that. Yes, that is an Eternal Servant in the process of construction. Come, I will show you some elements of its design."

As the group approached, Poplock could see what had looked wrong; the object was strangely incomplete, with the lower portion—the rear half of the Eternal Servant—looking finished, and the front half clearly only partly complete. This allowed a sort of cross-sectional view of the humanoid construct.

Kyri bent close. "Why, it looks like it has *skin*! The other ones didn't look like this."

"Indeed," Wieran said proudly. "The original Eternal Servants, while satisfactory in function, were sadly deficient in appearance.

I have been constantly improving the design and function since they were first created. Did you examine any of the others closely?"

"Well, we were really only introduced to one," Tobimar said. "What was the name...? Patina, that was it."

"Name? Introduced?" Wieran snorted. "Names I suppose are convenient labels, but do not make the mistake of thinking that because they move and can speak that they are anything but mindless mechanisms. Which unit was this?"

"Number Fifty-Seven of Murnitenzei," Hiriista said.

"Ah, I remember that one. I was experimenting with ceramic variants for covering. Very hard, durable, and with the right admixtures not overly frangible. A satisfactory design, but while possessing much ornamental utility did not meet the desire for more human-looking servants. Now *this*," he pointed to the skin-like material, "is a far superior covering. Go ahead, touch it."

Poplock bounced down and did so as the others took advantage of the invitation. "That's *artificial*? It feels like real skin!"

"Indeed it is artificial! My own creation, a combination of distilled saps, a *touch* of naptha, proper application of heat, and just the right alchemical treatment which yields a substance that will feel just like natural skin, *breathes* like natural skin for certain purposes, is waterproof, much tougher than any ordinary skin, and with the right materials and mystical energy infusing the entire creation can repair itself like skin."

"I'm more interested in the skeleton," Poplock said, perching on an elevated tool tray above the table.

"The *armature*," Wieran corrected with a bit of impatience, "is the central support as well as the channel for the mystical forces that motivate the entire Eternal Servant."

Poplock squinted; along the silvery-glinting steel he thought he saw faint traces of gold-tinted blue-green. "Thyrium, I see."

For just an instant he was sure he saw a narrowing of the ebony eyes, the sort that signaled a realization that one was more dangerous than suspected. *Oh, drought. I shouldn't have said anything.*

But the expression—if it was there—had disappeared even as he thought that. "An *excellent* eye, Poplock Duckweed. Am I correct, then, in assuming you are a student of arcane works?"

Mudbubbles! Okay, I guess I'll have to just recover as much as I can. "Well, I dabble a bit. Do clockwork stuff and I've fiddled around with alchemy. Really, I just noticed the similar lines here to the ones on Phoenix's armor."

"Hm. Well, yes, you are correct. Thyrium is not common but it takes very little, properly applied, to provide an excellent channel for all sorts of mystical forces." He went on to describe how this allowed him to provide the mystical force for operating the Eternal Servant in one location but have it available throughout the device.

"If you don't mind," Tobimar said at a pause in the description, "I'm curious about what you said about the Servants being purely mechanisms. I can see they're mechanisms, yes, but Patina spoke as if . . . it, I guess . . . was as intelligent as any ordinary person, and I've seen them performing a vast number of tasks. Some, like street-sweeping, might not be very hard to imagine being able to automate, I guess, but repairing stonework or cooking meals? These are complex tasks requiring judgment. I've heard of some magicians who have summoned or bound spirits to do such routine work, but those are still very much individuals, thinking beings, even if they're not as bright as the average human being. So how are you achieving this effect without what I think of as the cause, so to speak?"

Wieran studied Tobimar for a moment, then smiled again. "A penetrating question which deserves a good answer," he said finally.

I'm not sure I liked that smile. But was there really *anything wrong with it, or is it just that I started out suspicious of him? I hate this kind of silt-clouded groping around.*

Weiran led them to another part of the lab, this one with a tremendously complex mystical circle inscribed in it. Poplock studied the curving ranks of symbols and found himself, unwillingly, awed by what he saw. *I can't even begin to figure out everything that circle does. It's maybe the most intricate piece of magical design I've ever seen; makes the summoning circles for old Voory look like something a bird scratched in the dirt.*

Wieran was speaking. "During the development of the Eternal Servants, I had to address precisely this problem. It is of course immoral to have living intelligent beings performing your drudgery without recompense or choice, yet if an insensate construct is to do so, there must be some means to give it the capability to perform many tasks while not giving it sentience.

"Thus, the Learning Array!" he gestured grandly to the circle. "Only someone of my genius—of which there are no equals!—could have devised this solution to that seemingly insoluble problem. Here, and in similar arrays, I brought skilled individuals of all the key trades. The Learning Array impresses the entirety of their actions into these crystals here," he pointed to a matrix of crystalline discs which appeared to have been cut from huge gemstones. "I would present them with different challenges for their procedures—a missing piece of pipe for a plumber, a deficient or spoiled ingredient for a cook, and so on—and by varying these parameters the Array was able to distill the task's essence into a performance matrix—a matrix which I could then impress into all of the Eternal Servants.

"The matrices can be updated by the users or periodically by myself or my assistants, if and when desired," Wieran went on. "For example, as we have mentioned cooking, a few years ago certain dishes emerged and became popular around Kaizatenzei; I had one of the best chefs of this particular cuisine come here and extend the envelope of the cooking performance matrix, allowing me to revise the matrix on the existing Servants who were used for cooking duties."

He tapped a crystal on a low railing that surrounded the Learning Array. "Here, allow me to demonstrate. Master Tobimar, would you assist me?"

Poplock cursed inwardly. There was no good way to say "no" at this point, not with their displayed interest and avowed lack of suspicion of those in the higher echelons of power.

Tobimar *tried*, though. "Um...is it safe? My people are very nervous about magic applied to—"

"*Safe*?" Wieran looked scandalized—though to Poplock's eye the expression was a bit overdone. "I tested it first on *myself*, and many citizens—including Miri and Hiriista, both of whom are here—have been in this Array. I should think it is safe!"

"What was he recording on *you*?" Kyri asked. "That is...you aren't doing menial tasks, right?"

Miri laughed. "Oh, no, no. The Learning Array's useful for so much more than that. Remember you were asking if you could get one of the summoning crystals or a farcaller stone? Well, *this* is where you can get one, and the Learning Array helps with that!"

Mud, mud, MUD and DROUGHT. Stuck with our own earlier words.

"Well...all right." Tobimar took a breath and stepped in. "Does it...well, how does it *feel* when it's working?"

"It should not *feel like* anything," Wieran said, a touch of exasperation in his voice. "The whole *point* is to record the normal performance of someone's duty, or the normal signature of their essence, in the case of the crystals. If it felt odd, or painful, it could interfere with the data. Now...none of the Eternal Servants have ever been created with combat knowledge. If you could do a few simple combat moves, I can record those and give you a demonstration."

Poplock had hopped off onto Kyri's shoulder. He watched, trying to keep his face looking interested and carefree rather than grim, as Tobimar ran through a number of basic combat poses with his swords. The little Toad *was* pleased to note that Tobimar was sticking to poses not terribly unusual and certainly not connected with his *Tor* martial art.

After a few minutes, Wieran nodded. "Excellent. That will be sufficient for a demonstration." He went to the matrix of crystal disks and inserted a small, multicolored crystal into a slot below. A moment later he took it out and brought it over to what was apparently a completed Eternal Servant. "Expansion of directives," he said. "Provide access."

The Eternal Servant bowed and then a panel in the chest opened; this Servant had skin that looked more like pebbly leather but was otherwise much more human-looking than Patina had been, so Poplock found it a bit disquieting to see a piece of its chest just pop out. Wieran reached out, inserted the crystal into something within the Servant's chest, waited a few moments, and then pulled the crystal back out.

"Now," he said, stepping back, "demonstrate your recent directive expansion."

The Servant paused. "I do not have the requisite tools."

Wieran nodded proudly. "You see! It recognizes that it is missing a key element of the task, yet refers to that element as 'tools,' not connecting it with anything else." From a workbench nearby—*an enchanting bench, for making weapons I guess*—Wieran took two swords. "Use these."

The Eternal Servant took the swords and moved its arms as though weighing them. "These are not identical; some loss in efficiency will result."

"Acceptable. Proceed."

Instantly the Eternal Servant ran through the exact set of exercises that Tobimar had, duplicating his gestures precisely. *Well, that's impressive.*

"As you can see, right now it is extremely limited; there is no context showing the Servant that this is meant for use against an adversary; there is nothing to demonstrate the need to vary the approach, timing, and other aspects. To actually train a Servant to be a warrior would require two or more people in the Array, then tuning it to ignore all but the exemplar, and then a number of varied battle scenarios to generate a sufficiently flexible and defined envelope of operations. But I think it serves the purpose, yes?"

"Sure does," Poplock said. *The question I've got is what purpose it served for you.* He was also not entirely convinced that this would work to cover all the varied circumstances that such an automaton would encounter . . . but then, they hadn't followed any of the Eternal Servants around for any length of time; possibly they had routines to ask someone when they met some new situation.

"Kyri, why don't you get a pattern made for you?" Miri said brightly. "Then you could have a summoning crystal and give it to me or Tobimar. Or maybe we could get you a farcaller, and you and Tobimar could speak even when apart."

"Well, I don't want to impose—"

"It is no imposition," Wieran said. "In fact, I insist. Visitors of such unique nature and importance should be given the special attention they deserve. It will take only a few moments. Making the crystals will take somewhat longer, but that will not require your presence."

Poplock transferred back to Tobimar as Kyri entered the Array. *Our clever plan of acting like we had no suspicions kinda blew back in our faces. I'd really like to think there's nothing else going on here, but I wouldn't bet a single fly-wing on it.* He noted that Hiriista had not supported the idea or encouraged them to get involved, which was about as close as the *mazakh* magewright could probably get to telling them it was a bad idea.

"What about *you*, Poplock?" asked Miri, as Kyri stepped back out of the Array, finished with whatever it was that made the "pattern" for their crystals. "We could—"

"I am afraid not," Wieran said reluctantly, and Poplock was sure there was, in fact, real regret in those words. "I have tuned the Array for all of the types of beings known in Kaizatenzei, but an Intelligent Toad is something completely different. While the spiritual parameters will of course be *similar*, they will almost certainly not be identical, and the physical ones are highly divergent. I would require some weeks to perform the needed adjustments."

"Well, that's disappointing," Poplock said. "Having one of those crystals would be really neat. Maybe later, if we both get the time."

"I would very much like that. But I understand you have more pressing matters to attend to in the next weeks." He straightened from checking the matrix of crystal discs. "Well, allow me to show you a few more projects which should be of interest."

Poplock gave a tiny sigh of relief. *At least* one *of us won't be recorded or analyzed by whatever that is.*

I hope one will be enough.

CHAPTER 38

"Oh, *Light*, I hope people won't think this is all I do," Miri said, as she held up one of the blades and examined it.

Kyri felt a pang of guilt. "I'm sorry, I didn't mean to drag you down—"

"Drag? No, no. It's just that sometimes I think all I do is be 'Miri, Light of Kaizatenzei,' fighting things, tracking down problems, choosing new weapons so I can go out and track down more problems and fight more things."

"I think the people around here . . . and in the other cities, for that matter . . . see a lot more than that in you," Kyri said. "I haven't seen a single person who didn't smile when they saw you, not a single town we visited where the whole place didn't . . . well, light up when you arrived."

That amazingly delicate pale complexion looked even more perfect when touched with a blush of red. "Oh, Phoenix, I'm . . ."

". . . just doing your job, yes." Kyri laughed suddenly and looked down at the axe she'd been studying. "You sound just like me, you know. Like what everyone told me I sounded like."

The realization sank in, and for a moment she remembered—as clearly as if she were there—the fitted-stone streets of Evanwyl, the heads lifting and the smiles suddenly bursting out as she was seen, and she knew that what other people had told her was true. For a moment she was so homesick that her heart *ached*, but at the same time she suddenly understood Miri so very well. "Really. And I think it's just as true about you as I know now that it was about me."

Miri's wide blue-green eyes stared into hers, wide-eyed, and abruptly dropped away, the blush even more emphatic for a moment. "Well...maybe you're right. I try to make it so that people look forward to my visits." She shook herself. "All right, we're a lot alike, right? Except that I'm so tiny and you're so tall and beautiful like Shae. I wish *I* was like that."

Kyri felt herself blushing, but hoped that her own much darker skin hid it. "Don't be ridiculous. You're absolutely *perfect*. I wish I looked half as good."

"Can I tell you that *you're* being ridiculous?"

The two of them shared a laugh. "All right, look," said Kyri, "if you don't want to just look like we're grim warriors without any other interests—"

"Then you just keep doing what you're doing, Phoenix and Light Miri!" said Grithu, the weaponsmith who owned the shop. "A less grim and more fair pair of warriors I have yet to lay eyes upon."

"I think it's really the 'warrior' bit we were worrying over," Miri said. "But it may be that I'm just silly. Are you actually getting anything here?"

"Probably not," admitted Kyri.

"Alas, I would think not as well," Grithu said, tucking a strand of brown hair back under the band of cloth that kept it tied back while he worked. "I thank you for the privilege of examining your sword, Phoenix, and I confess that I cannot imagine you ever needing another weapon. If this and your armor is typical of the work of this Spiritsmith, I can but stand in awe and dream that I might one day be a tenth, no, a hundredth of the smith that he is."

Kyri laughed. "Thank you, Grithu. You're very good, you know; if you live as long as he has, you may well gain the same skill."

"Practice does perfect one, yes," Grithu agreed, then bowed and waved as they left.

"Well, *I* like my new fighting knives, even if I mostly don't use weapons," Miri said, spinning them expertly about in a complex flow of cuts. "But I'm hungry. I wouldn't expect Tobimar and Poplock to be back down for a bit, so why don't we get something to eat?"

"I certainly don't mind," Kyri said. She felt a bit left out at the moment, but tried not to show it.

But once they'd seated themselves at a table in the open-air dining square, Miri caught her gaze. "He should have let you come."

Kyri looked down. "Am I *that* easy to read?"

"As Hiriista would say, it's a matter of observation. You were suddenly a lot more quiet after I mentioned Tobimar, and you kept glancing back at the Tower whenever you thought I wasn't looking. It's obvious you're thinking about him."

"I guess it is." She took a bite of the *ourta* (a thick steak cut from a large fish in the lake, heavily seasoned) and swallowed. "He didn't *stop* me from coming. It's not like he has the authority to do that even if he wanted to, right?"

"He made it clear he wanted to ascend to the Great Light himself. Yet he took the Toad." Miri's lips tightened, and Kyri realized she was actually *angry* at Tobimar.

That realization suddenly relaxed the tension in Kyri's stomach. Impulsively she grabbed Miri's hand and squeezed it. "Thank you, Miri."

"For what?"

"Being angry for me, so I could see whether that was what I wanted to feel."

"And...is it?"

She shook her head. "No. No, I don't think so. You didn't hear our discussion before, but...if we're right, what's at the top of that tower is the most holy relic not just of *your* country, but of *his*—of his own religion, of Terian, the Light in the Darkness, the Infinite, himself. Climbing that tower's a pilgrimage for him, I think."

"But he took Poplock with him." The tone was still resentful, defending her against the wrongdoings of her friend, and Kyri laughed.

"Oh, Miri, it's okay."

Miri looked up, surprised. "But—"

"Really. Oh, I love Tobimar. And he loves me, to my astonishment. But Poplock and Tobimar traveled a lot longer together, and I think in some ways they'll *always* be a lot closer than he and I will. Poplock's able to be there without being...intrusive, when he wants to be. Hard for me to just fade into the background."

I'm not going to mention the fact that he's also there just in case there's a trap waiting.

Miri looked at her wonderingly for so long that Kyri felt her cheeks heating up again. "You really mean that," she said finally. "You were annoyed but now you're not."

"Oh, I'm still a *little*. Mainly because I really *do* want to see the Great Light up close, and I have to wait."

Miri smiled and shook her head. "Well, I hope he appreciates this. And I mean *really* appreciates you."

Kyri felt there was too much praise floating around for her to feel comfortable with, so she looked up and around. "So, if we're not going to be warriors, what do you do when you're not patrolling?"

"Um..." Miri looked embarrassed. "I, well, study the reports that have come in to see if there's other things I need to do. And I exercise, and I check up on things around the tower, and... what about you, what do *you* do?"

"Are we really *that* much alike?" Kyri was both amused and appalled. *When was the last time I played a game, just for fun? Read a book? Wasn't studying religion, swordplay, combat, or thinking about tracking down my enemies?* "Myrionar's *Balance*, I think the last time I did anything that *didn't* relate to being, or becoming, a Justiciar or Adventurer must've been when I was a child, playing with our figurines..."

The two looked at each other and the absurdity caused them both to burst out laughing again. "Oh, oh, *Light*, I needed that," Miri said finally, getting her breath. "All right, we're both career warriors. So let's just stop fighting that and go do some sparring? I've got these new knives that need an opponent, and you've got armor that I can't cut through."

"But *you* don't," Kyri pointed out as they got up to head for the training area Miri had shown them that morning.

"Don't underestimate what I wear just because it *looks* delicate!"

"All right, I won't. I certainly won't underestimate *you*, I've seen you in action. But I'll stick with hand-to-hand techniques and not use Flamewing."

"Oh, good, I don't feel like being bisected and cauterized at the same time," Miri said with a smile.

The training field was empty when they reached it—the midday sun was too hot for those not wearing comfort-enchanted armor. Kyri got into a guard pose and waited.

Miri advanced, knives flickering like lightning. The bewildering spinning movement baffled the eye, made it nearly impossible to guess the direction of the intended assault, and Kyri backed up, gauging not from the weapons but from the movement of the body and the shifting of the eyes where and when Miri intended to try to land her stroke.

Slash! Slash! Two strikes, quick as reflections dancing off water. Kyri barely parried them, but missed the boot that came up and struck her squarely in her midriff. The Raiment of the Phoenix blunted the blow but she still tumbled back, rolling and trying to come up in an advantageous position.

But Miri was *fast*—so fast she was already on the other side of Phoenix, *behind* her as she rolled to her feet. Kyri somersaulted forward, trying to stay out of reach of the deadly blades. *She's pursuing, so—*

The rear-directed sweep only *grazed* Miri's foot, but that still threw her coordination off, gave Kyri a vital split second to recover and face the smaller woman. For several more minutes they danced and ducked and struck and weaved, until finally Kyri saw an opening and kicked hard.

Miri flew across the field, tumbling like a rag doll, new blades scattered from her hands. *Oh, Myrionar, no! I put far too much into that kick!*

She ran forward. "Miri! Miri, are you all right? Balance, I'm so sorry!"

Miri slowly rolled onto her back and looked up as Kyri knelt down. "Ohhh...Well, well struck. I...left myself completely open that time. Thought I had you..."

She struggled dizzily, managed to sit up; Kyri braced her with one arm. "I'm sorry, Miri. I really didn't mean to do that! Are you all right?"

Miri's eyes looked still a bit dazed as they gazed into Kyri's. "No, it's all right. I asked you to spar. I just made a mistake."

She kept staring, and suddenly said, "By the Light...you have the most beautiful eyes, Phoenix."

And as Kyri was trying to figure out how to respond to that, Miri bent her head back, leaned a little forward, and kissed Kyri full on the lips.

CHAPTER 39

"You're actually *shaking*, Tobimar," Poplock said, a note of concern in his voice.

"What? Don't be ridiculous," Tobimar answered, feeling the muscles in his calves and thighs protesting as he went up another step, two steps, three—each step just a tiny bit higher than he was comfortable with. "It's just all...this climbing."

"No, it is not easy to climb to the top of the Tower," agreed Lady Shae; she and Master Wieran were escorting Tobimar, Shae ahead and Wieran behind.

That *did* make Tobimar a little nervous—if Lady Shae *and* Wieran were enemies, *and* this were some sort of a trap, he'd be several thousand feet in the air and beyond any help. But he *did* have Poplock with him, he had his training, he had his armor and weapons forged by the Spiritsmith himself, and...he *needed* to do this.

By preference, he'd have done this completely alone, without even Poplock. But the Great Light was the holy relic and symbol of all Kaizatenzei; there wasn't a chance in all the Hells that he would be allowed to approach it unattended. That meant he really did need to have someone with him, and Poplock was the best choice for that, not the least because he'd been with Tobimar long enough to know, really *know*, what this meant to Tobimar. *If it really is the Sun...*

He paused, catching his breath, letting the ache in his legs fade a bit. "How many steps *are* there in this Tower?"

"From the base of the tower to the peak—the Chamber of Light—are exactly eight thousand, eight hundred and eighty-eight steps of eight inches in height," Master Wieran replied from behind.

This has *to be the Sun. Eight is the sacred number, his symbol raised high.*

"Funny," muttered Poplock, as Tobimar resumed the climb.

"What?" he muttered. The echoing of their steps through the tower minimized the chance of being overheard.

"Well, *Shae's* an active woman with an obvious interest in keeping herself in peak condition, so maybe it's not surprising *she's* making you look like a newleg, but Wieran there doesn't seem to be bothered at all by the climb either."

That *was* odd. At the next short rest and for some time after they resumed, he surreptitiously studied Wieran, and concluded that Poplock was right. While he occasionally made sounds as though the ascent was difficult or tiring, Wieran did not in fact seem to be breathing significantly faster, nor did he appear to slowing down, as even Tobimar did. *Very odd. Unsettling, and it doesn't make sense. He's focused on his laboratory work. He doesn't have the time or inclination to stay in absolute top shape.*

But that minor concern was being pushed to the background as they approached the top of the tower. At this range Tobimar could *feel* the Great Light, an inaudible song, an intangible vibration, an invisible *Presence* calling him forward, radiating its power and essence through the stone and metal of the Tower as though it were the merest air. Though his legs were now leaden and filled with dull agony, Tobimar did not slacken his pace; he *could* not, not now, and he dimly realized that he had caught up to Lady Shae, had *passed* her, and he could see the landing above, twenty steps, fifteen, ten, five, one—

The last step gave onto a black floor, polished yet giving back only the faintest glint of light. The walls, too, were black, interrupted only by eight windows set equidistantly about the perimeter of this, the highest room in the Tower. The ceiling, too, was pure ebony black. But all of this was but the merest side note, inconsequential detail, for in the center of the room was the Great Light.

It floated without visible support, a sphere of crystal not quite three inches across, and from within shone a brilliant polychromatic refulgence, a rainbow light so rich and pure that it was *tangible*. The rays of light caressed Tobimar's cheeks as they passed, breaths of air glowing with ruby and amber and emerald and sapphire, the distilled essence of joy and power and of all that was *right*.

And at the very center he could see a spark of blazing blue-white, burning like the core of a thunderbolt unleashed yet restrained within that impervious shell. Tobimar found himself moving forward.

"Umm, Tobimar, are you sure you should do that?"

"Hold, Tobimar!" called a voice from behind him, tense with concern.

But there was no stopping, no holding him back. Before any could move to restrain him, Tobimar Silverun reached out and touched the Great Light.

For an instant nothing happened; he felt the crystalline smoothness under his fingers, saw the delicate inlay of silvery metal that formed a setting at the very top of the artifact, a setting with a slender black metal chain attached to it, but nothing save the light seemed at all unusual or remarkable.

Then without warning the light expanded, a brilliance beyond mere light blinding him...yet he found he could see, see something else, something *within* the crystal, something that should be small but that was not, that rose up, *towered* up, blotting out the walls and floor and looming like a thundercloud of onyx and shattered rainbow, a black figure draped in night-shadow and surrounded by light, the head a blaze of unreadable luminance, its waist belted by rainbow and prism, and on its chest a golden sigil that Tobimar had known since he was too young to walk. For all its incomprehensible size the figure still seemed distant, walled away, but there was no mistaking it or the aura of Power it radiated.

As Tobimar began to truly grasp what he had seen, the figure began to fade, the world around him to take on its structure again. But now he *knew*, and he sank to his knees and bowed low, then rose—realizing that there was no pain or stiffness in his legs, that indeed his weariness was gone as though it had never been.

"Are you all right?" demanded Lady Shae. "I warned you—"

"Lady Shae of Kaizatenzei," Tobimar said, and bowed. "I apologize for my conduct; I was seized by an impulse, and perhaps more than mere impulse, but still I committed an offense against your courtesy and hospitality by moving forward heedlessly."

He could not keep a wondering smile from his face. "But I have now absolute knowledge that *this*, your Great Light, is also what I have hoped and dreamed to find. This is the Sun of Infinity, Terian's Star, the greatest of His artifacts ever given to the hands of mortals, and I have the proof we sought." A rising triumph was in him, and his next words rang out with an echo throughout the Tower's highest room.

"This *was* my people's homeland, and my quest's end is in sight."

CHAPTER 40

For a long moment Miri was enveloped in pure sensation: the warmth on her own lips, the faintly spicy scent Phoenix must use as part of her morning ritual, the smell of exercise, the solidity of the arm supporting her. For that moment she was...happy.

And then her mind caught up to her impulse in a rush and she suddenly broke and rolled away. *What am I doing? What's wrong with me? I don't understand...*

But she *did* understand, and horror began to well up in her, even as Phoenix stood, staring at her in surprise and concern.

Her thoughts were still scattered, but she knew she had to say *something. Let the emotion drive your words, at least. Must be convincing!*

"I...I'm sorry, Phoenix! I didn't mean...I..." *What is that? It's babbling!*

The beautiful, severe face softened, smiled, and the great gray eyes caught Miri again in their gaze. "It's all right, Miri. I was...startled, I admit, but I'm not angry with you." She grinned. "How could I be angry at such a compliment?"

Relief—from both sides—filled her. *She's not angry with me! And she's not suspicious!* "Well, um, I'm glad you think it's a compliment...I didn't...well, I wasn't *thinking*, I just was a little knocked into shadow by that last blow, and I..."

Phoenix laughed and reached out, took her hands. "Miri, it's all right. Really. I'm sorry I can't, well, reciprocate, but I'm with Tobimar and I can't see that changing. We're *right* for each other, and we're both pretty much one-person-at-a-time people."

*Of course they are. I could see that in the way they look at
each other, often when they don't think anyone else is watching.* The
thought ached...yet try as she might, the black, corrosive rage
and hatred that would be *such* a good antidote for this confusing
and dangerous feeling *refused* to emerge. "I wouldn't want you
to leave him for me," she said, and to her utter bewilderment
a part of her *meant* that. *Oh, Father, I am so badly damaged. I
don't know what to* do! "...even if you would. I'm...needed here,
and you'll have to go on. You have your mission to complete.
He'll stay with you forever. I can see it."

Still, she wasn't letting go of Phoenix's hands, not yet.

"Yes...you're right." Phoenix smiled, looking up to the Tower
where Tobimar must by now be nearly at the top, then looked
back gravely. "I hope this won't damage our friendship."

That alien part of her spoke before the rest of her even
thought about the response. "No! No, I won't *let* it! We're so
much alike, we have so much in common, you're the first I've
ever had the *time* to get to know outside of the Guard... No, I
won't let it. But...I do need to think, I mean, to clear out my
head, if you know—"

A detonation of pure rainbow light *exploded* from the pinnacle
of the Tower, with a song of triumph and *good* that both burned
Miri's innermost soul and brought tears of joy to her eyes. She
saw Phoenix staring at the light, transfixed, even as the ecstatic
luminance slowly faded back to the normal shimmer.

"*Tobimar,*" Phoenix said softly, triumphantly. "He reached the
Great Light and it recognized him." The absolute certainty in her
voice stunned Miri.

"How can you be so sure?" Miri asked, trying to keep it from
being in the completely incredulous tones of her inner voice.

"Everything pointed us here, Miri. Both of us, not just me.
And this *place*, so filled with singing joy, with light and *good*
echoing out of every bird, every beast, every *stone*...something
of transcendent goodness had to have power here, had to have left
its mark across hundreds of miles of territory even in the midst
of the darkest corruption I have ever felt. What, then, *could* that
mean except something of one of the brightest and greatest gods
was here? Seven small cities and an eighth larger one, and the
legends of Terian's seven Stars and his Sun...what else *could* it
be? Terian's power *had* to be here." She looked up at the tower,

eyes shining. "I know what he has to be feeling. I felt it too, when Myrionar showed me that my faith had *not* been in vain, that I had *not* been deserted, that I, too, would be a Justiciar."

Miri nodded. "Of course. You're right. You must be right." She took a deep breath and released Phoenix's hands. "I still need to straighten out my thinking, though. If you'll please excuse me...?"

"Of course, Miri." She stooped and picked up the fallen blades. "Don't forget your new knives!"

"Oh, no. Thank you." Miri started away, almost at a run, then turned, waved, said "G-goodbye!" and then hurried away, nearly bumping into Tanvol, who was just entering the practice field.

Inside her guts began to churn. *I'm corrupt. I'm corrupt from* both *sides. My plans... I don't know if I can carry them out anymore! I don't* want *to, I think. But everything's ready! That light... Tobimar is the key we sought, Wieran says that the circle's analysis gave him nearly all the data he needed, all will be ready in a day, two, three at most!*

She reached her own apartments in a daze, not even remembering the exact route she had taken, and sank into a chair. The rolled-up scroll nearby taunted her with the knowledge that Viedraverion would be *laughing* if he knew about this.

Kalshae... oh, Father, Kalshae! The other Demonlord and Miri had shared certain bonds and affection as well. What would Kalshae do if she learned...?

Be honest, you know exactly *what she will do. The same thing you would have done to her if she did and thought and felt what you do: destroy the object of your affection, and possibly you as well. You've reached the final stage, the one that Yurugin and the others went down. You* care *about what happens to them. You don't want to hurt Phoenix. You don't want to hurt Tobimar, the* key *himself, who must be used to unlock the final seal.*

Kalshae would either kill her, or do her best to save her, to somehow bring her back to the proper Demonic point of view. They'd known the risks in what they were doing; the loss of three of the five major demons they had started with had emphasized that all too well.

But now it had happened to *her*, and Ermirinovas did not know what to do. "I have to at least be able to kill Tobimar," she muttered. "I have to. I *have* to. Hate him, hate him! I have to *want* to... want to..."

She felt her face screwing up painfully, an unfamiliar sensation, as she imagined herself slashing the Skysand prince's arm open, pouring its lifeblood out, and the pain in her chest felt as though she had driven the knife into herself, seeing the horror she knew would be on Phoenix's face, the betrayal, and the hardening of that face into the avatar of Vengeance that she was sworn to become.

My face is wet...I'm crying! *Oh, Father...oh,* Light, *I'm crying.*

And not in rage or frustration or fear, no. Crying because it hurt, it hurt so very much to think that she would be hated and despised by the companions she had traveled with for those weeks. And most of all by Phoenix, so much like Kalshae, yet the opposite in the most important ways of all.

A rap on the door startled her, and she looked up into semi-gloom. *I've been here... how long?* She controlled her panic, quickly wiped her face. "Who is it?" she answered, hoping that the slight hoarseness from her crying would not be audible. She grabbed up the shading stick. *Must hide the traces!*

"Shae, dear. Can I come in?"

Light, no! was her first thought, but that by itself would be a dead giveaway. She gestured quickly under her eyes, removing faint circles, then put the stick down as she said, "Of course." Her other hand gestured, bringing the lighting up.

Kalshae entered, wearing as usual the shape of "Lady Shae." Her true form—like Miri's—had once been something quite terrifying to behold for mortals (though still very beautiful from Miri's point of view). Now it was still something clearly inhuman, but more like a somewhat-monstrous version of her human form than anything else. "I thought you were going to be with the Phoenix all day?"

Instantly Miri thought of the *only* tactic she could take that might save her, at least for now. "I know, but by *Father* there is only so much of her self-satisfied innocence I can *take*. Especially since I've been playing the one being close to all of them and she's taken a particular liking to me."

Was there a flicker of surprise on Kalshae's face? She couldn't tell for sure. "Well, I can very much understand that. You've done a wonderful job, though. They're *absolutely* convinced that we're all their friends." Kalshae laughed, and Miri joined her, trying to make sure the laugh sounded natural. *And will that just make it more forced? I have to stop overthinking this! It will get us all killed!*

And even that thought was dangerous, because the *us* in that thought was not her and Kalshae and Wieran and the rest, but her and Phoenix and Poplock and Tobimar and Hiriista. *And Hiriista. Yes, he's truly their friend, I think. He wasn't a demon to begin with. If we test his loyalties I don't think Kalshae will like the result.*

"So how was your long hike?" she asked, to focus on a topic that should be interesting and much less likely to get onto dangerous ground for now.

"*Perfect,*" Kalshae said, her voice dropping throatily into an inhuman register—a sound that *used* to make Miri look forward to more private interactions, but right now sent a faint chill down her spine. *I'm worse than I thought.*

Unaware—hopefully—of Miri's conflicted state of mind, Kalshae went on. "He practically *sprinted* up the last sets of stairs, completely oblivious to our presence, and went right up to the Sun!" In private, of course, they were all quite aware of just what they were tampering with; no need for handwaving about "the Great Light."

"I saw the reaction from on the ground."

"Oh, practically everyone in *Valatar* saw it, at least to hear people tell it—even though a lot of them would have been indoors, or sleeping, or looking the other way. I'm going to announce that this was the reaction to one of our visitors. It will keep the people so very happy for the next day or so." She smiled, and her teeth were fangs; she was several inches taller, and her nails extended, crimson claws. "And that's *all* they'll ever need or want."

Miri's head snapped up. "That soon?" *Expression! Keep it eager! Not horrified!*

"Yes, that soon! No more waiting, Ermiri! We'll be *ourselves* again soon enough, once we have unsealed the Sun and taken its corrupted power into ourselves!" Kalshae laughed again, and she was a foot taller, skin with an unearthly sheen, and her eyes glowed red. "In a way, we were lucky the other three fell," she mused.

"How so?" asked Miri.

"Well," Kalshae said, and ran a finger slowly down Miri's face, and hooking the talon in the V at the front of her blouse, "if they were *here* we'd have to share all that power with *them*, wouldn't we?"

Miri gave her best smile, forcing her own body to shift, to change shade and texture in the way that was so familiar—but it was hard, *very* hard—and gave the joyful laugh she knew Kalshae expected.

And as Kalshae drew Miri to her, Miri knew she was about to have her acting ability tested beyond anything she had ever imagined.

CHAPTER 41

"Tonight's party is going to be the *big* one," Poplock said, looking out their window.

"Well, they *said* it was going to be a big one," Tobimar said. "What's so surprising?"

"Take a look."

Tobimar stepped to the window and looked down. A number of people were just approaching the gates in front of the Tower—people in very distinctive armor. Looking back, Tobimar could see more people in those armor designs in the distance. "Colors and Hues. Shades too."

"That must be why they were waiting before throwing this one. The dignitaries were all gathering; Lady Shae must've wanted as many to attend as possible. Leaving one or two for each city, there's still going to be like eighty of them here. All the Lights, for certain, plus a lot of the others."

Kyri and Hiriista joined them. "I guess they'll need a bigger dining room, then," Kyri remarked.

"They will need the *Grand* Dining Hall," Hiriista agreed. "I saw that in use exactly once, ten years ago ... it was, in fact, on the occasion of Zogen's retirement. I do not think it has been used since, now that I think of it. Lady Shae and the others tend to throw smaller parties, when they have time for such things at all."

Poplock wrinkled his face. *I don't like this at all.* "Phoenix, have you sensed any more of those flashes of bad things?"

She frowned. "A few times. I've sensed that huge, resentful

one thrice more; the cold-amused one twice. All of these times were either in the Tower's lower floor or out on the peninsula, toward the lake."

"So it wasn't a one-time thing. Something's definitely here—at least *two* somethings we don't want anything to do with."

"Then the question is who, and where," Hiriista says. "Have we met our adversaries already, and if so, who are they?"

"Wieran's still my top pick," Poplock answered firmly. "He's the brains of this place. Shae's not stupid, and Miri's sharp as a tack, but that guy could make both of them and all of us put together look like idiots. I'm laying my bet on him being the cold, amused one."

Hiriista hissed a laugh. "I think you may underestimate yourself and perhaps myself as well...but your point is well taken. For myself, I would beg to disagree in your bet, though I would agree that he is definitely one of our adversaries."

Kyri raised an eyebrow. "Why do you disagree with Poplock's judgment here? *Cold* certainly seems the most likely characteristic of Wieran; my gut feeling about him is that his smiles are almost all sham."

"There I would agree," Hiriista said, absently feeling about in a pouch and producing his scent-pipe. "That is not the part that jars with me."

"Hrrm," Poplock grunted. "You mean that you aren't seeing *amused* as part of his mindset."

"Exactly. I know you noted the anomalies of his body language and conversation; would you disagree?"

Poplock thought back over the few conversations they had had with the magical researcher. "No...no, I guess not. I don't get much sense of humor from him. It'd be quick and sharp and end fast, I think. More *resentment* than anything else."

"Then maybe he's the other one? Restrained by his position, and maybe something else, and resenting it."

Hiriista inhaled the scent, blew out, and nodded slowly. "Possible. But then the question is who is the *other*?"

"The...obvious choice," Phoenix said slowly, "is Lady Shae. I hate to say it, but she's at the center of everything. She's more focused and controlled than Miri; her big cheerful warrior-queen act could be just that, an act."

"What about Miri?" Poplock asked.

"That's *ridiculous!*" Kyri looked surprisingly outraged by the suggestion.

"Not so ridiculous," Tobimar said, looking at her curiously. "She's Shae's right-hand person, she goes everywhere, everyone trusts her; she could get away with literal murder without a chance of being caught."

Poplock noticed that Kyri's face was suddenly a shade darker. "Well...if any of you mention this to *anyone* else I will kick you over the mountains. But Miri kissed me yesterday."

The interplay of incredulity, shock, and other emotions across Tobimar's stunned face was so funny that Poplock began laughing uncontrollably.

"She...er...*what?* I mean..." Tobimar paused. "You know, that makes so much sense of her behavior now."

Hiriista was also chuckling. "Indeed, I had thought there were some unusual elements in her body language in her interactions with you; I had not interpreted them correctly."

"So what did you do?"

Kyri smiled wryly. "First I calmed her down when she realized what she was doing and panicked. Told her it was a compliment and I wasn't mad at all, but that you and I were already a pair."

"Well, I'm glad that was resolved," Tobimar said after a pause.

"Not disappointed I didn't ask about alternative possibilities?"

As Tobimar's face flushed visibly Poplock started laughing again.

"No!" Tobimar said finally, then saw her grin. "You asked that just to—"

"Of course I did," she said, and yanked the smaller Prince to her for a quick kiss. "I know we're *both* one-person people. And I also know there's *no* way you didn't think about the other possibility for at least a moment or two."

He coughed. "Um. Well, yes, I couldn't very well help it." Tobimar grinned up at her. "After all, she *is* very, very cute."

"Yes, she is. Not to mention smart, strong, and very talented." Kyri looked pensive. "It wouldn't be hard to fall in love with her."

"Still, how exactly does *that* tell us that she's not our person," Poplock said, returning to the original conversation. "Strikes me that this would be a great distraction tactic for her."

"Instinct," Phoenix replied promptly. "Her reactions afterward sent so many signals and they were exactly what someone with real affection that they hadn't noticed before would say and do.

I didn't get a *single* false note out of her. Plus...I never sensed any of these dark things until we got *here*. What's the chance that I'd only sense her dark side *now* rather than anytime during the months it took to *get* here? She spent a lot of time around me and I never got even the slightest sense of something wrong."

"Adequate evidence for now," conceded Hiriista. "We have often noted that you are extraordinarily good at sensing something 'wrong' in those contexts."

"Yeah," said Poplock, glancing back out the window. "So let's remember what we had our first group discussion on, eh?"

Hiriista froze, then let out a long, slow hiss of understanding. "Of course. If we are right, most or all of the Unity Guard are under some form of compulsion—"

"—by the bad guy, yeah. And here we're going to have most of 'em in the same room with us, the lonely bunch in one corner." Poplock shook his head. "If Shae and Miri *aren't* in on it, that's also the perfect time for them to eliminate the two as a problem, one way or another."

"What can we do about it?" Kyri asked after a moment. "We still haven't got the evidence we need to accuse anyone—at least, none of you have mentioned any?"

Tobimar and Hiriista shook their heads. Poplock hesitated, then moved side to side in his own equivalent of a headshake. "I haven't been able to move around as freely as other places, since they all know I'm not just a dumb toad. All I've been able to find on my own has been that there's at least one or two major underground installations we haven't seen yet. That's not exactly evidence. Sure, there's *probably* something down there that would tell us about our enemies, but by itself? Nothing."

"Then what *can* we do?" Kyri repeated. "I suppose we could decide to just run for it; if this was supposed to be a trap, that'd force them to follow us and reveal themselves."

"And if it *isn't* a trap?"

"At worst we've insulted our hosts," Poplock said after a minute. "But with all the goodwill we seem to have built up, I think we could get past that. We'd have to admit *why* we did it, and that might well force a confrontation—"

"—but with us then in a far, *far* better tactical and strategic position than simply walking into a room which may have four-score enemies waiting to capture or kill us, yes," agreed Hiriista.

"Then forget the party duds," Poplock said, bouncing towards his little niche with all his possessions laid out in it. "Get dressed for action."

"We're leaving *now*?" Kyri asked—though she was already in her room, the connecting door left open so they could hear her.

"I only see two choices—we leave as soon as we can, or we wait until they're all assembled in the room and then take a long hop."

"But in that case," Tobimar said, stripping off his dress shirt and stuffing it in his neverfull pack, "they'll all be assembled and ready to operate as a coordinated force, if they're our enemies. Unless you're planning on locking the doors?"

"It'd be a temptation if that's the route we're taking. What do you guys think?"

"Hsssss... both have their attractions, but I favor leaving as soon as possible."

"That's my preference too," Kyri said; they heard the flowing, chiming sound of the Phoenix Raiment enfolding her. "I hate running out on Miri and the others, but if we're going, let's go fast."

"I actually like the idea of getting them all in the one banquet hall and locking the doors behind them. Maybe sealing the doors somehow," Tobimar said. "But... no, then one or more of us has to be *right there* to pull that off. Too close for comfort. Let's get out of here immediately." The Spiritsmith's armor slid into place on Tobimar's body, even as Hiriista shrugged into his own armored traveling cloak.

"The next question is... how? We want to draw as little attention as possible."

"Well," Poplock said, leaning out as far on the window ledge as he dared, "if you guys weren't all really, really good I wouldn't suggest it... but if we go out this window and can scramble *up* to that ornamental curve to the righthand side, we could just maybe get in jumping distance of that floating bridgeway, which would let us clear a good half of the city by running along it. We'd have to either go through the building at the other end or drop down somehow, but..."

Hiriista stuck his head out and looked. "Something of a gamble, yes... but it has the virtue of keeping us mostly out of sight from the ground except from a small number of angles. And not many are using that bridge this time of day."

"Shame we can't all jump like you can," Tobimar said, squinting at the bridgeway. "It'd be easy then."

Kyri joined them and studied the suggested approach. "Yes, but I think we can do it. I like it, that will keep us out of the crowds in the streets for most of our escape."

"Where to *after* we escape, then?" Hiriista asked reasonably, settling his pack onto his shoulders.

"Play it as it goes," Tobimar said immediately. "We don't know how they're going to respond, and that response will probably decide us."

"All right, then, let's go."

Poplock scrambled onto Tobimar's shoulder and gripped tight. The Skysand Prince was the first out, edging his way carefully along the sill, then looking up to the ornamental fringing above. "Good thing this tower's made to look so pretty; there's a lot of handholds."

"Hurry *up!*" Kyri whispered behind them. "If someone looks even a little bit up—"

"I know!" Tobimar took a breath and then leaped upwards. His lean, dark fingers caught solidly on the scalloped ridge, and he was able to shuffle his hands sideways until he reached the rising curve and could pull himself up. He crouched down as low as possible, waiting for the others.

Kyri followed almost immediately, and—after a short pause—Hiriista. "What took you so long?" Poplock muttered to the *mazakh.*

"Making sure the window latched on the inside," Hiriista said with a spineridge-rippling equivalent of a chuckle. "If they don't realize we've already left, that should give them some confusion."

"All right, everyone ready?" Tobimar's eyes closed, and Poplock recognized his friend getting into one of his *Tor* "centers." "This is going to be the hard part. That's a pretty long jump, and if we miss it's a thirty-five foot drop. Not fun for anyone."

"Definitely not fun," agreed Hiriista. "But I feel an even greater sense of urgency right now. Let us be off."

Tobimar rose a bit from his crouch and rocked on his feet; at Poplock's inquiring glance, he said "Testing how well my boots are gripping on this surface."

Then he backed up as far down the curved ridge as possible, looked carefully at the suspended portion of the bridge—which looked a *lot* farther away now than Poplock had thought when they started—and then burst into motion.

It was a matter of a mere nine steps and a *leap*, but for Poplock the whole operation seemed to take about twenty times as long as it should have. Tobimar launched himself into space, and they *crawled* through the air, first rising, then beginning to descend, long before they had reached the bridgeway, dropping farther—*we're not going to make it!!*

But then Tobimar's hands lashed out and caught the silvery stone of the bridgeway; his body curled under and then flipped up and around, and with a single vertigo-inducing spin Poplock found himself sitting comfortably on Tobimar's shoulder on the wide, smooth stone of the floating bridge. Though it was apparently completely unsupported, the stone of the bridgeway felt as solid and stable as the paving-stones below had. *Amazing magical technique, there.*

Kyri's immense strength and much longer frame let her clear the distance more easily; she landed on the edge of the bridgeway feet-first, rolling forward and coming up easily.

Hiriista's jump was much more that of a lizard—a spring-loaded leap forward, arms outstretched, landing on the platform crouched like a cat and slowly straightening to his full height. He nodded to them. "Let us complete our departure, shall we?"

The three full-sized adventurers sprinted along the floating bridgeway. *We're making great time here*, Poplock thought. *No need to follow the turns and such of the roads, we're going right over their heads and their buildings.* "What about the building this one ends at?"

"Take a closer look," Tobimar answered cheerfully. "See? There's a spiral stair around the outside to let people get from ground level to the bridgeway without having to go through the building."

They had already crested the high point of the bridgeway and were on their way down. Still there was no one else on the bridgeway with them, and Poplock's occasional glances down through brief separations between sections of the bridgeway didn't seem to indicate anyone had noticed them yet.

"We just might make it out of the city without anyone realizing it," Tobimar said as they approached the slender building which lay at the end of the bridgeway; twin spirals of stairs dropped away on either side. The three runners barely slacked their pace as they reached the stairs.

"Let's hope so," Kyri said, only starting to breathe a little faster with the effort. "I don't want any fights where anyone else can get hurt. Ideally I don't want any at all."

The stairs streamed past below Poplock, and he kept an eye out in front. Within minutes they were off the steps and into the streets—only a couple of hundred yards from the entrance to Sha Kaizatenzei Valatar. In the slowly setting sun, Poplock could see that there were still quite a few people on the road, and that forced the group to slow. *Trying to run through the crowd would* definitely *get us a lot of attention.*

A hundred and fifty yards to go, and they were moving forwards easily; occasionally one of the people on the street would recognize one or more of them, but that just resulted in a nod or wave.

Then Poplock felt his own grip spasm on Tobimar's shoulder, even as the crowd separated slightly to reveal, dead ahead of them, Shade Danrall of Sha Murnitenzei.

"*Sand,*" cursed Tobimar. They were too close to evade or pretend they hadn't seen him. *Just have to act perfectly natural.*

"Danrall!" Kyri said cheerfully. Poplock had to admire how casual the greeting sounded; there wasn't a trace of the tension they all had to be feeling. "How *are* you? I didn't expect to see you here!"

Danrall's long, innocent face lit up. "Phoenix! Tobimar! And Magewright, what an honor!" He turned to Phoenix. "Yes, most of us have been summoned for a banquet in your honor; I am just arriving!"

"Well, then, we'll see you there in a little while!" Kyri said.

And in a single instant, *something* about Danrall changed. Poplock knew that if he were asked, he couldn't have touched tongue to the *exact* change, but he could see it clearly as anything. There was no obvious change in his expression, or posture, or tone, but somehow *all* of them were just different enough to send a screaming warning through the little Toad.

"Are you not going to the Tower now?" he asked; somehow he was still in front of them, rather than being passed.

"No, we'll be there in a little bit. Just taking one more walk before the sun sets."

"I think we should all go together," Danrall said. "After all, we should all get into our finest, and I am sure that takes time for you as much as it does for me." He bowed, but Poplock felt there was something...*sinister*...in that bow. "I would gladly escort you back."

"Thank you for the thought," Tobimar said, "but we'd just like to complete our walk and we'll head back on our own."

Danrall paused for a moment then, and the three of them began to walk past.

Then he turned, and with a shock of fear, Poplock saw a dark green *glow* behind his eyes.

"Return to the Valatar Tower," Danrall said, but the voice was no longer his, but a voice of flat, cold iron, as though a statue were speaking. "I'm afraid I must insist."

"*We* must insist," repeated other voices from every direction.

Surrounding them, scattered through the crowd, were others— Shades, Hues, even one Color—and each and every face was inhumanly calm, flat, and implacable.

"We must insist," they repeated, and moved forward as one. "Return to the Valatar Tower."

CHAPTER 42

"Balance!" Kyri cursed, but she already knew they couldn't afford to hesitate for a moment. She delivered a sudden, striking kick to Danrall, sending him tumbling backwards. The crowd scattered in confusion and consternation, leaving Kyri's little party mostly surrounded by Unity Guard who all now had the eerily emerald-glowing eyes. Their weapons sang from their sheaths almost as one.

Tobimar's twin-blades were also out. Hiriista gestured, and shimmering pearlescent light rose from a bracelet, became a whirlwind that surrounded them and pushed back their opponents for a few precious moments.

"Keep going towards the gate!" Poplock said. "Gotta bull our way through!"

"Capture them alive," Danrall said, getting to his feet. "They must not be killed. This directive is absolute!"

Well, that's one *edge we have. If we can take it.* "That means they can't take too many risks when fighting us!"

"And we don't have to be that restrained. Hate to do this, but..." Poplock muttered a few cryptic phrases and gestured; a streak of flame zipped from his tiny paw and detonated in the midst of the Guardsmen surrounding them. "Go, go!"

The blast *had* opened up a narrow passage, and the three larger people sprinted down it, the fourth tiny one still clinging to Tobimar's shoulder. "I thought you couldn't cast regular magic here!" she said, cutting with her sword at one Unity Guard who was already trying to close the gap.

"Can't do it *much*, too hard," Poplock said, and fired one of his incendiary bolts at another target.

"I was going to say that I wished you hadn't chosen a killing strike," Hiriista said dryly, "but it appears that you didn't."

Even those who had been in the center of the momentary inferno were rising, cloth scorched or completely turned to ash but otherwise showing little sign of having been struck with flame intense enough to have left its mark on the stone. "Myrionar's *Balance*, how—?"

"Surrender," Danrall said, and to her shock he was now *ahead* of them again. "We are to capture you, not kill you. Surrender!"

The *wrongness* of him screamed out at her, even more grotesquely evident in the surrounding perfection of Kaizatenzei Valatar; gritting her teeth, Kyri leveled a full-strength swing at Shade Danrall.

The great sword of the Phoenix, creation of the Spiritsmith, sheared straight through Danrall's own blade as though it were the merest twig and bit deep into the armor and through: three, four inches into the left shoulder beneath. It was not necessarily a mortal blow, but an agonizingly crippling one that would leave the injured man unable to fight for weeks or until he was healed.

Except that Danrall only winced, then tossed aside the useless stump of his sword and drew twin daggers—his left hand and arm moving almost as smoothly as if she had not struck him at all!

"Terian's *Light!* What in the name...?"

The other figures were moving faster, and an appalled Kyri realized that they were *faster* than either she or Tobimar—at least, without calling upon Myrionar's power for the speed to match them. And that would take time—

A tremendous impact struck her from behind. Her sword fell from her hand. She heard a shout, then a curse from Tobimar; his swords rang out like bells as she staggered, then found her arms caught by two of the Guard. She struggled, realized these people were extraordinarily strong as well; perhaps not as strong as she, but far more than she had expected. By the time she recognized her peril, both her arms had been forced behind her.

Hiriista gave a shriek of agony and she heard a heavy body *thud* to the ground. A darting, moving streak of brown was abruptly halted by a small net hurled with devastating accuracy. She was yanked around and thrown to the pavement, unable to twist out of the inhumanly powerful grasp of multiple Unity Guards.

With a tremendous effort she heaved herself half upright, shaking off the grasping hands through sheer Vantage strength. Picking up her sword, she spun from ground level, legs either scything down her attackers or forcing them to jump clear, and rolled to her feet.

She saw Tobimar's dumbfounded expression as one of his attackers completely ignored being impaled through the gut by one of the green-blue glittering swords, and then he fell to his knees as one of them struck him down from behind.

"*Tobimar!*" she shouted, and tried to lunge forward, but more hands caught her, a mace smashed her on the shoulder and momentarily numbed her arm, and as she staggered, one of them expertly took out her legs with a sweep and others seized her.

She was hammered to the ground twice to stun her, Flamewing was wrenched from her grasp (burning the one who did so, but even that seemed to only slightly bother him) and with two Unity Guards on each leg and one on each arm, they began to immobilize her. She struggled as much as she could, but it was useless. In minutes, she had been bound tightly with at least three different ropes; Tobimar, staggering groggily, was also tied up securely, as was Hiriista. Poplock appeared to have been wrapped in tight packaging material. *Not taking chances on him moving or going anywhere.*

Danrall gestured, and the Guards hauled her to her feet. Without so much as a word, they were unceremoniously dragged towards the Tower.

"Danrall! Danrall!" she shouted. *Get his attention! Stall! Do something!*

But Danrall utterly ignored her.

"Useless," Hiriista muttered. "The compulsion is complete. I do not know if they even know who they *are*."

"I'm not sure I know *what* they are," Tobimar said painfully. "I ran one of them through—"

"I saw. I cut Danrall deep through the shoulder; he's barely even bound the wound, and there's hardly any blood."

"Healing armor, maybe. Wound-sealing wards. And they're *fast*." Poplock said. "Couldn't you guys keep up?"

"It takes *time* to do that," Tobimar said. "I have to at least get a breathing space to focus, unlock the potential. By the time I could have done it, they had me trussed."

Kyri noticed that their captors weren't even bothering to *try* to keep them quiet. *It's as though there's nothing we can do that even matters.* The thought was absolutely chilling. "And with that power damping even my ability to draw on Myrionar, I need time and focus also."

The crowds parted before the Unity Guards—and Kyri now saw they'd been joined by others. *By the Balance, even if we could get free it wouldn't do us much good now. There's twenty-five of them surrounding us.*

"What is far worse is that they attacked us—honored guests and at least minor heroes, and the two of you unique visitors— quite openly," Hiriista said grimly. "This means they anticipate little need to continue their masquerade. Their preparations must indeed be complete."

"We were right to try to run," Kyri said. "We just didn't run fast enough and early enough."

The procession reached the entrance to the Tower and continued inside, straight through the doors; others of the Guards including Tanvol and Anora joined them. After a few more minutes they ascended a set of stairs and reached a huge set of double doors.

"Ah, we're attending the Grand Banquet as scheduled," remarked Hiriista. "This is the Grand Dining Hall."

As the doors opened and they passed through, Kyri felt herself go very cold all through. Poplock simply commented, "Not exactly what I was expecting in a dining hall."

The immense room was, Kyri realized, at the very center of the Valatar Tower, part of the original tower that held the Sun of Terian. Carved into the floor and surrounded by complex, precise designs, outlined by burning lamps and glowing gems, was a ritual circle—although to call it a mere *circle* was trivializing what was both a work of art and of dark genius.

"Blackwart's *Chosen*," she heard Poplock mutter as they got closer. "That's not good at *all*."

Standing in the center were three figures: Lady Shae, towering over the other two, wearing a simple dark robe that contrasted starkly with her usual subtly complex choice of dress; Master Wieran, gazing coldly at them as they were dragged into the circle; and Miri, still in her blue-green-crystal armor. For a moment Miri's eyes met hers, and Kyri was startled to see no triumph or malice, but wide blue pools of horror and sympathy.

"I am *so* disappointed in you," Lady Shae said, and even her voice was different; the timbre was deeper, the cadence sharper, the tone arrogant and weary at the same time. "Here we had pre- pared *everything* for you and you try to leave at the last minute."

In the center of the circle was a raised, eight-sided dais, deeply carved with complex symbology dominated by an eight-pointed star. And suspended over the very center of that dais...

"What are you doing with the Sun?" demanded Tobimar.

Shae laughed. "What are *we* doing with it? Nothing...yet. That is where *you* are going to be most useful, Tobimar Silverun, Seventh of Seven." She turned to those holding him. "Strip him of his armor and weapons."

Oh no.

"Oh, yes, we know who you are, Tobimar Silverun," she said, even as the Unity Guard complied with her instructions. "It was, indeed, fortunate that you and your allies were able to dispose of Misuuma and her people rather than the other way around, because you have a far greater purpose to serve in death."

"*That's* what happened to the Stars," Poplock said slowly, unbelievingly. "You *broke* them. But you couldn't just get rid of all the essence of the god, which is why—"

"It is far more accurate," Master Wieran said, gesturing to those holding the now nearly-naked Tobimar to place him on the dais in a particular location, "to say that they *used* the Stars, but that there were particular waste products which contaminated the area. *This* process will be much less wasteful."

"By the *Light*," Hiriista breathed. "You mean to steal the power of this god Terian directly."

"Exactly so," Shae said with a grin—a smile that revealed teeth far sharper than they had been. "Steal the power without its corruptive essence."

Now Kyri could sense the dark, cold, amused presence clearly. "It was *you* all along. I sensed you sometimes, but—"

"Yes, you couldn't be sure. We did not spend thousands of years working on this plan to be easily discovered." Shae stepped up and locked complex, elaborately enruned and crystal-encrusted shackles onto Tobimar's arms and legs, sealing each with a complex gesture and a drop of her own blood, drawn by a small needle. "There! All is in readiness, yes?"

Master Wieran nodded absently. "I believe so. I am perform- ing a final check of all arrangements now."

"Then we need to clear the circle of all non-participants. Consider yourselves fortunate—for various reasons, Master Wieran wants the three of you alive, for now. Although perhaps you, Phoenix, can be spared the pain of living to see what happens to your darling Tobimar."

"What?" Wieran's gaze was suddenly sharp and very much focused. "I said I wanted her for—"

"But *I* want to give Miri a chance for a little *fun*, and *I* am in charge here, *Master* Weiran." Shae was smiling and the tone was light...but at the same time dark, dark threats ran through every word. "Miri, you've had to put up with her sanctimonious clueless superiority for *months*, I think you've got *every* right to kill her now. As you told me just last night, there's only so much of that we can take." She gestured. "So go ahead. I'll let Wieran have the other two, but she's yours."

Miri stepped forward, and her hands distorted, her skin rippled and changed shade and texture, more armored, less human. "She's...mine?"

"All yours."

Without warning, Miri whirled, lunging for Master Wieran—

And was caught almost before she began by four Unity Guards.

Now Shae was not laughing or smiling; she looked both furious and sorrowful. "I knew it. I *knew* it! Ermirinovas, I *told* you to watch yourself! Now you're all contaminated, ruined, twisted, just like the others!"

"No! We're the ones who were twisted, Kalshae!" Miri shouted, struggling, her skin shifting color from a blue armor to light-skinned human and back in a chaotic pattern. "We can stop this! There's—"

"I have no intention of even listening. I know the dangers. But I'm going to help you, Miri, even though you don't want it now." She looked at the Unity Guards—Danrall with his handsome long face now vacantly grim, a Hue that Kyri didn't recognize in shifting violet armor, Light Dravan Igo like a mighty statue in his blood-red, Color Herminta Gantil in the blue-green of the sea—and made a sharp, savage gesture towards the door. "Take her down to my Meditation Chamber, the one at the very base of the tower, towards the lake. Perhaps it's not quite too late for her. But in any case she is *not* to leave until I release her. Tanvol, Anora, go with them. I want a *very* strong guard on her; if she tries to escape and the wards do not hold, you know how powerful she is."

Lady Shae—or "Kalshae" as Miri had just called her—watched darkly as Miri was dragged out. Kyri, seeing the shamed desperation in Miri's eyes, gave a tremendous effort and actually pulled halfway free of her captors, but it was futile.

Kalshae's burning gaze—now literally burning, with a red fire—locked on Kyri. "*You* were the trigger. I hope that what Master Wieran has planned for you is painful indeed."

"I would expect so," Wieran said, circling the dais with a precise eye surveying everything. "I had *thought* she would be a rather uninteresting specimen, but the evaluation scan showed that she was something far, far more interesting than anyone I had yet had the opportunity to measure. The analysis will undoubtedly extend to disassembling her—component by miniature component."

"Oh, *wonderful*," Kalshae breathed. Then she turned and gestured. "Clear the circle! Let the prisoners watch, just keep a close and keen eye on them. And once we begin, let none stray into the circle, for it will be death for you to do so!"

Kyri struggled, trying to draw on the strength of Myrionar now, but she felt that leaden weight impede her even more than before. *They can focus it?*

Of course they can, she answered herself. Even if this was a natural effect left from the last Chaoswar, these beings—*demons,* she now realized with certainty—would have learned how to best control and direct it.

Her struggles were utterly in vain; at the same time, she saw Hiriista and Poplock were equally unable to break free. And as she saw the circle begin to glow and a complex apparatus rise up around the central dais, she realized that it was already far, far too late.

CHAPTER 43

By the Seven and One... is there no hope?

Tobimar had never felt quite this helpless—not even the time he'd been cornered by *mazakh* in their own temple. At least *there* he'd been able to sell his life dearly, and choose to die on his feet, fighting, as long as his arms and skill held out. Here... "You seriously believe you can break open the Sun of Infinity and take its power?" he said, forcing incredulity into his voice. In honesty, he doubted that they would be *doing* this if they weren't very sure.

"It is not a matter of *belief*, Tobimar," said Master Wieran, his cold voice as calm and matter-of-fact as if they had both been talking the matter over at dinner. "*Belief* is for weak-minded fools who do not understand that there is only that which *is*, that which *may be* and can be tested, and that which *is not*. I *know* that I can do this, because I have examined all of the data, I have formed hypotheses and tested them, and I have verified all the steps necessary to reach a successful conclusion of this project."

The complex metal-and-crystal array of devices was aligning itself precisely with every angle and face of the eight-pointed star at Wieran's direction; behind him, Tobimar could see Kalshae producing four strange objects from a pouch at her side; they were similar to elaborate punching daggers, with a very narrow blade and four projections half the length of the blade facing forward with it and separated by several inches.

What are those? They don't look very useful as weapons, and she certainly doesn't need...

Kalshae stepped over—carefully avoiding any contact with Wieran's structure—and placed one of the things above Tobimar's wrist. With a shudder Tobimar realized that the very narrow blade was meant to transfix the limb into which it was plunged, and the four extensions would lock down into the matching holes he could now just make out around his wrists—and, he would guess, his ankles as well.

"And what do *you* get out of it, Master Wieran? They...or, I guess now *she* alone, get the power, but what is your interest?" He had no idea if these questions would be of use—if he couldn't figure a way out of this, nothing would matter soon enough—but it couldn't hurt.

"I *learn*, young man. Knowledge is the greatest power and the highest aspiration. The ability to investigate the essence of power itself—of the border between the numinous and the mundane, of the deific and mortal essence, *this* has always been my one, true interest."

"A study which requires very large scale operations and many...test subjects," Kalshae said, laying the other three of her daggerlike tools at their appropriate places. "We provided that, and he provided other tools or materials when we needed them. A mutually beneficial arrangement."

She turned to Wieran. "I am ready to perform the ritual. Is all in place?"

Wieran nodded. "All is in readiness. The completion of all our goals is at hand." He stepped back. "You may begin."

Kalshae nodded, and then began a slow walk around the circle, chanting in a language that Tobimar could not understand, but whose overtones were clearly Demonic. As she walked, Kalshae's transformation completed—seven feet tall, with a pair of spiraled, delicate horns rising from her head, her skin of an unearthly smoothness, shining more like porcelain than flesh, eyes now red, alien and deadly. Yet there was little of the monstrousness he had seen and sensed in other demons. There was evil here, yes...but not *only* evil.

"Lady Shae," he said, "you have been called that name for years. You have served as a strong, beloved ruler for all that time. I cannot believe that was *all* a fake, that there is nothing in you of the light. You have been here as long as Miri. You *care* for Miri in your own way—you wouldn't be so furious at Phoenix otherwise!"

Shae continued the chant, but he saw tenseness in her shoulders, the bunching of muscles at the corner of her jaw between phrases when she clenched her teeth. The eyes flicked at him, angry but unyielding.

Now she was spiraling in towards him. Periodically she scattered something—her own blood, Tobimar thought—across the circle. "You don't have to do this! You've built something wonderful and powerful and it doesn't have to be ended this way!"

She reached the raised eight-pointed dais, and for an instant—just an instant—her eyes met his and he saw a moment of uncertainty, of a wish to change the course of things from the one chosen. But even as he saw that, the eyes hardened their gaze. "It *will* end this way," she whispered as she leaned over him. And before he could react, she snatched up one of the daggerlike objects and drove it straight through his wrist.

Tobimar couldn't restrain a scream of shock. It wasn't entirely *pain*, not yet—that would come later, he thought—but it was definitely shock and the feeling of violation, of something impaling him and holding him locked to the table by gripping his own flesh.

"*Tobimar!*" Kyri shouted. "You monstrous—" The Phoenix Justiciar gave vent to some astonishingly inventive cures. "When I get free of this—"

"You will never *get* free," Kalshae said, a note of surprising weariness in her voice, and impaled Tobimar's opposite-side ankle.

Now that *hurt!* he thought, somewhat dazedly, as he heard his own scream echoing in his ears. *Through the ankle. Terian and Chromaias, that's agony!* He gritted his teeth, knowing now what was coming. The holdfasts on the eight-pointed altar, however, wouldn't let him get away. All he could do was endure.

But for what purpose?

A faint glow was now emanating from the table on which he lay, and he strained his head around to see.

Blood flowed from beneath his impaled wrist and ankle, blood slowly gaining a ghostly azure sheen as it trickled down a complex pattern of channels worked into the stone. Another shock of pain, and a third stream of blood began to run down the channels beneath his other arm.

Once more he wondered: *is there no hope?*

As the lightning-sharp agony repeated for the fourth time, transfixing his last limb, he looked over at Kyri and saw her eyes closed, her lips moving in prayer. *She's calling on Myrionar, even though she's in enemy hands, and the power is blocked.*

He remembered her story then, and Myrionar's words to its last Justiciar: "... *believe, and hold, and be true to Justice, and there is a way out for you.*"

That meant that there was—there *must* be—a way out for Kyri, if not for him.

But I was sent to her for a reason. And not just to help her against Thornfalcon. It means nothing *if I found my homeland and no one ever hears of it. Master Khoros wouldn't have just let me go here to die.*

He could feel coldness starting to creep upon him; *losing blood pretty quickly through those wounds.* But he clung to those other thoughts. Oh, he knew some other people—more cynical about Khoros' motives and approaches—might laugh at him for having faith in the ancient wizard, but Khoros intended them to achieve *something*, and something that, he was sure, had not yet been achieved.

The light was brightening, and now the Sun was responding, its luminance beginning to shine forth. *I can't let this happen. But I'm* helpless!

He felt fury rising in him even as his breath became shorter. *They will steal the very power of Terian and use it for their ends—and now that they've reached this point, what will happen to Kaizatenzei itself? This was all a trap, something perfected to bring in and hold one particular target—me—so they could use me as a key to...*

A key...

The idea was there, hovering just out of reach. But it made sense, somehow. Terian had given the Stars and Sun to his family. If the artifact of a god *could* be forced open, even with the knowledge and skill of a twisted genius like Wieran and the power of what he now knew must be a demonlord, then it must be *meant* to open somehow. There must be some way for those who *owned* it to activate it, to call upon that power in utter extremity...

And once more, the memory of Khoros, towering above him, face somehow hidden, a mouth with a half-smile beneath the five-sided hat...

Kyri... praying...

And then he remembered.

His breath was shorter now, and sweat stood out on his brow. He was faint and nauseated, but he drew in a breath. *Khoros said, "...But when all else fails, you may find strength in childhood prayer..."*

That childhood prayer. Said to have been the words of Terian himself, in the days of the founding of their line...

"Seven Stars and a Single Sun hold the Starlight that I do Own," he began, and Kalshae suddenly turned to him, eyes narrowing. Wieran raised his head from where he stood.

"These Eight combine and form the One, Form the Sign by which I'm known," he continued, speeding up as he saw Kalshae start forward. But the demon hesitated, and Tobimar managed a wan grin of triumph. *She doesn't dare interfere—her own ritual is in the process of completion too!*

"The Good in Heart can Light wield..." he said, and heard his voice echoing out, stronger than he had believed possible. *And one tiny change from the prayer,* "...The Length of Space shall be *MY* shield!"

And as the four rivulets of his own blood coalesced about him, the world dissolved in a thunderous blaze of blue-white flame.

CHAPTER 44

The detonation of azure-touched argent staggered everyone in the room, knocking Kalshae and Wieran to their knees. Kyri felt the grip on her arms loosen; she spun and kicked out, freeing herself, straining against the bonds on her. But as her sight recovered from the dazzling blast, she stopped, staring incredulously.

Standing atop the eight-sided dais was an immense figure, perhaps eight feet tall. The head was shrouded in a nimbus of pure white light, blurring the features so that the only thing that could be seen were a pair of piercing blue eyes and the hazy gold of the hair. A black cape streamed from the shoulders, a waterfall of ebony in stark contrast to the shimmering light that surrounded the apparition, light that coalesced into an ever-shifting sparkle of rainbow about the waist that seemed both source and product of the luminance that enfolded the figure. Just visible above the crossed arms, a small golden sigil, a sidewise eight, could be seen over the heart.

For a frozen instant no one moved, all staring at the impossible. Within that figure, a shadow within a shadow of light, Kyri thought she saw a smaller figure.

Then the light-shrouded head came up, and the apparition spoke.

"I am the Nemesis of all Evil. I am the Light in the Darkness. I am Terian, the Infinite."

Kalshae's face was salt-white beneath its tan, and she *cowered* back against the limit of the ritual circle. "You ... you cannot be here. You *cannot!* You made a pact—you *all* made a pact—with Father, with Kerlamion and all the other gods, that you would not, *could* not directly intervene!"

Kyri noticed that one—and only one—person in that room seemed unawed by the presence. Master Wieran's face held an expression as of someone given an unexpected and wonderful gift, and even as Terian answered, the alchemist-sage bent over his complex apparatus.

"It is even so that such a pact was made. And even though it was done with malicious intent, to allow that which has now come to pass, still I am bound by that oath. To intervene directly would, by that oath, precipitate a Godswar across the face of Zarathan." The shining figure nodded. *"That I shall not allow."*

A hint of a smile, sharp and dangerous. *"Yet there is nothing in that oath or any other that prevents me from awakening the power that slumbers within Tobimar Silverun, Seventh of Seven; that sleeps within his blood. Within* my *blood. So it is done, and I have written your ending, as surely as if I had taken up sword against you."*

The figure vanished in a rampage of blue-white fire, energy that tore through the room in a storm of actinic fortune that shattered her bonds, stripped the coverings from Poplock Duckweed and Hiriista, and hammered the Unity Guards to the ground.

Now it was Tobimar Silverun who stood on the dais, the wounds on his body shimmering with the gods-fire, sealing, welded by the power of the divine, and the Sun of Infinity was open, its shimmering polychromatic light pouring down upon the Prince of Skysand.

But in the same moment, Master Wieran slammed down a pair of levers within his mechanism, speaking a phrase in a language Kyri did not know. The waterfalling power was suddenly drawn downwards, through the dais, and swirled through the entire complex circle. Kalshae began to glow darkly, blue-black energy twining up around her as the azure-white shimmered around Tobimar.

Kyri stretched out her hand and Flamewing wrenched itself from a nearby pack; she kicked one of her captors in the face, caught the bundle he had been holding, and hurled it through the air. *"Tobimar!"*

Tobimar's eyes snapped open, shining with the awakened power but fully aware. The bundle came apart in midair as his aura reached out to meet it, and in a blur of motion and magic Tobimar was suddenly clothed, with his swords back in his hands. "Kyri! Get Miri, keep them from holding her!"

"But you—"

There was a scream of pain to her side and one of the Unity Guards was falling, gripping his ankle. "*Go,*" Poplock said from the floor, bouncing speedily around the circle. "I'll keep an eye on things here!"

"You will go *nowhere!*" Kalshae stretched out her arm and red-black fire coiled towards Kyri—

—Only to be blocked by the now blue-blazing swords of Tobimar Silverun.

Kyri gritted her teeth and turned towards her opponents. *Have to get through that door, to the stairs. They can't have gone too far yet.*

The Unity Guards were slower, moving in a confused pattern. Danrall's eyes were only half-focused, dazed, and Kyri realized that the brief manifestation of Terian had, somehow, disrupted the control or geas that had transformed him from the earnest young man to the implacable destroyer.

And I can feel Myrionar's presence again!

"I will be your rearguard!" Hiriista said, and unleashed a storm of shimmering bolts that battered at the Guards, further stunning and confusing them. "Go, and I shall be not far behind!"

She charged forward, shoving past the Unity Guards' halfhearted defenses, and burst through the door, praying even as she did so. *Myrionar, now truly I need my strength and speed and power. Give me what you can, for not merely my friends, but all of Kaizatenzei, needs our help now. And so does one who has repented, who cares and would seek salvation, I think. I will save her, if I may.*

Footsteps were behind her now, and their uncertainty was fading, becoming a staccato drumbeat of pursuit that was closing the distance, even as she turned, seeking the way down. Hiriista's hissing voice evoked more thunder and light, but she knew he couldn't possibly stop them all.

The question was *where*. Where was the entrance to...

And in the moment of thinking the question she knew the answer. *This ritual was done above the Valatar Throne. Where else would the entrance to the secrets be, than through that room, more guarded and more watched than any other?*

At the same moment, Myrionar answered her prayers. Golden strength flooded into her, with the singing, joyful certainty that Myrionar's presence had always given her. She sheathed Flamewing. Her body was light as a feather, and she streaked down the stairs, the sound of the Unity Guards now fading away, passing an open-mouthed servant like an arrow in flight. The Throne Room was closed now, but even as the Unity Guards posted there saw her coming she was past them, grasping the doors and *heaving* with all the strength of Vantage and godspower.

The doors of the Valatar Throneroom ripped from their hinges, battering the reaching Color and Shade aside like toys, and Kyri was through. She drew her sword, and Flamewing ignited in red-gold glory as Kyri saw that indeed the Valatar Throne had concealed a passageway down.

The Tower shuddered and she knew the battle between Kalshae and Tobimar must now be joined in earnest. *Please be all right, Tobimar,* she prayed, and then was heading down the winding staircase, three, four steps at a time. *They've gotten farther than I thought. The ritual took time, longer than I had imagined.*

The steps ended at a broad intersection, one hallway going straight forward, another going to left and right. *Which way?*

At first she had no clue; all three ways were dark, silent, polished stone and subtly-painted walls all identical, unmarred, unmarked.

The sound of her pursuers was increasing, and she gripped Flamewing tighter, brought its power to the fore, and in that brighter pulse of light, her eye caught something tiny but lighter colored, just at the limit of the light on the right-hand side.

A tiny scrap of blue-green.

Miri!

Kyri turned, sprinting as fast as she could now. "Hold on, Miri!" she shouted into the silent dark, and her voice echoed endlessly down the corridors.

"I'm coming!"

CHAPTER 45

Once more, I'm a fly in a battle of spiders, Poplock thought as he bounced around the perimeter, ducking, dodging, occasionally poking Steelthorn into someone so that his pursuers kept getting in each others' way.

Kalshae rose to her full height, the dark energy now seething around her, the simple robe evaporating to be replaced by water-pure crystal armor that had leapt to her from a casket nearby. "Ignore that Toad," she snarled. "Catch up with the Phoenix—now!"

"Overconfident, are you?" Tobimar said. His voice was different—more powerful, resonant, with a touch of Terian's own voice still present.

For answer, Kalshae leveled a blast of black energy—so potent that Poplock winced just *seeing* it—at Tobimar. The twin-swords caught it, held, as the Skysand Prince was slowly pushed backwards, nearly off the dais, before the blue-white power within him burned forward and dissipated the attack.

But Kalshae was already there, her own great sword slashing down to be barely parried by Tobimar's. She grinned, and Poplock did not like the confidence he saw. "You have gained some of the power of the Sun, yes. But so have I, as was intended."

She delivered a tremendous backhanded blow that sent Tobimar skidding backwards, off the dais and over, and then chopped the dais itself in half and kicked one of the chunks into the Skysand Prince's face; Tobimar barely rolled with the impact, and still there was blood on his face when he rose. "But I have wielded such power for millennia untold, while *you* are a mortal child just now learning what can be done with such strength. You shall have little time to learn!"

Ouch. She's probably right. It suddenly dawned on Poplock, though, that the fact she had just cut the dais meant that the ritual itself was over. *Which means...*

He held his breath as he bounced across the border of the ritual circle; if he was wrong, this could be very, very painful. But to his relief, he felt nothing happen as he entered the circle. *Notice she did* not *touch Wieran's little apparatus—kicked the chunk* over *the edge of the device.*

Something bothered Poplock about that—the way the power was waterfalling from the opened Sun down, into a shimmering mass centered in that assembly of devices, and then moving out in thin streams of light and dark to the two combatants. But he didn't have much time to think about it; Kalshae had summoned another ball of energy and hurled it at Tobimar.

Can't hold back here; she probably won't notice *the smaller stuff.* He gripped the elaborate setting on his upper arm and concentrated. "*GO!*" he shouted.

Blue-green energy coalesced and cascaded outward as the Gemcall activated. The torrent of the very essence of water caught Lady Shae, bowled her over just before she could strike Tobimar again, slammed her so hard against the far wall that chips and dust exploded from the polished stone.

She cursed and hurled a minor bolt at Poplock, but couldn't spare the time to make sure it hit because now Tobimar was on her, a whirlwind of blades surrounded by godspower. For a few moments, the two traded blows, and the entire tower shook.

Then Lady Shae laughed and leapt back, whirling her sword like a noisemaker at a party. "Oh, now, why don't we make this *interesting*?"

She slashed around in a complete circle, blue-black laced with poisonous green and actinic white. Tobimar hurdled the streak of cutting death, which passed far above Poplock's head.

And with a grinding, shuddering noise, the Tower above began to slide sideways, tilting, the entire Tower cut asunder by that single assault. Poplock felt his eyes bugging out twice as far as normal as he tried to grasp the fact that a single blow had just cut down the Valatar Tower, a tower two Chaoswars old, a tower built to hold an artifact of Terian.

Slowly the Tower of the Great Light continued its great, dramatic tilt, tipping farther and farther so the rosy sunset light now streamed into the roofless chamber and Poplock could see that it was falling, majestically and ponderously, towards the West. *Thank all the gods for* that; *means that it mostly falls to the peninsula and the lake.*

Kalshae bounded to the top of the broken wall, raining destruction anew atop Tobimar's head, and Tobimar was barely able to deflect the lethal barrage. "What a shame, I got turned around a bit; it's not going to fall on the city," Kalshae said. "But just the fall of the Tower will be more than enough to strike fear in their hearts."

Poplock ducked behind the untouched section of the dais and started wrenching at the points of the Gemcalling Matrix. *Got a couple more I can use.*

"I think a part of you *wanted* to spare them," Tobimar said, and Poplock heard a flurry of cuts. "You deny a part of yourself, Kalshae, and that weakens you. And I am not *quite* as untrained as you think. Khoros' training is not to be ignored . . . and here, let me show you a trick my friend Xavier taught me while we were traveling!"

Ooo, I know that one. Xavier had his defense that he couldn't teach, and then he had his offense . . .

Tobimar backflipped away from Kalshae, landing right in front of Poplock. The twin-blades crossed, and where they crossed, blue-white fire concentrated, expanded, became a spinning ball of coruscating power. "Here, Kalshae—*catch!*"

The sphere of energy streaked past Poplock at blurring speed and there was another Tower-rocking impact. Kalshae's curse was pained and disbelieving, and the little Toad grinned as he managed to shove the next gem into place. *Go get her, Tobimar!*

"A surprise indeed," Kalshae conceded, razor-shards of night-dark flame swarming about Tobimar, rebounding—for now—from the Spiritsmith's armor and Tobimar's parrying blades. "But if I keep you from concentrating, you shall never use that trick again!"

"But then," Poplock said, bouncing out from behind the stone, "you're busy concentrating on *him*." He touched the Calling Array.

Actinic violet-tinged light turned sunset to midnight and thunderbolts rained down throughout the tower, somehow missing both Tobimar and Poplock but hammering down on stone and Demon alike. *And Wieran? Wait, where in Blackwart's name is he?*

The white-haired experimenter was nowhere to be seen.

Tobimar had lunged as the lightning died down, and for the first time red blood bloomed from a wound, two wounds, three, on Kalshae, and she cursed in a demonic tongue. "Both of you will be something of a challenge. But I have no interest in challenges." Her hand dropped to the mechanism on her belt and came up with an amber-orange disc. *"Come forth!"*

Sunshine-colored light rose and faded, and Light Anora's staff abruptly blocked a stroke of Tobimar's swords. Kalshae smiled and turned towards Poplock. "That will hold you a moment, while I eliminate the smaller but annoying opponent."

She can do that with all the Lights. Except Miri, I guess. Why aren't any of them going against the orders, though? Why's Miri so different? Poplock dodged behind another chunk of stone as blue-black power ripped a hole in the floor where he'd just been. *This is bad. Stone won't shield me, just keep her from being sure where to aim. We've got to get Anora down, then somehow keep Kalshae from summoning more reinforcements.*

But he wasn't helpless yet. As he bounded from the temporary shelter, which was being shattered by demonic power even as he did, he aimed the clockwork crossbow and triggered it.

A stream of alchemical bolts stitched the air between Poplock and Kalshae. The aura about her diverted some, incinerated others—but as Thornfalcon had discovered months before, some things can hurt you even if they didn't quite reach you. Stinging vapors, an incendiary blast, acidic spray, and Kalshae was driven momentarily back. *That won't last long, though, and—*

In that instant, Tobimar Silverun took the opening and with a tremendous double-cut, cleaved Light Anora Lal in half, blue-white godsfire trailing along the line of the cut. Tobimar's expression was grim and sorrowful; Poplock doubted that Tobimar would have had the will to deliver such a horrific blow if it weren't obvious that the little Toad were in mortal peril.

Her legs and lower torso fell to the ground; the upper torso, arms, and head spun in air, hit the floor and rolled, presenting the severed end to Poplock's astounded view.

From within the fallen corpse gleamed metal and crystal and woven nets of fiber, and barely a trace of blood or flesh.

CHAPTER 46

For a moment, Tobimar found himself unable to grasp what he was seeing. Then, as Anora's upper half struggled to right itself and move on its arms alone, it penetrated.

Eternal Servants. They're fully human-looking Eternal Servants! But Wieran said...

He mentally smacked himself. It was obvious now that so much of what they'd been told were half-truths, evasions, and sometimes outright lies. The Eternal Servants the cities were given were practically toys, whose ongoing development was merely a mask for what Wieran was actually achieving.

He leapt forward and engaged Lady Shae again. *Have to keep her off-balance.* "Poplock—"

"On it!" The tiny Toad scuttled underneath Anora's unevenly-cut chest, as Tobimar matched blades with Shae. In the midst of an exchange of blazing blows which scorched both Tobimar and Kalshae, Anora's body stiffened and collapsed. "Yep," came the muffled voice from within, "pulling that stack of crystal discs works just fine."

Kalshae made an abortive move towards the mechanism on her waist, but was forced to keep her hands on her sword as Tobimar pressed her, hammering at her with both swords as hard as he could. *We're both unbelievably strong,* he realized as he saw the *shockwaves* from their blocked blows resonating in the floor, making dust and crumbled rock dance.

Distract her. Keep her off-balance constantly. "If they're nothing but Eternal Servants, why the recruits?" he demanded. "You call for these people and yet they're not the ones you have serving. Do you kill them? Sacrifices?"

Kalshae did not answer, though her grin widened.

A small weight was now on him, scuttling up but only reaching about halfway before being forced to hang onto one of the pouches at his waist for dear life. He lunged to keep up with Kalshae as she tried to disengage, and more realization burst in. "But no . . . no, that wouldn't work. Zogen Josan, he's not an Eternal Servant. They've seen him wounded. And Miri isn't."

As he leapt over a fallen fragment of stone, he saw that the Sun had finally fallen from its place, empty, a crystal shell. The jump was apparently too much for Poplock, too, as he dropped to the floor and bounced to the side. "What in the name of Terian have you been *doing* with those people?"

"Why would I tell you, Tobimar Silverun?" Kalshae asked calmly. "The knowledge would do you no good dead, and if you win and I lose, why should I smooth your path?"

"No desire to tell me whatever horror lies behind it and see my own reaction?"

She laughed, and the laugh was incongruously cheerful and jolly, the same laugh they'd come to love before the truth came out. "Oh, now, Tobimar, you're clever. Yes, of course there's some temptation. But I am rather good at resisting such—"

Without warning, as the two dueling figures spun past another clump of rubble, a tiny brown form hurtled upward and latched onto the slanting cylindrical mechanism at Kalshae's belt.

"Father *take* you!" Kalshae tried to reach down and rip Poplock off, but Tobimar's renewed assault and the fact that the little Toad had wrapped webbed feet and hands tightly about the device made this very difficult. Finally, though, she delivered a sharp blow with her elbow that dislodged Poplock, sending him tumbling drunkenly away across the stone; the holder of the summoning crystals dangled, still partially secured.

Sand and wind, that got us nowhere! A glance told Tobimar that Poplock wasn't, as he'd feared, dead, but the sluggish movement of the Toad showed he wasn't in full possession of his wits right now, either. *Think!*

As Kalshae spun her massive sword in a dark-flaming arc, reminding Tobimar forcefully of Kyri, he knew the only approach that might work. "Please, Kalshae, stop this. A part of you doesn't want this any more than I do."

Kalshae's blade streaked down, then across, up, around, dancing from one side to the other so fast he could barely parry them. But there was a tiny wrinkle between her brows. "You've already *shown* this! The fall of the Tower—where it will hurt almost no one! Your expressions and hurt over Miri—you care about her, the way I care about Kyri!"

Whoops. Used her real name. Well, I guess it doesn't matter now. He couldn't feel too bad about the slip; in the middle of battle it was *very* hard to keep track of the lies you were supposed to believe, and he felt he'd done very well to keep it straight this long.

"Kyri? The Phoenix's true name. I see." Her strokes were still vicious . . . but was it his imagination that they were just the tiniest bit less, that the room was not shuddering *quite* so violently with each monstrous exchange? "No, not the same way. We are of *Kerlamion's* heritage, she a direct one of his children, and we are bound by blood and the excitement of power and dominion, of the crushing of others beneath our heels and the ecstasy of ruin! Do not insult me by—"

He caught her blade between his, drove her back, and now he was *sure* there was hesitation. "You argue with yourself, not me. Perhaps you have found a way to resist the Light more than she, but you cannot have been unaffected. You even call it 'corruption,' when you know full well that it is *purification*. But you fear it, because it is part of you, a part that has been growing for thousands of years!"

She snarled, redoubling her attacks—but they were crude assaults, much less delicate, easier to block or evade despite the raw power, and he went on, feeling a rising hope. "Kalshae—*Lady Shae*—if our positions were reversed, you would hope I would fall, that I would become one of you. You would make these arguments to me. But you have *been* part of the argument. Can you tell me, in truth, that never have you felt a touch of pleasure at resolving another's problems? At being admired for your justice and your kindness?" He spun away, and realized that for the first time another attack was not immediately forthcoming.

She had paused, staring at him—yet not, precisely, at him, but more inward.

He made another guess. "Have you not found beauty where before you would have found ugliness, things opposed to your nature? Doesn't a part of you *want to stop this*?"

The huge sword wavered, and the dark flames were guttering lower, showing shades of lighter color. "I . . ."

"You don't have to give it all up. You can have this power as it was *meant* to be. You can be everything you've pretended to be, and Miri would *want* that. She would be *proud* to be part of that now."

Kalshae's sword had lowered halfway, and Tobimar, barely daring to hope, let his drop slightly, too. *Not leaving myself uncovered . . . but showing that I am not preparing to attack her in weakness. If she does not trust, there is no chance.*

But even as the hope dawned in his heart, her head came up, and black flame burned anew in her eyes. "*NO*," she said, and the refusal shook the Tower. "No, you will not divert me, you will not play on my corruption and make me betray the one who even now reaches out his hand to *crush* your world beneath him!" The great sword darkened the air with its power. "There *is* no hope for your pathetic Light here, for Kerlamion Blackstar walks this world and it will soon be his—and any who think otherwise are doomed! I will *prove* this to Miri, and she will be *cured*!"

Her hand darted to her belt, and Tobimar realized that they were too far separated for him to stop her, even as he started a desperate lunge forward.

She cast the crystal disc outward, shouting, "COME FORTH!"

Just as the disc struck the unyielding stone surface, it registered with Tobimar—and with Kalshae, whose eyes widened in disbelieving horror—that it was of shining, water-clear crystal, as uncolored as a breath of air.

A blaze of white light enveloped Kalshae and seethed about the point where the crystal had struck. An echoing, agonized shriek pierced Tobimar's ears as the light surged, vibrated back and forth, both nexuses of light brightening, expanding . . .

The explosion blew him across the Tower, shattered the remaining walls, cracked the floor itself. Tobimar found himself sliding off, plummeting through the air. But the godspower was still in him, and he realized that he could simply *will* the air to support his feet, and it did; he stood and then ran back into the broken tower.

A smoking black crater, crackling with light and dark, and the twisted remains of a cylindrical device were the only things remaining where Kalshae had stood.

Poplock eased his way out from a pile of rubble, looking pensively at the crater.

"And *that*," he said, "is why you don't try summoning yourself."

CHAPTER 47

Miri tugged in vain at the hands holding her. *Useless. They have been given very clear commands, and the power driving them is now . . . immense.*

The Unity Guards dragged her implacably down the shadowed corridor, and she felt the darkness *radiating* from ahead, a palpable malice and hatred that sought out the part of her that was as of yet still the original demon. But now the vaster part of her was something else, something that fought desperately against that immeasurable malevolence. *But I cannot do so forever. A day, a week, a month perhaps, but then I will fall.*

She laughed bitterly. The armored figures took no notice—they were completely dominated by their mission now, and no humanity was left. But it was so very ironic that she had fought hard and long to keep her destructive, vicious nature untouched, had denied the Light its foothold, and now, having finally opened herself up to the joy that she had battled so long, was waging a futile battle to *not* become what she had been.

And this close to such darkness, she dared not use her full power and expose her essence to something that might easily tip her back over into the darkness that waited so very, very near. *In fighting I might lose everything.*

If only I could weaken them somehow. But there was no way; by commanding that she be taken, Kalshae had automatically neutralized Miri's command over the Unity Guards and their armor. She wouldn't be pulling the same trick on them that she'd managed on the renegade Govi Zergul. The same thing would have happened to Kalshae if Miri had given the order; it was a safeguard they had both agreed upon, for precisely this sort of situation, and it had proven useful in the past when the others of their brethren had gone bad. Or, to be more accurate, gone good. Miri had fully intended to use that trick on Kalshae; she'd just been beaten to the punch.

Distantly from overhead came a shuddering vibration, then a muffled booming that seemed to come from all around. *Something's happening, something not in the ritual.* She felt a faint stirring of hope, but the smothering power of the evil that lurked beneath the lake nearly snuffed it out. *Almost there.*

Then a faint sound, but one that was closer, much closer. *A voice?* She stopped, and noticed that her escort had also paused.

"*Miri! I'm coming!*"

PHOENIX!

"I'm here!" she shouted back, and threw all the strength in her small body against the pinioning arms.

Now there was a distant glow, a golden point of fire, growing, and Miri felt the tug of a very different power approaching, contesting with and pushing back the darkness towards which she had been drawn. *Just a little closer, Phoenix, please . . .*

Dravan Igo and Anora stepped between Miri and the charging Phoenix. "Get her to the cell. We shall stop her."

Miri felt herself dragged back even faster than before, Tanvol and the three others trying to complete their mission while Dravan and Anora dealt with the intruder. Miri fought to slow herself, but it was useless; the Unity Guards were well-trained in how to keep a recalcitrant prisoner moving, and her own Light armor was being suppressed. She had managed to keep Kalshae from simply causing it to remove itself, but unless Miri could somehow get away from the Unity Guards under Kalshae's control, she wouldn't be able to make use of the armor or much of her own power.

She still clung to hope, but there was fear now, corrosive fear as to what might happen to Phoenix. *I . . . I really do think I love her. But against two Lights—*

Even as she thought that, there was an amber-orange explosion of light and Anora was gone.

What . . . ?

And suddenly she understood and laughed triumphantly, for the Phoenix was *there*, and Dravan grunted as the impact drove him back a full two steps before he could regain his footing.

Summoned! Kalshae had to summon Anora to her, which means something's pushing her hard! And Phoenix is here, so she escaped! And...

The Light of Myrionar surrounded her, keeping the darkness behind from quite touching her. Miri took a breath and reached deep within herself...

Strength *surged* up from within; she saw her skin transform from near-white to the blue-black of darkest sapphire, and the Unity Guards suddenly leapt back, realizing something had gone very wrong. She whirled and kicked out, making them back off another few feet, judging, analyzing.

But that, really, was their major weakness. Too much time analyzing, not enough acting. *"Kolvaka urdruon, heshok!"*

The Stone Prison erupted from the polished rock of the corridor, pillars spearing upward and downward from mere inches in front of Miri all the way back to the limit of her sight. Herminta and the violet-armored Hue Pini were impaled by stone columns, shattering the Guard Armor and crushing their central cores; black-bearded Tanvol and Danrall evaded that doom, but were hemmed in by the stone in all directions; so tight was the spacing between the columns that they could barely move, let alone escape to fight.

Phoenix was *hammering* at Dravan, and Miri was astounded to see that the huge, massive Light—one of the most formidable warriors in all Kaizatenzei—was utterly *unable* to do more than defend himself. He was being driven farther and farther back, closer to Miri and the bulwark of stone she had raised.

She has to know the truth, so she knows how to fight. "Phoenix! The Unity Guard—they're actually Eternal Servants!"

A moment of disbelieving shock, just as abruptly transformed to revelation and understanding, burst across Phoenix's face. Then her assault on Dravan redoubled, and suddenly the warrior's big blade spun away into the air, rebounding from the corridor wall. Phoenix's great sword Flamewing continued its arc, spun, and impaled Dravan Igo directly through the center of his chest, just above the breastline.

There was a faint splintering sound and a flash of light from the wound, and Dravan collapsed like a puppet with the strings cut...which was, Miri had to admit, essentially accurate.

Phoenix looked up to see the Unity Guards struggling within the stone cage and laughed. "Well, I came to save you, but you seem to have been doing fine on your own."

Miri tried to restrain herself but failed; she embraced the other woman as tightly as she could (eliciting a faint *"oof!"* sound) and then realized that she was still in her half-demonic form. "I...no, if you hadn't gotten close enough I couldn't have done anything. Not without...but we're wasting time."

"You're right. Tobimar's fighting Kalshae right now."

"Light's Mercy. How's he even *surviving?*"

Despite her obvious worry over Tobimar, Phoenix grinned again. "Oh, you missed the best part. Where *Tobimar,* instead of Wieran and Kalshae, opened the Sun and called Terian himself down."

Miri staggered to a halt, trying to process what the Phoenix had just said. "*Terian?* Tobimar *opened* the Sun? I...Phoenix, that makes no *sense!*"

"Oh, it makes perfect sense, which we can talk about later!"

She shook herself, and sprinted after the tall girl with the gold-touched blue hair streaming behind her. "The stone columns won't hold Light Tanvol forever, I should warn you."

"Doesn't matter. If we're all together I'll bet on the five of us against any *number* of Unity Guards—Shades, Hues, Colors, *or* Lights."

That depends on so very much, Miri thought, but she did not speak. There was, she realized, no point in it. Either they would win through, or they wouldn't, but there wasn't much point in ruining Phoenix's confidence now.

Sound of scratching footsteps ahead, with a pearl-glowing ball providing illumination, and Phoenix grinned. "Hiriista! You made it!"

The magewright was battered, with blood trickling slowly from a dozen minor wounds, but seemed otherwise unharmed. "And I see you have succeeded in your mission."

"I have. Though she helped free herself, too."

"I would expect no less from Light Miri." Hiriista had turned and matched their run instantly. "Now let us hope we are not too late to assist our friends above."

But as they emerged into the Valatar Throneroom, Miri saw to her mounting joy that Tobimar was already running through the ruined (*ruined? Great Light!*) doors, Poplock clinging to his shoulder.

Then her heart suddenly went cold and she stopped, even as Kyri ran forward and embraced Tobimar in relief; she found herself staring at the floor, not daring to move. After a few moments, she heard Tobimar say uncertainly, "Um...Miri?"

She found it almost impossible to look up. "Kalshae...?"

He also looked down. "I'm sorry. I tried to talk her out of it. I...almost succeeded, I think. But maybe I'm deluding myself. Anyway...I'm sorry."

A huge aching wound was ripping open in her chest. For a moment Miri couldn't understand what was happening. *What attack is this? A spell? I sense nothing, I...*

And then as a huge cry broke from her and her sight blurred to uselessness she understood. *No! I...don't cry...not over her!* Miri fought, tried to contain the tears trickling down her face as she dropped to her knees. "I...c-c-can't...stop!"

She heard a racking indrawn sob, recognized that it was her own, that the agony in her chest was tragedy and loss of someone who had been an ally and...at the end...more, but who couldn't be saved. "I...I should have found a way...Shae and I were always together, but, but, she, I mean, you *saw*, she wanted to save me, but I...I..."

The tears kept interrupting and she had no idea what she was saying, or what she *wanted* to say or what she *should* say, only that it *hurt* and there was nothing she could do, nothing left *to* do, because somehow she did not doubt Tobimar Silverun; Kalshae was gone, Kalshae the strong, the confident, the loyal and dedicated, her right hand and best supporter, Kalshae was gone.

A hand touched her shoulder gently. Two hands, one on each side. "I'm sorry, I truly am," Tobimar said gently. "I guessed that you two were...close. If I could have found another way—"

"*We*," Poplock said from the floor in front of her. "Because it was really both of us. I was the one who swapped the summoning crystals. So...if we could have found another way..."

"No!" She forced herself to stand, furiously scrubbed the tears away. "No, you didn't have a choice. If she stayed, if she was there for the ritual..." Now she saw the faint blue-white aura

that surrounded the Skysand Prince, and felt the power, even
more pure and clean than that of Myrionar, radiating from him,
and the wonder helped dry her tears, at least for the moment.
". . . and if you gained *that* power, then no, there was no choice."

"And we're not done yet," Poplock said. "There's a big loose
end running around."

She felt a familiar cold anger returning, and grasped it gratefully, used it as an anchor and touchstone to drive away the grief
for a little while. *"Master Wieran."*

"I'm guessing he's got *another* lab down there, one he didn't
show us, right?"

"Very right, Poplock. That is where he built most of the Guardsmen as well as the Eternal Servants, and where T'Terakhorwin
is located, the Great Array which is the source of most of his
power. If he escaped your battle—"

"—he did," Tobimar said positively. "He disappeared during
my fight with Kalshae."

Miri nodded. "Then he'll have gone to the Great Array. He'll
have sealed the doors and be preparing to destroy any that come
to get him. Of course, he'll also be hoping that Kalshae finished
you off."

"Well," Kyri said, grim-faced, "let's finish this."

"Don't let your guard down, guys," said Poplock. "He's going
to have a lot to greet us with, or I'm just a dumb toad."

Hiriista looked narrowly at Poplock. "What did you see?"

"That . . . device that Wieran had set up. It took in the power
of the Sun of Infinity and filtered it, split it into light and dark.
I guess if Tobimar hadn't been there, it would've just disposed
of the light stuff."

"Yes," Miri said, puzzled. "That was the whole purpose of the
setup; our work in opening and stealing the power of the Stars
had been, well, terribly inefficient. This was supposed to be much
better, much more."

"And," Poplock said, "you know, I was watching that process,
and what I saw was a *huge* pouring stream of power coming
from the Sun . . . and two *dinky little* streams of power going out
to Tobimar and Kalshae."

She froze. *The treacherous, backstabbing little—*

And then she had to laugh. "Oh . . . oh, I am not *used* to
these . . . these . . . flip-flopping emotional changes! But . . . we were

all planning on when we could dispose of Wieran, deciding exactly when he would no longer be necessary...and it seems he had already decided on how to deal with *us* when *we* were no longer necessary!"

"*Told* you he was smarter than everyone here. He had them fund their own project, and designed his mechanism to steal most of the power for his *own* purposes rather than theirs." Poplock nodded and then bounced back to Tobimar's shoulder. "Still, guess we have no choice but to go after him."

"None," Hiriista said firmly. "Every moment we delay gives him more opportunities to prepare."

Miri rose to her full (not very impressive) height. "Then follow me."

Once more they entered the passage behind the Valatar Throne; once more Miri strode down the central passage and then began the descent down the three hundred forty-three steps. About halfway down, her steps slowed. *I...have to tell them now. Before the battle begins.*

"What is it, Miri?"

"Phoenix..."

"Kyri," she said. At Miri's inquiring look, she smiled. "That's my real name. Kyri."

Oh, Light. I hope she will stay so kind when she understands everything I've done...how much of a true monster I've been, and how many I've created. "Then...thank you, Kyri. But I have to tell you something."

She took a deep breath. "Behind the doors...within the Great Array...are all the people we have taken from the cities over the past centuries. All of them."

CHAPTER 48

"*All* of them?" Tobimar repeated incredulously. Poplock felt the same disbelief, but Miri's expression was too deadly serious to really doubt.

"Well...a *few* have actually died. And a lot of them, the older ones, are probably close to death. But virtually all, yes."

Hiriista gave a rasping hiss of anger. "All imprisoned in tubes, yes? As the vision of Zogan Josan implied!"

"Yes," she whispered. "All held by Wieran in the Great Array, part of his grand experiment."

"Balance," muttered Kyri, and Poplock knew she'd seen it.

"Great," Poplock said. "He's got, what, hundreds of hostages, then. Plus whatever power and weapons he's set up."

Kyri looked at Miri and then touched her shoulder. "Miri."

The young woman—the former demon, Poplock reminded himself—looked up forlornly.

"I know you're thinking about how you helped all this to happen. And that you've lost someone precious to you. But right now, we need you to fight by our side. Don't worry about the past. All right?"

It was amazing how the little speech brought the light back into Miri's eyes. Poplock watched the delicate-looking girl straighten up and nod.

"All right, then. We know we *will* need everything now, so everyone get ready."

Poplock pulled out a bottle and drank the contents down.

Eeeeugh! I've gotta figure out how to make stuff that tastes as good as it works. But that'll kick me up enough to run with these guys for a little, anyway. He saw Hiriista drink his own pick-me-up and invoke swirling somethings that then entered the *mazakh*'s body. The golden fire of Myrionar glowed brightly from Kyri, and the blue-white power that still shimmered around Tobimar intensified, echoing the fire burning in the Skysand Prince's eyes.

"You all right, Tobimar?"

"I...don't know. I've never felt like this, ever. Like I see everything, hear everything, can *do* anything. I'm burning up inside, but the fire's rebuilding me, too." The familiar voice was still touched with the sound of another.

"Just don't forget who you are."

"Never," he said, but his voice shook. Then it firmed, and Tobimar set his jaw. "*Never,*" he repeated, with more certainty.

"All right. Everyone ready?" Kyri stood before the sealed doors. "Very well."

She drew Flamewing and held it up, and white-gold fire shone from the mighty blade. "Now the way shall be *opened!*"

But even as the blade came down, the doors swung silently open; Kyri stumbled slightly before she could recover from the complete lack of resistance. "What...?"

"Do not damage my doors, Phoenix of Myrionar," came the precise, level tones of Master Wieran. "There is no need for such violence. Enter, then, since you have all gathered to see my ultimate triumph!"

Oh, great. He knows we beat Kalshae, and he's still so confident that he's just letting us walk in.

WHOA!

"Hold it! Hold it!"

Kyri froze, foot almost ready to cross the threshold.

Poplock bounced down, studying the floor. Then he looked up, but the words he was going to speak died away.

Before the party lay the Great Array. Rank upon rank of gleaming tubes of crystal and metal, worked about and around with intricate symbols, descending in concentric seven-sided levels. *Seven. Another of the commonly revered numbers.* He hadn't counted, but he was sure that if he did, he'd find there were forty-nine levels to the Great Array; Miri had mentioned there were three hundred forty-three steps on the staircase they'd just descended. *Seven times seven, and seven times seven times seven. So he gets seven* and *three, two of the big numbers.*

In the ceiling, hundreds of feet above, the black stone contrasted with the complex brilliance of the inlaid and worked runes visible against the darkness. Directly below the peak of that great dome was a central space, and within that space stood Master Wieran.

He was surrounded by mechanisms of incomprehensible complexity; gold, steel, brass, thyrium, krellin, silver, copper, tubes and gears and crystalline retorts, wire in intricate coils, spiraling glass and vibrating springs, with seven consoles laid out around him, covered in levers and buttons and verniers, slots and sockets and racks of other unknown devices. He was hundreds of yards away, but with Poplock's now-enhanced senses there was no mistaking the brilliant white hair or the absolute confidence of his pose, the arrogant look in his eyes. No, not arrogant; *fanatic.* Master Wieran had the look of a prophet on the verge of apocalypse.

His doorstep sure echoed *that.* "Thanks for the invitation, but I don't know if I want to step across *those* symbols. Clever, the way you hid them in the cracks of the natural stone here. People coming through would be focused on you anyway, and even if they looked down, it'd look just like ordinary stone unless they knew what to look for."

Wieran's head tilted the slightest bit. "Perceptive, Poplock Duckweed. Good, you do not disappoint me. Then enter...if you can." He turned and bent over a complex device. Distantly, Poplock heard movement above them.

"Oh, *drought.* The Unity Guard is on its way."

"Precisely," Wieran said absently. "You can enter my laboratory—and, if you succeed, close my doors to bar them passage—or you can close the doors and face them directly, and then still have my own defenses to deal with afterwards. I benefit either way."

Poplock glanced around. Hiriista caught his eye, then bent over the symbols. "A complex ward. Three elements?"

The little Toad squinted. "No, four...*five!* See that? Looks like just a flaw in the stonework."

The noise of boots was beginning to grow louder. Kyri and Tobimar took up positions behind the two, while Miri stood over them, watching in case anything came from in front.

"Hssss! Clever. Brilliant. But that means that only all five can neutralize it. Or spirit magic."

Poplock suddenly stiffened. "Or one *other* thing." He turned. "Hey, Tobimar, switch places!"

Miri moved next to Kyri as the Skysand Prince stepped back. "What?"

"I think if you can concentrate your gods-power there, it'll shatter the ward without detonating it."

"You'd better be right," Tobimar said, casting a glance up the stairs where a flicker of light was becoming visible.

He drew back his twin-swords, as Poplock and Hiriista moved quickly out of the way, and paused a split second; the blue-white purity of Terian's power shimmered along his weapons. Then they came down, a double cut of deific energy.

The floor shuddered, but there was no great detonation, just a shattering of stone. "It worked! Inside, inside everyone!"

Figures were already visible, charging down the stairs as fast as they could now that they saw their quarry ahead of them. But Miri gestured and stone spikes grew from the walls and floor, barricading the steps for a few precious seconds. By the time the might of the Unity Guard began to break through the stone wall, Tobimar and Kyri had shoved the door to Wieran's laboratory shut and dropped the bar. "That should hold them for a little while," Kyri said.

"It will hold them for a very long time," Master Wieran said, his tone holding not a trace of concern. "Or, at the least, until I permit them entry. It was designed to withstand any force I envisioned attempting to assail me. Naturally," he continued, looking at Miri with contempt, "that included any attempt by you or your now-fallen accomplice to turn my own weapons against me. I have taken every contingency into account. I have visualized every scenario."

He glanced at Poplock and Hiriista. "A properly scholarly approach. You studied, you deduced, you acted, and were proven correct. I congratulate you. Few could analyze so complex a ward so swiftly. I welcome you, then, to my laboratory. Watch, then, as my ultimate experiment is finally concluded!"

Now Poplock could see the entirety of the Great Array, and he shuddered. *This is monstrous. It makes that sacrificial circle they were using to summon up Voorith look like something a kid scratched in the dust. I can't just go cut it; if I don't know what he's doing with it I could kill us all, or worse.* He saw Hiriista with a similarly shocked posture, his crest and scales down, body tight.

"So *that's* what you meant by benefiting either way; if we shut the door and died on the doorstep, you had no interruptions. If we passed the test to enter, you gained an *audience.*"

"And once more you do not disappoint. Yes, there should be witnesses to such a momentous occasion, but not ones incapable of understanding *what* they witness. You and Hiriista are truly worthy, even if your companions are not."

Kyri was not hesitating; she strode down the steps towards Wieran. "You will release your prisoners now."

Wieran cast an irritated glance in her direction, then placed a crystal in a slot before him.

Instantly a ring of lightning sprang from floor to ceiling, encircling the entire hall—straight through the point where the Phoenix stood. Kyri screamed, head flung back, hair standing on end, in a spasmodic dance that only ended when the lightning ceased. Tobimar cursed and yanked the girl backwards, bending over her.

"Do not *presume* to give me orders here!" Wieran snapped, eyes cold. "This is *my* realm. For *centuries* I have endured the constant interruptions, the demands on my time for trivial matters, so that I could reach my goal! Now that it is within my reach, none shall interfere!" The devices around him began to move and an aura of such power radiated from them that Poplock could *feel* it. "You shall stand and watch as I unravel the ultimate secrets of existence!"

CHAPTER 49

Poplock saw that high up in the air—between the inlaid portion of the Great Array on the ceiling and the levels of the floor—a seething mass of rainbow power boiled, rings of light and dark shimmering around it. Streams of power—seven streams—were flowing from that mass, shimmering with blue-white and light-devouring black, and touching the points of a seven-pointed star inlaid into the hundred-yard-wide circle in the middle of the laboratory. That star was itself beginning to flicker, and the complex mechanism at the very center—the mechanism at which Wieran was working—was humming. The air was filled with the tingling scent of lightning, the earthy smell of fermentation, the odors of a thousand chemicals mingled in a skin-crawling way.

Even as Kyri was steadying herself on her feet, Wieran touched two more crystal objects, then muttered something and activated what appeared to be a Calling Matrix. The air between them and Wieran acquired a pearlescent shimmer, and Miri, lunging towards the white-haired alchemist, rebounded from the shimmer as though from a wall of steel.

"Strike the Barrier as much as you like, Ermirinovas," he said. "I am quite beyond your reach."

Poplock saw Hiriista's posture shift. It was subtle—a human almost certainly wouldn't notice. But then the *mazakh* glanced sideways at him, and—without any words—Poplock knew what Hiriista was trying to say.

Stall him. Keep his attention.

Poplock gave a barely perceptible wink of one eye. *I don't know what he's seen, but I've got to have faith. He's analyzing this whole array, and—truth? I don't know enough to figure it out.* Hiriista, though, was a magewright, a master of magic made solid, of runes and symbols and gemcalling and summoning, one of the best in Kaizatenzei. If *anyone* could figure out that hideous array and find some weak spot, some key location, it would be Hiriista.

Poplock whirled and threw a vial of flame-essence from his neverfull pack. It burst and burned uselessly against the nacreous nothing that lay between him and his target, but succeeded in getting Wieran to look at him. He hopped up on Tobimar's head. "Ooooohh, I get it. You *did* steal most of the Sun's power. That's it, up there. Got to hand it to you—that was one-hundred-percent brilliant, getting them to do all the work so you could take the Sun's power for yourself."

Wieran snorted, but something about his posture encouraged Poplock. *He likes people recognizing how brilliant he is.*

"But these tubes...they've got all the people you've taken in them."

"Not *all*. Most, yes. A few have not survived all of the years, for various reasons, and there is, currently, one exception other than that."

Precision in everything. He can't abide inaccuracy. Can I use that? "Exception...Zogen Josan!"

"Of course. Can you tell me *why*?"

Desperate for intellectual conversation. He's hidden all this for centuries, he wants to talk about it now. And at the same time, he's focused on his work. If I keep him talking, he won't notice Hiriista. I hope.

"Umm...oh, with the hint here? Sure! He decided to retire, instead of dying in the line of duty the way all, or maybe most, of the others have." He paused. "Oh, and you had to have ways of covering up when they died..." He saw a faint smile on Wieran's face. "Ooooohh. Of course. *Because* they were so much more powerful than ordinary warrior types, they'd never 'die' unless overwhelming force wiped out any nearby witnesses. Zogen must've just been incredibly lucky that he never got *into* that situation, so you couldn't pull that trick off."

Wieran's tiny nod made him go on. "You couldn't afford a

chance that Zogen's nature would be discovered, so you swapped the real body back in when he came for his retirement party. Still, I'm missing something." He gestured at the ranks of tube and rune-covered caskets. "So you... what? Use their minds to run the Eternal Servants? So you can cut out the original mind and run them your way, whenever you want? But what's your purpose? That was useful for Miri and Shae when they were running the country, but what's in it for you? I don't get it."

"Bah!" Wieran slid two levers partway along a track, and the light around the seven-pointed star flickered more brightly, began to pulse in the runes and symbols that surrounded the star, spread a little farther up the Great Array. "You disappoint me, Toad. The Eternal Servants? Toys, a waste of time, a distraction which I tolerated because it cost me relatively little and kept my dull-witted but useful patrons satisfied until the time I no longer required their services."

Miri hissed something under her breath that Poplock didn't understand, but he was pretty sure it wasn't a compliment to the silver-haired alchemist-sage.

Keep focused. "But the Unity Guard—they had to be more complex than that. Most of the time they act just like their originals." Poplock thought for a second, then bounced his understanding. "I get it. They think they *are* the real people."

"What is 'real'? They have the same perceptions, sensations, knowledge, and capabilities—indeed, more so—than their flesh bodies. They are unaware of any difference, or of any loss."

Hiriista had wandered back, was moving in the shadows along the perimeter. Looking. Reading. Pondering. *Have to keep Wieran's attention... and I think I've got it!* "Hey, don't think that *I* am an idiot. You know perfectly well that 'real' means something in this context. The mystical connections between truth and falsehood aren't produced from nothing."

"Oh, excellent. You *do* think on occasion."

"Besides, you're wrong. They *are* aware of the difference and loss."

Now Wieran's attention was entirely focused on him. "What? What is this nonsense? I have perfected the process—"

"Maybe not quite as perfect as you think." Poplock deliberately introduced a hint of derision into his voice. *I know something you don't!* "That's one of the reasons Zogen Josan retired. He was having vague dreams of being in something that—having seen your lab—was one of your little storage tubes."

Wieran stared at him narrowly, but Tobimar said, "That's right. He mentioned those dreams a couple of times, and noticed people not being themselves."

"But that's not surprising," Poplock went on, "because the Unity Guards were just another of those stopgaps, something you made to keep Miri and Shae off your back. They weren't part of your *real* work, so you might not have put your absolute *best* into them. Am I right?"

Wieran leaned back, nodding slowly, as he wound some mechanism at his right up with a crank. A chiming began to sound out rhythmically, and the light chased the sound around the room. "You are correct, Poplock Duckweed. And I concede that if what you say is true, then I must not have applied myself entirely to the perfection of the Unity Guards. My regular research demanded most of my attention."

"So what *is* your goal?" Poplock said, returning curiosity and awe to his tone. "I can make out *pieces* of it, but this is all way, way beyond me. You've taken hundreds of people and you're maintaining their bodies, I'd guess, or most of 'em would've died years ago, but you're using their spiritual power to run those Eternal Servants and the Unity Guard. You've got the power of the Sun, and I can figure some of this array of yours is to channel that, but I don't get how it all fits together."

Hiriista, Poplock could see out of the corner of his eye, had made his way to the western side of the room. *Is the array a little . . . different there? No . . . looks like there's a secondary array there. Is that what he's . . .*

He caught himself before he let the distraction go too far. *Can't let Wieran realize what's up. Only his ego and his profession give me a chance here.*

Kyri and Miri had tried a few more attacks on the pearly barrier, but it was clear no simple approach would work. Maybe wrecking parts of the array would, but even they didn't need to be told how bad *that* could get, not with parts of the array connected to each and every one of the hundreds of tubes circling the room. And any assault of sufficient power to possibly break that barrier would certainly destroy ten, twenty, even fifty of the precious capsules holding the half-dead, half-dreaming hostages.

Now they were still, and he could tell that they'd realized he was stalling for some reason. Tobimar, of course, had figured it out earlier.

"I think you give yourself too little credit," Master Wieran was saying. "You managed to conceal your existence throughout your journey here, and are obviously an accomplished magician. But this is the result of centuries of labor; there is no surprise in not comprehending it at a glance. So let me ask you this: what is the distinguishing characteristic of true godspower?"

Poplock blinked and tried to think about what little he'd heard. "Um . . . well, it responds instinctively to the gods' commands . . ."

"Pfui! Inherently magical beings could say the same about their magic, or for that matter, you could say the same about your hands. Again!"

"Mmmm . . . it's drawn from the worship of others? The power of belief made manifest?"

"Closer, but still not there." Wieran adjusted something else and nodded. Poplock noted that the shimmering polychromatic cloud was smaller than it had been, and runes on the floor were now glowing much farther inside and outside the septagram's edge. "Again!"

Poplock scratched his head, which gave him an excuse to swivel one eye towards Hiriista. The *mazakh* magewright was crouched down, studying part of the secondary array intently. *Hope you're getting close, because I don't know how much longer I can keep this up.* "Er . . . I don't know. It's more powerful than other forces?"

Wieran snorted in contempt. "There are magicians who can shatter mountains, and gods who make hard work of just battering one down. No. Consider the characteristics of power. The power of magic depends on the belief both of caster and target to some extent. It can perform nearly any feat, as long as sufficient power exists. The mental powers, *rannon* or psionics, depend on the belief of the *user* alone—he or she must be confident in their use. They are more reliable, but more limited; one born without them cannot use them, those born with them can only use them in certain ways. The power of the physical—the simple warrior, the technology of those occasionally marooned on this world—depends on no belief, but simply works, is dependent on precise construction and not easily duplicated, though once duplicated it can be exchanged and used by others freely."

"Yeah, I got that."

"Godspower goes beyond all of these, yet is more constrained in a sense," Wieran went on, and the cloud above contracted again. "It penetrates the others—the shield of metal, the enchantment of the wizard, the mind-shield of the *rannon* master—as though they were not there, at the will of the wielder. It can be used to perform nearly any feat, if enough of it is available... but only so long as the god itself remains powerful, remains an active and conscious force, which is—nearly always—dependent on their having some number of beings who believe in, worship, the deity. I could not shield myself from your attacks, Phoenix, or those of your newly-empowered friend Tobimar, had I not also gained some godspower of my own to work with. This power is rare—the second-generation children of Kerlamion, alas, have very little of it, and thus Kalshae made poor use of the power she had gained. Had she realized the full potential of what I had given her, you would never have left the Tower.

"Yet what I have said is not absolute. There are at least two powers which may oppose even godspower and not be bypassed."

Poplock remembered his magical studies. "Spirit magic—that's one." *And who was the most powerful spirit mage of all, according to rumor?*

"Exactly. And so is the chi, ki, spirit energy of certain physical disciplines, which powerful warriors and others have been known to wield." Wieran's lecture suddenly made sense. *I was right! He's been thinking about this stuff for years, but never had a chance to tell anyone. Now that he's started, he can't wait to show off.* "Now, here, two more riddles: how is it possible that a sufficiently trained warrior—one without mystical training—can learn to withstand magic, break spells with a cut or a blow, parry power as though it were steel? And second, how is it that many mystical assaults can cause tremendous damage to their surroundings, yet trained Adventurers and others can survive, though battered, to retaliate?"

Those... are good questions. The first was such a well-known *fact* that Poplock had never given it much thought; of course a trained warrior could do that, how else could he or she possibly survive in a battle against a wizard? And the second... he remembered Kalshae severing the Tower with a single blow. Yet Tobimar had blocked many of her attacks, survived others, all of which should have cut him in half like a reed struck with a sword.

Which means... "Souls. Warriors gotta be focusing their will, their spiritual power, against their opposition. And destroying inanimate, unalive targets is easier than ones with spiritual power." *And that explains the power of the Spiritsmith's weapons and armor, too. Not magic...yet magic.*

"Precisely! I had to lead you a bit, but you did make the connection. So I deduced that there was a connection between the soul, the spirit, and the power of the gods. They require worship—the devotion of a mind and spirit to their cause. They are *constrained* by worship—a deity who is worshipped as a fire god will never be seen creating palaces of ice. And they can be opposed by spirit, such as the enchantments of a spirit magician, or the simple will of a strong-souled being. Thus I needed spirits for testing, experimentation—*sapient* spirits, mind you—"

"—and so you arranged a reason to bring them to you," Tobimar breathed suddenly. "These people..."

"By the Light," Miri said suddenly. "So *that* was the point of all this mechanism and enchantment, your emphasis on *efficiency.* You used only a *fraction* of the spiritual power of the prisoners to run the Eternal Servants, maybe even the Unity Guard—"

"Precisely, Ermirinovas. For the Eternal Servants I need scarce five percent of their available spiritual strength to keep them animate. For the Unity Guard, no more than thirty-five, save for the infrequent occasions they find themselves...pushed." He glanced at the doors behind them. "Of course, in this case I have severely limited their ability to draw on that power. I shall require it."

"So you've figured out how to make yourself a god," Kyri concluded with bitter certainty.

Wieran looked offended. "What? Utter rot. What sort of ridiculous figure of children's stories do you think I *am*?"

That stopped Poplock cold; he thought he even saw Hiriista tilt his head, but didn't dare even roll one eye in that direction. "Well...it did seem the logical conclusion."

"I am a *researcher!*" Wieran thundered. "A mere *god*? Why would I stop short of the ultimate goal? Think! What do all of these things share? What is the single ineffable quality that *all* of them have, from the basest matter to the greatest Power, and the single limitation they *all* must deal with?"

Poplock thought furiously. *What quality do they* all *have? That a spear or sword has in common with a spell of flame or a* mind-reader's power or a god's rage or a spirit-mage's enchantments? What limitation do they all share?

After a few moments he gave a bounce-shrug. "I can't figure it. Sorry, but I'm just a Toad."

"They *exist!*" Wieran snapped. "They are things which *are.* And they are limited in that they cannot create or do *anything* without taking something in exchange. A sword must be swung with enough power to strike, a god must draw upon its resources to act, a psionic master must withstand the cost of drawing upon their power. Even magic, which can *seem* to create things from nothing, requires a source of magical power with which to do it.

"Yet once...in the Beginning...there was true Nothingness, and from Nothingness Something came." He looked around them, and Poplock felt a creeping sensation going up his body. "There, behind the essence of them all, *above* them all, is the key to true power, the power to make things *be* or *not be* without the demand to have something else *not be* or otherwise give up its essence to perform your bidding, the power to transcend all barriers of possibility—the power of Creation itself!"

Oh, drought. He felt Tobimar's shoulder tighten in shock.

Wieran gestured to the now rapidly diminishing cloud of shimmering power. "Undirected godspower—freed of its constraints, no longer directed by a mind! The power of alchemy and symbolism, arrays of gemcalling, summoning circles, patterns of mind and memory written in spirit power! The power and patterns of two demonlords, recorded and adjusted to my desires!" Poplock saw Miri's fists clench. "The concentration of mental energy and the will and spirit of hundreds, all focused within this array, constraining and guiding even godspower—and the array, focused upon *me!* When the channeling is complete I will perceive the fabric of *all* realities, and finally be able to rend it asunder to see the ultimate, and *I will become that Ultimate! I will know ALL because all things will be as I envision them!*"

Insane was the first thought that came to mind, but Poplock realized that it didn't matter. Wieran might well be mad, but he might also be *right*—and even if not, the powers he described, all focused into him, would then simply make him a mad god with the delusion that *all creation* was his to behold...and change.

And then Hiriista spoke.

"Well, then, I think we had best prevent that, hadn't we?"

Even as Master Wieran whirled and a blaze of light started from the surrounding mechanism, Hiriista, Magewright of Kaizatenzei, unleashed a mighty torrent of power against the secondary array on the far wall. Bolts of lighting, incandescent blazes of fire, hammerblows of the earth itself, the swirling implacability of water, all detonated against the array, driven by the spirit of the greatest magewright of Kaizatenzei, and the wall and ground *cracked*, splitting the pattern.

Instantly Poplock felt a terrifying weight of darkness surge outward, a feeling of triumph and dark rage and hatred. "Guys..."

"You *fool!* Do you know what you have done?"

"Unleashed something you bound here, something bound for ages," Hiriista said equably.

The ground shuddered, and Poplock remembered the prior earthquake.

Wieran glanced upward, but already the array was flickering, destabilizing. His head whipped around. "You. You *played* me. *Me!*"

"You made it easy," Poplock said.

Wieran's eyes went cold and calculating again. "The entire experiment is ruined, ruined at the last possible moment. I have no time to complete it. I will have to start over." The look he gave them all—and that lingered on Poplock—was of such icy fury and hatred that Poplock found himself seized with an impulse to hide; Tobimar actually stepped back. "I shall not forget this. You have deprived me—deprived the *world*—of the greatest discovery in all the histories that have ever been." He bent over the control consoles once more. "I will *remember* you," Wieran said, and those four words were distilled, corrosive venom.

The pearlescent wall flickered and vanished. Instantly Tobimar and Kyri lunged down the stairway, but Wieran stepped backwards, entering a spherical capsule barely five feet in diameter. The capsule sealed up behind him.

"Not *that* easy!" Kyri shouted, even as the room shuddered again. Tobimar ran to assist her; from his shoulder, Poplock could get a look through a small window set in the capsule—

Mudbubbles. "Don't bother, guys. He's not in there anymore."

Hiriista gave a disgusted hiss. "Teleportation. Far-travel. He had even *that* contingency planned for as well."

"Worry about that later," Tobimar said, a note of frustration and worry rising. "You said you unleashed something. Those earthquakes are it *moving?*"

"I am afraid so. But it was the only thing I could do to interrupt Wieran; that secondary matrix was placed there long before the main Grand Array, obviously shortly after Wieran arrived, and its only function was to keep whatever-it-was caged up."

"No, no, you did the right thing," Tobimar said. "But what—"

Miri, who had been standing frozen ever since Hiriista's action, finally spoke, in a voice so small and terrified it sounded utterly unlike her. "Sanamaveridion," she whispered.

"Sanama . . . who?"

Kyri had gone pale. "Great Balance, no. It can't be. But I know that language . . ."

"Oh, yes, it can be," Miri said, voice shaking. "Sanamaveridion, one of the greatest of the Elderwyrm, the Dark Dragons, the Shadows of the Sixteen."

CHAPTER 50

Kyri felt as though the floor was not merely shaking, but had fallen away into an abyss of horror. "*Elderwyrm*? No, Miri, that can't be, they're *legends*, stories people tell to scare each other at night, they—"

"*I was THERE!*" Miri snapped, tears starting from her eyes. "I *saw* him—Light forgive me, I *guided him* in the destruction of the Lords of the Sky!"

That brought Kyri up short, and she *looked* at Miri, really looked at her, with the sight granted by Myrionar, and now that Miri was no longer hiding her nature could *see* the truth, the whirling confused mass of light and dark within the human shell. It sank in, *really* sank in, that Miri, the dynamic, diminutive, beautiful Light of Kaizatenzei, was something ancient beyond easy understanding, something that had once been a Demon of the highest ranks.

"We have no *time* for this!" Tobimar shouted, grabbing both their arms and pulling, dragging them with him. "If such a monster is rising, what do you think it will do to Valatar—to all of Kaizatenzei—if someone isn't there to *stop* it?"

She tore herself free. "Wait, Tobimar! We can't! The people—"

The Skysand Prince cast a tortured glance around the ranks and ranks of tubes, within which were sealed so many.

"Leave them," Hiriista snapped, heading for the doors. "They are preserved and maintained for the moment. If we cannot stop this new horror, *all* will die. We have neither time nor knowledge to release hundreds safely, nor do we know if they will be ready and able to flee even were we to succeed."

"Worry more about whether we'll be running straight into the Guards," Poplock said. "They *were* just on the other side of that door, you know."

Myrionar help these people, she prayed. *They have been imprisoned for so long, do not let them be entombed.* Then she nodded. "Ready."

"No," Miri said, a hollow, tragic note in her voice. "No, you are not."

Then she set her jaw, and her armor glowed with blue power. "But we shall *have* to be. Kaizatenzei will not fall."

Hiriista pulled the bar from the door and cast it aside. Nothing immediately thrust the door open, so he and Tobimar pulled the portals wide, Kyri and Miri standing ready.

Not entirely to Kyri's surprise, there was no one there; a faint glow of light receding away showed that the Unity Guard were retreating, unwilling to risk the collapse of the underground. *They'll probably set up an ambush at the exit above ground, perhaps outside the Tower, or what's left of it.*

"How long do we have?" Poplock asked. "Feels like the shocks are increasing."

"Minutes," Miri said grimly. "With the seal weakened, the Dragon is throwing all his power against the remainder. This will weaken him, of course, in turn, but that will not matter much if he breaks free...and without Kalshae and the old Towers as resonance points I cannot reconstruct the trap I caught him in the first time."

"Ohhh," Poplock said, looking impressed. "So you two got him to do some of the big dirty work, take down the major resistance of the Lords and wreck their cities, then used the Seven and One *themselves* as a trap against him. I'll bet even Terian didn't expect *that.*"

They were sprinting up the stairs now, halfway up and rising. Miri gave a wry smile. "Oh, I'm *sure* he didn't. If he had, it would not have been possible. But they *had* already placed the Towers in the pattern of his power, so when Sanamaveridion approached the Tower of the Sun, we were able to trigger Terian's own strength in his own pattern to seal the Elderwyrm long enough for us to get our own bindings on him."

Another shock, this one strong enough to make them stagger, and cracks spiderwebbed the walls. "Balance, I don't know if we're going to make it."

"We *have* to. If a Dragon assaults the city without someone to stop it—"

"The Unity Guard—"

"Have not a chance in all the Hells of my Father," Miri said bleakly. "They are strong, yes . . . but not as strong as Kalshae or I, nor as strong as either of you." She glanced at Poplock, and for the first time since they entered Wieran's laboratory, gave a genuine smile. "Perhaps as strong as you, Poplock. Or perhaps not."

"Fear me," the little Toad said with an answering smile.

"No sign of them yet," Tobimar said as they reached the top of the stairs and headed for the next flight, the one leading to the throne room. "Where will they be?"

"Outside the Tower," Miri said decisively. "Without Kalshae or Wieran driving them, they'll be more themselves, and won't want to stay inside a collapsing building. Now that I think of it, they *may* even accept me again as commander; I don't believe they will remember the sequence in which they were controlled."

"That would be wonderful," Kyri said, letting a bit of hope rise.

Now through the Valatar Throneroom, and another quake that shattered decorative crystal; Kyri went down, rolled back to her feet, reinforcing the power she had already called up. *Myrionar, Justice will not be served at all if we fail to protect the innocent here!*

As they emerged from the Tower, they saw the Unity Guard— nearly all of them—gathered outside, staring at the fallen Tower and the surging, tumultuous lake whose waters were swirling and boiling like a pot about to boil over.

"*Light Miri!*" The cry was filled with relief. Light Tanvol caught her up in a great bear-hug, then set her down as though afraid he had committed an impropriety. "What has *happened*?" he demanded, and the others Unity Guards crowded around. "We came to ourselves before a set of locked doors in the depths of the Tower, and the ground began shaking! Then we come out and see the Tower is *fallen*! What is happening? What are we to do?"

Kyri saw Miri hesitating, and realized that the once-Demon didn't know what to tell her allies.

"We have been betrayed completely by Master Wieran," Hiriista

said, and the look of pure gratitude that Miri bestowed on the
mazakh magewright could have lit the world. "Lady Shae fell in
her attempt to stop him from stealing the power of the Great
Light, and he had found ways of using even the Unity Guard to
his ends. But now the dark monster he had imprisoned and used
for his plans is about to emerge."

*Brilliant. It fits everything they would know, what the towns-
people will have seen, and leaves Miri trusted and loved.*

The ground *heaved*, and the lake *bulged* up, sending a wall of
water twenty feet high thundering towards Sha Kaizatenzei Valatar.

But the Unity Guard were gathered and had purpose once
more; together eighty and more strong, they called on the powers
given them and built a mystic wall, a shield that shuddered but
held long enough, weakened the surge, so only a thin sheet of
water rose to run swiftly through the streets of Valatar.

"Go," Miri said, her voice back in its accustomed confident
tone. "We will face this threat. You must stand by to save the
people, protect the city—for this will be a hard-fought battle
indeed, and we will not be able to watch for all the consequences
of our actions or those of our enemy."

The Guard began to disperse, but Tanvol and one of the other
Lights hesitated. "But surely we could—"

"*Go!* Surely you have suspected the Lady had given me my
special place for a reason. This is a battle you cannot win—a
battle you cannot even *survive.*"

As Tanvol looked at her uncertainly, the earth reared up like
a steed preparing to bolt. Screams and curses and the sounds of
shattering stone and glass filled the air, even as the great lake
beyond rose up in a mountainous moving mass of water that
dwarfed the prior surge to insignificance.

But it *continued* to rise, something within forcing the water
upward on a scale so titanic that Kyri froze, momentarily unable
to even comprehend what she was *looking* at. The far end of the
peninsula split down the center, a yawning chasm into which
water poured. The rising power split the mass of water with a
roar that struck with a physical force, nearly felled her again,
sending waves hundreds of feet high to left and right. *Balance,
the destruction that will cause around the Lake! How far will
those monster waves go?*

But at the same time the water began to retreat, draining

away to fill the space vacated by the impossibility that was rising from the lakebed. Water streamed in thundering cascades from glistening ebony and red scales the size of houses, and two blazing green eyes opened, glaring down at the cowering motes before it as bottom-mud and stone fell away, inconsequential as dust from a man's boot. Farther back, halfway to the horizon, vast pinions surged from the roiling water, stretching out, out, casting shadows across land and water as though great banks of cloud had suddenly materialized, and with a mighty *heave* something the size of a mountain lunged skyward, and hung above them, floating unbelievably in the sky, casting the entire city and all about into black shadow as though night had replaced day.

Sanamaveridion, the Elderwyrm, was free.

CHAPTER 51

Kyri stared in utter horror, unable to move. *Too big. Too powerful. By the Balance, I'd heard* stories, *but they were just that,* stories. *The Dragons couldn't be that immense, it was impossible.*

Nevertheless, it stretched above and before her, miles long, darkening the sky as though something had rent the bright blueness asunder and torn a strip half its width down the center of the heavens.

"Now! We must act *now*, Kyri!"

The voice brought her mind back to herself, unparalyzed her shaking limbs even as she heard the screams and panic behind her, and she looked down. "Act? Miri...Miri, what can we *do?*"

"You are the *Phoenix Justiciar* of a *GOD*," she said, and her eyes—no less terrified than Kyri felt—were at the same time filled with a frightening determination. "If you and I and Tobimar cannot do something, nothing can. He is stretching, taking this moment in pure pleasure of release, but that will end very soon and turn to rage."

Kyri drew Flamewing, felt a ludicrous comfort in its heft and strength, even though it was less than a thorn before the monster above them. "What do you..."

"I will...distract him, at least for a while." Her smile was wan. "I was after all one of those who imprisoned him, built this entire country around him, sure in the knowledge he would never be released." Her tone said *it's all my fault* as loudly as if she'd spoken the words. "He will be more than willing to give me his undivided attention. You must stop that wave, break it. I know you cannot get both sides of the lake, but at least one..."

She almost protested again; even as they were receding at unfathomable speed those waves were nearly as huge as the Elderwyrm that had given them birth. But she knew she couldn't afford the time. *A minute, maybe two, and they'll strike the shore on both sides.* Nearby areas were already hit, no chance there.

She nodded; then, as Miri started to turn, her back stiff, her eyes a bit too-bright, Kyri recognized the truth.

She doesn't intend *to survive. She's going to do the best she can against that... monster, and she knows she's going to die.*

Kyri stepped forward, not even sure what she should do—what she *could* do—to stop the girl who had been a Demonlord... and then she *did* know, after all.

She grabbed Miri and planted a kiss of her own on the smaller woman's perfect lips. As Miri's eyes widened comically, Kyri gripped her by the shoulders. "You *come back*, you understand me? Because for all of what you've been... it's Light Miri that I know, and it would hurt me—hurt *us*—to lose you."

Miri's hand had come up to touch her lips as though she couldn't believe what just happened; she looked around and saw Tobimar, Hiriista, and Poplock nodding agreement. And then her face lit up with a brilliant determination that buoyed up Kyri's own spirits. "Then... somehow... we have to *win!*"

Kyri smiled as Miri turned again and ran—not heavily, not as one going to a foredoomed end, but as Light Miri of Kaizatenzei, the irrepressible, ever-cheerful defender—towards her mountainous opponent. Then the Phoenix Justiciar closed her eyes and concentrated.

Myrionar, what a test you have set before us now. But I believe in you. I feel the barrier between us is weakened now, in this moment, and I must ask you for all you can give. Somehow, let me be Justice and Mercy, let me shield those who sheltered us along our path, and then... and then I must help duel a Dragon.

She could *feel* the golden-singing power in her, and she was right, that heaviness that had impeded her *was* weaker—but so was Myrionar; she knew the god was dying, it had told her so.

So many in danger, Myrionar. I know I ask much, I ask so much, of you who are already so weakened—

You ask nothing I would not wish for myself, answered the Voice she would never forget, so calm and cool, at once so familiar she felt she had heard it all her life, and yet so different she knew it was no one she had ever met. *I give you all that I can... and I will show you the way.*

Her body *screamed* at the influx of power, but Kyri had been prepared; she remembered, all too well, the ecstasy and agony of the ultimate strike she had leveled against the Summoning Gateway in Thornfalcon's mansion, and knew that this would be—*was*—far worse.

And then she saw the wave coming at her—coming at her a dozen times over. For a moment she could not comprehend, could not *tolerate*, the concept, the inundation of images of simultaneity, couldn't imagine where she was, *who* she was.

But the Voice spoke to her, weakly but clearly, one last time. *You can tolerate it, you can grasp it, because you must. You are more than you were, Kyri Victoria Vantage, and you must endure and* accept *what you are, for only the power of the Phoenix—multiplied—will suffice for this moment.*

Kyri grasped that reassurance and command as though it were an actual lifeline. *Myrionar has never asked me to do anything I couldn't do. So I can do this.*

She opened her eyes and *looked*.

Before her the wall of water towered higher, ever higher, two hundred, three hundred, five hundred feet, beginning to curl and collapse in what would become an unstoppable surge of roiling mud and shattered debris. Behind and at either side of the wall the shore looked different... yet, really, the same, for it was all *Kaizatenzei*—all the places she had seen and passed in her travels, and as each of her looked, to one side they could see, in the distance, another golden blaze of light, barely visible yet to her inhuman sight so clear: a woman outlined within the heart of the Balanced Sword.

She/they raised their/her arms and called forth the power of Myrionar, and about them all appeared their namesake, a red-auric flaming firebird that *screamed* forward, god-fire against implacable water. The energies of a god detonated in a shockwave across the monstrous breaker's entire front, sending the vanguard of the wave skyward in a plume of white and gold a mile high and *pushing*, shoving, refusing passage to the unstoppable, and Kyri felt the *weight* descend upon her, the piling-up of uncountable

tons of water threatening to drive her back, to crush her beneath
its impersonal, pitiless bulk, to shatter even the power of a god
by the sheer, vast indifference of nature.

But Kyri Vantage would not yield, not even to the entirety
of an inland sea. She felt her selves reaching out to each other,
separate and together and now interlinking as though hands
stretched across the miles between them, and braced themselves
against the bedrock of Kaizatenzei. *No farther! This far, but no
farther!*

The pressure crested, and she felt even Myrionar's power
wavering before that absolute force, and *still* she refused to yield.
The faces of all she had met along the way now swam before her
mind's eye—Hulda and Zelliri, Tirleren and Demmi and Hamule,
Kittia in Kalatenzei with her wild hair and hidden depths, Reflect
Iesa accepting a difficult prisoner with trepidation and relief,
and for a moment she almost...*felt* them, some already looking
up to see both horror and hope before them with the towering
wave faced by the golden defenders, others blissfully unaware of
anything wrong, and she somehow found the strength to brace
herself again, refuse to give a single *inch*...

...and the water stopped, the pressure began to fade. It was
receding, flowing away without even the force to rebound.

With a sensation like a thousand bowstrings vibrating after
they are released, Kyri found herself back to her singular and
original self; she wobbled and collapsed to one knee.

I did it, she realized, and the thought filled her with awe and
wonder. But at the same time she realized how fleeting that victory might be. *All that monster has to do...is fall, and another
wave—worse than that one—will be born.*

And I really don't think I can do that again.

CHAPTER 52

Tobimar watched Kyri dissolve in a blaze of golden light that streamed off to the south and west with a mixture of awe and worry. *What ... is she doing? She's going to* stop *that wave? Can she? Will she ... survive?*

It was somehow so obviously typical that Kyri made a point of telling Miri that she had to come back alive, while not promising to do so herself.

Unwillingly, he found his eyes drawn to the floating monstrosity above. Sanamaveridion was stretching, lazily flapping one gargantuan wing, then the other, barely moving, hovering as though he were nothing but a red-black cloud. A low rumble, as of the purring of a cat the size of a city, reached Tobimar's ears.

"Well, he's happy for *now*," Poplock observed dryly. "But once he decides to celebrate with a little dancing ..."

"Terian's *mercy*," Tobimar heard himself whisper. "What can any of us do against ... *that?*" he asked, chilled to the core of his soul by a glimpse of the cold, hungry eye of the Elderwyrm. He saw Miri running towards it, to the broken point of the peninsula, but could not even *imagine* what the ex-demon thought she could accomplish.

Auric-ruby light *erupted* all along the southern shore, causing the mountain-sized head above to slew around in startlement; just as suddenly it snapped around to the north, where Tobimar thought he saw, not a flash, but a *darkening*, as though for a moment a living bolt of night had crossed from horizon

365

to horizon. Tobimar could not see what happened there, but to the south, the great wave shuddered, then collapsed, flowing back into Enneisolaten, the great lake called Sounding of Shadows, to join the rest of the water as it tried in white-foaming torrents to fill a void nearly as deep as its creator was high in the sky.

"*So, you avert disaster once, twice, little creatures, servants of tiny gods. Well done.*" The voice of the Dragon was thunder and earthquake, sound and force in one, and the chuckle that followed was the threat of storm and avalanche. "*I can spare a few more efforts for you to counter. How many will it take, I wonder?*"

Kyri reappeared in blue-touched gold, the color of Myrionar, and went to her knees. "I...stopped it. But all he has to do is *fall* and—"

"Do not worry, Phoenix," Hiriista said. "There shall be no more such waves." He grasped a necklace from which hung a drop of amber like distilled sunshine. "By the Pact of the Call, by your Essence bound, I call you forth, Shargamor's Shadow!"

From the depths of the amber shone a light the color of a tropical ocean at noon, a blue-green as pure as dawn and mountain streams. Abruptly that light became a flare, the sun rising through the depth of the sea, streaking out and detonating within the lake.

The water *shone*, and then rose up, a curling wave a thousand feet high, and within that wave a shape, streamlined, deadly, black of eye and white of tooth, with a fin projecting from the water that cast shadow like the Castle of the Dragon.

With a rumbled, startled curse, the Elderwyrm leapt higher into the air, circling and staring. Then it chuckled again. "Ahhhh, a Great Summons, but still, a mere echo of the Lord of Water's power. You prevent wave and ruin for perhaps...ten minutes? Fifteen, at the most. If, that is, I remain above the water. Perhaps I will not."

"Or perhaps you will, if you want to face me, Sanamaveridion!"

The venom-green eyes widened and a growl shook leaves from the trees. "ERMIRINOVAS...you should have run while I was lost in the sensation of release. I *see* you now, and I will *REND* you, reduce body and soul to nothingness!"

"Is she insane? He's right, she should have run." Tobimar hated the quaver in his voice, but he couldn't help it; despite the godspower that still lingered within him, *this* was something utterly beyond his imagination.

"She is not as helpless as you think. And neither are you. Do you not remember what Terian said ere he left?"

Tobimar blinked at Hiriista, and then suddenly goggled in disbelief.

For Miri, diminutive Light Miri, was *growing*, rising, *towering* now, great shining wings of her own stretching from her back, shimmering with sapphire and silver, as was her entire body as it continued to grow. "You may *try*, Sanamaveridion," Miri answered, and her voice, too, was greater—yet still touched with the innocent determination of her ordinary form. "But I will not let you destroy what I—what *we*—have built here."

The laugh was almost enough to knock Tobimar from his feet; it vibrated in the ground and blew small clouds aside. "*You* will not let *me* destroy? You are strong, yes—but of the second order, not the first, and you know as well as I that even the first children of Kerlamionahlmbana himself would fear to face me or any of my brethren! And for what will you die? Mortals who were once your playthings? Ha! A fine jest indeed, you who were once the destroyer, using my own power to obliterate the Lords of the Sky, now stand hopeless before me—"

"*Not* hopeless!" Miri cut him off, and drew herself up—smaller far than her opponent, but still tall enough that she could reach down and with an effort lift the fallen Tower, lever it up, and lift it back to its place; with a blaze of light the severed pieces were rejoined. "I have more hope than you imagine, for I have found purpose where I had none, and friends where I had enemies. Perhaps it is a fool's hope—but hope it is."

Tobimar had been racking his memory to recall what Hiriista had asked him, and finally shook his head. "No, Hiriista; it's... foggy. I barely remember that time; Terian was speaking and I was...elsewhere."

"Then understand that you are no less than Miri or Kyri," Hiriista said, even as Kyri herself rose from the ground and the red-gold Phoenix fire reignited about her. "For Terian the Infinite said: '... *there is nothing in that oath or any other that prevents me from awakening the power that slumbers within Tobimar Silverun, Seventh of Seven; that sleeps within his blood.*'" Hiriista paused, and a chill went down Tobimar's spine as the magewright finished: "'*Within* **my** *blood.*'"

Suddenly everything made sense. *Why is my family, alone*

of all in Skysand, not blessed by the appearance of Terian's card, but called, required to act? Why have we always been hunted by demons wherever we go? Why was my blood the key for forcing open an artifact forged by Terian himself?

Because we are ... I am ... of his blood. When Terian came from beyond and gave us the Seven Stars and Single Sun ... he must have begun our line, too.

Hiriista nodded, even as a shudder went through the ground, Miri blocking a blow from one of the titanic wings—and holding strong against it. "Now you see, Prince Tobimar Silverun. The power you borrowed may be fading ... but that power dwells, also, within you, and Terian Himself said He had awakened it. If you can only find a way within yourself to tap it."

Kyri leveled a blast of godsfire that forced the Elderwyrm to back off, and for a moment she hovered in the air, the wings of fire he had seen once before now holding her aloft next to the hill-sized head of Miri. Then Tobimar closed his eyes.

Once more he drew on the discipline and focus that Khoros had taught him, the *awareness*, sought the connections between action and reaction, past and future, choice and consequence, and almost instantly, still borne up and made greater by Terian's power, he *SAW* it, a webwork of peril and possibility interwoven from the sky to the earth and all in between. He could see the immensity of their opponent and the vector of his assault, the poise and preparation of the girl who had once been a demon, the flow of godspower from many points into the Phoenix Justiciar, and more: the Unity Guard, evacuating people from trembling buildings, tending the injured, shoring up weak points, preparing—in case the unthinkable happened—for a desperate last stand. And more: deep below, the pattern of life, slowed yet active, in rank upon rank of sealed capsules, whose existence resonated with the Guardsmen above. And hovering in the air within that silent vault ...

The experiment was interrupted. Some of Terian's power remains!

The sense of that power *sang* to him, echoed the power still dancing about him, throbbing in his veins, pulsing in his soul, and without even thinking about it Tobimar *called*, reached out—

And the rainbow-shimmering energy, the last power of the Sun of the Infinite, streamed up and out, passing through stone and air and wind, and poured into him. He felt his blood resonating with that response, and something more, something *greater*, rising from within to meet it—

Rainbow mist and polychromatic dust abruptly ignited in blue-white fire, and Tobimar suddenly *knew* what it felt like to be a god. The world was as clear and simple as a child's toy, and even the towering monstrosity above was just another monster, nothing to fear.

Even as Tobimar felt a part of him quail at this terrifying shift in perceptions, he knew he had to act; the Elderwyrm was preparing to strike Kyri and Miri with a lunge of the sky-spanning head.

He channeled argent-sapphire power into his body as he had always done with his own discipline, and the world slowed to a snail's crawl, to the imperceptible slowness of ice melting in the sun. The light was around him, beneath him, and he was running, *sprinting* through the air as though it were solid ground. Even Sanamaveridion's charge was sluggish, a glacial movement scarcely worth adjusting Tobimar's motion for, and the cold emerald eyes were widening as Tobimar streaked towards him, a running bolt of lightning, and channeled his full power in a double-cut with the Swords of the Spiritsmith.

The impact of the deific-powered blow smashed the Dragon's head sideways as though he had been struck by a ten-mile-tall giant wielding a mountain as a club. The gigantic body slewed around and plummeted from the sky, plunging into the lake from which it had come; the water from the impact fountained three miles into the air, but even as it came down the waves were subsiding, rippling to calmness, shimmering with the blue-green energy of Shargamor.

Tobimar looked at his swords in awe, and then back at Kyri; she and Miri were staring at him, and their smiles were so dazzling that they nearly outshone the aura of Terian about him.

"It's not done yet," he said, and knew, somehow, they could all hear him. "But by the *Seven* we have a chance to finish it!"

Sanamaveridion's head erupted from the water and he lunged skyward. "*Terian*? No . . . no, one of his spawn, a little godling whose power has been awakened. Very well; defend yourselves, god-children!"

The Dragon drew in a breath with a whistling roar, and even the supreme confidence of the godspower was not enough to keep a new chill from going down Tobimar's back. *He's going to—*

The mighty jaws opened and spat forth a column of white-hot fire two thousand feet wide, straight for Tobimar.

Remember the discipline of Tor! Brace, focus—and CUT!

Even as he cut down, directing will and force towards the Dragon, Kyri Vantage did the same, and a blade of Phoenix-fire joined Tobimar's blue-white cross of flame. The Dragon's raging incandescence met their counterstrike with an impact that shocked the water below to foam, and *split* down the center.

Half of the white Dragon-flame went left, half went right, but it was sundered enough to bypass Sha Kaizatenzei Valatar. Even so, the fires blasted their way across the landscape, carving twin paths of devastation from the shoreline to the horizon, impacting finally in a flare that left a scar on the mountains ringing Kaizatenzei, more than a hundred miles away.

That was enough to shock Tobimar from his momentary transport to godhood—and, from the looks on their faces, Kyri and Miri as well. *Who knows how many people just died in little villages, or walking the Necklace road, in that holocaust?*

We have to stop him now!

Grim-faced, the three defenders turned back and braced themselves against the onslaught of Sanamaveridion.

CHAPTER 53

"I'll be Light-damned sad to see you go," said Tamilda, Color of Ruratenzei, as they stood at the gates of the City of Sunlight. "Especially since right now we're shorthanded, with most of the Guard called to Valatar for some big fancy celebration."

"I'd stay if I could," Condor said, looking down at the squat, solid woman in her gold and silver armor. "But I really want to get there in time. I think the people I want to meet *must* be at that celebration."

"Yes," the Odinsyrnen Color agreed, "And even if they're not, Lady Shae will surely have word of them for you. But take this." She put a crystal disc, in which Condor could sense some mystical power, into his gauntleted hand.

"What is it?"

"Message of commendation and recommendation from the Reflect—and me, of course. That'll get you past the Guard fast, right to the Valatar Throne."

Condor winced internally. *I'm being the hero here, but if I guess right, my target's their guest of honor at this celebration.* Having seen the Unity Guard in action a couple of times now, Aran Condor was now very doubtful that he'd survive assaulting the Phoenix with a lot of them around, if they had even the slightest interest in keeping her alive. But this was exactly what he needed if it turned out his target was gone by the time he got there. "Thanks *very* much, Tamilda. Could you convey my sincere thanks to the Reflect? If I'd known, I'd have done so in person." He paused, then shook his head. "No, actually, I *should* do so in person."

Tamilda used a word that he suspected was extremely rude. "Reflect Sygak knows you're in a hurry and took a lot of time out of your quest just to help us solve a few local problems. She wouldn't want you to waste time just to come back to say thank you, especially if you're in so much of a Light-lost hurry that you feel you shouldn't even wait until morning. Now go, get moving!"

Condor couldn't keep from cracking a smile. "Oh, all right, as you wish. But *do* convey my thanks."

"No worries there. Now—"

A quiver ran through the ground, and the head-high grasses all about shook, a rattle and a hiss that was followed by the susurration of beating wings as birds and a few Least Dragons took to the sky in startlement.

"Hmmm," Tamilda said. "Haven't felt a quake that strong in a while. Maybe the firemounts around Alatenzei are getting restless. I—"

A stronger shock hit, this one causing Condor to stagger and the shorter, more stable Tamilda to sway. "*That* wasn't an ordinary earthquake," Condor said.

"No...and that hasn't stopped, either."

The ground was continuing to vibrate, and a third quake hit, far stronger; screams echoed from within the city amid sounds of shattering glass and creaking stone.

But Condor had noticed something, a swift ripple streaking through the grass from right to left and diagonally from south to north with the last shock. "It's coming from the southwest somewhere!"

He concentrated, and the power came; he felt the red and black wings stretch from his armor, and leapt up, arrowing into the sky. *Get up high enough and I'll be able to see, maybe, what's going on.*

A minute later, at nine thousand feet, he stopped and looked, his Justiciar-born sight piercing even the growing dimness of the evening, now able to see a line of the shore stretching away about a hundred miles distant, vanishing over the horizon in each direction. To the east-southeast he suddenly *felt* something, as though a monstrous power were no longer hidden but had stepped into full hideous view.

No; not *as though*. Something *was* rising into view, above the far edge of the horizon, where—as near as he could guess—Sha Kaizatenzei Valatar should be on its long peninsula, and the shadow of a huge bat-wing appeared, stretching out, even at this distance so clearly visible that Condor's mind went utterly *blank* trying to grasp how huge the thing must be to be seen from so far away.

Then he saw the horizon itself moving, and horror truly came home. *That's . . . a wave. A wave hundreds of feet high, maybe more.* The great comber stretched from one side of the lake to the other, as far as his vision could reach in either direction, and Condor realized that this oncoming mountain of water would utterly *erase* everything in its path, possibly scouring the land clean all the way to the base of the surrounding mountains.

Myrionar, no. The thought, useless as it was for a False Justiciar to have, came to him as the enormity of it all sank in. He couldn't see Evening Dawn, far off to the West, or Hishitenzei beyond that, or the other cities and villages he'd passed, but he knew them all and remembered the people he'd helped, or who'd helped him on a quest none of them realized was dark and selfish: Tamilda, now organizing people far below to start rescue and cleanup, oblivious to the fact that only minutes remained before something inconceivably worse came to wipe the city away; Istiri and Mallan, probably just having finished repairing all the damage the *bilarel*'s attack had caused the farm; Venn and Vann, the two twins who'd stolen his coin purse and led him on a laughing chase through half of Hishitenzei; Falura Seven Nails and her three children who'd needed his help solving a mystery that almost ended in three more deaths; and others, all about to be destroyed by a power beyond anything Condor had ever . . .

No. Not quite beyond *anything*.

He reached back and drew the Demonshard. Instantly he felt the hungry, cold desire of the blade and its puzzlement at sensing no target nearby.

"I have heard it said, Demonshard, that Kerlamion's blade can cut anything, be it flesh or steel or a wall of purest force, and strike beyond its mere reach, breaking power and shattering strength. Is this true?"

A sensation of assent. *Yes.*

"Then show me this power, for I give you a target worthy of

your own parent." He focused, showing the Demonshard the great wave, now looming even higher, five hundred feet and more. "A stroke to cross the horizons, a single cut that shatters the power of an ocean, severs speed and chops height, that none I would protect are harmed. That is what I want."

A feeling of contempt. *I don't save, I destroy. Weakling. Unworthy.*

Condor growled under his breath. "I told you you'll do as *I* say, sword. Or by Myrionar, I'll drop you into that maelstrom and you won't be found—if you're *lucky*—until the next Chaoswar!"

Unwilling acceptance. *If I must. At least I'm unsheathed.*

"*Can* you stop that wave?"

Smug confidence. *Try me.*

"Let's hope you're as good as you think."

He rose higher and higher, judging the line, the angle, the course. The cut must intercept all of the tsunami, in a single stroke. He regretted that he couldn't do the same for the other shore, but that simply wasn't going to be possible. Then he whirled the Demonshard three times and brought the great black sword down in a cut that traced a line from one horizon to the other.

A streak of black *ripped* the air with a horrific shriek, emanating blue-white death that echoed the eyes of the Lord of All Hells, and shot outward, carving a dark shadowed path beyond the shore of Enneisolaten that *exploded* in a fountain of white, opening a vast *rent* in the freshwater sea into which the oncoming monstrous wave *fell*, dropping from sight, plummeting to impossible depths beyond sight or imagination. The darkness lifted and only a boiling line remained of what had once been a wave the size of a moving mountain.

Condor stared in awe for a few moments, then murmured, "Thank you, Demonshard. Well done."

He felt a grudging acceptance of his thanks from the dark blade, and then raised his eyes. "What about *that*?"

For the first time, the sensation from the blade was uncertain.

"What?" Condor was stunned. After what he'd just seen, after what the King of All Hells had said, he'd thought there was truly nothing beyond the Demonshard to destroy. "What *is* that?"

An image came, of a great black dragon casting cities into shadow darker than the now-coming night, a black dragon that was the opposite of every image of the Great Dragons that Condor had ever seen, and now he *truly* knew horror. A childhood story meant to frighten children had risen from myth into horrid reality. "An *Elderwyrm*?"

Assent.

Faint distant flashes of light; gold, blue-white, and something *staggered* the mighty Dragon.

Then he looked down and saw the devastation in Ruratenzei. A final shock had brought down hundreds of homes, cracked the surrounding walls, damaged the castle itself. He looked back, to where—he was sure—the Phoenix Justiciar and his—or her—companions dueled a monster out of legend, and sighed. *I suspect the battle will end—one way or another—before I could reach them. And there are people below who need my help* now.

Condor sheathed the Demonshard and let himself drop, plummeting down towards Ruratenzei. He landed next to Tamilda, who was bellowing orders to a group trying to brace a precariously-tilting wall. "I'm not leaving now. You need help."

She looked at him with a suspicious air. "I just felt one of the darkest things I have ever sensed, Condor, watched living malice radiate from you from one side of the world to the other. I appreciate your earlier help...but I need to know what that was before I accept any more."

Good senses. He nodded. "We have little time, so...the short explanation is that I made a bargain for the power to track down a very personal enemy of mine. I'm not sure it was a good bargain, and I'm stuck with the consequences. But I've so far kept it from hurting anyone else."

Tamilda's sharp black eyes searched his own narrowly. Then she finally nodded and stepped back. "I see you tell the truth. All right, then, I won't deny we need your help!"

With a relieved smile, Condor ran to the wall, calling up his full strength, and pushed the question of the Elderwyrm to the back of his mind. *Either they will deal with it...or they will not, and in that case I may have to face it. But that is something for the future, and these people...these people are something for the* now.

CHAPTER 54

I've never felt this *useless in my life,* Poplock admitted to himself.

He was sitting on Hiriista's shoulder, having bounced away from Tobimar when he'd gone to try his luck against the Elderwyrm, and both Poplock and the magewright were basically just spectators. Hiriista occasionally selected one of his many matrices and hurled a spell at the gargantuan reptilian monstrosity, but for the most part they could only watch as their three friends contested with an awakened god.

The cataclysmic struggle, the waving of forest-sized wings and unleashing of energies capable of breaking mountains, the shocks of power and boiling heat of battle, had created seething clouds overhead in what had been a pristine sky dotted with stars. Lightning flickered within the clouds, the power of storms now the merest backdrop for a battle beyond imagination.

"Isn't that completely useless?" he muttered as Hiriista sent a screaming bolt of ice at Sanamaveridion.

"Not *completely,*" the *mazakh* answered. "Even the power of the gods *can* be worn down by enough mundane or ordinary magical power. It just takes a great deal of power to do it. But our friends are doing their best to wear the Dragon down." He sorted through the multiplicity of amulets again. "I will admit it is something of a forlorn attempt, but it is all I can do."

"More than I can manage," Poplock said. His little clockwork crossbow and all its darts put together probably couldn't even have gotten the Elderwyrm's attention, even if the range hadn't been literally miles beyond anything Poplock had ever imagined shooting. He'd already triggered the couple of Gemcalls that he had available, for what miniscule and undetectable difference they might have made, and if he *really* wanted to, he could probably throw a couple more spells that *might* reach the monster.

He glanced back into the city, seeing the broken houses, the floating bridges that had cracked—some pieces now dwindling away into the sky—the smoke rising from fires. *I'm not even going to be very useful* there. *But maybe more than I am here.*

But he couldn't keep from watching. Everyone's lives depended on this battle—maybe the lives of everyone on the *other* side of the mountains, too. After all, once Sanamaveridion was done with Kaizatenzei, why wouldn't he head south and start wrecking anything that caught his eye there?

A tremendous wing-buffet struck Tobimar from the sky, sent him plummeting into the roiling water below; but even as Poplock felt his little fingers digging *hard* into Hiriista's scaly shoulder, he saw the Skysand prince shoot skyward again, the blue-white aura of Terian clear and bright. Kyri, a brilliant point of gold light surrounded alternately by a red-gold firebird and a blue-and-gold balance, struck the Dragon so hard its head was driven down, halfway underwater, even as Miri managed a midair kick to the thing's armored gut.

Poplock had his farseer out, and he heard the grimness of his voice as he spoke. "Oh, this is getting *bad*."

"What do you see, my friend?"

"Look for yourself." He handed the miniature spyglass to Hiriista, who resized it by touching it to some crystal on his chest.

Hiriista let out a long, baleful hiss as he studied the situation. Poplock knew what he saw: Tobimar's face, bloodied and battered, Miri's utter exhaustion written in her pale cheeks, Kyri's weary, slowing movement that brought each of the Dragon's blows ever closer to finishing her. Even with powers of god and demon, the three were reaching the limit of their endurance and the powers that supported them. Sanamaveridion was not unscathed—he was bleeding from a dozen places, one eye was swelling shut, scales were rent all along his head and neck—but he was clearly not even close to the end of his strength.

"What if we got *all* the Unity Guard in on this?"

Hiriista shook his head. "I am unsure whether they even have a way to *reach* him, so far away. Besides..." and the reptilian voice had a note of furious, painful empathy, "look."

Poplock looked and saw one of the Hues suddenly clutch his head, stagger, and collapse. Looking around, he realized that several other Unity Guards were down, with the others trying desperately to revive them. "What is going on? I don't—"

The little Toad broke off, suddenly understanding. "Oh, Blackwart's *grace*. The capsules. The room's starting to collapse on them, isn't it?"

Hiriista nodded slowly. "That is my guess, yes."

"You weaken, half-gods and fallen demons!" Sanamaveridion's voice boomed. A raging column of fire was split again by a desperate lunge of the Phoenix, but this time vertically; part of it plunged with a screaming hiss into the lake and spewed hot, sulfurous mists across the city, while the other part passed just above most of the city—blasting the Tower and turning it to burning, useless splinters as it collapsed in ruins atop the broader base of the Valatar Palace, which cracked dangerously.

"*Drought*. Even if they *win* this battle, the damage will be huge." He glanced to the multiple scars across the landscape from prior attempts by the Dragon to obliterate Sha Kaizatenzei Valatar. *No telling how bad the damage really is; I can't* see *it from here, really, and it still looks awfully bad to me.*

"And they have little time left before it becomes moot," Hiriista said slowly. "Shargamor's Shadow says it is fast losing strength. Another five minutes, and the waters will no longer obey any save the law of wave and destruction."

"Well, *mudbubbles*."

Hiriista shook his head, and Poplock felt the shoulder slumping. "I fear we are, indeed, doomed. Without some other factor entering the equation, some outside element, I think we are about to see our friends die. And we, ourselves, will not outlive them for long."

Poplock stared up and wished he could argue, but he could see the way his friends were weakening. *They may not even* make *it to the end of those five minutes.*

But... "Wait a minute. Say that again."

"I fear we are—"

"No, no, the rest of it."

"Without some other factor?"

That was it. "An *outside element!*"

He dove into his neverfull pack. *Where? Hid it away safe. Where . . .* here!

He pulled the matrix off his arm and tugged hard on the prongs. "Come on!"

"I do not know what you think you are going to do," Hiriista said, taking the ring-shaped Calling Matrix from him, "but I will help."

The magewright pulled the currently-drained gem from the socket and looked at Poplock's proffered replacement. "This? It is flawed, and not terribly magical at all. I—"

"Just lock it in!"

The magewright shrugged and took the clear gem with the blackish inclusions. "As you wish." His taloned fingers delicately repositioned the crystal and pushed just *so*, and it was seated in the matrix. "It is done."

Poplock shoved the matrix on his arm again. *How would this work? Not attuned, got no time to work through it . . .* "By the gift I was given and the hope of the legend, I call you—*COME FORTH!*"

The gem *detonated* in a spark of pure white light, spraying sand-sized shards outward to abrade and embed in skin, shattering the Matrix itself, sending a screaming wave of pain through Poplock. *Broke . . . my arm. Lost the gem. Stupid, stupid!*

But as Hiriista shook his head, they heard another voice, a voice that spoke from the empty air, air that shimmered with pure black night speckled with stars, as though they looked through some spectral gateway to the sky.

"I cross the void beyond the mind; the empty space that circles time. I see where others stumble blind, in search of truths they'll never find. An alien wisdom is my guide.

"I am . . . the Wanderer."

From that darkness, gripping his elaborate staff, white light playing about him, the Wanderer stepped, his blond hair shining faintly in the night from the flickers of the desperate combat. "A True Summons, touching on my own essence. I sense it was felt even by my original." He looked up. "And a desperate enough reason to try it. An *Elderwyrm*, huh? Should've guessed it was something like that in here."

"I don't know if you can do anything . . . but you were the only thing I could think of."

The wizard's smile flashed out. "Oh, I think I can manage

something. Hmm. Twilight Cannon? No, probably not quite bad enough for that. But this is still a very, very bad situation..."

For a moment he stood, studying the uneven battle between Dragon and defenders, and then smiled again. "Yes, actually. Time for a spell that I've wanted to use for a *long* time, but wasn't ever quite appropriate before. Too much collateral damage. But in this case, you've already got something giving you *plenty* of collateral damage. Magewright, have you anything that could convey a message to your friends?"

Hiriista didn't bother asking how the Wanderer knew what he was, just took out a pair of rings and put them on. "We can speak with two of them using these—it will last but a few minutes, though."

"That's all we need." The Wanderer stepped forward. "Tell them that the Dragon *must* be confined to the open water, and they *must be clear of him.*"

Hiriista relayed the message, choosing Miri and Tobimar. "What?" came Tobimar's voice, edged with exhaustion. "Why? We might manage that for a minute or so, but—"

"Do it, Tobimar!" Poplock said. "Trust me—we've got a plan!"

"All right, I'll trust you. *KYRI!* Me, you, and Miri are going to wall him in! Miri knows how to do it, a three-sided seal!"

"We'll run out of strength—"

"We *already are! Do it!*"

Blue-green, red-gold, and blue-white energies suddenly shimmered from three points as the three combatants darted away—Miri once more standing at the very end of the peninsula, Kyri far off to the right, Tobimar far to the left—and the triple light stretched out, touched, and then *grew,* a triangular box reaching from the depths of the water to the clouds above. Sanamaveridion snarled and threw himself against the wall, but though they could see sparks travel its length and Miri stagger as though she'd been struck, it held—for the moment.

"This is *pointless!*" the Dragon roared, half in puzzlement, half in anger. "A minute, perhaps less? And then you will be exhausted!"

"Wanderer..." Poplock said.

The youthful-looking mage grinned, a sharp and dangerous expression, and then his face grew grave as he raised the legendary Staff of Stars. "Don't worry. They don't have to hold him long."

"Distant beyond measure, source of every dawn
Blazing in the heavens, hope when all is gone..."

Sanamaveridion's eyes saw the faint white light, and widened. *"Wanderer?"*

The Dragon redoubled its struggles, suddenly aware that it might well be in danger. Miri staggered and went to one knee, her power streaming out so swiftly that her gigantic form was shrinking. The barrier rippled now like a curtain, and Tobimar and Kyri bobbed like corks in the air...but it still held.

"Reach beyond the sky, opening the gate
Bridge the gap 'twixt world and light, heed you now
my call..."

Abruptly the roiling clouds above were pierced, racing away from the point above Sanamaveridion, and Poplock thought he saw a single faint point of light within the stars, a point starting to brighten.

"From the depths beneath I summon now your fate
Come now, final destroyer, enemy of night—
SUNFALL!"

The point of light suddenly widened, as though a door the size of Kaizatenzei had been opened, and from that door blasted a ravening pillar of inconceivable incandescence, so unbearably bright that Poplock whimpered and shielded his outraged eyes and Hiriista gave vent to a pained hiss. The column of pure distilled destruction *smashed* into Sanamaveridion, spanning him from wing-tip to wingtip, and the scream of the Elderwyrm shattered every remaining window in the city, a scream that was as abruptly cut off.

Poplock peeked from beneath his good arm and felt his mouth drop open.

Towering above the lake, rising in still-flaming glory, a massive fireball trailed a stem of steam and smoke and incandescence, a mushroom cloud that overshadowed the lake.

Of Sanamaveridion, there was no trace.

For several long moments they stood simply looking at the slowly dissipating monument to destruction, and then—as the Wanderer's summoning bowed and began to disperse—Poplock finally found his voice.

"Someday you have *got* to teach me how to do that."

CHAPTER 55

"Don't go in there *now!*" Tobimar protested.

"I *have* to!" Miri said. "There's no telling when the rest of the Palace will collapse, and there's one thing I absolutely *have* to get out of there before that happens."

"Something that won't survive the collapse?"

"Maybe. But you know what such a collapse will do. It could take weeks or months to find it, and we'll have to concentrate most of our work on reaching Wieran's lab before *it* finishes collapsing on the Unity Guard."

Miri sprinted through the slightly-sagging doorway of the Valatar Palace before anyone could raise more objections. *My past has to be finished, and I have one more deception to play—this one on the* other *side.*

She couldn't risk anyone else finding that scroll; even she wasn't sure of its full capabilities... or what it might do to someone not allowed to use it. Besides, if she could recover it, it might have some of the exact answers that Kyri was seeking.

And rescuing the Unity Guard was essential, too; a few were dead or nearly so, but apparently the chamber had not yet completely collapsed. But as soon as the immediate emergency ended and anyone started examining the bodies *closely*, there would be horrified questions, and they *had* to have the right answers for those questions.

Even as she ran up the broken stairs, skipping over gaps in the stonework and trying to ignore the faint groans of the structure and sifting hiss of breaking rock, she made herself relax inwardly. *Maybe they won't forgive me when they find out. But that's all right; I probably don't* deserve *forgiveness. Kyri's accepted me, and I think that's more than I could ever have asked for.*

Her room had half-collapsed; her bed was crushed under a massive slab. But the large vanity desk was still intact, and on it, the scroll rested, face-down. She snatched it up—

And froze as she saw the cheerful, smiling human face looking out of it, the form used by Viedraverion.

"Why, Ermirinovas, how fortuitous!" he said in his usual calm, friendly tones. "I had almost given up on being able to contact you this day. How *are* things there?"

Father's Hells! This was almost the worst possible situation. She wasn't prepared, she hadn't even *begun* to try to figure out how to tell her story. Now she'd have to *improvise*, and improvised stories were always dangerous.

Remember the cardinal rule of lies: tell as much of the truth as you can. "Not terribly well, to be honest. Your little miracle-worker, the one you found for us? Wieran? He backstabbed us *all*."

"You mean he had his own agenda and betrayed you for the power of the Sun of Terian? How shocking." The lack of surprise in his tones was matched by the lazy smile. "Your outrage would be more justified, I think, had you not been planning to betray *him*."

"*He* wasn't the major problem. But the resulting conflict unleashed the Dragon, and so I now have a much . . . larger problem."

"Yet you are speaking with me, so obviously *he* was dealt with. Which is very impressive."

"Well, we did not lose *all* of the power to Wieran. It proved . . . barely sufficient."

"So, you and Wieran completed your ritual, he betrayed you *just* before you could do so yourself, and had to use up what you had gained to deal with the Elderwyrm you had yourself led there and imprisoned. Something of the completion of a circle there, I see."

He is absolutely—and deliberately—infuriating. She didn't rise to the bait. "Yes, I suppose so. I did have one question: we did not see that assistant, Tashriel, around when Wieran completed his work. Do you know—"

"Oh, yes. He completed his assistance with Wieran and

I recalled him immediately. I was a bit concerned with the alchemist's ultimate intentions, which—I see—were more than adequately founded."

She nodded. One minor question answered, and so far no problems. "Well, I have other things to work on. What did you want, Viedra?"

"Tsk, tsk, so hasty. But yes, you have your own business to attend. I wanted to let you know that henceforth I may be rather less available. Father's getting a bit testy, the plan's looking a bit shabby at the seams, and so on." The cheerful and casual way in which he said this gave her a crawling sensation up her spine. *No one should be so relaxed about failing Father.*

"Well, given how things have fallen out, we probably have little need to speak at the moment. I wish you ... good luck."

"Oh, wait, one more thing," Viedra said, holding up his hand.

"As always with you. What?"

The smile widened. "Where is Kalshae? I need to speak with her."

"Dead." She didn't have to work to put anger and loss into the single word. "Wieran's betrayal cost her everything."

The smile did not fade. "Oh, I rather think it was something else ... don't you, Miri?"

She stiffened. "What?"

The hand suddenly shot out *through* the scroll and grasped her arm. "I think I'd like the truth now," he said.

Miri collapsed to the floor, feeling her strength and power drain out of her as though through a broken cup. *What ... how is he doing this? Viedraverion's stronger than I am, but I should be able to fight it; instead, I'm barely slowing it!*

The smile widened, and she thought she saw the teeth glitter unnaturally. "Ahhhh, so very *not* demonic, my dear. Stunningly human, or more, I think. So *that* is how it actually played out. Wonderful, wonderful. Exactly as I had hoped."

She had thought she had faced horror before, but those last words dropped her into a pit of terror such as she had never imagined. "Wh-what? You hoped—"

"I *planned* on your becoming purified, yes. I expected that it would be you, and not Kalshae, though it could have worked with her too. The entire sequence worked *precisely* as I had hoped."

"You're ... not ... Viedraverion ..." she said slowly, feeling the coldness that was not just from the loss of her powers.

A smile so wide it was now clearly inhuman. "A revelation too late, my dear. No, I am not the prodigal son of the Lord of All Hells. Yet there is a certain...kinship between us."

It dropped its disguise and for one instant Miri *saw* the truth, knew what implacable and ancient evil grasped her arm now with a hand the size of her forearm, shaggy with fur and armed with talons that could sever her in a gesture, and she tried to scream, but found herself unable to even so much as gasp.

"Oh, do not be so afraid," he said, and she suddenly wasn't, feeling confusion rising in her. "I have no intention of killing you, none at all. There mustn't be the slightest suspicion of anything wrong *now*. They've solved all the problems here, you're all such good friends, and there's just a small adjustment I have to make."

"C-condor..."

"Oh, my, yes, you're quick, even when I'm working on your mind, sorting out the memories and eating the ones you really shouldn't keep. Condor mustn't catch up with them *yet*, and under *no* circumstances should they even know he exists until he does catch up with them. Everything depends on timing, you know. Proper timing."

She felt her memories slipping away, fought desperately to hold onto them, but her fading awareness told her that it was hopeless, that she was fighting... "L...Lightslayer..."

"Oh, now, there's a name I haven't heard in a long, long time," he said, with a trace of some accent she didn't recognize. "But yes, that is indeed one of mine. A shame you can't remember *that* either, because if you could simply tell *her* who I was, she might just escape the trap."

The glittering smile was now the entirety of the world. "But you won't remember enough to tell her *anything* except what I want you to."

The world faded away.

Miri started up from the floor. *Tripped as I turned. Don't rush, not in a collapsing building!*

She gripped the communication scroll tightly. *I got away with it. He doesn't suspect anything!*

Now I can warn them!

Her heart lighter once more, Miri ran as swiftly as she could, towards her new friends.

CHAPTER 56

"Push...push..." Light Tanvol directed as Kyri, Tobimar, and Miri levered up a huge brace-beam. Tanvol and several Hues and Shades were holding the temporary supports for the building steady. Kyri felt the strain in her arms, her legs, her back. *We finished... no,* Poplock *finished, with an incredible summons— that hideous battle, and we've been on cleanup for... how long? Fourteen hours, at least; look at how high the sun's risen. But this is the last!*

In a way, it had been incredibly fortunate that the vast majority of the Unity Guard had been called in; most of them were still up and working (*which means the laboratory hasn't completely collapsed... yet*), and their power, speed, and tireless willingness to work meant that they managed to accomplish in hours what might have taken many days, even weeks. Poplock, too, had been invaluable; without the tiny Toad to wriggle down narrow cracks, sensing and hunting, there would be many people still buried under rubble. Now, the only people left trapped... would be under the Castle.

"Steady.... Almost there..."

With a sudden *thunk*, the beam seated itself in the notch cut for it. *"Done!"*

A weary cheer went up all around, and the three of them sagged to the ground. "Oh, thank the *Light*," Miri said. "Now maybe we can rest...just a little."

Tobimar nodded his agreement. Despite the hard stone of the street beneath and the pervasive stench of bottom-mud and fire, it was still a taste of the heavens to simply sit and breathe without having to expend any other effort.

"I wish we could allow that, Light Miri," Tanvol said, and Tobimar looked up to see that the entirety of the Unity Guard was making its way to them—some limping, some with the dragging footsteps of the utterly exhausted, but all of them coming, and their expressions were not comforting. "But before we rest—and then attempt the most dangerous and difficult work of excavating Valatar Castle—there are things that must be explained, serious things."

Tobimar saw Miri swallow hard, even as she stood and looked with superficial calm at the broad, black-bearded Light. Tobimar stepped up to stand at her side, as did Kyri; Poplock hopped to her shoulder, still favoring his one foreleg despite Kyri's quick healing of the bone shattered by the explosion of the Wanderer's crystal. Hiriista stood behind, close enough for support, far enough to give her room.

"Then ask, Tanvol, and I will answer. But I hope the questions will be short and the answers needed not overlong, for we are all bone-weary—as are you."

Tanvol inclined his head, but his expression was hooded, suspicious. "You have always been one of our most trusted and loved comrades. Yet this..." he trailed off, obviously unable to find words for the moment; Tobimar couldn't blame him.

"...This...cataclysmic battle, and the events before it, have left me and the others wondering what exactly happened, how all of this *could* have happened. We remember being gathered to Valatar for a celebration. We remember entering the city...but the memories fade from clarity near to sunset. When next we are clear on who we are, we are running up steps from the depths of the Valatar Castle, steps that none of us recall ever having seen. Light Anora is nowhere to be found. And you appear, with a story of Master Wieran having betrayed us somehow, and then that... that *monster* appears from the lake and you send us away...to transform into something beyond anything we imagined."

He studied her. "Who *are* you, Lady Miri? *What* are you? What did Wieran do? Whence came that monster—for it seemed to many of us that you knew exactly what it was, *knew* what terrible thing was causing the earth to quake as it shook off the bonds of earth and stone. What are the answers to these questions, Light Miri?"

Miri hesitated, an agonized expression on her face, and Tobimar's heart twinged in sympathy. *She doesn't know where to begin.*

Kyri stepped forward. "Lady Miri—"

"No!" Tanvol said, and his deep, powerful voice was absolute. "I mean you no offense, Phoenix; I have seen your power, your courage, your willingness to risk all for our city, and for that I honor you. But we wish our answers to come from *her*."

Kyri looked for a moment as though she would argue, try to shield Miri anyway, but Tobimar caught her eye and she closed her eyes, then opened them and bowed to Tanvol.

"It's all right, Phoenix," Miri said softly. "They're right. I do need to explain."

"But—"

"I'll tell them the truth." The blue-green eyes were suddenly terrified—and not of death, because Tobimar knew she could face *that* as courageously as any.

She's terrified because she might lose everything she was fighting for, just... what, hours? after she realized that it was what she was fighting for.

Then she straightened and her voice firmed. "You were told that Master Wieran had betrayed us—and that was true. A monstrous betrayal indeed, seeking the power of the Great Light for a purpose none of us suspected." She gave a bitter smile. "But in a sense, you had all been betrayed since before you were born. I... Lady Shae and I... had been manipulating this country's development for longer than you can imagine, wearing different guises, changing your histories, your legends, your *world*, all so that we could, ourselves, steal the power of the Lights."

The Unity Guard were staring at her with incomprehension that was slowly shading into horror. "You...?"

She drew herself up, taller now than she had been, and those beautiful wings appeared, shimmering with gemlike sparkles, yet dangerous and terrible as well. "I am Ermirinovas Leshkivinahlmba, Daughter of the Second to Kerlamion himself, and I had planned long since this theft and destruction of all things good, the debasement of the Light into a weapon of the demons and a source of power for myself and my most trusted ally and aide, Kalshae Vunalivieria, daughter of Erherveria the Accursed, whom you knew as Lady Shae."

Just as abruptly she shrank back to the tiny, innocent Miri

they had first met, but with an expression of abject sorrow on her face. "I *had* planned that. But in the end...I did not *want* that. I wanted Kaizatenzei to *live*. I wanted to see you all live, and build Valatar and all the cities higher and brighter, and for that I fought as you saw.

"But you can lay many crimes against my name, and I am guilty of them all, including most of the wrongs done to you by others such as Wieran. Kalshae and I lured Sanamaveridion here, used him to destroy the Lords of the Sky who dwelt here, then betrayed and imprisoned him so that we could take the power of the Seven Stars and the Sun—for so they were truly named—for ourselves. We encouraged Wieran to perform his experiments, which are responsible for your lost time and for those of you who have collapsed without explanation or understanding."

There was a quaver in her voice, and Tobimar stepped forward and laid a hand on her shoulder. She did not look towards him, but her own hand came up and gripped his fingers so tightly it hurt...but he did not pull away. "I...I knew what he was doing, and I didn't care. I've...I'm a monster, I know. I just...woke up, I suppose, a few weeks ago, started to think I wasn't sure I wanted this thing I'd worked towards for so long, and then I *knew* I didn't."

Tanvol finally found his voice. "You are a *Demon*?"

She nodded.

Shocked, unbelieving murmurs ran through the assembled Guard...and then the murmurs began to take on a darker tone.

"But she has changed," Kyri said. "And she was willing to die, if necessary, to protect you. I think that's worth giving her a chance, at least, if not the respect she had before."

"But how do we *know* that?" Danrall demanded, pushing through the crowd, and shouts of assent went up. "We saw you fighting that monster, but it surely would have killed you anyway!"

"You're right about that part," Tobimar said, feeling he'd better at least remind them he was there. "But if you *watched* the battle—with the training all you Guards have had—you know that all *three* of us put ourselves in a lot of *extra* danger trying to protect this city. There were a lot of blows we could have avoided if we weren't trying to keep the Elderwyrm from wiping you all out."

"Still, he has a point," said a middle-aged woman, heavily

built, leaning on her lance. "If she's as old and devious as she says, the whole thing could be a trick. How do we know it *isn't*?"

"Because *I* tell you she speaks the truth," came a weary, pained voice behind them.

The Unity Guard whirled, but Tobimar had already seen enough to make his jaw drop.

"Every word is true, even though she could easily have placed the blame squarely on *my* shoulders," Lady Shae said, and her voice held a touch of wonder. "She could have blamed Wieran alone, or the two of us. Yet she did not."

"Shae?" Miri's eyes seemed to have doubled in size; Tobimar thought that Poplock's had too, though not with such a joyous smile. "*KALSHAE!*"

Miri's leap cleared the entire assembled mass of Unity Guard. She landed just before Lady Shae, who was barely dressed in the ragged remains of what Tobimar assumed had been the under-armor for her battle gear.

Shae looked at her, and the two stood, swaying the tiniest bit from injury or exhaustion.

Then Shae's gaze dropped, and Miri lunged forward, embracing her and crying uncontrollably. Slowly, uncertainly, Shae's arms came up and returned the embrace.

"So, I hate to interrupt the reunion, but last I saw of you, you weren't exactly on our side," Poplock said.

Lady Shae's laugh was more a snort. "No, indeed. Though I was rather less effective than I had expected. A trick worthy of a demon, little Toad."

"Fear me," he agreed. "Am I going to have to do that to you again? It might stick, the second time."

This laugh was the great, loud, cheerful one Tobimar remembered. "I would say that you couldn't manage it a second time, but I think I have learned my lesson. No." The wonder had returned to her voice. "No, you won't. When that . . . attack of yours dispersed me, I was caught in Wieran's trap. I was *enveloped* by the power of the Sun of Terian, and I felt my anger and hatred dissolving as though they had been the morning dew before the sun. By the time I managed to drag myself free and try to bring myself back to some semblance of solidity, well . . ." She smiled down at Miri, still with her face buried against Shae's side. ". . . well, I wasn't who I'd been, but instead the person I'd been making myself."

She met Tobimar's gaze. "As you knew, and tried to make me accept. I thank you for trying; it helped, when I was realizing what I was becoming."

"You...are *both* Demons?" Tanvol asked, with the tone of a man still trying to grasp the impossible.

Miri pulled herself free and wiped her face roughly with one arm. "Yes. Well, no, not *now*."

"Say, rather, that they *were* demons, but are no longer," Kyri said.

"I will vouch for them both," Hiriista said, finally speaking. "You all know me. You have worked with me for many years and know that I have ever and always been a resource you could trust, though I am not one of you—and therefore not subject to any influence they or Wieran may have used."

Tobimar could *sense* the relief slowly working its way through the crowd. *That could have become* very *ugly.*

Light Tanvol sighed and suddenly sank down to sit on a nearby piece of fallen bridge. "*Light*, I don't even know what to think. But by the Cities we need your help, Lady Shae, Miri. If we can trust you..."

"Trust *me*," Poplock said. "They're all right now."

Shae shook her head. "But can they ever trust us?"

Danrall looked around at the other Unity Guards, then laughed. "Well, Lady Shae, the fact is we've never *seen* you do anything wrong. Or Light Miri. Maybe...maybe this will mean we won't ever *completely* trust you again, but for now? We're the *Unity Guard.* Our job's to protect Kaizatenzei, and you're the ones who can tell us how we can do that best, at least for now. So... I guess what I'm saying is, we *have* to trust you."

"At least for now," Tanvol said. "So...let us lay these issues aside, Lady Shae, Light Miri. We all require rest...and then we must enter the Castle, brace it, and seek the survivors within!"

Kyri smiled, and went to embrace the other two women. After a moment, Tobimar went and added his own, at which point even Shae began to cry a little, and Tobimar didn't mind that his eyes stung a bit with empathy.

Miri thought she might lose everything; *Shae must have thought she* was *going to die. And now, just maybe...they've* won *everything instead.*

CHAPTER 57

"Viedraverion, when are you going to return my property?" Balinshar demanded.

"When I am *finished* with him, and not one minute before. Father *told* you to let this go. Do not presume too much on my well-known good nature."

Balinshar's eyes narrowed. "Well-known *now*, but I remember you somewhat differently, oh, some ages back, before the Fall."

Unexpectedly perceptive of Balinshar. "I spent millennia playing human roles to tear down civilizations, Balinshar. One thing I learned well was that one can gain much with a quiet word and patience. Especially," and It caused Its shape to change, growing, the skin turning stony-gray, "when one *can* choose the other path."

Balinshar's fanged mouth twisted in annoyance. "Bah. In any event, *you* had better not be relying on your Father's good will so much; he's becoming annoyed with you, and everyone knows it." The black-fanged grin was mocking. "Perhaps your fortunes are about to change." The connection was cut in that instant.

Just as well; he'll brood about my keeping Tashriel and not think more on that other subject. Tashriel was *vital* to the final portion of the plan, though almost certainly not in any way that anyone else would guess, and Balinshar definitely wouldn't.

Miri had played her unwitting part *perfectly*, right down to returning to the palace to retrieve the scroll—which had of course activated upon contact, as he had planned. The alternative courses had also been planned for, with appropriate arrangements made

393

for each—Miri not retrieving the scroll, Miri not falling to the influence of the Light, Kalshae falling, both dying, et cetera, all planned for. But his predictions had been correct and the course he had most hoped for had been run.

Weiran escaped? Well, that may become interesting in a year or ten, depending on where he escaped to, and with what. He will certainly be most put out by our little band of heroes, but they'll be dead long before he has any opportunity to try for revenge.

It stood and put the scroll away. *Condor will be helping rebuild on the other side of the lake; I'm sure he's trying to be the hero by now—Miri's reports certainly indicated that—and he won't be able to leave a devastated town. So he will not catch up with Phoenix yet, not until the proper moment.*

It made a note to Itself to make sure that the agents It had planted there centuries ago were ready to act just in case Condor put on a surprising burst of speed. *Timing is the absolute essential element here. Can't have him interrupt the rebuilding of Kaizatenzei Valatar and their heroic departure. I'm certain there will be a small but important Temple to Myrionar there before she leaves. That must be properly dedicated.*

Judging from what he'd seen in Miri's memories—both those things she'd witnessed and those things she had been told—there were other likely events. *Kalshae is probably not actually dead, though I have no doubt that being disintegrated that way must have been painful. But my, my, my, that little Toad is clever. I look forward to seeing what tricks he can come up with in the ultimate confrontation.*

The Elderwyrm, on the other hand . . . *hit with what appears to have been part of the Sun's core. Were it merely something like, oh, one of the* rannai *cannon the Reborn Empire used to use, or even the thermonuclear toys Earth's playing with, he'd be back fairly quickly.* However, the fact that it was a piece of the *Sun*—the light of the world—had symbolic and thus mystical significance which undoubtedly injured Sanamaveridion's spirit gravely. *And, of course, the fact that it was one of the Wanderer's tricks might make it even harder to deal with. No, I think that he'll be long in returning . . . which will likely make the rest of the Elderwyrm cautious in their rising.*

Then there was Kerlamion. The time was nearly right to let Kerlamion decide the great plan was unraveling and to dismiss

"Viedraverion" in disgust. Not *quite* yet, but soon, very soon. Kerlamion and his pedestrian and rather boring plans of dominion were, in the end, futile, and the amusing thing was that the King of All Hells did not realize this. *It all goes back to that ancient conflict, so far that I'm not sure any of them realize their motives anymore, let alone how completely their little dances of death and revenge are choreographed by others.*

It of course understood those motives perfectly; after all, It had arranged that conflict, just as it had arranged all of what was happening here.

A knock on the door of the nearly-bare room caused It to turn. "Enter, please," It said.

Bolthawk and Skyharrier entered and bowed low. It returned the bow with a slight nod. "Welcome, both of you."

"You called us," Skyharrier said, still carefully avoiding using even pronouns that might designate anything about It. That wasn't so important anymore, now that neither he nor Bolthawk dared show their faces in Evanwyl anymore, but old habits died hard. "You said that you had some good news for us."

"I do indeed, my friends." It smiled, and was pleased to see that they still flinched at the expression. "I have been giving thought to the problem you posed, Bolthawk."

"You mean about our numbers. As in, there's only two of us left, and it's going to be Balance-damned hard to recruit any new blood."

"There are *three* of you, technically. Condor has not, after all, been killed or otherwise removed from the Justiciars, he's merely on a rather extended mission. But still, there *are*, as you say, only two of you available. And while it *is* true that Justiciars' Retreat is very difficult for those not of the Justiciars to find, it is not at all impossible. And *if* that happens..."

"My apologies, but we can, I believe, envision the results well enough, Patron," Skyharrier said.

"Yes, yes, I do tend to ramble, don't I? Well, in any event we are missing four: Silver Eagle, our beloved Thornfalcon, Mist Owl, and Gondor's foster father Shrike. If we are discovered—and we will be, I assure you, because our friend the Phoenix has been far from idle and will be on the way back here very soon—you were correct that we must have more allies, more sword-brothers... more Justiciars, in short."

Bolthawk shook his head. "Takes too long—why, even if we *weren't* on on the Watchland's kill-on-sight list—how ironic *that* must be for you, eh?—even if we weren't on that list, I say, we wouldn't have half the time we need to train even one newcomer, let alone four."

"I entirely agree with you," It said, and smiled more broadly. "So I have found a far better solution."

It gestured, and in the darkness at the far side of the room was movement. The movement sharpened, became three figures walking with a faint creak and clank of armor. The smell of polish and oil carried with it another odor: the faint, sweetish-foul stench of something long dead.

Bolthawk gave a curse, bringing his gauntleted fists up to guard position, while Skyharrier paled, and half-drew his weapon, backing up with a terror that was sweet to smell indeed.

"Oh, how, now?" It asked, and now It laughed, even as the three figures stopped just behind it. "Is this how you greet the comrades you had just now said we need?"

"Oh, great *Balance*..." murmured the ashen Skyharrier, and Bolthawk's hands trembled.

Silver Eagle, Mist Owl, and Shrike bowed, surrounded by the smell of the grave, as Its laughter echoed throughout Justiciars' Retreat.

"But...but Mist Owl was *burned!* To *ashes!*" Skyharrier finally managed, his voice shaking. "And that...that's Gareth Lamell, the Eagle *before* Rion Vantage, buried years agone! He should be *bones!*"

It turned to them slowly and let them see the lambent yellow light in its eyes. "You have allowed yourselves to forget, or perhaps never realized, the truth. You are *bound* to me, your oaths given and accepted, my power bestowed upon you.

"Did you think that there was *any* way for you to escape?" It smiled, and the two living Justiciars shrank back. "There is no escape from *me*. If you serve me well enough—and live—then when the final act of this play is concluded, I *may* release you.

"But if you serve me *poorly*, you shall have no release...not even death."

It looked upon their horrified faces, and knew that all was ready, now, for the final act.

GAZETTEER FOR ZARATHAN

NOTE: Some elements of the Gazetteer may be spoilers for *Phoenix Rising* and *Phoenix in Shadow*.

Overview

Zarathan (more properly Zahr-a-Thana, World of Magic) is a planet of generally Earth size and composition. It is presumed to be the source of all magic in all universes. The main continent (and the only continent commonly known) stretches approximately four thousand, eight hundred miles north to south and, at its widest, is about the same east to west (it averages between two and three thousand east-west over most of its extent, however). It can be generally divided into three regions: Southern Zarathan, which is most of the continent south of the Khalal mountain range; Northern Zarathan, which is everything north of the Khalals plus the very large island/miniature continent of Artania; and Elyvias, a subcontinent peninsula shaped something like a gigantic Cape Cod and separated from Southern Zarathan by the Barricade Mountains.

The history, geography, and peoples of Zarathan are all affected greatly by the apparently cyclical "Chaoswars" which bring periodic conflict to the world and are associated with massive mystical/deific disturbances which, among other effects, distort or erase memories and even records of prior events—up to and including those of the gods. Thus, while the generally known history of Zarathan stretches back over half a million years, clear records are rarely available for anything older than the most recent Chaoswar, and even the gods themselves can only partially answer questions pertaining to events beforehand.

Countries

There are several countries on this continent, but it should be made clear that "country" on Zarathan is not quite the same as "country" in the modern civilized world of Earth. Most of the area claimed as a country's territory is actually relatively wild and untamed and dangerous; only cleared areas around cities and major roads tend to be safe for travel. The overall population of the countries is therefore much lower than might be expected, given that the average standard of living is closer to that of twentieth-century Earth in many ways than it is to the medieval era that one might first assume, seeing no factories and noticing that the sword is still a common weapon. Following is a list of the important countries of Zarathan (there are others not listed, but these are the ones significant either overall, or specifically for the Balanced Sword trilogy):

STATE OF THE DRAGON GOD

Called variously the State of the Dragon God, The Dragon-King's Domain, The State of Elbon Nomicon, and other appellations, the actual name for this country is a very long string of Ancient Sauran words that boiled down means something like "The Country founded in the days of the Dragon-God's First Creation, That Endures Eternally." It is the largest country on the planet, stretching from the western edge of Southern Zarathan all the way to the Barricade Mountains in the east, and from the southern coast all the way to the Ice Peaks in the north. In a governmental sense, the State of the Dragon God might best be described as a theocratic libertarian state.

The capital of the State of the Dragon God is called in Ancient Sauran Fanalam' T' ameris' a' u' Zahr-a-Thana T'ikon, but commonly (and to the Saurans and Dragons, painfully) called simply "Zarathanton." It is the most ancient city, and the largest, on the continent, with some buildings over five hundred thousand years old and a population of roughly 200,000 inside and immediately outside its walls. Other important cities within the State of the Dragon God borders include T'Tera (also called the Dragon God's City), Artani (a city of trade with the Artan of the Forest Sea), Dragonkill, Bridgeway, Odinsforge (also the name of the mountain range in which it is set), Salandar, Thologondoreave (an independent city of the Children of Odin), Shipton (known to the Saurans as Olthamian' a' ameris) and Hell's Edge.

THE EMPIRE OF THE MOUNTAIN

Nearly as large as the Dragon God's country, the Empire of the Mountain actually straddles the Khalals, claiming much of the territory north of the Ice Peaks to the Khalals and some territory to the north and east above them. Ruled in unbroken power for hundreds of thousands of years by the God-Emperor Idinus, most powerful wizard ever to live, the Empire has always had an uneasy relationship with its neighbors. While Idinus is not, strictly speaking, evil, he has motives and goals that are unclear to others and this has led on occasion to war on a titanic scale. The capital of the Empire of the Mountain is Scimitar's Path, at the base of Mount Scimitar—tallest peak of the Khalal range at sixty thousand feet. There are several other cities, the most important of which are Kheldragaard to the west and Tor Port in the east. It is an ironclad theocracy ruled directly by the Archmage himself from atop Mount Scimitar—where he remains virtually always.

DALTHUNIA

Dalthunia used to be an ally state to the Dragon God, a modest-sized country which broke away from the Empire due to a very bad set of mis-steps by some of the Empire's local rulers, eventually triggering a local revolution. For some reason the Archmage—after a short demonstration of his power which showed that if he wished, he could take Dalthunia back at any time—allowed Dalthunia to remain independent. At the time of the story, however, Dalthunia has been a conquered state—whether by internal revolution or some subtle external invasion is unclear—for a couple of centuries, and very little is known about it other than that they do not welcome visitors. They clearly have powerful magic and probably deific patrons, because scrying and ordinary espionage have not been effective. The capital of Dalthunia is Kymael, named after the instigator of the revolution.

EVANWYL

A small country between the northeastern portion of Hell's Rim, the Khalals, and the Broken Hills, Evanwyl is an almost forgotten country at the time of The Balanced Sword trilogy; its great claim to fame used to be its connection to the civilization that lay on the other side of Heavenbridge Way, the only useful pass through the Khalals. But that was before something happened during the last Chaoswar, something that turned the other side to the monstrous Moonshade Hollow and the Heavenbridge Way into Rivendream Pass. Now Evanwyl's only function is keeping the things that exit from Rivendream Pass from entering the larger world. Governmentally, Evanwyl is a monarchy (ruled by the Watchland) with the monarch's power moderated by his subordinates and advisors the Eyes and Arms, and by the powerful influence of the faith of Myrionar, the Balanced Sword, especially as embodied in the Justiciars of Myrionar and the high priest called the Arbiter. The city of Evanwyl is the capital; its population is between four and five thousand people in total.

SKYSAND

Situated on the far northeast corner of the continent, Skysand is a country which is mostly desert with considerable volcanic features and with some interior and coastal oases (around which are built its few cities). A theocratic monarchy, Skysand is ruled by the Silverun family under a complex set of rules administered and watched over by the temples of Terian, the Mortal God; the capital is also named Skysand and is situated in a natural harbor with a periodically active but generally harmless volcano on the southern side. Cut off from the rest of the land by the high and volcanic Flamewall Mountains, Skysand trades by sea with other countries around the continent, its most prominent exports being magical gemstones which are found in great quantity and diverse assortments in the desert and mountains.

ARTANIA

A huge island or small continent a thousand miles long and a few hundred wide, Artania is the claimed homeland of the youngest of the major species on Zarathan, the Artan (sometimes called Elves). Few other than the Artan are allowed beyond the capital city, Nya-Sharee-Hilya (which means "Surviving the Storm of

Ages"); this city is run on rather militaristic lines but it's uncertain as to whether this reflects the overall government, or the fact that the city is often the focal point of invasion attempts.

WHITE BLADE STATE

Located in a circle of mountains in the far northwest of the main continent, the White Blade State is a rotating monarchy, with rulership cycling regularly between the ruling families of the five main cities. How the individual cities determine their ruling families varies, making governmental changeovers...interesting at times. Naturally this also means the capital city changes with regularity. The "White Blade" is a symbolic, but extremely powerful, sword which is held by the current ruler; it is said to be the gift of the patron god of the White Blade, Chromaias, and each of the five cities are devoted to and named after one of the five gods of that faith (Chromaias, Stymira [Thanamion], Amanora, Taralandira [Mulios], and Kharianda).

AEGEIA

A small country walled off from the rest of the continent by the mountain range called Wisdom's Fortress, Aegeia is a theocratic state which is ruled much of the time by a council of twelve nobles, but at other times by the literal incarnate Goddess of Wisdom, Athena, in the capital city of Aegis.

ODINSFORGE RANGE/THOLOGONDOREAVE

The Children of Odin claim this as their homeland, and politically the entire mountain range is treated as a sort of neutral ground with the Children of Odin having priority in disputes. The area immediately surrounding the general location of Thologondoreave ("Cavern of a Thousand Hammers") is acknowledged to be sovereign territory of the Children of Odin; as the exact location of Thologondoreave is a well-kept secret from most people, with powerful enchantments and even deific protection, in practice this makes most of the Odinsforge Range their country, an island in the middle of the State of the Dragon King.

PONDSPARKLE

Possibly the smallest country in the world, Pondsparkle consists of one small city and the surrounding area near a small lake a few miles in extent. Pondsparkle is the permanent home for a large number (several thousand) of the Intelligent Toads and the site of the first and still primary temple to their god, Blackwart the Great.

KAIZATENZEI

A country unknown to the outside world until *Phoenix in Shadow*, Kaizatenzei is a country set in the midst of Moonshade Hollow—and is every bit as beautiful, fruitful, and pleasant as Rivendream Pass and the outer part of Moonshade Hollow are monstrous, corrupt, and deadly.

The name of the country translates to "The Unity of Seven Lights," with the Seven Lights of the name being seven cities or very large villages which served as the center of safety and power against the evil surrounding them, and who began working together once they discovered each other's existence. The discovery of what is called the Light of Unity caused them to found a reasonably central capital city called Sha Kaizatenzei Valatar, which means something like "soul-light heart city of the Unity of Seven Lights."

Other Locations

ELYVIAS

Not, strictly speaking, a country, but a subcontinent, Elyvias used to be a larger portion of the continent, with additional area extending up nearly to Tor Port, but according to legend a battle between Elbon Nomicon and the Archmage Idinus caused a cataclysmic restructuring of the whole area, sinking a large chunk of the continent and creating the distorted conditions within. Elyvias has several countries and significant cities within its borders (Firestream Falls, Shuronogromal, Thunder Port, Thelhi-Man-Su, Zeikor, Artilus) but is severely cut off from the rest of the world both by the physical barriers of the Barricade Mountains, Blackdust Plateau, and Cataclysm Ridge, and by the mystical disruption called the Maelwyrd which surrounds the entire peninsula to a range of up to forty miles, with only a mile or two of clear-sailing space inside the Maelwyrd, near land. Magic also tends to work differently in Elyvias and the civilizations there have developed differently in the last several thousand years.

THE FOREST SEA

Stretching from the Great Road and the Odinsforge Range in the east to the Barricade Range in the east, the Forest Sea presses against the Ice Peaks and surges around them in the east, up into the Empire of the Mountain. Stretching for three thousand miles, the Forest Sea is broken only by tiny enclaves within it and by the narrow clear-cuts around the cities and Great Roads. Somewhere within is hidden the Suntree, which the Artan on the main continent use as temple and center, but most of it is utterly unexplored, filled with danger and possibility.

"HELL" AND HELL'S RIM

Created, it is said, from a cataclysmic mystical confrontation between the powerful Demons and the Great Dragons in the days before human beings walked the planet, the region called "Hell" is a place of twisted, distorted magics, impossible conflicting terrain, and monsters found nowhere else. No coherent picture has emerged of the place within, and few even attempt to go there; passing Hell's Rim, a steep barrier of high peaks, would be too much effort for most anyway. The only pass through those peaks is sealed off by the fortress city, Hell's Edge, which exists almost solely as a barrier between "Hell" and the rest of the world.

ICE PEAKS

Like "Hell" and Elyvias, the Ice Peaks are a reminder of one of the conflicts of history, though long enough ago that the precise nature of the event isn't known. The Peaks are magical, solidified ice for the most part, meaning that they are beautiful, transparent or translucent, and very, very hard to pass, given they have nothing growing on them. They form one of the natural borders between the State of the Dragon God and the Empire of the Mountain.

People of Zarathan

Many different species share this continent—many relatively peacefully, others...somewhat less so. Following is a summary of the most significant peoples of this world.

HUMANS

Human beings on Zarathan are basically the same as they are on Earth. Generalists, humans are something of the chameleons of the civilizations, showing up in any profession, any part of the world, in large numbers. They are probably the most common of the intelligent species.

INTELLIGENT TOADS

Called the Sylanningathalinde, or "Golden-eyed," by the Saurans, the Toads claim to be the oldest of the intelligent species, even pre-dating the Dragons and Demons. They are in general a fun-loving but insular people, and mostly stay near to the pond they are born and raised in. Toads are given one name in their larval (tadpole) stage and, when adults, choose a significant second name. They vary tremendously in size, from dwarfed individuals a few inches long up to some four feet from nose to rump and weighing two hundred pounds.

SAURANS

Averaging eight feet in height with massive bodies, armored tails, heavy, clawed feet and arms, and a head sporting a very large fanged mouth, Saurans resemble nothing so much as a miniature Godzilla. They claim to be direct descendants of the Great Dragons, and the Ancient Saurans—somewhat larger and clearly superior in many ways—are supposedly ranked as equals with the Dragons. There are very few Ancient Saurans left. Generally even-tempered, and a good thing, since when angered they are terribly dangerous.

ARTAN

Very humanlike, Artan tend to the delicate in appearance, with hair and eyes of exotic colors; they are extremely controlled in emotional displays as a rule. They often live in wilder areas—forests and mountains—but not, despite some assumptions, because they like to live "close to nature"; they prefer to be hard to find and have a sort of racial paranoia that they are still being hunted by some nameless adversaries who supposedly chased them from beyond the stars to Zarathan. The Rohila are technically the same species, but are otherwise separated from them in culture, behavior, and associations, aside from being also isolationist.

CHILDREN OF ODIN/ODINSYRNEN

Short, broad, tough as stone, these appear to be—and in many ways are—the classic dwarves. However, they are not a species of hard-drinking and fighting warriors, despite appearances and the fact that their patron pantheon includes Odin and Thor. According to their legends they were literally created by Odin, who forged them in Asgard from the heart of a world, using Thor's hammer to do the striking. While their greatest city is indeed underground, the Children of Odin are equally at home above ground and are nearly as flexible in choice of profession and environments as human beings.

WINGED FOLK/SAELAR

Generally human in appearance but with a set of huge but compactable wings, the Saelar are almost certainly the result of some mage's experimentation a few Chaoswars ago. The records are, however, lost, and they breed as true as any, so they are now an uncommon but widely-spread species, most heavily concentrated in the region of the Broken Hills.

MAZAKH

Often called "snake-demons," "snake-men," and other more derogatory terms, the *mazakh* were originally the creation of the demons they worship (the *Mazolishta*) who literally constructed them from a number of other species. In appearance they are actually somewhat less snakelike and more like small raptorian dinosaurs. Generally raised in a hostile culture that trains them for warfare and lack of empathy, the *mazakh* are still not inherently evil and some leave the service of the *Mazolishta* and join the greater societies above; these are called *khallit*.

Gods and Beings of Significance

The gods and their choices affect nearly everything on the planet. There are, literally, hundreds if not thousands of deities worshipped on the planet; for purposes of The Balanced Sword, only a few are of great significance, however. In this section are also included a few individual beings who may not be, strictly speaking, gods, but who have influence on that level.

MYRIONAR

God of Justice and Vengeance, Myrionar is at the heart of the action here. In the grander scheme of things Myrionar is a fading god whose influence is vastly reduced from what it was, but that may be changing. Represented as a set of scales balanced on the point of a sword.

TERIAN

The Nemesis of Evil, the Light in the Darkness, Terian is also called Infinity as he is referred to in prophecy as "The Length of Space." A deity of unswerving good, Terian is also ranked as one of the most powerful of deities on anyone's scale. Represented by a human figure mostly in black with a cape or cloak clasped with a golden sidewise-eight figure and head blurred/concealed by a blaze of light.

CHROMAIAS AND THE FOUR

Generally portrayed as good, the Chromaian faith is extremely... flexible, especially as it manifests all aspects of magic and power. Symbolized by a four-pointed jack-like object with crystals of four different colors at the points and a clear diamond at the center.

EÖNAE

Goddess of the world(s), Eönae's focus is on nature, with control over the natural elements (earth, air, fire, water, and spirit) the common manifestation of her power. She is commonly allied with Shargamor, a demon of water turned to the light, who is mostly focused on storms, streams, rain, and so on. Symbolized either by a woman (young, medium, old) with green and brown hair, or by her signature creatures, the Eönwyl, which are essentially god-empowered winged unicorns.

ELBON NOMICON AND THE SIXTEEN

One of the most ancient pantheons, the head of this group of gods is Elbon Nomicon, Teranahm a u Gilnas (Great Dragon of the Diamond), supposedly father to all Dragons and a being of almost incalculable power. The Dragons tend to slow, long duty-cycles on Zarathan, either sleeping for ages or travelling to other planes of existence, with only a few physically present on Zarathan at any given time; it is, however, rumored that Elbon Nomicon's own home is at the center of the Krellin mountains at the extreme southwest tip of the continent. The symbol of each dragon is its chosen gemstone; Elbon's personal symbol is a stylized lighting bolt with rays extending out from it.

KERLAMION

The Black Star, King of All Hells, Kerlamion is one of the most powerful of the gods as well as one of the original Demons. He symbolizes destruction and conquest and thus attracts only the worst sort of worshippers; he is however often quite active and those who please him may often get material aid. His symbol is, predictably, either a black starburst or a humanoid outline of pure black.

THE MAZOLISHTA

Great Demons who are the patron gods of the mazakh and other creatures of darker natures, there are several Mazolishta whose names are rarely spoken; the only one appearing directly in The Balanced Sword is Voorith, whose focus is life, forests, and such—in a corruptive and destructive sense.

BLACKWART THE GREAT

God of Toads (and anything else he happens to like), Blackwart manifests as a gigantic black toad, hence the name. While not powerful on the scale of many of the gods, he is much more savvy than many give him credit for (just like his people). He is symbolized by a stylized set of pop-eyes and a smile, or by a black toad figurine.

THE WANDERER

A supposedly human wizard, the Wanderer is a figure of popular legend across Zarathan; stories about him go back at least one and possibly two, three, or even four Chaoswars. An extremely powerful magician, the Wanderer is most known for his unorthodox approaches and apparent immunity to destiny; it is said he originally came from Zaralandar (Earth) which may explain his unique nature. Even the "he" is somewhat in doubt as the Wanderer has appeared in dozens of different guises throughout history, men, women, children, and even occasionally Artan, Child of Odin, or other species.

KONSTANTIN KHOROS

The most powerful spirit magician known, Khoros is regarded with trepidation, awe, and fear by almost all beings of power. He is a master manipulator, whose goals may be good but whose methods are at best harsh and at times dark indeed. He has devastated the plans of demonlords and kings, of gods and villains, often without being himself physically present. In The Balanced Sword, Khoros is known to have had contact with all three of the main characters and be directly involved with some of their actions.

THE SPIRITSMITH

An Ancient Sauran with a history stretching back at least half a million years to the Fall of the Saurans, the Spiritsmith is the greatest known artificer on the planet, and the one asked by gods and heroes for the mightiest weapons and strongest armor. He forged the original Raiment for all the Justiciars.

VIRIGAR AND THE GREAT WOLVES

Not, strictly speaking, a god by the standards of Zarathan, Virigar is the King of the Great Werewolves, or Great Wolves, which are the most individually feared monsters on the planet. Great Werewolves (seen in their weakest form in *Paradigms Lost*) are soul and energy eating shapeshifters whose only vulnerabilities are silver or powers similar to their own. Virigar himself is the most ancient and powerful of their race, and is a bogeyman to even the gods themselves; one of his appellations is "The God-Slayer," and he has apparently earned this title multiple times in history.

THE ELDERWYRM

Little more than a dark, dark legend at the time of The Balanced Sword, the Elderwyrm are said to be the opposite numbers of the Great Dragons—equally powerful but as evil and destructive as Elbon Nomicon and the Sixteen are noble and constructive.